That One Small Spark

Jules Dalla-Libera

This is a work of fiction. Names, characters, businesses, places, events, and incidents are either the products of the author's imagination or used in a fictitious manner. Any resemblance to actual persons, living or dead, or actual events is purely coincidental.

ISBN Print 978-1-7642597-1-2

ISBN eBook 978-1-7642597-0-5

Published by Jules Dalla-Libera

Visit jdlbooks.com.au

Cover design by Adrian Dalla-Libera

This is for all you gorgeous readers out there who love escaping into the fabulous, fantastic worlds of fantasy just as much as I do. Life is hard enough. Reading should be a retreat, a pleasure, a sanctuary. I hope you enjoy this little oasis I've created, where you can forget about the mundanities of life and immerse yourself in my fairytale world filled with magic, spice and ludicrously beautiful men.

You were looking for a new book boyfriend, right?

Author's Note

If you're a history buff or *Outlander* fan, you might recognise some of the names in this book. That's because quite a few of them - Agnes Sampson and Geillis Duncan included - were real people swept up in North Berwick's late 16th century witch trials.

In researching this book, I uncovered their stories, then wound them around my own. So, while they were certainly real people involved in those very real events, I created their characteristics for the purposes of fictionalisation, entwining my own imagining of their personalities and interactions around my own fictional version of events.

As for Scotland's witch trials, they were very bloody real. In 1590, the Scottish witch craze began with the trial of a 'coven' from East Lothian, who were accused of meeting with the Devil and conjuring up storms to destroy James VI on his return from Denmark with his bride, Anne. In the 150 years that followed, thousands were accused, tortured and executed for witchcraft.

Like certain characters, my depiction of how witches were brought to trial and their confessions extracted is inspired by historical accounts. As such, it is graphic in nature.

On that note, please be aware this book contains references to a past abusive relationship, past physical abuse and stillbirth. There is also frequent use of profanity, as well as depiction of blood and gore, death, murder, execution and graphic violence. The spice is also pretty spicy, so get ready for several explicit sex scenes.

This may be a faerie tale, but it is dark and steamy in parts, so mind these trigger warnings and care for your mental wellbeing.

Language & Glossary

Because I'm Scottish and this book is set in Scotland, you'll find it's written in British English, rather than American English. Expect colour rather than color, materialised rather than materialized, and so on.

You'll also find the spoken language is not correct for the period. This is a style choice. In crafting these characters, I found myself more interested in the accessibility of the language than the accuracy of it. And as a Scot with a dirty mouth, I also quite enjoy swearing, so there is much more of that than there would have been back in the 16th century.

Alongside the naughty words, there are certain Gaelic and Scottish words and names from Scottish mythology interspersed within the text that you might not know the meaning of, or may find hard to pronounce.

As a fantasy reader, I know how irritating it can be to attempt unfamiliar words as you read, so here is a small glossary to refer back to.

Kirk [*kurk*] Church

Bairn [*bayrn*] Child

Clarty [*klar-tee*] Dirty

Eejit [*eed-jit*] A stupid person

Samhain [sah-win] An ancient Gaelic festival, celebrated on the night of October 31st

Gallus [*gah-luss*] Cheeky, mischievous, over-confident

Haar [*hahr*] Fog

Ken [*ken*] Know

Besom [*biz-um*] A term of contempt for someone who is cheeky or annoying

Nicnevin [*nik-neh-vin*] A witch or fairy queen from Scottish folklore

Sluagh na Marbh [*sloo-ah nah marr-v*] Host of the dead

Eachlair Ürlar [*ech-layr oor-lar*] A witch from Gaelic folklore

Baobhan-sìth [*baa'van shee*] Vampire faerie seductresses from Scottish folklore

Slàinte mhath [*slanj-a-vah*] Cheers in Scottish Gaelic

Chapter 1

Blood. *So* much blood. It's all I can see. All I can smell.

I lick my lips, tasting copper.

No one can lose this much blood and survive. Surely.

Slick pools stain the bedsheets. Not red, not like blood should be, but black. In the dim light, it creeps across the fabric like a shadow, reaching out to me like it has a mind of its own.

'Elspeth.' Agnes's voice snaps my attention to her, much harsher than usual. Wild strands of silver escape her braid, but her eyes are clear, her expression controlled.

'Sorry,' I murmur, turning to scrub my hands. Steam curls around my fingers as I dry them, then pick up a fresh towel. I pace back to the bed and hand it to Agnes, who takes it without looking up.

A wretched scream breaks against me. Unwilling, my eyes hitch from Agnes's skilful hands past those pale thighs, smeared glossy and dark with blood, tracking up, up, to find an even paler face. Skin waxen, a glassy sheen of sweat coats Tibbe's features. They are twisted in agony, almost unrecognisable. Eyes screwed shut, another scream escapes her.

One hand on Tibbe's swollen belly, Agnes motions to me with the other. 'It's time.'

I eye the bruising stretching below her hand. A darkened inflammation where there should be none. My guts twist.

'Are you sure I can't get someone–'

'There is no one else,' Agnes interrupts, her gaze flicking to me as I hesitate. 'Not close enough to be of use, anyway.'

'But what use am I?' I plead.

I brew ale. I don't deliver babies. I can't stop anyone from dying.

The only reason I'm here is because I was foraging nearby. That, and I can never say no to Agnes.

She observes the panic painted so clearly across my features, her expression softening to reveal the encouraging smile I know so well. 'Plenty, pet. Now, get over here.'

I force my feet forward, just as another flood of anguished screams pours from Tibbe and my resolve stutters. Clenching my jaw tight, I keep moving. I kneel beside Agnes and hastily tie back the auburn tangle that is my hair. 'What do you need me to do?'

'Her placenta has ruptured. We need to get the baby out for the bleeding to stop.'

'Will the baby...?' Unable to get the rest of the words past my lips, I let the question hang. Tibbe isn't due for another month, maybe two. She shouldn't be labouring this early.

'I don't know. But if he is to have any chance at all, this needs to happen now. Just follow my lead. It should hopefully move quickly.' Agnes gives Tibbe's calf a squeeze. 'Alright, Tibbe. On the next big wave, I need you to push. Can you do that?'

A low moan churns through Tibbe, her eyes opening to fix on me. Terror surges behind them, mirroring my own. She looks so young. *Too* young at only 15.

You were married at that age too, my mind prods.

I grit my teeth. *And look how that turned out.*

I sweep the thought aside, along with the entirely shameful one that follows hot on its heels. The one stoked by relief that I never found myself in Tibbe's position, despite those five miserable years of marriage.

Reaching out, I grasp Tibbe's hand and squeeze it. Ignoring how feverishly hot it feels, I say, 'You can do this, Tibbe. You're almost there.'

I don't know this girl, and she doesn't know me, but she must see something in me that gives her strength. A determination to do better, perhaps. Her grip tightens on mine. 'Yes,' she rasps past dry, chapped lips. 'I can do th–'

Her entire body tenses, her timid words cut off by another tortured cry.

'That's it,' Agnes says, implausibly calm. 'Push, push. You're doing so well.' Quieter, she says to me, 'Bring more towels.'

Reluctantly, my gaze tracks down between Tibbe's thighs, where blood spills out of her. *Fuck, this is* not *good.* I race over to scoop up more towels, staggering back to Agnes with many more than she'll need. Hopefully. She mops up the worst of the blood, soothing Tibbe with soft reassurances as I sink to my knees.

Tibbe slumps back, breathing ragged, barely catching her breath before another surge racks her.

'Push, Tibbe,' Agnes urges, discarding another blood-soaked towel. 'Almost there.'

Sure enough, I can see something straining to get out of her. Another push and I can see it clearer. Confused, I whisper, 'That's not a head, Agnes.'

It should be a head. I don't know much about delivering bairns, but I know heads are supposed to come first.

'No, it's not.' For the first time, I hear strain in Agnes's voice. I turn sharply towards her, but she keeps her words low as she continues. 'Baby is breech. He should have had more time, and he hasn't turned.'

'What is it?' Tibbe says between gulped, panting breaths. 'What's wrong?'

'Your baby is coming out arse first.' Agnes's reply is breezy, a bewildering contrast to the expression she conceals from Tibbe. 'Nothing to worry about. We'll get him out on the next push.'

Tibbe has no more time for questions before her body seizes. She screams with each push. One, two, three, and a scrawny body slithers out, slimy legs following.

'That's it,' Agnes soothes, supporting the tiny body, slippery with blood and swathed in a strange waxy coating. 'Another push and we'll see the head.'

But we don't see the head, on the next push or the many more that follow. With each lurch of agony, Tibbe shrieks, blood pulsing out of her, while the baby's head remains stubbornly stuck.

'Too early,' Agnes murmurs, more to herself than to me.

Regardless, I reply, 'What's happening?' My hands flutter at my sides, looking for something to do, some way to help. Never in my life have I felt so useless. Tibbe is fighting for her life, for her baby's life, and here I am doing my best impression of a house plant.

'It happens sometimes with breech births. The head is much bigger than the body, so we get the body out, but the head remains trapped in the birth canal.' Her urgent words are quiet, barely audible over Tibbe's jagged moans. 'We need to get his head out or he won't survive.'

Unbidden, my thoughts fly to my mother. Agnes had been there to guide both me and my brother into the world. Had it been something like this that had taken him? Grief tightens around my heart. Was this how my mother had died? Crying, tormented, her lifeblood coursing out of her in an inexorable, indifferent rush?

'Come, hold him.' Agnes wrenches my attention from the past, a past I had been far too young to remember, never mind comprehend. She guides my hands to support the small, slick body, then hurries to her healer's bag.

In my trembling hold, he feels far too frail. Too delicate, too vulnerable to be out in this unforgiving world. 'Too early.' My whisper echoes Agnes's words. 'But that's not your fault, little man, is it?' My eyes dart to the bruise on Tibbe's belly, to the welts on her legs. Anger slips through me, sharp and searing. Stumbling in a breath, I let it go, along with my fury. It is futile, and it will not help here.

Agnes returns to kneel beside me, holding a pair of forceps. Growing up with her healer's bag in my home more often than not, I am familiar with all of the tools it contains. But that familiarity doesn't make the sight of this particular tool any less daunting. Its cold metal, scissor-like construction resembles more an instrument of torture than a life-saving device.

Trying not to jostle the baby, I fit myself around Agnes as she adjusts the forceps. Tibbe stirs, glancing down. Her glazed stare catches on Agnes's hands and her eyes fly wide, somehow conveying even more terror than I had seen there before. Another moan cascades from her, before Agnes hushes her.

'It's alright, Tibbe,' she says. 'I'm going to use these to ease your baby out. It won't hurt him.'

I note what Agnes doesn't say. That it won't hurt Tibbe. Still, with as much blood as she is losing, the alternative may be something much more permanent. I swallow, smoothing my thumbs over the baby's bloodied belly.

'On the next swell, I need you to push hard,' Agnes continues, not giving Tibbe time to find more fear. With a glance, she asks if I'm ready. I nod, although I'm not sure how convincing it is. She eases the forceps into place. I wince but don't look away. If Tibbe can bear this, I can bear witness to it. Hopefully without fainting.

With a strangled cry, tension ratchets over Tibbe's body, and although she is markedly weaker now, she jams her eyes closed and heaves a strong, solid push. Guided by the movement, Agnes pulls confidently with the forceps, twisting them to one side, before the baby slips free, and with an expert flick of her fingers she has cleared his nose and mouth.

Suddenly, my arms are full of screaming, slippery baby and I can't look away from his furious little face, screwed up and squawking loudly. He is alive. After all of that, this tiny, fragile thing is actually alive. Enveloped in a tremendous sense of wonder, I am only vaguely aware of Agnes clamping and cutting the cord, before she turns her attention back to Tibbe. It takes a long moment, but eventually my wonder shifts, my gaze cutting past the angry squawks, past the flailing limbs.

Tibbe. Unlike her baby, she is making no sound at all. She's not moving either.

'Agnes,' I say, her name a frantic question on my lips.

'She will be fine,' Agnes replies, her tone brooking no argument. Head bent, she is reaching inside Tibbe, feeling, searching.

That unbearable sense of uselessness floods me once more. 'What can I do?' My question rattles around inside me, *what can I do, what can I do*. I need to fix this. I need to do something to help.

Without looking up, Agnes replies, 'Just care for the bairn. He needs you most right now. I'll bring his mama back to him.' Her searching hand finds something, and she pauses. 'Take him to the bench and get him cleaned up. Check his nose and mouth are fully clear. Listen to his breathing and feel for his heartbeat.' She sounds so calm, so entirely unflustered. It's baffling.

Still, I do as I'm told, rising carefully to my feet to carry the tiny wailing bundle over to the bench, where fresh towels and a warm bowl of water wait. Over my shoulder, I hear Agnes humming to herself, and although I don't recognise the tune, I allow the melody to calm me as I check inside the baby's nose and mouth, then count his heartbeats. I'm gently wiping the blood from his face and body, when the sound of a loud shivering inhale snaps my attention back to the bed.

It's Tibbe. Tibbe is breathing. Tibbe is alive, just like her son.

An untended knot, serrated and dense, unravels inside me. This is not my mother, not my brother. What happened to them has not happened here. I release my gnawing fear and let it wash away, focusing instead on beaming at Tibbe.

Quickly and without any real knowledge of what I'm doing, I swaddle the baby and he settles slightly, seeming to like being tucked somewhere warm. Looking anywhere but at the mess between Tibbe's legs, I walk the baby over to her, placing him in the loving cradle of her arms. Immediately I feel the loss of his ferocious heat, missing the dense weight of his body against mine. Those thoughts scatter, though, as I watch Tibbe's features shift.

Love. Unbreakable, unfathomable, unknowable. All that love for one tiny creature who almost cost Tibbe her life.

As exhausted as she looks, she is radiant. Her ghostly pallor is gone, replaced by a healthy flush. Once glazed and brimming with panic, her eyes are clear and bright, dancing with adoration as she gazes down at her baby. Even her hair looks healthier somehow, less sweat-slicked and more glossy, fuller even.

My eyes track to Agnes, who has efficiently cleared away the bloodied towels, cleaned and covered Tibbe with a blanket, and is now washing her hands at the bench. 'Agnes, what did–?'

'I told you I would bring his mama back, and that's what I did.' She cuts through my question with that same unshakable tone. It's one I know from experience is not worth arguing with.

And yet, I do. 'But how?' I protest. Lowering my voice and turning from Tibbe, I continue, 'She looked *dead*.'

'She wasn't dead. There's no bringing back dead.' There is a severity to her words now that I don't recognise.

My brow furrows. 'So, what *did* you do?'

Agnes sighs. 'I am experienced in this. I've been delivering bairns for decades.'

'I know that, but...' I start, before hesitating, trying to find my words. Confusion nips at me, but it's more than that. A chaotic emotional turmoil laps at the edges of my mind. 'But it doesn't always work out like this.' I bite my lip, holding Agnes's steady, assessing gaze.

With another sigh, she pulls me into a hug. It is firm, familiar and feels very much like that first look Tibbe gifted her son. Filled with unbreakable, unfathomable, unknowable love. 'No, pet,' she murmurs into my hair, 'it doesn't.'

Tears sting my eyes. I sniff them back, drive them down. 'It was just luck, then?' I ask, pulling away, abruptly needing to know why some survive and others don't.

Agnes ignores my embarrassingly petulant tone and moves to cuff me round the ear. I duck and she misses. On purpose. She hasn't actually cuffed me round the ear since I was nine, when I stuffed mice in my pockets because I thought they'd make better friends than the children at school. They got loose in her house, and we had to set my cat, Cheetie, on them.

'Some luck,' Agnes admits. 'Some skill.' Her face stretches into a teasing smile. 'And a little midwife magic, of course.'

A smile kicks at my own lips. 'Sure,' I say. 'Magic.'

Still, when my eyes drift back to Tibbe, I can't help but wonder at the extent of her recovery. I eye the bruise on her belly, wondering at its faded colouring.

My musings are interrupted by a heavy knock.

'Come,' Agnes calls out, the play in her voice vanished.

The door opens to reveal Tibbe's husband, Donald, filling most of the doorframe. Balding, bulky and much older than his adolescent third wife, he glares at Tibbe, then at Agnes. 'It's done?' he rumbles. At Agnes's tight nod, he continues. 'The bairn is a boy?' It is a demand rather than a question. Again, Agnes only nods.

I wonder whether, like me, she doesn't trust her words not to lead her into trouble.

Donald strides to Tibbe's side, where she waits, eyes cast down. 'Give me the bairn.'

Tibbe clutches the baby tighter, looking for a long, tense moment like she will refuse, then lifts him gently to her husband. Donald is noticeably less gentle receiving the baby. There is no look of love, or anything like it, as he assesses the child like he might consider a bull he is buying to stud.

'Isn't he perfect?' Tibbe's voice is tremulous and so very young.

'He'll do,' Donald replies, dropping the baby back in her arms. 'You have one day, wife, before you get out of this bed and back on the farm.' His dark eyes scan Tibbe. 'There's chores needing doing.'

'She'll have three days of bed rest.' Agnes's voice rings clear and confident across the room, meeting Donald's weighty, unflinching stare. 'She lost a lot of blood. She needs to recover.'

Donald flicks a disdainful look over Tibbe, who has shrunken in on herself significantly. 'She looks well enough.'

'She requires rest to recover properly,' Agnes replies, her tone resolute. 'She might look fine–'

'She is needed on the farm,' Donald cuts in. With one meaty hand, he hauls Tibbe out of bed. She grasps frantically onto the baby and only just manages to keep to her feet. She is naked, her legs still stained with blood. She no longer glows. She looks broken, cowed.

My earlier fury streams to the surface. 'She almost died, you fucking bully.'

'What did you call me?' Donald's eyes swivel to me, his expression a black, forbidding thing.

'A bully,' I repeat, ignoring the fist clenching at his side. 'She almost died, because of you. Because of what *you* did to her.' I spit the words before I choke on them. 'She wasn't ready to labour. You beating her forced that baby to come early. The only reason both she and the baby are alive is because of Agnes. You should be thanking her, not talking to her like she's something you'd wipe off your shoe.'

A whimper escapes Tibbe. Donald releases her arm and she collapses onto the bed, somehow keeping the precious bundle she holds from tumbling to the floor.

'How dare you fucking talk to me like that in my own home, you uppity little bitch.' Donald's tone is dangerously low, his demeanour past menacing. 'I'd have thought Menzies hammered better manners into you.' He pauses, a perilous smirk smearing his expression. 'Perhaps he's been gone too long. It's what, six, seven years since he passed?' He doesn't wait for a reply before forging on. 'Long enough for you to require a reminder.'

Agnes steps in front of me. Whether she does it to protect me from Donald, or protect him from me, it does nothing to tamp down my rage. I step around her and slide an equally hostile smile onto my lips.

'What are you going to do?' I snarl. 'Hit me, like you hit Tibbe? Punch me, like you punch Tibbe? I think you'll find I don't make quite such an easy target as a broken 15-year-old girl.'

'Elspeth.'

I bat Agnes's warning aside. 'Come on, old man,' I taunt, discreetly checking the dagger concealed within my skirts. 'Let us see what you've got.'

Donald's eyes dart toward Agnes, uncertain now. He doesn't know what to make of me. Then his expression shifts. I see it happen; the instant he finds his way back to himself. He remembers he is bigger than me, better than me. He remembers he is a man, and well within his rights to put me in my place.

He reaches for his belt.

Marking the movement, absorbing the look of insidious hatred shrouding his features, I am momentarily jolted from the present and sent back in time. Back to a time when *I* was broken, when *I* was cowed.

I see Malcom before me. Cold loathing lines his expression. Danger radiates from him, warning me of what is to come. I am to be taught a lesson. I am to be put in my place.

Agnes's warm hand slips over my arm, bringing me back, before she once again steps in front of me. My skin crawls as breaths escape me in short, painful gusts. *He is not here. He is not coming back. I am free. I am strong. Stronger than I was. He has no power over me now.*

Gradually, my breathing slows, my panic receding to allow my vision to clear.

Donald's smirk is returned; deliberate, delighted, knowing. He sees my fear. It pleases him.

But my fear is not for him. It is for a dead man. And so, it too is dead.

I square my shoulders and stare him down.

Whatever Donald sees in me now, it enrages him. 'You little fucking whore,' he spits, menace slipping and sliding around his words. Belt forgotten, his hands curl into fists as he steps toward me.

Time slows as my fury soars, refusing to be packed down any longer. It swells, rising, surging...

A sudden silvery blue spark explodes behind my eyes.

What the fucking fuck?

Stunned, my fury vanishes, and with it, the inexplicable shimmer.

All the way unnerved, I haul in a few deep breaths and look around warily. With effort, I take in Tibbe, head down, her arms curled protectively around her baby. Donald, a few paces away, halted mid-stride and gaping at me open-mouthed. Agnes stands between us, the guardian and protector she has always been.

'Witch,' Donald hisses, hastily gathering his wits.

'Excuse me?' Agnes replies coolly, like accusations of witchcraft aren't tantamount to a death sentence.

'*She* is a witch.' Gaze narrowed, sneer foul, Donald's words are as dangerous and ugly as his expression.

'She is no such thing,' Agnes replies. She hasn't so much as taken her eyes from Donald, but I know the countenance she wears. It is solid, steady, and utterly unyielding.

Finally, Donald's attention shifts from me to Agnes, where it transforms into befuddled slackness.

'She is no such thing,' Agnes repeats, tone fluid, rhythmic.

'But her eyes...' Donald's words drift away, as slack and empty as his features. After a moment, he echoes, 'She is no such thing.'

'That's right,' Agnes agrees, and I am apt to agree with him as well. That spark had scared the bejeezus out of me, but now, now... I suppose it must have been some strange trick of the light. Or maybe I was just incandescent with rage. Yes, that makes *complete* sense. 'Now, leave us alone so I can tend to your wife and child.'

Without a word, Donald turns, stumbling as he steps out of the room.

'Tibbe will have three days of rest,' Agnes calls after him.

Expression now ominously vacant, Donald nods as he closes the door. 'Yes, Mistress Sampson. Three days.'

Skirts swishing, Agnes spins to face me. 'Are you alright, pet?' Concern fills her words as deeply as her expression.

I blink, struggling to focus through the haze that is my mind. 'Yes?' My reply is less an answer and more of a question. 'What... what happened? Did I do something?'

'Nothing to worry about.' She squeezes my arms, and I feel the disquiet drain from me. Watching it go, she carries on, 'Good. Let's finish cleaning up here. Once I've checked Tibbe and the bairn over, we can be on our way.' She smiles at me, offering me that same warm, reassuring look that has soothed me a hundred times before.

My own smile is weak, but I nod and set to work. I might not know much about birthing, but I know plenty about cleaning. It's something I can do, even through this peculiar haze that refuses to lift.

Mind drifting, I busy myself with a mop, my gaze enamoured by the swirling black that follows each pass I make across the floor. It's only as I coast closer to the bed that my eyes rise to meet Tibbe's.

There is horror there. Genuine, undiluted horror.

I don't understand it, or the protective hand she coils around her baby, but I know it's nothing to worry about.

Nothing to worry about at all.

Chapter 2

North Berwick has been my home my entire life. I know its streets, I know its people, I know its many, *many* quirks. For the most part, I think myself happy here. Or, with little else to compare it to, I'm at least as happy here as I might be anywhere.

There is one thing I would change about living in North Berwick, however, if I could.

I would very much like it if the village's more devout inhabitants would refrain from spitting on me.

I stop, placing a hand against the rough stone wall bordering the kirk, and use the back of my skirts to wipe the gob of spit from my boot.

So unpleasant.

Having disappeared in a swirl of dust and righteous indignation, the offending parishioner is long gone now. Not that I would have done anything to her in retaliation. There's only so much futile fist waving you can do before it becomes clear the act is pointless.

Turning towards the arched wooden doors of the kirk, I roll my eyes at the new sign I see posted there.

The alehouse is the Devil's schoolhouse.
Alewives are the Devil's schoolmistresses.
Repent now and save your soul from the demon drink.

I can't say I'm particularly fond of the term alewife, but I do brew ale to earn a living – and those devout women despise me for it.

Immoral, they say.

Wicked, they whisper.

Sinful, they spit.

Like almost every woman I know, I learned how to brew ale as a young girl. A skill usually passed down from mother to daughter; it's one that provides women a way to fill their bairns' bellies when food is scarce. But, while brewing ale to feed one's family is acceptable, brewing ale to sell to the masses is most definitely not. In those pious women's eyes, I am leading North Berwick's citizens astray, encouraging their drunkenness and debauchery by tempting them with my filthy wares.

Sighing at the absurdity of it all, I turn back towards the market. I need to find my malt merchant and have a word with him about his prices.

I set off at a brisk pace, startling as a sudden gust of wind churns around me, whipping up my hair and wrapping a crumpled piece of paper against the front of my cloak. Before it falls away, I gather it up and scan the familiar typeset.

The Newes of Scotland, October 15, 1590

Noting a disturbing rise in devilry among his subjects, His Royal Highness, King James VI has made a formal appeal to the nation to join him in his noble and godly fight against witchcraft.

Following his return to Scotland with his newly coronated queen, Queen Anne of Denmark, the King has spoken of all the Queen's brother, the King of Denmark and Norway, Christian IV, is doing to eradicate witches from his lands.

"The witches of Denmark are laying siege to our neighbours to the east," King James said in a stirring speech to parliament. "Needless to say, King Christian is working tirelessly to stamp out all traces of witchcraft and its associated devilry, within both Denmark and Norway."

During his speech, King James made mention of the storms that cursed his crossing from Denmark to Scotland earlier this year, asserting they were conjured by Scottish witches hell-bent on eliminating both His Royal Highness and his Queen.

"We Scots are not of a type to lie down and let evil take us," King James said. "I will do my utmost to uncover the root of this torment – and from there, exterminate all witches from this land."

His Royal Highness appealed to every citizen to be on the lookout for signs of witchcraft.

"Witches hide in plain sight," King James said. "It's up to each and every one of Scotland's fine citizens to be watchful for mischief, mayhem and evil. I cannot fight this alone. It should be a personal point of duty for Scots to root out and expose the witches amongst us.

"Whether it's a neighbour, friend, or even a family member, a witch is a witch. I beg all Scots to do the Lord's work and expose any person suspected of witchcraft, so they might be brought to justice."

The Court of Judiciary in Edinburgh advises all complaints associated with witchcraft should be directed to the complainant's local court, where they will be investigated thoroughly under Scotland's Witchcraft Act of 1563.

I mutter a curse, balling the page into my fist. I know government propaganda when I see it. Know this is nothing but a tactic to encourage people to turn on one another. To keep them scared and keep them in line. And it's certainly not the first of its kind I've come across either.

Since the king's return from Norway, he has made a profusion of appeals to root out the *evils of witchcraft*. Newspaper articles and learned tracts, pamphlets and posters, from Sunday sermons to the shouts of town criers, it has all worked in congruence to whip the masses into a frenzy, ensuring the word *witch* is on everyone's lips and never far from their minds. Predictably, witches have since been unearthed in every village, town and city. Although from what I've heard of it, those who accuse often have something petty to hold against those whom they condemn. The general feeling seems to be if you don't like someone or something they've done, simply accuse them of witchcraft.

A good burning at the stake will teach them a lesson.

Abruptly, I am ill at ease, a precarious sense of foreboding washing over me. I no longer want to speak to my malt merchant. I want to speak to Agnes.

As if summoned, I see her rushing along the high street beyond the throngs of the busy market. Desperate to tamp down my unease, I pick up my skirts and hustle to catch up.

'Agnes!' I call out. Chilly autumnal air fills my lungs as I weave around inconveniently large knots of people that dawdle on the high street, skipping as I dodge ankle-shattering cartwheel ridges hidden beneath the mud. 'Agnes. Wait!'

Her silver braid swinging, Agnes spins around, catching me before I barrel into her. 'Elspeth?' she says worriedly. 'What is it, pet?'

I take a moment to catch my breath, then smile, allowing my friend's comforting presence to cast away some of my lingering concern.

'Nothing,' I lie. 'I saw you and thought I'd see what you were doing.' Glancing down, I check for her bulky healer's bag. 'I'm not keeping you from anything important, am I?'

'No, pet,' Agnes replies. 'Nothing like that.'

A distracted frown creases her brow, and my own brows draw together. 'What's wrong?'

Agnes pauses. 'It's Geillis,' she admits. 'Nobody's seen her for the past three days.' She shakes her head and glances around. 'It's not like her to disappear. She has people who depend on her. She'd never forget that.'

Geillis Duncan works as a maidservant in Tranent, a small village that lies some way to the south-west of North Berwick. Like Agnes, she offers her services as a healer, and while I personally don't see much of Geillis, I know the two of them regularly swap remedies and help each other out when needed.

'I've not seen her,' I say. 'But that's not unusual. I can't remember the last time we met.' Which is not strictly true. My mind flashes to the revels in the woods all those months ago at Beltane. Where I inadvertently saw a lot more of Geillis Duncan than most people ordinarily would.

'I've asked around,' Agnes continues, mercifully unaware of the images I'm attempting to drive out of my mind's eye. 'Here and Tranent, nobody has seen hide nor hair of her.'

My words of comfort are cut off when a small, raggedy boy hurtles into us. 'Mistress, mistress,' the boy shouts up at Agnes, clearly agitated.

I don't recognise him, but then, I don't make a habit of looking too closely at the town's dirty-faced little boys.

'What is it, Rab?' Agnes says.

Of course *Agnes* knows him. She likely caught him as he shot out of his mother.

She attempts to calm the boy by placing a hand on his shoulder. It doesn't appear to work. He continues to vibrate in front of us.

'They're comin' for you, mistress,' Rab manages. 'The men fae the Court are comin' for you.'

Cold fingers walk their way up my spine. I stare at the boy, then at Agnes. She appears calm enough, but the hand she removes from Rab's shoulder comes away trembling.

'Why?' I demand. 'What do they want with her?' I push down the desire to shake him for more information.

'It's Mistress Duncan,' Rab starts. 'I heard the men talkin'. They catched her up too and now they're callin' her a witch. They say they're comin' for you next, mistress.' He glances up at Agnes, a look of anguish screwing up his clarty wee face.

'Right. Thank you, Rab,' Agnes says evenly. 'Run along now.'

'But, mistress,' he tries, but Agnes shoos him away and the boy takes off along the road at a run, no doubt eager to share his news elsewhere.

Panic grips me. What can I do? I can't let them take Agnes. I want to run, but I don't know where to run to. Can Agnes run? Not likely. Those knees of hers are always giving her gip.

Agnes interrupts my flitting, terrified thoughts, gripping my elbow and turning me back the way I came. I let her lead, as she steers us off the high street and down a narrow alleyway. A little way along, she pulls us to a stop, angling us into a doorway so that we are hidden from view.

'Good, yes, let's hide,' I say. 'We'll stay here until they're gone, then we can find a better place to hide you.'

'No.' Agnes shakes her head. 'I'm not going to hide from anyone. I just need time to explain.'

Tangled confusion rushes over me. 'Agnes, you can't let them take you.' Just as I had wanted to shake Rab, now I have a strong desire to shake my friend. Violently, if need be. 'The wee boy was talking witches. He said they think Geillis is a witch. That they think *you're* a witch. We *know* what they do to witches, Agnes.'

Terror threatens to overwhelm me, my head swimming with visions of racks and thumbscrews and jagged iron collars.

'I *am* a witch, pet,' Agnes says calmly, in the same way as she might have said, I am a librarian, or I am a little peckish, how long is it going to be until dinner.

Now my head goes entirely blank.

'What?' I try. 'What?' My mind stutters and my mouth refuses to make any further attempt at words.

'I am a witch,' she repeats. 'I have been for a very long time.'

For some reason, my mind flits over the haze of last night. To Tibbe and her baby. To Donald's slack face. To the vicious headache that followed me home and trailed me into the early hours of this morning.

Not helping. I shake those thoughts away.

My focus finds Agnes once more. 'But they'll burn you for it,' I whisper.

'They might. Or they might not.' Agnes places her hands on my arms. I feel the warmth of them through my cloak and the thick sleeves of my wool dress. 'If they want to question me, they'll find me one way or another. And I'll only make myself look guilty if I run.'

Stunned, I simply cannot comprehend her baffling composure. 'A witch?' I say weakly. 'Why didn't you tell me?'

'It wasn't just my secret to tell,' Agnes replies. 'I'm part of a coven. We are all sworn to secrecy. It's for our protection, and for the protection of those we love.' She lifts one hand to cup my cheek.

'But you didn't... you wouldn't do...?' I stammer.

'No,' she spits, anger colouring her voice now. 'I would never use the craft to hurt anyone. None of my coven would. We use what power we have to help people. Why do you think I'm such a good healer?' Her face softens with a small smile.

'You have powers?' I ask, curiosity pricking at my terror.

'Some of us do, others not so much,' Agnes explains. 'It really depends on the witch. My coven was fortunate enough to be granted our magic by the Queen of Elphame. It allowed us access to quite a bit of power.'

While my thoughts had been slowly catching up, processing Agnes's revelations, my mind stutters to a halt once more at the mention of faeries.

'I'm sorry, what?' I splutter. 'The Queen of Elphame?'

'Aye.' Agnes's smile broadens slightly. 'I can't explain it all now, though. We don't have time.' She peers out of the doorway to glance up to the high street. 'I can't imagine we have long.'

'Yes, but *faeries*?'

I can just about wrap my head around the fact that witches might be real, but faeries seem a step too far. Sure, there are all the legends, the myths, but they're just stories. Living, breathing faeries simply cannot be something that exist.

'Like I said, we don't have time to get into it,' Agnes says. 'But aye, faeries are real. The Queen of Elphame is real. There is a whole world beyond the veil, full of faeries and goblins and so much more. I wish I could have had the chance to talk about it all with you before now. To explain it all properly.'

'I saw you on Beltane,' I blurt out. Heat rises in my cheeks, my thoughts racing over all I witnessed that afternoon in the woods. Of the peculiar pagan celebration Agnes had been a part of, but later told me nothing about.

'Did you indeed?' Agnes's reply is warm, touched with humour. 'And why didn't you tell me?'

'Why didn't you tell me!' Hurt crawls its way up my throat, squeezing my words.

'Oh, I am sorry, pet.' Agnes pulls me into a hug. 'I wish I could have.' Her arms feel strong and warm and familiar wrapped around me.

Her hugs have been a staple in my life up to now. They comforted me when I skinned my knee as a bairn. Reassured me when I first got my period and thought I was knocking on Death's door. Supported me when I broke down and told her of Malcom's ways. Through everything, Agnes has been there. Always. The notion that now she might not be is unfathomable, too vast to comprehend.

'It's too late for me to explain my truth,' she continues, dragging my attention back to the here and now. 'But it's not too late for you to find yours.'

I draw back to search her face, seeing the ways the years have lined it with evidence of her life, her laughter. 'What do you mean, *my* truth?' I ask, wilfully blocking out the angry shouts of angry men up on the high street.

'You'll need to speak with your da about that,' Agnes says. 'To start you off, at least.'

'My father?' I realise vaguely how dense I sound repeating everything Agnes says, but it's about all my mind can manage as it wades through each of these new truths.

'Aye, ask him to tell you about your mother,' she says firmly. Pausing to think, she continues, 'Now, we should just about have time for this. Close your eyes.'

I do as I'm told without comment, although it goes against the grain. She moves closer, her breath warm on my face as she murmurs something I can't quite make out. With a gentle kiss on each of my eyelids, intense, golden light explodes behind them.

My eyes jolt open.

'What in the name of holy hellfire was that?' I blink away stars until I can see normally again.

'I gave back your Second Sight,' Agnes explains. 'That should help you find what you're looking for, when it's time.'

'Wait, what?' I'm tired of feeling so confused. 'What do you mean give *back*?' As far as I'm aware, I've never had the ability to see anything magical or otherworldly.

'Your da will explain,' Agnes says, still inexplicably calm. She takes a deep breath. 'Now, I suppose I should go and let these men find me. They won't stop until they do.'

My ears pick out the commotion getting louder, nearer. Not so far away now.

'Please don't go to them,' I plead. 'You need to run.' A strangled sound escapes me as I try frantically to think. 'You could ask the Queen for help. Or you could... you could hide in Faerie. They won't find you there.' The words tumble out of me, my mind tripping over their peculiarity. Could Agnes do that? Visit Faerie, like she might travel to Dirleton or Tantallon?

Her eyes searching mine, Agnes gives me a sad smile. 'No, pet. I couldn't,' she says with a small shake of her head. 'I couldn't leave Geillis and the rest of my coven to face this alone. It's not in me to abandon them.'

I want to ask why she feels like she can abandon me, but I don't get the chance. Agnes pulls me into a fierce hug and I am enveloped by it, by her. Instead of arguing, I try desperately to draw strength from the familiar feel of it, from her incomprehensible composure. But still, I feel the searing sting of tears behind my eyes, my chest constricting painfully as I try to hold them back.

No, no, this can't be happening.

Before I can say anything else, Agnes steps back, resolve setting determined lines onto her face as she gifts me a tight smile. 'Now stay here, pet,' she says, placing a firm hand on my shoulder. Then she backs out of the doorway, and I watch, unable to move, as she hurries along the alleyway and strides out into the watery sunlight that fills the high street.

Feet pinned to the ground, all I can do is listen as my heart pounds in my ears. Two beats, five beats, ten.

Then I am free.

I pick up my skirts and run. Bursting out of the alleyway, I whip my head left and right, frantically seeking Agnes's blue cloak, her silver braid, trying to catch any glimpse of her in the jostling crowds.

There. I spot her sitting high up on horseback, wrists bound in front of her.

I'm about to cry out, to run to her, when the man sitting behind her abruptly turns the horse and digs his heels into its flanks. They take off at a canter, with a dozen more men on horseback chasing close behind.

Heart in freefall, agony carves up my chest. As hot tears, furious and futile, drift down my cheeks, I can do absolutely nothing as I watch my best friend being carried away by angry, dangerous men, careening down the high street, scattering crowds as they go.

Chapter 3

Spilling through the front door, I find my father propped against a pillow, a book lying open on his lap and his mouth slack, gentle snores escaping him. I push down my frustration and drag a chair over to the bed, hesitate, then shake him gently to wake him. At any other time, I would leave him to sleep. I know how often he wakes confused and disorientated if roused.

But I need answers. And the only one left to give them to me is him.

'Da,' I say, pleading. 'I need to talk to you.'

His eyes flick open. He gazes around blankly.

Fuck.

My father has had fewer and fewer lucid moments over the past few months, and I can see immediately that this is not one of them.

'Da, please,' I try again. 'They took Agnes. She's gone. She told me to talk to you. I need you to come back to me.' I take both of his hands in my own, gripping them tightly. Probably a little too tightly.

'My sweet girl,' he says. 'What did I do to deserve you?' His eyes find their focus, but his vacant smile tells me he's still not here with me.

'Agnes told me to ask you about Mama,' I say, almost begging now. 'She said I need to find out the truth. *My* truth.'

At this, his eyes sharpen slightly and his gaze fixes on me. 'The truth,' he says, voice soft. 'Aye, I suppose it is about time for that.'

I let out a deep breath I hadn't realised I'd been holding. 'Tell me then, Da,' I say. 'Please, I need to know.'

Still somewhat dreamlike, my father soothes his thumbs absently across the backs of my hands and sighs the words that cause the bottom to drop out of my world for the second time today.

'Your mama isn't dead, Elspeth.'

Shock steals my reply. I cannot speak, can barely think.

But it seems I don't need to. My father has a story to tell.

'My dearest Hester,' he begins, the frailty in his words matching the bones of him. 'She was in so much pain. I could hear her screams, but I couldn't go to her. You were so little. I had to make sure you stayed asleep, so you wouldn't worry about your mama hurting so. I rocked you and held you, staying out of Agnes's way as she helped your mama labour.

'Then things went quiet. Far too quiet. I waited as long as I could, listening to that quiet. But then I couldn't take it anymore, I needed to know what was happening. I carried you in here and Agnes was kneeling by the bed, where you are sitting now. Your mama was lying where I am, pale, so pale. There was so much blood, it was everywhere.'

In the echo of his words, I am transported to last night, to Tibbe's bedside.

I blink away the image and refocus on my father.

For a moment, he drifts, and I worry I've lost him. I squeeze his hands and open my mouth to speak, before he continues, misery contorting his features.

'Agnes told me she had to do it, that she had to ask for help. That she couldn't let them both die. Agnes and your mama were such good friends. Even in the state I was in, I could see what it was doing to her to see your mama like that.

'I started to ask what she meant, who she had asked to help. You see, there *was* no one else. If a midwife with Agnes's experience couldn't help her, then your mama was beyond saving.

'But I didn't get a chance. Before I could say anything, the front door swung open and in came the strangest creature. A faerie... some sort of faerie, I'd never seen the like.'

I tense, breath catching in my chest. Just like Agnes, my father – my very ordinary father – is talking of faeries. Like they actually exist.

He carries on, seemingly lost as much to me, as to his story.

'This creature strode past me, going straight to your mama. It placed one hand on her forehead and the other on her swollen belly, then started chanting something in no language I'd ever heard. Out of nowhere, it was as if a bolt of lightning hit your mama's body. Her whole body lurched upward in the bed, then she fell back down and heaved in a long, deep breath. Her eyes popped open, and she looked around wild-eyed, before fixing on the creature.

'I'd never... I'd never seen her look so scared.'

His voice cracks, and my throat tightens to hear it. I want to tell him that it's alright, that he doesn't need to tell me the rest.

But he does. I need to hear it.

Clearing his throat, he continues, words wavering. 'She began to scream again, the most agonising howls. Agnes hurried to the end of the bed, propping up your mama's knees. She told her to bear down, bear down. Your mama pushed, pushed, pushed, and out he came. My wee boy. He was so small, so blue. So quiet.'

His voice breaks again, and despite the tears that spill from my lashes, I do not tell him to stop. Cannot tell him to stop.

'Agnes did her best to bring him back. She rubbed him, thumped his back, breathed into his tiny mouth. But there was no helping him. I looked to the creature, just standing there, watching. I knew it could help him, like it had helped your mama. But it didn't. It just watched as Agnes placed the little mite in your mama's arms. She let out the most terrible keening sound at that. She looked so beautiful, lying there with your brother. But there was so much agony. I couldn't move for it.'

He exhales, eyes glossy with his own unshed tears, reliving it all too clearly in his mind's eye. Reliving the raw torment of losing his child, who had never had the chance to live. Of seeing his beloved wife in pain, and the defeat in not being able to help her.

Swallowing hard, he continues. 'I looked back to the creature, and for a moment, I thought I saw that same agony, mirrored in its peculiar features. But then it was gone, its face a mask once more as it said, "It is done. Now, you come with me."

'Your mama looked to me then, feverish, then she looked down at you, still sleeping so soundly in my arms. Tears poured down her face, and something in me snapped. This rage I felt, for my son, for your poor distraught mama. For this creature in *my* house who had done so much and so little, and now wanted to take *my* Hester away from me. I wanted to hurt it. To make it pay.'

Steel having flashed suddenly through his words, he sighs again, his voice gentling as he fixes his frail gaze back on me.

'But before I could do anything, before I could even move to place you somewhere safe, it turned to me, casting one hand up in the air. It chanted more of its incomprehensible words, and I was stuck. I couldn't move. It felt like freezing water had been poured over me and I had turned to ice. It soaked into my body, my bones, my mind.

'I could do nothing but watch as it passed Agnes, who was knelt on the floor shaking, and stood before me. I looked in its extraordinary face, watched as its gaze narrowed, and saw something at war behind those bizarre, inhuman eyes. I was still frozen. I tried, but I couldn't stop it from placing its hands on you. It closed its eyes and chanted. I'm so sorry, love, I couldn't do anything. I couldn't, I couldn't. I could only watch as it cast this bright, bright light over you, wrapping you up in it. Then the light was gone. Disappeared completely.

'I asked it what it had done, pleaded, but it ignored me, turning to place your brother in Agnes's arms. Then it gathered your mama up, like she weighed no more than a child herself. It took her. I don't know where. It took her and I couldn't...'

Silence falls over the room and I stare at my father, wondering if there is more, *needing* there to be more.

But he just lies there, quiet and calm, detached from it now. Not at all like he'd just told me a story that changes the very parameters of my life.

My mother is alive. *Alive!* But she was taken. Stolen from us.

Still holding my father's hands, I shake them.

'Where is she now, Da? Where did it take her?' I say, hoping desperately he's not all the way gone. I'd seen it happen so many times before. Completely lucid, and then, vacant.

He remains quiet, staring at me but not seeing me. I look into his eyes, pale watery blue to my green, and I will him to come back to me.

'Please, Da, please. I need to know where Mama was taken.' Desperation coats my words so thickly I can almost taste it.

'It was a faerie. A faerie took her,' he murmurs, his expression unfocused. 'The Queen of Elphame will know. A faerie took her. You need to ask the Queen.'

I start. *The Queen of Elphame?* First Agnes, now my father. *What is going on?*

I try again, try to cajole my father to return to me with more pleading words that he does not, or cannot hear. After several long moments of this, I give up and adjust his pillows, settling him back down to sleep.

Standing, I roll my shoulders, trying to decide what to do next.

I need to know what happened to my mother.

I need to know what that creature did to me.

I need to help Agnes.

I need to make a plan.

Chapter 4

I check over the contents of my pack. Not for the first time, or even the second. Anxiously, I let my hands roam over the packages of food, the change of underclothes, the dagger. I reach into the pocket of my skirt, touching the rowan ward concealed there.

I haven't the slightest idea what I will need for this trip, or even how long I might be gone. But I am ready.

As ready as I can be anyway.

Mentally ticking off all the things I've done to prepare, I can't think of anything I might have left out.

Having arranged for some acquaintances to cover my brewing obligations, I'd told my customers that I am leaving on family business, that I may be gone some time.

And Agnes. *Agnes.*

I shove down my tears. I've had enough of those.

As much as it twisted me up inside, there had been nothing more I could have done for Agnes. She'd been taken to Edinburgh, that much I know. But for me to pry further, to try to visit, I know well enough how that might shine unwanted light in my direction. When it comes to catching up witches, the authorities tend to look to those who are closest to the accused, and it's no coincidence how often they end up cast into chains alongside their loved ones.

While I would do almost anything to help Agnes, I know I will achieve precisely nothing by getting myself locked in an iron collar beside her. That is no way to get her free.

My eyes fall to my father.

In the days since his revelation, he has rarely been lucid. Even when I'd been able to talk with him, he had refused to say more, explain more. It had felt like a light had been snuffed out inside his head.

Beside the hearth, the old widow Ogilvie sits, patiently darning the elbow of one of my father's shirts. I'd asked her to look out for my father and had been only mildly surprised at how happily she'd taken up the request. I've long suspected Mrs Ogilvie of having a fancy for him. Not that he ever paid her much notice in return.

That's Da. I tick him off my list as well.

Now, is there anything I'm missing?

I have few friends, and none that are close, none who will likely miss me. Once upon a time, I had Malcom, but even when things were good, I'd never thought of him as a friend. Now, I have Agnes, and my father, but there are no others I would need to notify of my leaving. Certainly no family to speak of.

Distractedly, my mind wanders over how others might consider me lonely. But I have never minded being alone and have always been quite content in my own company. I like being self-sufficient, self-contained. Even before Malcom, when I was wee, I was the same.

And after Malcom… I try not to think about how hard I'd had to work to recreate my own sense of independence after he died. Not wanting to be reliant like that again. So reliant I couldn't get away.

Pushing myself out of my head, I pick up my cloak and shawl, wrapping myself against the chill October night. I take the few steps to my father's bedside and see that he is asleep. Knowing it's better that way, I lean over and brush a kiss against his forehead, feeling it smooth and soft in slumber.

'Goodbye, Da,' I murmur. 'I love you.'

He doesn't stir as I straighten, nod to Mrs Ogilvie, and pick up my pack. I take one last look at the three small rooms that have been my home for so long now. At the walls that have seen so much of my life. I wonder when I will return, when I will see my father again. What state he will be in when I do.

I scold myself for my melancholy. Navel gazing has never helped anyone, and it certainly won't help me where I'm going.

Knowing I'm as ready as I'll ever be, I walk to the door, open it quietly and step out, where darkness envelops me and has me shivering at the creep of winter in the air.

Having picked my destination carefully in the days before, my journey up the large hill looming over North Berwick is a hard trudge, if uneventful. While I try to stop my mind from travelling the same ground it's worn away over the past few days, staying out of my head during the long walk is difficult.

Finally, I reach the top of the hill, breathing deeply, each exhale billowing out in front of me in a white, puffy cloud. With the full moon hanging low in the sky, it illuminates farmland sprawling below, reaching out to the tiny twinkling lights of the villages along the coast. The black seas beyond appear still and serene from up here, but I know just how rough they can get, having watched many a wild storm blow through.

Turning, I find the pile of wood I'd stacked there yesterday. Thankful there had been no rain, I check it over, before taking out the flint stone and small pile of kindling I'd carried from home. In a practised motion, I flick the flint stone and soon have the lit kindling sparking under the firewood.

Up on the hilltop, the winds sweeping up from the sea are stronger than they had been down on the coast. While I know this will help the fire catch faster, I can't help but curse those bitter tendrils working their way under my cloak, making my exposed cheeks and nose sting as they burn to vivid pink.

This had better bloody work.

In truth, I have no idea if this very dubious plan of mine *will* work. Or what I will do if I simply remain up on this hilltop, with nothing to show for my efforts except frostbitten extremities.

It will work. I cling to my positivity, even as my sanity feels like it may have deserted me. *It* has *to work.*

Stamping my feet and feeling utterly ridiculous, I check the bonfire is fully ablaze, then make my call to Nicnevin.

Sometimes referred to as a goddess, sometimes a witch, sometimes as a grand high faerie, Nicnevin is a being even I – who have never had any desire to get caught up in stories of the supernatural – have taken note of over the years.

Leading the *Sluagh,* Nicnevin is said to capture the souls of the dying and take them... well, I'm not quite sure where she takes them, but the fact that she can take them *anywhere* is a scary enough prospect.

What I *am* sure of, though, is tonight – Samhain – is Nicnevin's night.

As one of the nights when the veil between the human and faerie realms is at its thinnest, Samhain is the night when Nicnevin is most often seen riding the skies within the *Sluagh*, collecting souls and listening keenly through that slender veil for mortals who are unwise enough to catch her attention.

While I hadn't been keen to wait the few days for Samhain, I'd been unable to conjure up any other way for me to gain access to the faerie realm. If I am to make it to Faerie, to the Queen of Elphame, this is the night to do it. And Nicnevin is the one to take me there.

Self-consciously, I continue my call, yelling out Nicnevin's name into the darkness.

I stop to listen, hesitating, doubting.

And then, I hear it.

The *Sluagh na Marbh*.

It is here.

One minute, there is nothing but the harsh, whipping wind and eager crackle of the fire, the next, a cacophony of noise crashes over me. It is a vociferous roar of thundering hoofbeats and the wild barking of frenzied dogs, distorted by feral and furious screams of torment that do not sound in any way human.

Trailing the commotion, the *Sluagh* emerges into view, a horrific manifestation that aptly demonstrates why it is named the host of the dead. It remains translucent, otherworldly, as its swarming hoards touch down, led by towering grey riders sitting atop ghastly black steeds. Wraithlike, the hooded faces of the riders are gone, missing, replaced by dark gaping holes that seem to drink in the light. Spectral, near invisible, the captured souls wail their torment, hemmed in by snarling hounds that strain and snap against unseen tethers, keeping the eerie masses in check.

The clamour of it, the turmoil, it is immense.

A crone steps out from the midst of the hoard, and I try desperately to keep my terror from overwhelming me as I watch her transform from immaterial to material with each light, skipping step.

Even at first glance, it is evident why mothers would use this creature to scare their children. While I can't recall my own mother doing so, I remember plenty of children at school whose mothers had terrorised them with the threat of gifting them to Nicnevin if they continued to misbehave.

There is just something so innately *menacing* about her.

Shrouded in a long grey mantle, she picks her way around the bonfire, stepping right up to me before stopping abruptly and placing her hands on solid, lumpy hips. With fine wisps of silver hair drifting over her shoulders, she has a face that is so deeply lined, I wonder whether there might actually be more wrinkle than face. She is old, incalculably so, and also, far from easy on the eye.

Pointed ears protrude at an angle, and a long, crooked nose juts out above thin lips and a receding chin. It is her eyes that transfix me, though. Those bright violet eyes seem to pull me closer the longer I stare into them.

'Close your mouth, stupid girl,' the crone barks, her voice shrill. 'You will catch flies.'

I think it likely this old hag would enjoy snapping her yellowing teeth over some unsuspecting fly, but I choose not to voice this.

'Nicnevin?' I whisper. I am torn between feeling utterly aghast at this living, breathing representation of the faerie realm, and being dumbfounded that my plan to summon her actually worked.

'Yes, girl, that is me,' Nicnevin replies sharply. 'I heard your call. What is it that you want?'

Her eyes bore into me, and I stare back, mesmerised, unable to shut out the uproar that envelops us. Stamping hooves, baying howls and anguished wails continue to twist around my ears, driving out any hope of coherent thought.

'I have a busy night,' she prompts, terse, hurried. 'Come on now. Spit it out.'

I try to make my mouth form words, try to articulate a sentence that might actually make sense. 'Lady Nicnevin,' I manage, trying for a low bow. It can't hurt to be polite, after all, especially when dealing with faeries. 'I called you here to ask you to take me to Faerie.' Considering, I quickly add, 'Please.'

Her narrowed gaze burrows deep into my bones. 'Why do you want to go to Faerie?'

'I need to speak with the Queen of Elphame.' I shoot for confident but don't quite get there.

'And why do you think the Queen would want to see something like you?' She drips disgust onto the word *something*, and takes her time to look me up and down, the hollow sound of laughter echoing within the hoard.

Rude. I square my shoulders. I may be out of my element dealing with this old crone, but that doesn't mean I will let myself be talked down to. 'That is my business,' I bite out. 'Not yours.'

Nicnevin pins me with another look that goes straight to my soul. 'Well, if that is how it's to be, girl, I will continue on my way.

Lots of souls to capture. I don't need to be dallying, wasting my time on uppity little sprigs like you.'

She turns to leave, and I startle. I know of no other way into the faerie realm, and I've already wasted so much time waiting for Samhain. My guts twist thinking of Agnes trapped in a cell. I need help. I need answers. I need Nicnevin.

No matter how snappish she is. Or how disturbing her eyes are.

'Please, stay,' I almost shout. 'I will give you a gift!' Faeries like gifts, I am sure of it.

She swings back around, not bothering to conceal her blatant interest. 'What kind of gift?' she asks, her face creasing into an alarming smile. 'I do so enjoy getting gifts, you know. No one ever thinks to give me gifts anymore... not with my looks fading so.' She cackles softly, running her hands in extravagant curves over her bulky form.

Again, soft peals of laughter resonate through the hoard.

My mind cycles, frantic. What can I offer? I don't imagine Nicnevin will think much of the food in my pack, or of my underclothes. Even my dagger is quite ordinary. I try to think back over the stories I have heard of faeries, of what they like, things they appreciate.

'A memory,' I say, triumphant, recalling a faerie story I'd heard at Agnes's knee. 'I'll give you one of my most treasured memories.'

Nicnevin nods, seemingly appeased. 'Yes, that will do very nicely.' She spits into her palm, then grasps my unwilling hand in an unnervingly strong handshake. 'Done, sprig. You have yourself a deal. You give me that memory and I will take you to Faerie.'

I look at my hand, grimacing at the wetness. 'Was that really necessary?' I ask, wiping it on my cloak. 'The spitting?'

Nicnevin cackles, louder this time. 'Not at all. I just wanted to see your face when I did it.'

Abruptly, she is much closer, and I jump, wondering how the hell she moved so quickly without my notice. Her gnarled hands lift to cup my temples, and I draw on all my available willpower, forcing myself not to shy away. Her eyes snap shut and deafening silence surrounds us as the hoard falls wholly, utterly silent.

Urging my own eyes closed, I conjure a memory, one of my most golden. One of my mother.

We are out on the heath, wrapped up in one another, surrounded by heather and a vibrant assortment of wildflowers. The sun burns bright in the sky, and we have nothing to do but play. I rest my small head on her lap, relishing her soft touch as she draws long strokes through my hair. I look up at her and ask her to sing me a song. Happiness curling through me, I listen as she sings the most beautiful song I have ever heard.

I smile, savouring the sweet ache of the memory, then open my eyes, swallowing around the tightness in my throat.

Then it is gone, the memory vanished, torn away to leave something blank and empty in its place. Stunned, I search the void it has left, my mind contorting around it, prodding the deep gouge where the recollection once rested.

Nicnevin's eyes flash open, her mouth spreading wide in another alarming smile. Her tone is just as disturbing as she steps back and says, 'Interesting.'

Before I can ask what exactly she finds so interesting, she snakes out one of her twisted hands to grasp my wrist, then drags me toward the hoard.

Anticipating our departure, the immense stallions stamp impatient hooves, their faceless riders wrestling their reins in an attempt to keep them under control. Spit flying from their mouths, the ethereal hounds snap savagely at me as I pass, and all around me, sorrowful wails recommence their cacophony.

I scramble behind Nicnevin, dancing desperately around the edges of the hoard as I try to keep up. Out of the corner of my eye, my attention snags on my boots. They are... transparent. As is my cloak, my legs. All of me.

Incredulous, I wave my free hand in front of my face.

I can see through it. I can see all the way through my hand.

My dishevelled mind succeeds in tossing out a few of its more noteworthy curses, before the world fades away and I descend into blackness.

Chapter 5

I wake with my face in a pile of foetid, scratchy blankets. My head, heavy and hazy, doesn't quite belong to me and I only just manage to lift it to hack out a lungful of thick fust. Blearily, I blink once, twice, then use my knuckle to remove a rather dense lump of crust lodged in my eye. Happily, the movement rewards me with the touch of an actual, solid hand, rather than some ghostly version of one.

Good start, Elspeth. Big improvement.

Shoving myself up, I turn to sit, not particularly enjoying the blurry fog still slithering over me, but needing to see where I am. Through the sludge, I try to encourage memories of last night to play out in my head, only to realise there's not much of anything after I was dragged into the hoard. It's all just eerie snippets of movement and the ungodly noise that had surrounded it all.

I look around.

Is this Faerie?

It really could be anywhere.

Apart from the blankets, the room is bare. Stone walls, stone floor, stone ceiling... Much like a cell.

A shot of panic courses through me.

I'd made a deal with a faerie, but what had I actually agreed to? Nicnevin had consented to bring me to Faerie in trade for a memory, but no part of the deal had specified in what state I would arrive. Or what would happen to me after.

How could I be so stupid?

Rising hurriedly, I brush myself down and look around, urgently seeking anything I may have missed. *There!* My pack and cloak sit tucked behind the blankets. Comforted I have at least this, I grab the pack and check its contents, making sure everything is there and is as it should be.

Now it's time to see if my stupidity has gotten me locked in a Faerie dungeon, destined never to see daylight again.

I swing my pack over my shoulder and my cloak over one arm, then pace to the door. With a tentative twist of the handle, the door swings towards me on soundless hinges. Relief surges through me and I peek my head out, only to find the stone hallway beyond entirely empty.

'Hello?'

Answered by nothing but echoes, I determinedly pick a direction and start walking.

Like the room – cell, whatever it had been – the hallways are made of stone, bare of any decoration. High on the walls, golden balls of light burn brightly within sconces, powered by what I can only assume is magic.

'Hello?' I try again.

Again, nothing but echoes answer in reply.

My anxiety builds as I continue to wander the warren of deserted hallways, finding door after door locked. Finally, one opens into a vast, imposing hall and I hesitate at the doorway. Hindered by an undeniable sense of trepidation, I force my footsteps inside, knowing I must find someone, anyone, if I'm to learn where my questionable faerie deal has landed me.

As my feet carry me forward, I stare up in wonder, my mouth dropping at the sight of an enormous chandelier, which floats, suspended some four or five yards below the soaring cathedral ceiling. Around it, a multitude of gauzy draperies hang, swaying in a breeze I'm not entirely sure is there. While the walls again are bare, large stained-glass windows splash the hall with colour, giving the daunting space a sense of being much cheerier than it has any right to be.

Turning slowly to take it all in, I notice a small figure bustling through another door at the far end of the hall.

'Hello?' I call out, hesitant.

Noticing me right back, the tiny man observes me, pausing for a beat, before coming at me, pumping his short legs in an impressively fast run. I falter backwards right before he slams to halt, a fretful edge to his coal black eyes as he takes me in. Dressed in a red felt suit and matching cap, he fidgets in front of me, looking like he has a dozen other places he would much rather be. 'You must be her,' he says, his small voice high and reedy. 'The one Lady Nicnevin brung here. She'll want to see you now you is *finally* awake.'

I squint out the nearest window. It doesn't help. I still have no notion of what time it is.

Not that it matters. Whether the hour is late or early, my sludgy mind tells me whatever sleep I managed had been far from restful.

Offering its own opinion on the unidentified passage of time, my stomach takes this opportunity to make its thoughts known.

'And I suppose you'll be wanting food an' all,' the little man chirps.

Before I have the chance to protest, he turns on his heel and pelts back the way he came.

'Alright then,' I say to no one in particular, then, not entirely sure what to do with myself, I take another amble around the hall.

It doesn't take long.

The stained glass is placed too high to see out of, and aside from faded velvet lounging chairs positioned along the walls, there is nothing else of interest apart from the large wooden table set with a dozen chairs at the centre of the hall.

I'm hovering beside said table when Nicnevin sweeps in some moments later.

Moving with a lot more pace than one would expect from a creature of her years, she surges toward me. Unsure whether my eyes are playing tricks on me, I blink, certain I see the fabric of her skirts skip away in front of her, like it's trying to stay out of her way. Behind her, the little man charges, somehow managing not to spill anything from the large tray he carries.

'Ah, sprig, I see you're finally awake.'

For fuck's sake. What do these faeries have against sleep?

Forcing down my sleep-deprived petulance, I grit out a smile. I need to remain civil, at least until I work out where I am and what exactly is happening here.

'Good day, Lady Nicnevin,' I say. *That's an excellent start.* 'I am sorry if I overslept, but we were out all night. From what I can remember anyway.'

'Yes, yes, a most fruitful collection. I do enjoy a good reaping on Samhain.' She draws out the syllables as she says *saaah-win*, smiling that same horrendous smile I remember from last night.

The sight of it making me distinctly uncomfortable, I shift my weight awkwardly from one foot to the other. I might need to keep her on side, but I'd rather not consider too closely whatever devilry makes her smile so.

Searching for something, anything else to look at, my attention catches on what the little man is doing. Balancing atop one of the chairs, he sets out a small feast, moving each item carefully from his tray onto the table. The scent of roasted meat winds its way to my nose, and my stomach forcefully announces what it thinks of the smell.

'Mathe has kindly brought you some sustenance, little sprig.' Nicnevin looks pointedly at my stomach. 'It seems you might be in need of it.' She then stalks toward the table, where the little man pulls out a chair for her, waits for her to sit, and shoves it back in.

I hesitate, then follow. After Mathe dutifully does the same for me, I drape my cloak and pack over the chair beside me. 'Thank you, um, Mathe?'

Hazy with distraction, I absently wonder whether his name means the same in Faerie as it does at home, where the word *mathe* means bear. This man couldn't look less like a bear... unless he's hiding some kind of ursine magic within that diminutive frame.

'You is most welcome, human,' he replies, and I realise I am staring. Unconcerned by my unintended rudeness, he bows, then scurries away, leaving me alone with Nicnevin.

Forcing my attention back to the table, to her, I see she has piled her plate high with food and is in the midst of pulling apart what looks to be a very large squirrel. I watch, hypnotised, as her long, gnarled fingers tear meat from delicate bones, before sliding pieces up towards her snapping yellow maw.

I rip my gaze away. Even as my stomach rumbles its heartfelt protest, I know I will not eat here. Despite being somewhat clueless as to the ways of Faerie, even I know I must not eat food within the faerie realm. Beyond that though, beyond those nebulous warnings the faerie stories offered, I know eating at the table of someone such as Nicnevin could never lead anywhere good.

She glances at my empty plate and her greasy lips curve into a knowing smile. 'So,' she says.

'So,' I repeat. 'I suppose I should be on my way. I assume you carried out your end of the deal and we are in Faerie?'

'Yes, of course, sprig. Old Nicnevin would never renege on a deal.'

Shoving aside my fervent dislike for people who talk about themselves in the third person, I remind myself I can't afford to put this deeply unsettling faerie offside by revealing what I truly think of her. The fact that she talks about herself in the third person is probably the least concerning thing about her.

'Thank you, then,' I offer tightly. Wanting suddenly to be far from Nicnevin and her intrusive violet stare, I push back my chair to stand, the noise of scraping stone reverberating around the cavernous space overly loud in my ears.

Observing me with interest, Nicnevin interrupts my designs to escape. 'I have to wonder, little sprig, in which direction do you hope to go?' She cocks her head to one side, that knowing smile of hers firmly back in place. 'Do you happen to know the lands of Faerie well?'

I stop, awkwardly stuck between sitting and standing. While my plan to get to Faerie had been shaky at best, my plan to find the Queen now I'm here is admittedly non-existent.

Maybe there will be road signs I can follow?

'No, you don't, do you? Perhaps then, I could assist with that.' Lifting the napkin from the side of her plate, she wipes her mouth daintily. 'Lawrens, could you come in here?' Her rasping words twist oddly in the air, seeming to gain volume the further away they travel.

Still unsure whether I should be sitting or standing, I watch as perhaps the most disconcertingly attractive man I have ever clapped eyes on enters the hall. At the sight of him, my arse makes the decision for me and hits the chair beneath me with an ungainly thump.

Dressed plainly in black boots, black trousers and a black shirt, he wears his impressive height with confidence, his finely sculpted form making itself known with each long stride. Flowing and fluid, his movements highlight broad shoulders that cut down to a narrow V at his waist, and as those long legs of his carry him ever closer, my breath falters as his face falls further into focus. With inky hair framing sharply pointed ears and even sharper cheekbones, he is undeniably beautiful, but with his thin lips, cut jaw and aquiline nose, there is an indefinable strength to his perfection.

As beautiful as he is, though, what I can't seem to tear my eyes from are the twining shadows that curl and creep over him. Twisting black tendrils shift and slink over his skin, creating an ever-changing tapestry at his neck, his throat, his hands. I can't see any more of him – sadly – but I am somehow sure the shifting marks must cover him entirely.

Nicnevin turns and winks at me. 'Pretty, isn't he?'

Having reached the table, Lawrens pulls out the chair opposite mine and sits, eyeing me carefully with a slate grey regard.

Ignoring the urgent desire to sort my sleep-mussed hair, I sit on my hands to avoid the temptation to make myself look more presentable. *Stop it, Elspeth. You are not here to ogle faerie men.*

No matter how... pretty they are.

In the six years since Malcom's death, I have not experienced even an inkling of interest towards any man. While I'd be the first to admit the selection on offer hadn't exactly been tempting, even now, with damnable perfection staring back at me from across the table, I feel something deep within me roil against the idea of letting a man get close to me again.

I decide I won't like this Lawrens. He really is far too beautiful. And honestly, what kind of person can he be if he willingly spends time with Nicnevin?

'I've had a chat with young Lawrens, and he has kindly agreed to be your guide while you are here in Faerie,' Nicnevin says, interrupting my musings. 'He will help you find the Queen.'

Noting the sneer in her words as she mentions the Queen, I assess her, instantly suspicious. 'Why would you help me?' I ask guardedly. Their eyes dart together in meeting, then shoot away just as quickly, but whatever passes between them is too fast for me to catch.

'Why, my little sprig, I brought you into the faerie realm. Do you not think that makes me feel responsible for your safety? I can't have you wandering off and being eaten by the first angry pixie you meet.' Nicnevin spreads her hands on the table in front of her in a gesture I assume is an attempt at sincerity. 'Faerie can be a dark and dangerous place. Especially for a tasty little morsel such as you.'

Her tone is syrupy, her words contrived, but at her mention of tasty morsels, I can't help but think of those pale fingers of hers sliding greasy pieces of meat into her mouth.

I swallow thickly.

Trying to marshal my thoughts, I consider my options. I can wander out into Faerie and try to find the Queen with no idea of where I am going. Or I can trust Nicnevin and her so-called guide.

I slide my gaze to Lawrens, who is lounging in his chair like he's been poured into it. He has still not spoken, but his eyes twinkle as he looks back at me, his mouth kicking up at one side.

In my mind, suspicion wars with pragmatism.

Then curiosity creeps in.

'So, you're saying Lawrens will fend off angry pixies and such?' I aim the question at Nicnevin but continue to stare at the dark fae in front of me. 'How will he do that exactly?' I somehow manage to tear my gaze away and find Nicnevin grinning broadly, the creases around her terrifying eyes growing ever deeper.

'Oh, Lawrens is more than capable of taking care of a few pixies – and anything else that may happen your way.' She draws towards me conspiratorially, and I can't help but lean towards her in return. In an exaggerated whisper she explains, 'He has shadow magic.' Resting back in her chair, she abruptly drops her grin. 'He can be ever so frightful when he wants to be.'

Prickles sting the back of my neck, and I shift away from her disquieting violet stare to consider Lawrens again. Studying his fingernails, his grey eyes lift to meet mine. His lips do not curve into a smile this time.

My heart stutters, although I'm not sure what exactly it is responding to. Whether it's my mind's response to the apparent danger Lawrens presents... Or something lower down that's reacting to his other attributes.

To hell with it.

While I may have proved myself to be woefully underprepared for this little adventure, I am nothing if not practical. And thinking on it, I know there is no other practical option available to me. I might be handy with a blade, but I have no idea whether I'm up to the task of facing down the many unknowns within Faerie. I need someone who is if I'm going to reach the Queen.

If the likes of Nicnevin considers Lawrens dangerous, he must be fairly fucking dangerous. And at least he knows where he's going.

Fine. That's decided. But I need to get one thing settled.

'Alright,' I say. 'He can be my guide. But I need a little something from him first.'

Lazily rolling back his sleeves to reveal muscled forearms, Lawrens allows his seductive gaze to rest on me. 'You have my interest, Red.' His clipped drawl shimmies over me, curling down low to stoke heat in my belly. He raises his brows in question. 'What could you possibly have to ask of me?'

Pointedly ignoring the way his voice resonates and the tempting tease of his lips, I can't help but bristle at the use of yet another irritating pet name. 'It is *Elspeth*, Lawrens, not Red. I have a name, please see to it that you use it.'

Amusement plays over his features. 'And mine is Law. Only Nicnevin insists on calling me by my full name.'

Nicnevin coughs a rasping laugh. 'Full name. Very droll, Lawrens.'

'Yes, yes, Nicnevin.' He waves a hand at her. 'You're not really one to talk.'

Puzzled, I glance between them.

Noting my expression, Nicnevin explains. 'Every fae and his dog has a rather long and boring title. Phaedria Aesculapias Duron of Gaelesophie, First of her Name, Princess of the Flower Meadows, Singer of Enchanted Melodies, and so on.' She shrugs, trying on innocence for size. 'I was just pointing out that poor Lawrens holds no such title. He remains undistinguished... Apart from his reputation, that is.'

'Anyway,' Law cuts in, sounding bored. Turning to me, he prompts, 'You had something to ask of me?'

I blink at the directness behind his regard, then firmly pull myself together. 'Yes, a promise.'

I know faeries cannot lie, and as such, any promises they make are binding. If a faerie makes a promise and then breaks it, they have essentially broken their word, or in other words, lied. From what I understand of the stories surrounding such things, the consequences are not exactly pleasant.

I aim that directness right back at him. 'I want you to promise not to harm me.'

Law glances at Nicnevin, notes her slight nod of agreement, then leans forward and steeples his hands. 'Fine. You may have that promise.'

Recalling my earlier concerns regarding my deal with Nicnevin, I am reminded to be wary of faerie contracts and promises. 'And you require nothing of me in return?' I ask cagily.

Law raises a brow. 'Unless you want to agree not to harm me in return?'

Despite myself, I snort out a laugh. I cannot see how I could possibly harm him if he's as dangerous as Nicnevin suggests. Watching his own flicker of a smile, I reply, 'Unnecessary, I think.'

At this, Law nods once, appearing serious once more. 'Red, I promise not to intentionally harm you on this journey of yours to see the Queen.'

'Thank you, Law*rens*.' I let out my accent, so that the r in his name rolls around my mouth to make a point.

What kind of bloody name is Red, anyway.

Unsure if promises, like deals, require a handshake, I stretch out my hand. Law dips his gaze to take in the gesture, then – thankfully choosing not to spit into it first – he clasps my hand in his.

His calloused hand warm in mine, I hold on perhaps only a moment too long, marvelling at the shadowy spirals that snake down his forearm, coiling over the back of his hand and reaching, reaching–

A tiny silvery blue spark flashes between us.

My eyes widen in alarm as Law looks up at me sharply, then shoots his gaze toward Nicnevin. Slugging back her wine, she seems not to have noticed, and after a beat, he relaxes. Not giving me time to consider what exactly that strange spark had been, he drops my hand and abruptly stands, offering a curt nod to Nicnevin, to which, she gives him a close-mouthed smile and nods in return.

Shifting his regard back to me, he softens his features with a slant of a smile. 'Well Red, as you do not seem to be eating, we should be on our way. It's a long way to the Queen's palace and we only have our feet to take us there.'

Chapter 6

Following Law, I step through the imposing front door out onto Nicnevin's cobbled courtyard, turning in place to get my first proper look at Faerie. A drab, grey building looms over us, giving me a crick in my neck as I stare up its high walls and daunting stone turrets, where ghastly gargoyles perch, appearing to be doing the most unspeakable things to one another.

Evidently having seen it all before, Law walks ahead without looking back. 'Keep up, Red,' he calls. 'There are a lot more impressive sights to see in Faerie than this crumbling pile of stone.'

Hitching my pack onto my shoulder, I hurry to catch up and, stepping out into the lush woodland beyond, it isn't long before the commanding figure of Nicnevin's estate disappears from view behind me.

As I try to match my pace with Law's, I can't stop my attention from drifting over my surrounds, neck craning to take in the soaring canopy above, and gawking stupidly at the otherworldly splendour of it all.

All around us, endlessly luxuriant leaves tremble and sway in a fluttering breeze, flaunting lavish shades of green, framed by cloudless azure wherever the canopy opens up to the skies. Along the path, butterflies glide by on vastly oversized wings of the most spectacular colours, stopping here and there to dip into jewel-like flowers that twinkle in such a way that I imagine they might be flirting with me.

I force my gaze back to the path when I notice I am falling behind, urging my focus down to my feet and compelling them to move faster to keep up with Law's much longer stride. In the growing silence, my mind coasts reluctantly over how I feel now that I am alone with him. About how wise my snap decision had been to trust him. Can I really trust him to keep me safe? To get me to the Queen?

I glance over, taking in his exquisite profile, the black hair that sweeps back from his face to reach soft stubble at the nape of his neck. My fingers twitch, longing to reach out and touch it.

Perhaps the more pressing question is, can I trust myself with him?

Enough Elspeth, you have absolutely no interest in males such as him.

'What are you thinking about so furiously, Red?' Law turns to me, cocking one brow, and looking even more disgustingly attractive.

I see no reason to lie. 'I'm thinking about how I have absolutely no interest in a male such as you.'

'A male such as me?' His brow arches higher as his lip quirks.

'I have no interest in any males, thank you very much,' I answer primly.

'Oh, so you have more interest in females, perhaps?' Law's eyes sparkle suggestively. 'If you so desire, I could facilitate you in your search. We will get you to the Queen first, of course. What comes after though…' He lets the suggestion hang, accompanying it with a shrug of his shoulder.

Heat creeps into my cheeks. 'That's not what I meant,' I reply tersely. I consider leaving it at that, but waiting a beat, I find myself wanting to explain. Although I am unsure why. With Malcom, I constantly had to explain myself, to defend my actions. Following his death, I'd worked tirelessly to push past that desire to explain, to defend, to justify. Still, I find myself saying, 'I was married. A long time ago,' adding somewhat hotly, 'to a man.'

'A long time ago?' he replies, tone just this side of teasing. 'You can't have much more than a quarter century, Red. How much life have you had the opportunity to live?'

I bristle at being condescended to. 'I might be young, but that doesn't mean I haven't lived.'

As my sharp words escape me, I realise I probably shouldn't be quite so terse with such an allegedly dangerous fae. But there's something about Law's easy manner that keeps making me forget my status as breakable human.

He seems to ponder my statement, apparently unbothered by my brusque tone. 'So, would you say then, that you humans live *more* because your lives are shorter?'

I can't stop my eyes from rolling. 'I can't tell if you're being facetious to try to get a rise out of me, or you're actually attempting to romanticise my life. If it's the latter, I can tell you there is absolutely nothing to romanticise about life as a human.' I pause. 'The humans I'm acquainted with, anyway.'

I consider brushing it off, letting it go, but I'm feeling tetchy from lack of sleep, and his dismissive, teasing tone is getting right under my skin. 'Life as a human can be brutal,' I push. 'It can be horrifying.'

My mind flashes to women I'd known being burnt at the stake. To men I'd drunk ale with, hanging from the gallows. I think of sunken-cheeked children starving after yet another crop failure. Feeling almost selfish, I think of my time with Malcom.

I shake my head to clear the image of my former husband towering over me as I'd lain broken on the ground.

'We take joy where we can,' I hurry on, 'but don't start thinking we live some enchanted existence because we know our lives are short. That we are somehow able to make our lives more meaningful because we know we have fewer years between when we are born and when we die. For some, their lives are mercifully short. Death is a kindness.'

Having run out of steam, I walk on, silent. Law remains quiet beside me. Out of the corner of my eye, I see the shadows at his neck curling in a way I'm sure feels contemplative.

'I apologise,' he offers, after a few more moments of silence. 'I did not mean to offend.'

I regard him, trying to decide if he is merely apologising in the hopes that it will cease my monologuing. 'Apology accepted,' I say warily.

'So, what of this husband then?' Law tries. 'I take it from your tone that he is no longer your husband.' He looks to me as if seeking something. 'Or perhaps, that he is no longer of this world so that he can call himself so.'

I turn to stare straight ahead, teeth gritted. 'He is no longer of this world.' My hands clench into fists, unbidden. 'And this world is no worse off for it being so.'

'I see,' Law says. 'Well, if that is the case, I will not mourn the fact that I never got to meet him.'

I look back at him sharply, trying to gauge his expression. No longer displaying any hint of mockery, he appears instead to be done with the conversation. The unexpectedness of it unbalances me. I really don't know what to make of it. Or him.

It hadn't been like that when I first met Malcom. I had known where I stood with him. He had been sure of himself, but he wasn't pushy with it. He had a shy smile, a quiet way. It had been one of the first things I'd fallen for when he arrived back in town after his years away as a soldier. I had been nothing more than a child when he left, but when he returned, I was a woman. Or at least, I'd considered myself as such. All of 15, I'd been just a silly wee lassie really. But he had turned my head, in the same way my new womanly curves had apparently turned his.

I push down those thoughts. Malcom has no place in my life now, alive or dead.

'How long until we reach the Queen?' I ask, trying to drive my dead husband out of my mind.

'Feet hurting already, Red?' Glancing down, Law appears to notice my hurried stride.

I utter a curse. 'Infuriating male. Can you not answer a straight question when it is asked?'

Law stops on the path, arranging his features into a sombre expression, before bowing deeply. 'I apologise profusely, mistress. I'll be sure to make the utmost effort to answer all questions put to me from now on.'

Gallus eejit.

Making a tsking sound, I continue walking. I like being made fun of even less than I like being condescended to. 'Well, go on then,' I call over my shoulder.

'Go on where?' he asks, jogging to catch up. Even in that casual jog, he moves with such feline grace, such elegant movement.

'Go on and answer my question, you smartarse. How long will it be until we reach the Queen?'

God, how I hate relying on anyone. Back at home, I had worked so hard to retain my independence, pushing against the limits of what independence I'd been granted because of my gender so I could live freely and rely only on myself. And now I am here, having to rely on this unknown fae who I find hard to read and who is most certainly a smartarse.

'Travelling at this pace,' Law says, breaking through my bitter musings, 'I would expect to reach the Queen's palace within four, maybe five days.'

Five more days in Faerie. Five more days until I get answers to my questions and the help I need for Agnes. *Hopefully.*

I rearrange my pack so that it sits more securely on my shoulder, carefully considering the provisions it holds. I will need to make sure they last.

Five more days. *With Law.*

I try for a deep, calming breath and focus on my stride, noticing only now that he has slowed his own stride to match mine.

***

Hours later, we sit just off the path, Law resting beside me as we lean against an ancient tree whose sturdy branches twist high into the canopy. Soaking in the melodious sound of birdsong, my feet finally at rest, I take the opportunity to examine the luscious sights surrounding me.

Gnarled bark at my back, I reach out a hand and run it over the soft blades of grass at the base of the tree, listening as they seem to sigh with each pass of my hand. Up on a nearby branch, the most fantastical bird peeks down at me from behind a curved beak of shimmering gold, fanning a tail of fuchsia and teal that sweeps to the ground. Beneath it, tiny balls of fluff skitter hither and thither, occasionally releasing unimaginably loud honks that cause the undergrowth to shiver.

Over the long miles that led us away from Nicnevin's estate, I'd missed all of this, finding myself lulled by the repetition of watching one boot fall in front of the other, tiredness playing its part in stealing my attention from the sights around me. As I look around now though, I can't help but feel at home here. Despite its luxuriant, almost dreamlike quality, its peculiar sense of *other*, what I've seen of Faerie so far has felt oddly familiar, almost welcoming.

Perhaps it isn't so dangerous here after all?

Idly, I wonder whether I even need Law to be my guardian, my guide, whatever the bloody hell he is supposed to be. If I only knew which way to go, I'm sure I could make it there on my own.

At least he had remained blessedly quiet during the rest of our walk, perhaps put off from making further comment by the look on my face. I have been told on more than one occasion that my face is rather... expressive.

Thankfully, he remains just as quiet now.

Tilting my head to capture the warmth a sunbeam offers as it breaks through the canopy, I sigh my contentment and let my eyes drift closed. Just for a moment.

Waking with a start, I see immediately that Law is gone, and glancing around, I see my pack is gone too. Breathing rapidly, I feel the beat of my heart rising along with my panic.

What had I been thinking? I can't do this alone. I am in Faerie. I have no food, no weapon, no idea of where I am or where I am going.

Forcing myself to stop, to calm down, I take a deep breath, then two. I need to think.

I stand and look around, but can still see no trace of Law or my pack.

'Hello?' I call out, voice tight. I hate how high and nervous it sounds.

'Hello,' a small voice calls back from the undergrowth to my left.

'Hello,' another voice says from behind a tree to my right.

'Hello, hello, hello,' similar little voices echo all around me.

I spin around. *What in the world is going on?*

'This isn't funny,' I pronounce, trying to make my voice sound more confident than I feel.

A high-pitched chorus chanting *this isn't funny* seems to come from all around me.

A touch of anger trickles through my fear. I don't like tricks. I have no time for that kind of nonsense, here in Faerie or back at home.

'Just give me back my pack,' I call out, more certain now. 'You can keep the shadowy eejit, if you must.'

Gleeful giggles carry over me like a breeze.

'What will you give us for it?' one voice asks.

'Nothing,' I say in reply. 'It's mine.' I continue to turn around, still unable to work out where the voices are coming from.

'How about a kiss?' says a different voice.

More delighted laughs twitter around me, joined by whistles and cheers.

'You are delusional if you think that will actually happen,' I bite out as I hunt around, trying to find the source of that last call. I think it came from some red-berried shrubbery on the ground to my right. 'Aha!' I shout, bending down to make a gap in its branches.

Damnit. Nothing there but more shrub.

I straighten to see Law sauntering back from the other side of the path, hands in his pockets, inky coils at his throat rearranging themselves nonchalantly.

'Where the hell have you been?' I demand. My earlier fear and panic forgotten; anger takes control now.

'Call of nature,' he says with a shrug. He whistles as if to further the point.

'Bloody typical,' I fume. 'You're supposed to be protecting me. You think it's acceptable to just wander off while I'm asleep, leaving me to who knows what in these woods?' Not for the first time in his presence, my hands ball into fists.

Law looks at me perplexed, and not the least bit apologetic. 'You seem to be well enough,' he says. 'If a little pink in the face.' Then, after a moment, he adds, 'Are you well, Red?'

'No, I'm not bloody *well*. Some thieving wee tree sprites have taken my pack and are holding it hostage.' I gesture to the greenery around me. 'They keep laughing at me.' I notice then that there has been no laughing, indeed no noise at all since Law returned.

'Tree sprites, you say,' he says patiently. 'Well then, that is serious. Perhaps we should ask them to give your pack back?'

'Do you not think I tried that?' I work my jaw to unclench it.

Law whistles again, then calls out, 'Tree sprites, please would you be so kind as to give the mistress back her pack. It seems to be very important to her.'

Something small jumps out of a nearby tree, landing on the mossy ground beside me in complete silence. It appears to be a small male creature, rounded through the belly, with chubby little legs. His skin is a rich brown, his eyebrows heavy over eyes that seem far too big for his face. In his arms, he holds my pack.

'We are sorry,' he says, expression grave.

'We are sorry,' the surrounding greenery echoes.

While the little creature stands beside me, he does not look in my direction, does not speak to me at all. Instead, he has his head bowed deeply before Law.

'We did not know this human belonged to you,' he continues.

'We did not know,' the trees repeat.

'Never would we have snatched up the human's belongings if we had known.' He chances a quick glance up at Law. It's a long way up. His head only reaches to the height of Law's knee.

'Never, never, never,' the trees chirp, and I wonder whether I'm imagining the roiling sense of despair that churns around me.

Law smoothly removes his hands from his pockets, his eyes fixed on the creature. It steps back abruptly, as if in fear. Looking to me, Law says, 'Not a tree sprite. A pixie.' He directs his attention back to the pixie. 'It's not me to whom you should be apologising.' He points a long, elegant finger in my direction. 'It's her.'

'We are s..so very sorry, mistress,' the pixie stutters, turning to face me.

'Sorry, sorry, sorry,' echoes around me. 'Please forgive us,' one voice adds desperately.

The pixie skips neatly over to me and reaches up to return my pack, hands shaking. He looks to be suffering such abject misery, I start to feel a little sorry for him.

'Apology accepted,' I try warmly. I have no idea why this stout little creature should be so terrified, but I don't want to make matters worse for him.

Could Law really be the source of such terror?

He circles back to Law, head bent low again.

'You are excused,' Law says, his expression solemn.

As soon as the words are out of Law's mouth, the pixie leaps up the nearest tree and disappears.

Letting his solemnity drop, Law allows a small smile to lift one side of his mouth. 'See, no harm done. You are in one piece, you haven't been ravaged by pixies – or tree sprites, for that matter – and you have your pack returned to you.' He nods his head at the pack in question. 'I gather nothing is missing?'

Feeling stupid for not checking straight away, I open the pack to carefully catalogue its contents. 'Everything is there that should be there,' I confirm. 'That doesn't mean you're off the hook, though.' I angle a narrowed gaze his way. 'No leaving me alone while I'm sleeping in future.'

'Perhaps you should consider not falling asleep in the middle of the day,' he counters.

I contemplate telling him where he can stick his suggestion, but choose to rise above it. Instead, I point up the tree into which the pixie had vanished. 'Why such deference?' I ask. 'That poor little thing looked utterly petrified of you.'

'Poor little thing?' Law scoffs. 'What happened to *thieving wee tree sprite*?' Smirking, he turns to start back toward the path, leaving me to swing my pack over my shoulder and hurry to catch up.

'Don't avoid the question,' I say.

'As Nicnevin alluded to, I have something of a reputation, Red.' Law casts a glance at me as he walks on. 'Perhaps you should be a little more deferential as well.'

I snort softly. Still, I can't help but think of the fear in the pixie's voice. The reverential way he had bowed to Law. I look him over again.

Should I fear this fae? Should I be more respectful of the danger he apparently presents?

Admiring his perfect aquiline nose, the strong cut of his jaw, that teasing glimpse of a smile, I find that I do feel something for him. Some sort of strange... pull. A tug right from my centre.

Since Malcom's death, I have held myself back from falling into any kind of relationship, but I've also learned in that time to look for more in the folk I meet. To find what lies hidden, and to trust myself to deal accordingly with what I uncover.

Reaching deep, looking beyond his beauty, I find I cannot seem to dig up any fear for Law.

He turns to hold my gaze, his mouth curving in a way that makes it seem like he knows exactly what I am thinking.

My stomach flips.

Apart from that.

That reaction to him is what I should fear.

Chapter 7

As dusk closes in, I try and fail to push past my tiredness. I open my mouth to ask Law what our plans are for the night, when he steals my words and replaces them with his own.

'There is a small tavern up ahead,' he says. 'We will stop there to rest.'

I narrow my eyes, wondering whether all that dark and dangerous magic of his extends to reading minds. Immediately, my thoughts turn carnal. Just the idea that he might be able to read my thoughts makes my mind go to the worst possible places.

Why does it do that?

I blush furiously and fervently hope he cannot indeed read my filthy mind.

'No, I cannot read your thoughts, Red,' he says, as if he truly can. 'But your face really is quite expressive. And I can tell you are getting fatigued.' He glances at my feet. 'Your tread is getting heavier.'

'You're paying attention to the way I'm walking?' I ask, turning my gaze to him, suspicious.

Law smiles as he continues to stare straight ahead. 'I pay attention to everything.'

I don't entirely know what to make of that, so I decide to bring us back onto safer ground. 'Is it a magical tavern?'

'The tavern itself has no magic, but it's more than likely there will be other magical peoples that choose to take their rest there.'

I consider him as I watch a shadowy tendril twist up over his ear, then coil down the side of his cheek. 'And should any of these magical peoples be of concern to me?'

After thinking on it, I'd concluded the pixies, while troublesome, had not been particularly dangerous. They had meant me no harm. As for the rest of Faerie's so-called magical peoples, I'm not so sure I can say the same.

My eyes fall back to the path. Up ahead, a break in the trees shows a tavern, as promised, welcoming us with twinkling lights.

'Of that, I cannot say,' Law replies.

'Well, what *can* you say?' I sigh exasperatedly. I hate feeling out of my depth. Hate not knowing where danger lies, and how to defend myself from it. 'Can you not tell me something useful of Faerie? Of how things work here? What I should be wary of?'

'Apart from me, you mean?' He turns to give me a quick wink.

'Yes, apart from you.' I can't stop my mouth from twisting into a small smile.

'As your guide, I suppose I am duty-bound to provide you with guidance. It would be remiss of me to let you wander off into danger's embrace without at least giving you some understanding of where certain dangers lie.'

'That would be greatly appreciated, thank you.'

'Where is our starting point then, Red?' he continues. 'What do you know of Faerie?'

I dismiss the pet name. I'm quite sure he's only using it to rile me. After taking a moment to think, I start, hesitant. 'I know that the faerie realm is separated from the human realm by some sort of magical veil, and as a human with no magical powers to speak of, it is near impossible for me to pass through that veil alone.

'In saying that, I know the veil is supposedly thinner on certain days of import. That's why I chose to call on Nicnevin on Samhain. Everyone knows that is her... special night.' I grimace as I recall the vague glimpses I'd caught while being carried along within the *Sluagh*. 'I knew she would be listening out, as it were.'

Law nods, motioning for me to continue.

'As for the faerie realm itself, I can't say I know all that much.' My eyes dart towards him. 'I know the stories. Everyone does. But past childhood, I... stopped believing.'

'I'll try to not be offended by the fact that you considered my home and my entire species undeserving of belief,' Law replies, tone unreadable.

I forge on, inexplicably feeling the need to explain myself. Again. 'I had no time for magic in my life. There was too much of the *real* to contend with.' I pause. 'But a good friend of mine had a lot of time for magic, it seems.' Thinking of Agnes makes my heart twist in my chest, and instinctively, my tired feet pick up their pace. 'She is a... witch.' Saying it aloud still feels bizarre. 'Although I didn't know that until very recently. I'm still not sure what it means, but thinking back on it, she may have tried to instil some knowledge in me over the years, relating to magic and,' I wave my hands in Law's direction, 'you magical folk.'

He allows a small smirk to rest on his lips but remains silent as my words bring us to the door of the tavern.

Up close, it seems a very ordinary tavern. I am almost disappointed.

Clad in stone, it extends up over two levels, making it large enough to house eight or so rooms, presumably with a dining room and kitchen below. Wooden shutters secure the windows, and a jauntily painted sign above the front door proudly displays the name *The Chipped Tea Kettle*.

Law opens the door and ushers me in. The entryway I step through leads directly into the expected dining room, which holds a dozen or so tables of varying sizes, and a wooden bar at one side. Inside, the windows are unadorned with draperies, and sawdust scatters the floor, working hard, but not quite managing to cover stained wooden floorboards. At one side, a large fireplace throws a warm, flickering light over it all.

I cast my gaze over the room. A few of the tables are occupied, but none of the tavern's diners bother to look up as we enter. To my inexperienced eye, no one looks like they might be apt to cause me harm.

But then, what do I know.

I choose a table that puts us as far as possible from the room's other diners, and Law seems happy enough to follow. To my annoyance, he doesn't look at all like he's spent most of the day on the road. I feel sticky, dusty and more than a bit rumpled, while he appears just as he had before we set out. He doesn't have even a hair out of place.

He catches me staring. 'Yes, Red?' His dark brows arch in question.

Before I can answer, a stout serving maid bustles up to our table. Dressed in homespun sackcloth, she has a pouchy face and dark, thinning hair scraped into a tight bun at the back of her head. She stares at the table instead of looking directly at either of us.

'What can I get for you?' Her words sound tight as she chances a quick look at Law.

Shadows shift in soft whorls down the side of his neck to the top of his chest, which is revealed now his cloak is draped over the chair beside him. He angles a smile at the maid. 'Wine, if it pleases you,' he says easily. 'And a bowl of your finest stew.'

She nods quickly and turns her attention to me. Having taken furtive bites of my provisions through the day, I am admittedly still hungry, but it's my thirst that bothers me most of all. I waver.

'You're going to have to imbibe eventually,' Law pushes. 'You will not last long on this quest of yours if you don't.'

'Water?' I ask, uncertain. Surely the water will be safe. Well, as safe as it is at home, which, if I'm honest, is not very safe at all. Safe from the dangers of magical compulsion, though? My parched throat tells me I'll have to risk it.

'Just water for me, please,' I say, more determined this time.

The maid bobs a curtsy, still avoiding eye contact with Law, then bustles away.

'This witch friend seems to have warned you of the dangers of eating and drinking in Faerie.' Law looks questioningly at me.

'Yes, she did, in a way,' I reply thoughtfully, taking a small parcel from my pack and placing it on the table. I think of the endless faerie stories Agnes wrapped around my childhood. I wonder now if she had meant them less as entertainment, and more as a guide.

Tapping the parcel distractedly, I carefully unwrap its tight packaging.

Law screws up his nose. 'What in all hells' name is that?' he says in disgust. 'It reeks.' He pushes himself further back in his chair, as if to put as much distance as possible between himself and the little sack in front of me.

I look at him like he must be slow witted. 'Haggis.'

'It smells repellent. Are you supposed to eat it or bury it?'

I laugh. 'Eat it, of course.' I dig my fingers into the little sack, scoop up some brownish gristle and pop it into my mouth. 'Delicious,' I pronounce, mouth full. 'Would you like to try?'

'And how do I know you're not trying to cast some spell on me?' Law puts on an expression of mock horror. 'What do I know of food from the human realm, apart from the fact that it apparently smells like death. Enticing me to eat this... supposed foodstuff... could be your way of enchanting me.'

I narrow my eyes at him. 'I don't think anyone would ever enchant a haggis.' I push the meaty little sack towards him. 'Go on, try it.'

'Alright, a deal,' he counters. 'I will try a bite of your haggis, if you take a bite of my, ah here it is, fine repast.'

From her tray, the maid takes a bowl of steaming stew and a mug of wine, placing them in front of Law. Giving the haggis a wide berth, she then puts a mug of water in front of me.

'Thank you,' I say. I look up to offer her a smile but find myself smiling at her broad back as she hurries away.

'Don't tell me. Your reputation precedes you,' I say dryly, nodding my head in the direction of the retreating serving maid.

I still cannot fit this perception others have of Law with how he has behaved since we met. Sure, the shadows on his skin are peculiar, sure, he has gotten under my skin at times, but his actions so far have done little to make me fear him.

Needling, insistent, that little voice inside me reminds me appearances can be deceiving. No matter how far I dig, I have no way of knowing for sure what truly lies beneath.

'I try to make friends wherever I go,' Law replies with a sharp smile. 'Now, do we have a deal? I'll taste yours if you taste mine.' That sharp smile turns lazy, feline.

I ignore the innuendo and gather back the little sack from the middle of the table. 'No more deals. I've had more than enough of those.' I scoop more haggis into my mouth and watch Law gag. Then, taking a tentative sip of water, I roll it slowly around my mouth. It tastes clean and crisp, and not at all like the brown filth North Berwick calls drinking water. I conclude that it must be safe enough and drain the entire mug.

'Your loss, Red.' Law heaps his spoon with stew and makes an exaggerated sound of pleasure as he chews.

Ignoring the tantalising aroma of braised meat and warming spices that drift over to me, ignoring just how much I long to have something warm and hearty in my belly, I shake my head. 'No, thank you. I'm perfectly happy with what I have,' I say, pointing to the haggis. 'What I would like, however, is more information. You asked earlier what I know of Faerie.'

I hold up one finger. 'A human should not eat or drink in Faerie. Food and drink can easily be enchanted. If I were to ingest enchanted food or drink, my will would no longer be my own.'

A second finger joins the first. 'A human should not dance in Faerie. Music can also be enchanted. If I were to start dancing to faerie music, I may never stop.'

I lift a third and final finger. 'A human should not give a faerie their full name. A faerie that knows your full name has power over you.'

'Very commendable,' Law nods. 'Despite your apparent disbelief regarding Faerie's existence, you have managed to acquire quite a few truths.'

I consider this. 'Yes, I've been wondering whether Agnes – she's the witch I was telling you about – perhaps did that on purpose.' I pause. 'Also, the lives of you *guid folk* are of the utmost interest to many Scots. I suppose a lot of it just becomes ingrained.'

Chewing thoughtfully, I swallow and flick up a fourth finger. 'Oh, and iron.' Law winces ever so slightly, the inky loops on his skin stuttering in their movement. 'A human can protect themself from fae using iron.'

'And do you happen to be carrying any iron, Elspeth?'

I start at Law's use of my actual, given name. Frowning, I reply carefully, 'No Lawrens, I am not carrying any iron.'

While he cannot lie, I certainly can. I do not blink as I stare back at him, keeping my expression neutral even as I think of my dagger. If Faerie really is as dangerous as everyone keeps making it out to be, I prefer to meet it prepared.

I let a few heartbeats pass before I continue, 'Now you know what I know, I want to know what you know.' I force myself to smile, to sound gracious. 'If it pleases you, sir.'

The tension in Law's face fades. 'But of course. Fair is fair, Red.'

I carefully breathe out my own tension, happier than I'd like to admit to hear that silly pet name again.

'Right, let's start with a bit of history,' he says, scraping up the last of his stew and spooning it into his mouth. He pushes the bowl to one side and brings his mug of wine closer.

'Once upon a time...' he stops and smiles teasingly at me.

'Very good, Law.' A small grin escapes me. 'Carry on with your faerie story.'

'Once upon a time,' he continues, 'the faerie realm was whole, ruled over by the Queen of Elphame. Under said Queen, a gaggle of nobles governed various courts within the realm, controlling all day-to-day comings and goings, but overall, answering to her. Everyone answered to her.'

He takes a sip of wine and leans back in his chair. 'Now, while she may not look it,' he lifts a hand to his mouth to whisper exaggeratedly behind it, 'don't tell her I said this, but Beatrix is *really fucking old*.' He lowers his hand. 'This Queen you are so eager to meet has been in power for centuries. And she was alive for centuries before that.'

I prop my elbows on the table and cup my face in my hands. While Law certainly knows how to get under my skin, when he talks like this he has a way about him that makes me want to listen. I might even be tempted to call him captivating.

It also doesn't hurt that he's somewhat easy on the eye.

'Why does that matter?' he continues, mercifully unaware of my thoughts. 'Throughout Beatrix's exceptionally lengthy reign, Faerie, on the whole, enjoyed relative peace. So she got comfortable, let her guard down. The trouble with staying in power so long, though, is that you're bound to make a few enemies. And the Queen had apparently amassed some powerful ones. When those enemies attacked, she was not prepared.'

'What did they want?' I ask, interrupting the flow of his story.

'What do you think?' Law raises a knowing brow, signalling to the serving maid for more wine. 'Power.'

'What happened, then? She's still in power now, so it couldn't have turned out so badly?'

'She rules over the Seelie Court, yes,' he nods. 'But the Unseelie Court, she has no control over.'

'The Unseelie Court?' I'm glad to see the maid bringing me another mug of water in addition to Law's wine. I drain that one too.

'Faerie as it is now – as it has been since the Queen's enemies rose up against her – is separated into two courts: Seelie and Unseelie.'

'Who rules over the Unseelie Court?' I check Law's reaction as I interrupt again. With Malcom, I'd learned the hard way that some men do not like to be questioned or interrupted. To my carefully trained eye, Law seems unphased.

Thinking on it, I consider how utterly unphased he has been all day. Despite my undeniably short temper and my resulting sharp words, he has not reacted at all, simply letting it wash over him without giving me anything back. With Malcom, I'd known to be careful, I'd learned to be smaller, to be less *Elspeth*. If I'd talked to him the way I have to Law… No, that simply wouldn't have happened. No matter how awful I'd felt, no matter how bad my mood, I would have tidied it away, kept it contained. If even a stray muttered word made its way to Malcom's ears, the consequences would have been–

No. I force the thought away. He has no power over me now.

Malcom had worked so deftly to diminish my sense of self, but I'd worked even harder after his death to re-establish it. Now, I refuse to let him shape me. I refuse to let him have any control over how I go about my life, over my actions, the way I interact. I will continue to be careful of Law, but I will not be scared. I will not make myself smaller.

'No one,' Law replies, bringing me back to the moment. 'There is a head of each Unseelie territory, but they have learned to rule together. For the most part, each territory keeps to itself. There have been skirmishes, of course, but nothing they haven't been able to get past.'

'Why did they not just take it all?' I ask, more focused now. 'If they were more powerful, why not take the Seelie Court as well?'

'While the Queen had only a small army, she wasn't completely unprotected. She rallied and fought back most admirably. After some lengthy battles with heavy losses on both sides, Seelie and Unseelie came to an agreement that each would retreat to their own lands and live separately henceforth.'

'Sounds like a wise decision,' I say, thinking of the grief caused by land wars and power struggles between the Scots and English.

'Sure, sure,' Law agrees airily. 'But relations between the two courts are not what you'd call amicable. There are fundamental differences between Seelie and Unseelie that cannot be overcome. Tensions rise, which often leads to violence between the two courts.'

'What kind of differences?' I ask, intrigued.

'As it is still ruled by the Queen, the Seelie Court mostly sticks to the old ways. While fae may be rather morally ambiguous,' Law shrugs a shoulder, 'the Seelie still believe in restraining their wilder instincts. They believe in a somewhat stricter moral code, you could say, than the Unseelie.'

'And the Unseelie?'

'The Unseelie are *not* so interested in restraining their wilder instincts. It was one of their main motivations behind rising up against the Queen. They see no harm in indulging in hedonism and desire. As a result, the Unseelie Court can be somewhat chaotic, more dangerous. Especially for the likes of you humans.'

I hesitate before asking, 'And what court are you from, Law?'

He gives me a wry smile as shadows swirl and sway across his throat. 'I am courtless.'

'Courtless?' I'm confused. 'How can you be courtless? Are you not one or the other?'

'No,' he says evenly. 'One can choose.'

He turns his attention away from me to focus on his wine, and it doesn't take any of my subtle reading skills to see that while he seems more than happy to discuss Faerie, he's far less inclined to talk about himself. Despite wanting to know more, pry more, I pull back, allowing him his space.

Abruptly, a faerie appears at our table, materialising as if from nowhere. Or perhaps not from nowhere. I think she'd been sitting at a table in the corner.

Still, though. It's not right they can move like that, appearing and disappearing. It's incredibly disorientating.

Law folds his arms, looking unperturbed. 'Eachlair Ürlar,' he drawls. 'Can I say how enchanting it is to see you again.'

With a jolt, I note his use of her full name. Had that been some kind of power play? What is going on here?

Tall and willowy, the female that stands before us is undeniably exquisite. With a delicate heart-shaped face framed by waves of decadent indigo, her skin has a silver tinge that makes it appear almost luminous. Her perfect lips curl back in a snarl. 'Don't use your word games on me, boy.' With words crisp and cold, her snarl transforms into an icy smile. 'How have you been faring since last we met?'

Outwardly, Law is all civil elegance. Only the shiver playing along the shadows at his forearms gives away any hint of strain. 'How kind of you to enquire,' he says, tone detached. 'Things have been much changed, I have to admit.'

'Changed for the better, I hope?' With her icy smile fixed in place, cold waves of power flow from her. This is not someone I would choose to cross.

'That's surely a matter of opinion,' Law replies.

She nods, as if in agreement, although the expression on her face is anything but agreeable. Then she turns to inspect me. 'You should watch this one, little human.' Her tone is still stark, but her expression not quite so terrifying. 'There is more to him than his pretty face suggests.'

'But you do think I'm pretty?' Law cuts in, a forced bitter lightness in his tone. He taps his fingers against the table as if to make a point. 'Well, if that will be all?'

Looking down her nose at him, she nods again. 'Yes, that is all.' Her words are as brusque as her movements as she casts her cloak over her shoulder and leans in closer. Dangerously close, some might say. 'Just know that I am watching you. Carefully.' She presents him one more chilling glare, before she turns and sweeps out the door.

Law drains his wine, his gaze determinedly on anything but me. Before I get the chance to vomit the many, many questions I have for him, he is up and out of his chair. 'Let me go and see about getting us some rooms,' he mutters, walking away without looking back.

Chapter 8

The morning sees us back on the road, where there are conspicuously more travellers than there had been yesterday. I'm not sure whether this part of Faerie is better travelled, or I simply didn't register as much passing traffic during yesterday's decidedly hazy journey from Nicnevin's estate, but either way, I am glad everything is not quite so hazy today.

More than glad, actually. Relieved.

As with any bad day, I'd known I wasn't quite myself. I just hadn't been able to do anything about it. I'd spent the night in the skies doing God-only-knows-what with Nicnevin, then after very little sleep, I'd been thrown into the reality of having to function in a new realm.

Now, with a full night's rest behind me, my mind is clear, and my reactions are my own, rather than a product of my surroundings. Aside from hating not being in control, of myself, of my situation, I also like to think I am nicer to be around than I had been yesterday.

My eyes flick to Law, embarrassed by how snippy I'd been, wincing as I remember my monologue on human suffering. He hadn't deserved any of it.

Law had been tasked by Nicnevin to take me to the Queen, charged with keeping my helpless human self safe. He hadn't been high-handed about it, hadn't been surly about carrying out such an undertaking. He hadn't used the fact that we were alone, or the fact that he could easily overpower me to make me feel in any way uncomfortable.

He had been... nice. Friendly, even. This dangerous, dark fae so many dread had been nice, even when I had not been particularly nice to him.

Breathing out a sigh, I force myself to move on. I can't change what's done, only what's yet to come. And hopefully, with me acting like less of a snippy bitch, the remainder of our journey together will be far more comfortable.

With my grumbling stomach pushing me out of my head, I'm about to ask when we might stop for lunch, when the path opens out to reveal a clearing, where some sort of celebration is gathering steam.

'What's this?' I ask, ignoring my stomach's pitiful protests.

'A wedding, by the looks of it,' Law replies.

My spirits lift a little at the mention of a wedding. Despite not being a huge fan of the five years that followed my own wedding, I love wedding celebrations as a general rule. The happiness, the dancing, the high hopes for the future, it all just makes for the loveliest of days.

Reading my expression, Law narrows a look at me. 'Why, Red, would you like to attend?'

'No, we couldn't!' I reply immediately. 'We've not been invited. We don't even know who's getting married.'

He glances around at the gathering crowds of fae. 'It looks to be a big enough event. I don't imagine they'd notice two more.'

'Maybe,' I admit. 'But the fae we've met so far seem to have taken a strong aversion to you. Do you have any reason to think the happy couple and their nearest and dearest will be any different?' Staring pointedly at the shadows shifting over him, I continue, 'It's not like you're inconspicuous. They're *going* to notice you.'

Law considers this, not seeming to take offense to my drawing attention to his disagreeable reputation.

My conscience twitches. *I also have somewhere to be.*

'And we need to get to the Queen's palace,' I add. 'Stopping for revelries along the way isn't going to get us there any quicker.'

'Those are valid points,' Law says. 'But your stomach is making another. We need to eat. You may be happy to eat from your pack along the way – don't think I can't smell that revolting filth by the by – but I need to find food, and here seems as good a place as any to get some.'

'And your...?' I wave a hand up and down to indicate his general appearance.

In answer, he raises the hood of his cloak and promptly vanishes within its depths. With the sun high in the sky, I know I should be able to see his face. It should be right *there*. But it's not. All I can see within his hood is deep, shadowy darkness.

Icy prickles sting my skin at this unpleasant reminder of the *Sluagh's* faceless grey riders.

'What?' I murmur. 'I...'

As my mind stumbles, the shadows concealing Law's face twist away into nothingness. My breath hitches as his indecently beautiful features return, a mischievous smile playing at his lips.

'What the fuck was that?' I ask, skin still crawling.

'*Shadow* magic, Red.' he replies. 'Or did you think this was all it was?' He raises a hand to indicate the inky swirls weaving there.

I consider this. 'Um, no?' I try.

When Nicnevin mentioned Law's magic, she'd made it clear it was something to fear. Like something a *lot* of people would fear. With it all still being so new to me, finding out he had magic that could protect me on my journey had been enough information for me in that moment. Then, in those foggy hours that followed, my mind had been otherwise occupied with all of the *everything* it'd had to process. As a result, it had apparently filed his magic under need-to-know-only, content instead to be distracted by the shadows that twisted over his damnably perfect features.

'Well, kind of,' I admit.

'Well, that's *kind of* insulting,' he retorts, glittering grey eyes mocking me. 'Formidable reputation. Feared throughout Faerie. You really think that would come as a result of having shifting shadows etched on my skin?'

'Alright then,' I say, very maturely opting not to call him a smartarse again. 'What *can* you do?'

'That's for me to know and you to find out,' he quips back with a wink.

Fucking smartarse.

'Child,' I sigh aloud.

'Says you,' he pronounces, then turns away as if talking to someone else. 'I have centuries on her, and she's the one calling *me* a child. The audacity.'

'Centuries,' I reply cautiously. 'How old are you exactly?'

'What an impertinent question.' Law sniffs in playful outrage.

'You're the one who brought it up!' I pinch the bridge of my nose. This conversation is making *me* feel old.

'Around 287, I'd say, give or take a few years.'

Stunned, I temporarily lose my ability to form words.

Law is fae, so I'd known he would likely be older than he appears. But even so, it is undeniably disorientating talking to someone who appears to be about 30, knowing that their real age is closer to ten times that.

'I'll take from your silence that you think I look good for my age?' he asks.

I hitch a brow. 'You could say that,' I reply dryly.

Turning his amused gaze from me, he casts it over the crowds that have amassed in the time we have stopped to talk.

Fae of all shapes and sizes gather towards the opening of a vast pavilion set at the back of the clearing. Laden with food and drink, large tables crowd together inside, while outside, further tables fill up as more guests arrive. In one corner, a band sets up, made up of what appears to be four hirsute gnomes and a violet-haired fae of dazzling beauty, poured into a dress of molten gold.

'Seems like the celebrations will be starting soon,' Law says. Nodding his head in the direction of the pavilion, he continues, 'With so many folk coming and going, I think we'll be able to join unnoticed, sneak some food, then sneak back out again.'

'Are you sure?' I ask, worried both about causing a scene amongst all of these unknown fae, and the fact that stopping here will delay our journey.

Law disappears within the hood of his cloak. 'Quite sure.'

The voice that comes from inside the cloak is still his, still familiar, but I can't seem to shake my earlier unease. 'Is there any way you can pull back on that darkness a little? So it doesn't feel like I'm conversing with the Grim Reaper?'

'Having crossed paths with him on several occasions, I can tell you he's not as eerie as you might think. His reputation is much inflated.'

'You cannot be serious,' I splutter. 'You have *not* met Death.'

But I get no answer as he grabs my hand, turns, and pulls me into the melee.

As we make our way through the crowds, my attention is quickly drawn from Law's outlandish statement to the multitude of fae that surround us. While there are plenty like Law who appear human, there are plenty more that are so far from that, I have to work hard not to gawk.

Tiny creatures no bigger than my thumb flutter through the air in a flurry of iridescent wings and excited chirrups. More extremely hairy gnomes, similar to those tuning instruments on stage, stump around on cloven feet, rumbling to one another and growling out laughter. Tall, slender fae with skin resembling bark gather in knotted groups, talking animatedly and swishing their willowy limbs.

Everywhere I look, there is something new to see, something so fantastical and strange, I have to look twice to take it all in.

I shift my gaze up to the canopy above, where coloured balls of magical light pulse within glimmering garlands, intricately intertwined with vibrant banners that sway in the breeze. Complementing this, fabulous flower arrangements create further splashes of colour surrounding the various dishes that weigh down each sturdy wooden table.

In the middle of it all, the happy couple stand, greeting their guests and accepting a wealth of well wishes. Glowing with unmistakable joy, the bride grins broadly under a floral coronet, made from the same flowers as the arrangements embellishing the tables. Hand twisted in hers, the groom nods and smiles beside her, conversing with their guests, his gaze continuously drifting back to his wife, as if he simply cannot keep his eyes from her for long.

'They look so… happy,' I sigh, following Law to an empty table at the very edge of the celebrations.

Keeping his back to the other guests, he takes a seat at the bench and allows the shadows to clear within his raised hood. He quirks a smile in reply, heaping food onto his plate. 'You'd hope so, given the circumstances.'

I remove my own cloak, suddenly aware of the peculiar warmth within the clearing, then set it down next to my pack. As scents of garlic, rosemary and nutmeg knot my stomach with hunger, I let my greedy gaze roam the culinary delights in front of me. Alongside numerous dishes I don't recognise, there are plates of fire-roasted fish, scales charred and eyes bulging, neatly arranged next to steaming bowls of stew, containing large chunks of meat mixed with root vegetables and rich gravy.

Law breaks off a chunk of freshly baked bread and the smell drifts over to me, making my mouth water and my resolve waver.

'You were not expected here, Red,' he says, tearing my rapt attention from the bread in his hands. 'It's highly unlikely anyone would have enchanted this food. It's a wedding. No one is interested in enchanting anyone. They have more pressing matters to attend to. Celebrating takes precedence over enthralling humans, I'm quite sure of it.'

I open my pack, removing a bannock to place it on my own plate. It looks sad and somewhat miserable sitting there, surrounded by such delicacies, and my stomach dissents rowdily as I contemplate it.

'No,' I say sadly. 'I'll stick with this.'

'At least this thing you're eating now doesn't smell as bad as that other one,' Law replies, his nose wrinkling. He tears off a smaller piece of bread and dips it into the pile of stew on his plate, sending more of that baked bread scent wafting in my direction.

Doing my level best to ignore it, I break off a lump of the bannock. Sitting in my pack for the past three days has made it drier than I'd like, but I nibble at it anyway. To distract myself from the misery of my meal, I consider the questions I'd been forced to fold away last night.

Opting to skirt the subject of his courtless status and the quite obvious sore point of Eachlair Ürlar, I decide to start with some basic geography. I am under no illusion I could make it to the Queen without Law showing me the way, but still, knowing more of what we're journeying through might make me feel a little less overwhelmed by the great unknown that is Faerie.

And from there, who knows where I might be able to steer the conversation.

'Last night you explained how the court system works here, with the Seelie and Unseelie,' I start, testing the waters, while keeping the word *courtless* out of my mouth.

If Law is surprised by the change of direction the conversation has taken, he doesn't show it. 'Yes.'

'So, where are we now?' I ask. 'In which court? Seelie or Unseelie.'

'If this were an Unseelie wedding, you'd know about it, Red. And I wouldn't be suggesting you eat the food.'

'Seelie, then?' I push.

'Yes, we've been on Seelie lands for some time.' He takes the large jug of wine from the centre of the table and pours some of the bright, berry-red liquid first in my mug, then in his own.

'But not the whole time?' I surmise, purposefully ignoring the mug of wine in front of me as Law takes a sip from his own.

'No, we started on lands governed by the Unseelie, at Nicnevin's estate. She lives not far from the border of the wildlands, so we walked out of Unseelie, through those, then spent the rest of our journey on Seelie lands.'

It doesn't surprise me one bit that Nicnevin is Unseelie.

'Will we stay on Seelie lands until we reach the Queen?' I ask, trying to wrap my head round the route we might be taking, but failing miserably without a map to refer to.

'Mostly,' Law replies, spooning more food from the various large serving dishes onto his now empty plate. 'The fastest path to the Queen's palace will take us through lands governed by Unseelie, but I don't think we should see any trouble there. It's a well-travelled route we are taking.'

I pop the last crumbs of the bannock into my mouth, coughing at its dryness. I wish I had something to wash it down with. I'd drunk as much water as I could stomach before leaving the tavern, but after a morning of walking, my throat is once again parched.

Eyeing the wine in front of me contemplatively, I ask, 'Have you seen any water jugs?'

Law doesn't bother to look around. 'No.' His mouth curves to reveal an artful smile. 'It's wine or wine at fae weddings, Red. That's all part of the fun.'

I think of the gorgeous, amber-coloured ale I make at home. I've supplied plenty of weddings with my ale over the years, although for celebrations such as those, I typically tweak the fermentation process so that it's stronger than the everyday stuff I usually brew. All part of the fun, same as in Faerie.

'Alright, next question,' I push on, determined to keep my mind occupied and away from the far too tempting smells surrounding me.

Law raises his brows but remains silent as he continues to eat.

Just as he had last night, he seems happy enough to answer questions on the subject of Faerie. Now, I will test the theory that he is not quite so happy imparting specific information about himself.

'What is it that you do for Nicnevin?' I ask, keeping my tone casual.

Pausing, he assesses me. 'Why do you want to know?'

'I think, given our situation, it's relevant,' I reply, unsurprised by his answering my question with a question. 'We will be together for the next few days. I am under your protection, as it were. I'd like to know a little more about my guide and guardian.'

Swirling the wine in his mug before taking a long drink, Law remains quiet.

'Do you work for her?' I prompt. 'Are you friends? Lovers?'

Spluttering a cough, Law wheezes out an inhaled lungful of wine. 'You just made me imagine Nicnevin naked.' He coughs again, bashing his chest with a fist. 'Hells below, *no*. I work for her.' Something cold flits across his expression, there one second and gone the next.

Noting it but unable to discern what it means, I push on. 'And what kind of work is it that you do?'

'This and that,' he replies tightly.

This is like getting blood from a stone.

'So, is it unusual for her to send you halfway across Faerie, accompanying some human on a quest to seek out the Queen of Elphame?' I push my plate to the side, leaning closer so I can observe Law's face as we talk.

Curling shadows twirl swiftly over his throat, but his expression remains carefully neutral. 'Through the many years I have worked for Nicnevin, I have learned to expect the unusual,' he replies, tone entirely too even.

I ponder this. It doesn't answer my question, but it does give me something.

I narrow my eyes. 'And are you going to tell me anything more about what your work for her entails? Or should I just give up now?'

As much as I'd like to know more, I also know now that Law has *centuries* of experience talking around things. If he doesn't want to tell me something, there's no way to make him.

'You should give up now,' he says, his measured smile confirming my suspicion.

As I observe that smile and the teasing twinkle that accompanies it, a spark of heat unspools low in my belly. It doesn't seem to matter how frustrating I sometimes find this fae or how oddly off-kilter he puts me, there is something inside me that *tugs* me toward him. Silently, I assess him, the effortless ease of him, wondering if he feels that same pull, or if it's simply my body's instinctive response to being close to someone so obscenely attractive.

'But you're happy to be here with me?' I ask, prompted by an unexpected eagerness to know how he might feel about me. If he feels anything at all for me. 'On this errand for Nicnevin, I mean,' I add hurriedly.

I don't want him to *know* I'm eager.

Law's grey gaze twinkles some more, suggesting not only that he knows exactly what I had been asking, but what his smiles do to my belly. And certain areas below there.

'You're asking if I want to be here, Red?' he says. 'With you?'

Damnit to hell. So much for subtlety.

A blush rises to scorch my cheeks. 'I just wanted to know if you are as happy doing this as you are doing whatever else Nicnevin asks you to do,' I say, back-peddling desperately. 'That this is not a burden for you.'

I could really do with some of that wine right now.

'Actually wait, answer this first. Do you in all honesty think this wine could be enchanted?'

'In all honesty, I have no way of saying,' Law replies easily, continuing to enjoy my discomposure far too much. 'I do think it's highly unlikely though.' He pauses, appearing to weigh something in his mind. 'How about this? If the wine is enchanted, I will do everything in my power to save you from whatever dangers it brings.'

Taking time to turn over this promise, I cannot come up with any way it might lay trouble at my feet. It sounds like quite a good deal actually, having all of his supposedly vast and scary powers directed towards keeping me safe.

'Deal,' I say, thinking I've been involved in far too many faerie bargains, deals and promises since stepping into this world. Agnes would probably have something to say about that.

Shit, Agnes.

Determinedly pushing down the guilt curling up through my gut, I suck down a long draught from my mug. Light, bright and ever so slightly sweet, the wine slips over my tongue and down my throat, creating an instant warmth that rushes down deep inside. I have to admit it is far from unpleasant.

Observing me, Law cocks his head slightly, a hint of amusement playing around his eyes. 'Worth it?'

'I'll let you know later,' I grimace, swallowing another large mouthful. Having witnessed the fallout from many a wedding at home, I know the aftermath is typically much grislier when wine is served in addition to my ale.

Law lets out a low chuckle and I am reminded of the reason I'd felt pushed to imbibe.

'Are you going to answer my question? Or avoid this one too?' I ask, aiming a wine-emboldened gaze his way.

'You asked if I am as happy doing this as whatever else Nicnevin asks of me,' Law replies, smoky eyes on me. 'Yes, I remember, and no, I will not avoid this one.'

I take another slug of wine in anticipation of his answer. I can't work out if it's the wine or my apprehension over what he might say that is making me feel ever warmer. I use my hand to fan myself and remain quiet.

'Yes, Red, it is indeed pleasing to be here,' he says, pausing before adding, 'with you.' He reaches for his own wine and takes a sip, his plate long since emptied and placed to one side. 'And so far, yes, I have found myself happier doing this than what Nicnevin usually asks of me.'

I shove away the surge of pleasure that floods me at hearing this. Despite his earlier rebuff, or perhaps because of it, I still want to know more about what he actually does for Nicnevin.

'Why do you do it then?' I urge. 'Why do you work for her if you don't enjoy what you do?'

His face, previously easy and open, shutters and becomes guarded. 'That I cannot say,' he replies, tone hard. 'What I will say is that I don't have much influence on the matter.' His guarded features turn cold at the edges as he adds, 'But I am working to change that.'

Not liking this change in him, but knowing well enough it is directed at Nicnevin rather than myself, I search for a way to change the subject, to distract him. I take another sip of wine and turn my gaze to my surroundings, searching for inspiration.

Having tuned their instruments and settled in, the band is finally starting up. On the grassy space in front of them, the happy couple stand, heads together, talking quietly. The tables around them are full, occupied by a dizzying array of the weird and wonderful, each guest eating their fill and beginning to get merry.

This gives me an idea.

'Hey Law,' I say.

He looks at me as he pours more wine into each of our mugs.

'Hey Red,' he replies, a small smile softening his careful features.

That's a start.

'I was wondering why all the other tables are packed full, but ours isn't.' I gesture to the empty bench space beside us, the dishes still piled high with food. 'I know we don't know anyone here, but surely that wouldn't stop other guests from joining us. Apart from all the food we have here, you'd think some of them would simply want a seat.'

There are more than a few guests standing at tables where there is no more seating available.

'No one will be joining us,' Law says, shaking his head. 'I warded our table before we sat down.' At my apparent confusion, he continues. 'It will make anyone who thinks of coming over to sit with us feel overcome with a sense that it's not such a great idea.'

'Oh because of your...' I say, waving a hand in the direction of his face.

'Yes, because I don't want them to see my face. We don't want to make a scene, remember?'

I wonder if I catch a certain sadness within his words and consider whether he is as indifferent about his reputation as he makes out.

Forcing myself to stop staring, I take another sip of wine and compel my attention back to the band, who after having started on an energetic number, have now drawn a large crowd onto the makeshift dancefloor. As I watch the fae dance, my hand taps in time on the bench beside me, then sensing Law's attention, I glance back at him. He is observing me, expression serious.

'Do you not want to watch the dancing?' I ask.

'Not particularly,' he replies, features remaining watchful, unsmiling. Considering how effortless Law usually is, I find this solemnity somewhat unnerving. I am pushed off-balance by it. Again.

'Do you want to dance, then?' I'm caught off-guard by my own question.

Where the fuck did that come from? Had it been the wine? Law? Or just this bizarre situation?

'What happened to rule number two?' he replies. Raising two fingers in a salute, he lifts the pitch of his voice and puts on an absolutely dreadful Scottish accent. 'A human should not dance in Faerie. Music can also be enchanted. If I were to start dancing to faerie music, I may never stop.'

Embarrassment wars with laughter as a flush floods my face.

Laughter wins.

Seeing Law smile back at me, I realise I like this male. I like the easy way he is with me. The way I feel like I can say anything to him, be myself around him. While he has closed himself off at times, I recognise this is more than likely a measure he takes to protect himself. I know well enough the desire to shut down when someone gets too close to something I have no wish to discuss.

Feeling it out, I realise I've developed a tentative confidence in Law, this fae I had not even known two days ago. While I'm obviously a long way from knowing him properly, I am surprised to find that I would very much like to do so.

'You promised to keep me safe from enchanted wine. I thought you might be willing to extend that promise to enchanted music.' I'm pleased to find my voice sounds more confident than I feel.

'Oh, you did, did you?' His eyes crinkle at the corners. 'That's very presumptuous of you.'

'The wine is making me feel presumptuous,' I say. 'And I really do want to dance.'

Law hesitates, seeming uncertain, then reaches across the table to untuck a wave of hair I had pushed behind my ear. My heart skips an almost painful beat as it makes note of just how close his face is to mine.

'If we're going to dance, let's not make too much of a show of the fact that you are human,' he says, pulling back. 'I'm not the only one who can cause a scene simply by being me.'

'You think they wouldn't want a human at their party?' I ask nervously.

'I think most of those here would see no problem in it, but there may be some you wouldn't want the attention of. We might be on Seelie lands, but not all Seelie are as restrained as the Queen would like to think.'

I nibble at my lip. 'Do you think it's a good idea, then? To dance, I mean?' My head is spinning slightly. 'Maybe we should just leave.'

Law leans in again, his grey gaze centred on me. 'I will keep you safe, Elspeth,' he says, his words a warm flutter over my skin.

I cannot breathe, cannot think.

I am sure I should feel offended. I shouldn't need a male to keep me safe. I am an independent woman and can look after myself. Although, I'm not entirely sure that's true here in Faerie.

Acknowledging that now familiar tug in my chest, I consider something I *do* know. That I should absolutely not feel as drawn to this male as I do.

Law waits, patiently watching all of this play across my face.

Tug.

My breath catches.

Well, fuck it all.

'Let's dance,' I breathe.

Chapter 9

Law's gaze darkens with something I might be tempted to call desire, before being swept behind a mask of shadows within the hood of his cloak. This time, the shadows are not as deep or as dark as they had been before. Light catches the sharp planes of his face, the sparkle in his eyes, the glint of mischief in his grin.

Before I can change my mind, I stand and hold out my hand, letting Law lead me into the churning throng of dancing fae. Surrounded on all sides, I feel the press of bodies, the beat of the music, the wine singing in my veins.

Then he pulls me close, and it all falls away.

His embrace is irresistible. Everything about it seduces me.

It is the heat of him, the scent of him, the *rightness* of him. It very nearly overwhelms me. But in a way I *want* to be overwhelmed. By this. By him.

With my mind far from my footwork, Law guides me in a dance I'm entirely unfamiliar with, leading me smoothly over the grassy dancefloor, his own aptitude making up for my lack.

Warmed by his hand at my back, my own rests on his shoulder under his cloak, where taught muscle shifts under the light fabric of his shirt. With each sweep of movement, I relish the feel of him a little more, savouring the way our bodies meld together as we move with the rhythm of the flowing, graceful beat. Breathless not with the pace of our movements but with the sublime sense of having him so close, I chance a look up into the depths of his hood. Where shadows shift, solemnity remains, that easy grin of his gone. I feel the desire in his touch but cannot gauge his expression, and can do nothing more than return his pensive stare while my heart beats ever faster.

He is the one to break our gaze, spinning me away, then drawing me to him and dipping me back. With my hair brushing the grass and blood rushing to my head, laughter bubbles up and escapes me, before I am up and spinning again, that strange solemnity seemingly abandoned.

Time hurries by with the passing of more songs than I can count, until I can no longer deny the faintness I am feeling. The heat, the wine, the dancing. Law. They're all working together to make my head swim.

Regret tugs at me as I pull away from him, and immediately, I feel the loss of his body against mine. 'I need to sit down and get some air,' I explain.

'I have that effect on females,' Law replies, playfulness dancing in his tone. 'Take a seat. I'll see if I can find you something to drink other than wine.'

'I thought you said they *only* serve wine at faerie weddings?' I chide.

'I'm sure I can magic something up.' Even though I cannot fully see his face, I imagine the expression it holds, one brow arching to echo the curve of a smile.

Law stalks off toward the pavilion and I slump down on an empty bench nearby, my leaden feet unwilling to return me to the table we'd shared earlier. With most of the guests dancing and their attention turned fully to revelry, I let my unfocused stare skim over the crowds, swallowing thickly as I try to ignore my spinning head.

Before long, I catch sight of Law exiting the pavilion holding a mug of what I hope is water. He is still some distance away when his course is intercepted by the fae singer in the golden dress, apparently not required by the band for this particular number. Interested in a way I'm not sure is healthy, I watch as Law stops to greet her, most of the shadows concealing him twisting away within the hood of his cloak.

Does he know her?

Judging by the overfamiliar way her hand lingers on his chest, she certainly seems intent on getting to know him better. If she hasn't done so before. While I can't properly gauge Law's expression from this distance, I observe as they continue to talk for far longer than I'd like.

Wine whispering in my ear, a surge of jealousy washes over me, and a rush of anger follows hot on its heels. Turning abruptly from Law and the dancing crowds, I swivel on the bench to face away from the celebrations. Feeling stupid for getting caught up in my emotions, I close my eyes and work on breathing deeply to clear the knots in my head.

'Bride or groom?' a deep voice says.

Eyes flashing open, I look up to see a fae male standing a few paces back from where I am slumped. Stockier and more muscular than Law, he has a broad, pleasant face with a heavy brow, deep-set eyes and a carved jaw, his dark hair falling past his shoulders and looking to my eyes, suspiciously like seaweed.

'Excuse me?' I reply.

'Are you here for the bride or groom?' he clarifies.

Right, I am a guest at a wedding. An uninvited *guest at a wedding.*

'Bride?' I try.

'I'm here for the groom.' He smiles, showing even white teeth. 'Third cousin, twice removed, or something like that.'

My stomach flips and I grimace, a cold sweat breaking out in its wake. I take another deep breath in an attempt to steady myself. 'Fucking faerie wine,' I say through clenched teeth, more to myself than to the stranger in front of me.

'Pardon?' he says, leaning in slightly.

'Too much wine,' I explain. 'I'm not feeling great.' I swallow again as another full body sweat rolls over me.

'Can I get you anything?' he asks, concern warming his voice.

'My friend is supposed to be bringing me water.' I glance over my shoulder and spot Law with his back to me now, still talking to the far too beautiful fae singer. 'He seems to have been waylaid though.'

'How about a walk to clear your head? It should be cooler beyond the tree line. There's a small lake just over there.' He points to a gap in the trees, not far from where we are now.

Suspicion flares bright and hot inside me. 'I'm not going for a walk with you. I don't even know you.'

'My apologies, mistress.' He bows his head, his smile sheepish. 'My name is Calder. I'm not much of a fan of celebrations such as these, you see. Too hot, too noisy. I usually look for any excuse to get away. It seemed like I could kill two birds with one stone by accompanying you somewhere quieter, where you could perhaps clear your head.' He steps back, as if to give me space. 'I didn't mean to alarm you though. I will leave you in peace.'

Bowing his head again, he turns to leave.

Weighed down by the press of fae at my back, the unceasing beat of the music shifting around me, I shove down another wave of nausea. With the wine still clouding my mind, making my head feel heavy, I suddenly want nothing more than to dip my feet in the lake's cool water, to splash it on my feverish skin.

'No, wait,' I say quickly. 'Calder, is it? Thank you for thinking of me. It is a bit much, isn't it?' Casting aside my better judgment, I stand. 'A walk to the lake would be lovely.'

With a bashful air, Calder nods hesitantly, raising one arm for me to hold. I stumble as I take it, then prop myself against him as we walk around several empty tables toward the gap in the tree line he had indicated earlier. As soon as we are past the bounds of the clearing, the temperature drops sharply.

Was that some kind of faerie magic?

Coherent thought still isn't easy to come by, so I let my mind still, focusing instead on putting one foot in front of the other as we walk down the slope. Picking our way through the trees, it's not long before the lake comes into view, and when I finally look up from my boots, a soft sigh escapes me.

With dusk not far off, the last of the day's sunlight sparkles its iridescence over the water, a gentle breeze creating ripples on its surface. Without thinking, I bend to unlace my boots, removing them and my stockings before stepping into the water. Glancing down to see the hem of my skirts already soaked, I find I simply cannot care. I curl my toes into the thick, almost muddy sand, relishing the feel of the water lapping around my ankles, cool and delicious against my heated skin.

Smiling, I throw a glance over my shoulder at Calder. He stands watching me from shore, his expression severe. Eyes intense, his mouth a grim line, he no longer looks the bashful male he'd been only moments ago.

My smile falls away and panic edges its way towards me. I realise my mistake as I force my mind to focus. I don't know this male. I don't know why he might bring me here. From the look he is giving me, it's clear his talk of caring for my wellbeing and wanting to get away from the crowds had only been a ruse. That look says he wants *me*. Preferably no longer breathing.

Shit, shit, shit, how could you be so stupid?

'What do you really want?' I ask, mind racing, wondering how fast I can run. How fast he can run.

'You,' he says simply. While his expression is unchanged, his eyes seem darker now, ominous in their promise. He rolls his head from side to side, the resulting *crack* breaking the stillness over the water.

'Why?' I ask, thoughts fluttering uselessly, unable to think of how I can possibly get out of this. I can only just hear the sounds of the wedding, a distant drumbeat on the breeze. Would anyone hear me scream?

'You are human,' he replies.

Not much of a talker now. It's like a switch in him has been flicked. Like the male I'd spoken with earlier has been replaced by another. A fae much darker, much grimmer, much more intense.

My mind flashes to the way Malcom had been much the same way. When some tiny, inconsequential thing would irritate him and instantly he would no longer be Malcom. He would be something darker, something much more prone to violence.

Urging my mind to clear further, I weigh my options.

Running won't work. My feet are bare, and I know I won't win in a foot race, running uphill through woodland in bare feet. Screaming won't work either. We are far too far from the wedding, and the music too loud. Fighting is out of the question too. This fae is all muscle and more than a head and a half taller than me. Furious with myself, I think of the dagger lying well out of reach, in my pack back at the table.

There is nothing else I can think of to do but stall, in the hope that Law will notice I am missing and come to find me. While I despise the idea of simply waiting for him to rescue me, my addled mind cannot throw out any other way out of this.

'How did you know I was human?' I ask.

Nostrils flaring, he says, 'I can smell you.'

Well, that's disturbing.

Every nerve in my body quivers as I try to keep the tremor from my voice. 'And? What is it that you plan to do with me?'

'Humans are a great delicacy to my kind.' His hands clench into fists, muscles bunching in his arms as he flexes them.

Double shit.

'What *is* your kind?' I ask, keeping my eyes locked on his. He hasn't moved towards me yet, but he seems to be readying himself, stretching and flexing – and, *ugh*... rippling – while his feet remain planted on the sand.

'Stupid human.' His words strain past perfect white teeth, something under his skin shifting, looking very much like it wants to break out. 'So self-absorbed.'

'You didn't answer my question,' I push. I don't particularly want to make him angry, but I need to keep him talking. To delay whatever he seems to be gearing up to do.

'I am a kelpie.' Something entirely unhuman undulates under his skin, the bones in his face pushing up and out, rearranging their structure to reveal something new. Something sinister.

Tamping down my terror, I rack my brain, trying to scrape together anything I might have learned about kelpies.

Stupid human, indeed. My brain comes back with nothing.

While I know it will not save me, something primal in me screams at me to run.

Fuck it.

I run.

Or, at least, I try to.

Knees bent to launch myself back up onto the sand, I realise immediately I've left it too late. Rippling with magic, the male that had once been Calder bursts towards me, his fae form shifting as he tackles me, transforming into a slick, seaweed green horse that knocks me violently back into the water. Moving purely on instinct, I make a desperate attempt to roll to the side, but my movement is hindered by the weight of my now sodden dress. With the water around me transformed into a roiling mass of muscled limbs and snapping razored teeth, I wrench myself to my hands and knees, frantically trying to scramble back and away.

I don't move fast enough.

A hoof clips my side and pain scorches through me. Winded, I turn, swinging wildly with clenched fists, hoping to connect with something vital, but my throws meet nothing but solid muscle. It's like I am brawling with a slick stone wall. Another hoof clips my temple, and stars explode behind my eyes. I fall back, my vision filled with a chaos of flashing dagger-sharp teeth and stamping hooves, a frenzied wall of seaweed green crashing down towards me.

This cannot be it. This can't be the end.

Images of Agnes, my mother, my father hurtle through my mind.

I need to help them.

An image of Law, eyes twinkling, his mouth curving into a smile.

I need to live.

Suddenly, intense silver light envelops me. I can't work out where it's coming from, it just seems to be everywhere, all at once. Blinded by its intensity, I squint fiercely in an attempt to see beyond it, to find Calder. I need to know where he is so I can get the fuck away from him. Desperate, I squeeze my eyes against the glare and manage to make out the shape of the kelpie shying back, rearing up above me.

Panic seizes me. When those forelegs come down, they will crush me.

Just as abruptly as it had come, the light stutters and dies.

Shrouded by its sudden loss, I scramble back, trying to get my feet beneath me. The lake surges over me and I still can't see anything, can't stop the water as it rushes into my mouth, but somehow, somehow, I am not crushed by those heavy, hammering hooves. Coughing uncontrollably, blinking to force my eyes to adjust, I keep hauling myself backwards, trying to crawl further from wherever the hell Calder is now.

I swipe at my eyes and find him only a few yards away, head tossing violently, hooves stamping in chaotic movement. As my vision clears, I hope feverishly that his does not.

It takes less than a moment for that hope to wither.

Nostrils flaring, the kelpie shrieks, having found its focus once more.

Me.

Dragged down by the drenched burden that is my dress, I heave myself up to stand on shaking legs, refusing to face my fate lying down. I hold my ground and grind my jaw, thinking of nothing and everything as I obstinately stare down death.

Death comes at me at a gallop, lathered in froth, shrieking, fixated only on me.

Then, there is darkness.

It is a darkness so complete, I wonder whether I am, in fact, dead. Whether perhaps death took me so rapidly, there had been no time for what surely would have been an abundance of pain.

But no. There is still sound.

Wild snorting, splashing water, thundering hoofbeats.

I barely have time to register the return of my blind tumultuous terror, before the endless black disperses, here one breath and gone the next.

Out of the darkness, Law emerges, striding out of the foliage and onto the sand. Haloed by a roiling mass of shadowy vines that twist out from his body and whip riotously around him, he extends a hand, into which a broadsword made of midnight materialises, sparkling stars glinting along its razored edge. His every movement liquid and lethal, he swings the sword in a sweeping arc and lunges at Calder.

Its attention drawn by this much larger threat, the kelpie shifts direction, turning from me to charge Law on the shore.

Time slows, seconds becoming minutes, Law's inky sword drinking in the light as it continues its arc. Soaring, spectacular, it slashes the air, curving inexorably downward to slice clean through Calder's broad, thickly muscled neck. Carried forward by its own momentum, the kelpie continues its charge, even as its severed head slips to the sand, its legs folding underneath it as it slams heavily to the ground.

My legs abruptly unwilling to hold my violently trembling weight, I drop to my knees and sink into the sand.

Chapter 10

Heaving in deep breaths, I close my eyes, trying to stop my mind from spiralling. While I know the pain will come, at my side, at my temple, shock is keeping it at bay for now. What holds my attention instead are the thoughts that are doing their very best to admonish me, scold me, shame me.

It all keeps coming back to how *stupid* I feel. How fucking brainless I must be to have listened to Calder. To have followed him, to have trusted him.

Absently, my mind drifts over what led me to this, kneeling battered and soaking next to the corpse of a murderous fae. My thoughts stutter as I recall the heat of my attraction when I danced with Law. The jealousy I felt watching him with the singer. The gut-wrenching nausea that followed.

'How could I be so... stupid?' I murmur, unable to come up with another word to better describe my idiocy under the weight of my self-loathing.

'I was wondering much the same thing.' Law stands a few paces away, sword in hand. The shadowy vines have retreated, but his face remains hard. 'I had thought your survival instincts better than this.'

'Believe me, so did I,' I reply. Part of me wants to bury my face in the sand and keep it there. Another part wants to throw myself at Law, to allow the heat of him to drive away the numbness I am feeling, the shock over all that just happened.

I do neither.

'We should move,' Law intones, his voice as hard as his features. 'There could be more of them.' Broadsword coiling away to smoke, he takes the few steps to where I kneel and extends a hand. Hesitating only long enough to watch the shadows on his skin stretching toward me, I reach out and allow him to haul me to my feet.

I stand on somewhat steadier legs and make my way to where I'd left my boots and stockings, picking them up and hugging them to my chest. I am utterly drenched. My hair hangs in a wet snarl around my face, my dress clinging sodden and heavy against my skin, and with dusk ushering in the promise of evening's chill, I am left shivering as I wait, dripping on the sand.

Law looks out over the lake, then back at me. Cold seeping into my bones, I'm unable to stop a shudder from racking me. At the sight of it, his face softens.

'Are you well, Red?' he asks, his voice easier at the edges.

I must look a pitiable sight. I stand straighter, squaring my shoulders. 'I will be,' I reply. 'I just need to get dry.'

'We should get back to the wedding to pick up your cloak. Do you have any other clothes you can change into?'

'I'll make do,' I say, thinking of the underclothes in my pack. Eyes flicking to the kelpie, now in two parts where it had once been one, I add warily, 'Should we do something about that?'

'No,' Law replies, some of the hardness returned to his voice. 'But we really should go. I'd prefer not to be standing next to its corpse when it is discovered. By whomever discovers it.' His eyes sweep the lake again.

I bend to slip on my stockings and lace up my boots, unable to stop shivering.

'The walk up the hill will help with that,' Law offers.

Nodding, I reply, 'Let's go then.'

We walk in silence back to the edge of the clearing, where Law pauses to assess the scene. With darkness setting in, the celebrations appear to be intensifying, growing louder, wilder, more raucous. While most fae seem lost to the music, swaying and spinning within the chaos of the dancefloor, some have separated off in twos and threes, getting intimate on the grass, on tabletops, against tent struts.

Unable to stop myself from gawking, I make my feet move, quickly falling into step behind Law as he skirts the edge of the revelry, stepping neatly past lovers adrift in the throes of passion.

Back at our table, I find my pack and cloak untouched, and send up a thanks to Law's wards. I remove the spare underclothes and hold them in my hand, unsure of what I should do next. Apparently sensing my dilemma, Law nods tightly, before turning to give me privacy. He has lost much of the hardness that held him at the lake, but tension still rolls off him.

'I'm sorry,' I offer the strained lines of his back.

'For what?'

'For being so bloody idiotic,' I sigh. 'For leaving. For making you chase me down and kill that... thing.'

'Kelpie,' he provides.

'I know. He told me. Right before he told me he was going to eat me.' I snort softly at how ridiculous that sounds.

'Becoming someone's appetiser is amusing to you?'

Warming myself on the colour returning to Law's voice, I explain, 'Not even slightly. It just hit me as absurd is all. Last week I was living a fairly normal human life. Today I find myself dancing at a faerie wedding and almost getting devoured by a murderous horse.'

'Kelpie,' Law corrects.

'Either way, I really am sorry I put you in that position. Nicnevin gave you the task of protecting me and I didn't make that easy for you with my foolish decision to go down to the lake.' Dragging a hand through my wet hair, I concede, 'There was the wine, that woman, it all just made my head spin. Still no excuse though.'

Facing away from me despite the fact that I remain fully clothed, Law tilts his head in question. 'What woman?'

'Well, female, you know what I mean. The singer,' I reply, aware of how unreasonable it is for me to feel jealous, but unable to stop myself from adding, 'the staggeringly gorgeous one with her hands on your chest.'

Law chances a look over his shoulder, sees that I am wearing my dress rather than my underclothes, and turns to face me. 'That's not jealousy I detect, is it, Red?' Apology apparently accepted, the tension in him is gone, and he seems returned to his relaxed – some might say, charming – self.

I blush to the very roots of my hair, unable to find a grownup reply that doesn't involve the words fuck and off.

Eyes glittering, Law goes easy on me. 'Yacinda is an old friend. I'm not sure I'd say staggeringly gorgeous, but attractive, yes. Not that it matters. Her interests lie elsewhere.' Observing my questioning look, he continues, 'She'd likely be more interested in bedding you than bedding me.'

Understanding dawns on me, and I feel monumentally stupider now. Not only had I been squeezed by jealousy over a male I have no right to feel jealous over, that jealousy had been completely misplaced. I want to curl up in a ball and hide from the shame of it.

'Right, well,' I mutter, studiously looking anywhere but at Law. 'This is a banner day for me, it seems.'

I blow out a breath, exhaustion washing over me. Shock over the attack, shame over my foolish choices, confusion over my feelings for Law. It all piles on top of everything else that's happened over the past week. Losing Agnes. Discovering the truth about my mother. Finding out many of the things I'd thought were make-believe are actually very goddamn real. And some of them want to eat me. I feel like I might just crumple under the weight of it.

I glance up, my weary gaze landing back on Law. While he appears relaxed, inky coils shift over his exposed skin, seemingly in search of something. I am unable to read his expression. Is that pity? Disappointment? I can't tell.

Shivering, I look down at the underclothes in my hands. I really should get out of my wet dress. The situation will not look any better if I end up sick on top of everything else.

'Could you turn round again, please?' I ask.

Nodding, Law turns to face the revelry.

As quickly as my numb fingers allow, I remove my wet clothes and place them in my pack, continuing to shiver as the brisk evening air races over my skin. Somehow, I manage to dress myself in my dry underclothes, taking what little warmth I can from the cotton camisole and knickers. I bend to wring out my hair, wanting very much for it to stop dripping down the back of my neck, then slip on my cloak and pull up the hood.

'Finished,' I say.

'Feeling warmer?' Law asks, turning around.

'Somewhat,' I admit, although I'm still far from comfortable.

'There are ways to warm up further,' Law suggests, a playful smile tugging at the corners of his mouth. He tilts his head to indicate a pair of lovers nearby, one lying on the tabletop, her ankles wrapped around her partner's neck and her bare breasts bouncing with each of his thrusts.

I cough out a short laugh. 'Pass. Getting carnal in front of others isn't really my thing.'

Law's eyes flare and I'm gratified to see surprise in his expression. While I may not have centuries of sexual experience under my belt, I am no coy virgin. True, my own experience on the marriage bed had been far from spectacular, but I had taken my place there for five dutiful years. Skin crawling, I recall how Malcom had been anything but imaginative in the bedroom. Mercifully, he had also been short-lived.

Recovering quickly, Law lifts his brows, asking a little too casually, 'What is your thing?'

Feeling somewhat lighter, I decide to tuck away the things I can't change. For now, at least. I know I messed up. I know this is a messed-up situation. I know things are likely to get even more messed-up in the near future. But mental hand-wringing has never gotten me anywhere. Changing my attitude so that I can get shit done most certainly has.

Shame be damned. I press a little twinkle into my own eyes and say, 'That's for me to know and you to find out.'

Law grins, rubbing one hand over the back of his neck.

Seeing his face open up like that, I can't help but grin back.

While I have no idea where this journey will take me, for now, I am just happy to be alive. Happy to be able to spend more time with Law. This insanely attractive male who just saved my arse and I haven't even thanked him for it.

'Thank you,' I offer, sobriety chasing away my smile.

Law quirks a brow. 'For what?'

'For saving me,' I say, unable to look away from his steely grey regard. I still hate that I'd *needed* to be saved, but that's another thing I know I cannot change now that it's done. All I can do is make better choices next time.

'Any time, Red,' he replies steadily, his gaze just as intent. 'Just don't make a habit of it.' After a long moment, he finally looks away, searching the ground for my pack, then picking it up and handing it to me. He raises his hood and turns to leave. 'Best be on our way.'

'Where are we going? Is there another tavern nearby?' I ask, trailing behind him as he makes for a gap in the tree line. It's not the same one I'd taken to the lake. Instead, it looks to be a continuation of the path we'd been on earlier.

'No, we won't make it to the tavern I had hoped to use tonight.'

Guilt twists in my gut. We should be much further along by now. Again, knowing there is nothing I can do about that, I ask instead, 'Where will we sleep?'

Under his hood, Law's head tilts toward the skies. 'Under the stars.'

Before us, the path widens, and I hurry a few steps to walk at Law's side. Away from the many coloured lights that had lit the clearing, murky darkness falls over us, and it is by dim moonlight I see him take something from his pocket. With a murmur, an orb of light appears in his hand, illuminating the path in front of us. He releases it and it bobs just above our heads, keeping pace as we walk.

'Faelight,' he explains. 'I don't need it, but I thought it likely you might.'

'Thank you,' I say, eyeing it in wonder. 'What do you mean you don't need it?'

'What kind of shadow wielder would I be if I was blinded by darkness?'

'Truly? You can see in the dark?'

Law nods but doesn't say more. I wonder if I imagine the tightness around his eyes. Seeming to want to change the subject, he continues, 'I'd like to put some distance between us and the wedding before we stop for the night. I don't want any drunken, naked fae tripping over us as we sleep.'

'Will we be able to make up the time we lost?' I ask.

'We still have maybe three days before we reach the Queen's palace. Don't worry, Red, we didn't lose so much time. We can make it up.' Lit from above, Law looks over to give me a reassuring curve of a smile, inky black hair spilling over his face.

My heart kicks out in my chest.

'I do have a slight detour I'd like to take tomorrow,' he adds, apparently unaware of what I am thinking this time. 'It's more or less on the way.'

'What kind of detour?' I ask, partly intrigued, partly frustrated by the idea of losing more time.

'There's a fae I've heard of in this area. She's known for her insight into all things magical. I want to ask her advice.'

I wonder what kind of advice Law might need. He'd seemed to be very much in control of his magic back at the lake. It doesn't take any effort for my mind to conjure up how he had looked, power rolling off him, surrounded by that shadowy turmoil and entirely focused on ending the kelpie. If that's what he is capable of, I understand now why he is feared. Knowing he holds such power – and that he wields it seemingly at Nicnevin's behest – it's easy to see how a reputation such as his could flourish.

But should *I* fear him?

I know all too well the risks of getting close to a dangerous man. Malcom had certainly been dangerous, but only to me. There had been no violence elsewhere in his life. He hadn't started fights with other men, hadn't been aggressive around anyone else. He'd kept all of his violence for me.

I study Law's profile, stark against the faelight. I don't yet know him, not at all. If we'd met under other circumstances, where he hadn't been charged as my protector, where he hadn't sworn that he would not harm me, would I be safe with him? Safe from him?

With no answers forthcoming, all I can really say is that I feel safe with him for now. I like him. I feel that insistent tug towards him. But I will not let that cloud my judgment of him. I will do my best to judge him on his actions, rather than his reputation. I will look to what's on the inside, rather than settling on whatever he presents to the world.

Forcing myself back to the present, I ask, 'Advice about what exactly?'

'About your magic, of course.'

Chapter 11

Dappled sunlight caressing my face, I wake to the heat of Law curled around me. We'd fallen asleep with a chaste distance between us, but somehow, during the night we must have found one another.

Keeping my eyes closed to savour each sensation, I delight in his warmth, the rhythm of his heartbeat, the feel of his hard, muscled body bound close against mine. With every inhale, I feel his steady, even breaths echoing my own as I breathe in his scent, holding onto it like I can claim it as mine. Claiming me in his own way, Law has his arm slung over my waist, his hand tucked deep inside my cloak. He stirs behind me, and as curling fingers begin to trace lazy circles on my exposed stomach, I realise it's not just his muscled body laying hard against me.

Emphatically ignoring the heat rushing to meet his touch, I cough pointedly.

His hand stills, then pulls my body even closer to his, before settling on my hip. Telling me he wants me close, but leaving me free to pull away. I consider how I absolutely do not want to do that.

But I have to. We have places to be.

'We should get going,' I murmur, the words unwillingly slipping from my lips.

His reply is rough with sleep. 'Should we?' He stretches, turning onto his back, and I immediately grieve his absence.

I sit, pushing down my regret while pulling my cloak more tightly around me. The chill of night may have faded, but morning's bitter fingers wrap eagerly around me now Law is no longer sharing his warmth.

A hiss escapes me as I stand. Peeling up the hem of my camisole, I find a wicked bruise at my side, a vivid reminder of my clash with Calder. I touch ginger fingers to my temple, wondering if there is a bruise there too. Supposing there isn't much I can do about it if there is, I check my clothes to see if they are dry. Having hung beside the fire overnight, they are at least no longer sodden, so I fold the underclothes into my pack, then glance back to see whether Law, silent as he's been, has perhaps fallen back asleep.

One arm propped behind his head, his grey gaze rests on me, smouldering with banked heat.

My heart stutters, causing my mind to stumble over why the hell I'd made the outrageous decision to leave him there, alone, with that unmistakable invitation evident in his trousers.

Agnes, a small, faraway voice prompts.

Yes, Agnes, the hazier part of my mind agrees.

My eyes slide down Law's body, my aching core forcing a deal. *Later*, she says. *We will revisit this later.*

Deal, my mind agrees, apparently just as entranced by Law as my lady parts. *We just need to put some miles behind us first.*

I find my way back to his face, to that enticing kick of his lips. My lady parts purr. *Sure, sure, but let's do this one little thing now.*

Quite certain I shouldn't be taking life advice from my vagina, I shrug and do as I'm told, her thirst for Law giving me the confidence I need to hopefully pull this off.

Urging heat into my own gaze, I lock eyes with Law, then slowly unfasten my cloak, letting it slip off my shoulders to puddle on the ground. Left only in my camisole and knickers, I bite my lower lip, then stretch, long and luxuriously, making a show of lingering over my curves and tossing my hair over one shoulder. Offering him my cleavage, I bend to retrieve my dress, then pull it on. Eyes still fixed on his, I fasten the buttons, slowly and deliberately, and give him a little wink when I'm done.

I expect one of his wicked smirks. Instead, something dark flashes over his expression, before he quickly conceals it, scrubbing his hands over his face and muttering a low, unintelligible curse.

'Come on,' I prompt, suddenly unsure of myself, but all too aware of time ticking away. 'We need to go. Especially if we have to detour to see this wise woman of yours.'

After dropping his bombshell last night, Law had told me of what he'd seen during the kelpie's attack. Talking with Yacinda, he had turned just in time to see me disappearing beyond the tree line, hanging off Calder's arm. Urged on by his earlier promise to keep me safe, he had followed me into the woods, then arrived at the lake to see that huge burst of light exploding not just out of the ether, but out of *me*.

In my head, the notion I might have magic just doesn't seem to fit. I'm not a witch. I'm not fae. I am just a plain, very ordinary human.

With that being said, I *am* intrigued. Who wouldn't be?

Law rearranges himself and stands, suddenly in my space, hunger written across his features. My breath catches as I am spun off-balance by him, again. All I can see is the heat in his eyes. All I can feel is the heat of his body, crowded against mine. I'm temporarily overwhelmed by thoughts of every single thing I would like to–

Not now, Elspeth. Later. We made a deal.

I take a deliberate step back and busy myself with gathering up my cloak from the ground and putting it on. Looking around for my pack, I see it lying next to the dying embers of the fire. I scoop it up and sling the strap over my head.

'Ready?' I ask, perhaps a touch too brightly.

Law shoves a hand through his hair and turns. 'Not even remotely.'

My mind quirks but I choose to let it lie, instead pushing my thoughts towards my goal, toward moving forward, then follow him through the trees and back onto the path.

We walk through the rest of the morning, talking about small things along the way, and slowly blowing away the heat and tension between us.

The conversation is easy, coming and going as we pass other fae on the path and little villages interspersed between the trees. Little more than a dozen or so houses, a tavern and perhaps a shop, there is not much to each village, but I soak in the sights, marvelling at all the different types of fae we see. For the first time, I see fae children, playing together, laughing, scrapping, in much the same way as human children do at home.

As we talk, I can't help but notice our conversation focuses more on my life than on Law's, but I'm happy enough for now to let it play out. Content in his company, I understand some folk take time to open up.

And if he doesn't? I decide that's his choice.

At the wedding, I'd pushed him for more on his dealings with Nicnevin, trying to get a handle on the old crone's angle. But beyond that, Law's personal life is *his* business.

He doesn't owe me anything, after all. While there is undoubtedly an attraction between us – I simply can't deny that insistent pull towards him in every step I take – Law is here, by my side, at Nicnevin's insistence. I'd certainly like to get to know him better, but I'm in no position to push.

So instead, I tell him of my life in North Berwick, about my love of brewing ale, and of living with my father. While I skirt the subject of Malcom, I tell him of my father's worsening condition, and the helplessness I feel seeing him fade day by day. Explaining how his health seems to have declined since losing my mother, I go on to talk of how I'd discovered the truth about her disappearance, about my hopes of finding her here in Faerie. From there, conversation turns to Agnes, and as my throat tightens and tears threaten, I know my words in no way convey the depth of everything I feel for my friend. Of just how important it is I get the Queen's help.

It is around lunchtime when Law takes a turning off the main path, steering us towards a small wooden cottage nestled within the trees. Having asked for directions along the way, he seems confident this is the wise woman he has heard of.

To my eyes, the cottage looks the epitome of homely. Set over one level, the small building is made from the rounded limbs of trees stacked in lines to create walls, with a neat, thatched roof on top. Smoke curls lazily out of a pebbled chimney, and potted flowers add a splash of colour at either side of the bright yellow front door.

Law knocks twice and steps back to stand beside me. From inside the cottage, someone hums a song I don't quite recognise, and I listen, trying to place it, distracting myself from thoughts of whatever revelations this encounter might unearth.

The oddly melodic humming grows louder until finally, the door opens, swinging back to reveal a fae female dressed in a dark blue dress and starched white apron. While she looks to be in most ways human, it is her face that quite obviously sets her apart. Appearing almost like a mask, the upper section of her face from her left jawbone to her right temple is that of a cat, covered in fur of lush brown brindle centred by a small pink nose and long, busy whiskers. With dark brown hair pulled back in a loose bun, she has one pointed fae ear and one large cat's ear, but perhaps most unsettling in their asymmetry are her eyes. While her right eye looks human, her left cat's eye is large and green, centred around a black slitted pupil that currently holds all its focus on me.

'Ah, Elspeth,' she purrs. 'I was wondering when you would arrive.' Her small mouth spreads into a smile, revealing a neat row of sharp white teeth with two longer canines at the front.

'You know who I am?' I start, forgetting my manners entirely.

'Of course,' she replies. 'Our paths have crossed before. Although given the circumstances, you cannot be blamed for not remembering.'

Confused, I say, 'I'm sorry, when exactly did we meet?'

'Many years ago, although it seems not so long for me,' she says, smiling again. 'Time passes differently for us fae.'

I glance quickly at Law, who remains silent, letting me take the lead. 'Yes, I've heard that somewhere before.'

'I'm sorry, dear, I should introduce myself,' she continues. 'I am Sydok.'

'Pleased to meet you, Sydok,' I reply. 'Again.'

'And you are Lawrens,' Sydok says warmly, turning to Law.

Aside from Yacinda, Sydok is the first fae who has greeted Law without seeming fearful – or in the case of Eachlair Ürlar, threatening.

'Law, if it pleases you, Mistress Sydok,' he replies, bowing his head.

'Won't you both come in,' Sydok says, glancing amiably between us. 'I'm making nettle tea. Perhaps you would like a cup?'

She turns and steps back inside, leaving me and Law to follow. Law places his hand at the small of my back, giving me the confidence I need to walk forward into this strange, yet seemingly friendly faerie's home.

Eyes adjusting to the dim light, I'm hit by a disturbing sense of vertigo as I take in the dimensions of the room in which I find myself. From the outside, the cottage had seemed cosy in its size, likely made up of two or three small rooms, much like my own home in North Berwick. Blinking, I look around at a much larger space than should be possible, with doors leading out to further rooms I'm sure a house of this size should not be able to hold.

I look to Law, who has followed me inside to stand in front of the now closed front door. Relaxed, he waits there, hands in his pockets.

Perhaps unsurprisingly, he seems wholly unbothered by the home's unusual dimensions.

Over in the far corner of the room, Sydok picks up a happily whistling kettle and carries it to a small wooden bench, where she busies herself brewing tea and pouring it into clay cups. With her attention on her task, she calls over her shoulder, 'Take a seat. Feel free to make yourself at home.'

Warmed by the rolling purr in her voice, I make my way to an adorable little sitting area, finding three plump chairs arranged around a small chipped table. As Sydok continues to hum the same not quite unfamiliar melody, I ease myself into one of the chairs, being careful with my bruised side, while Law pours himself into another. A few moments later, Sydok arrives with the tea and hands us both a cup.

Settling herself, she blows coils of steam from her tea, her gaze finding mine over the rim of her cup. 'What is it that you would like to know, dear?'

With a quick glance at Law, I reply, 'Well, Law suggested we come to you to ask about my magic. Or what he thinks is my magic. I still don't see how I could possibly have any.'

'Of course you have magic, dear,' Sydok says, smiling another of her sharp-toothed smiles. 'You are fae.'

Chapter 12

I jolt, almost dropping my cup and its steaming contents in my lap. Setting it down gingerly on the table, I turn my attention back to Sydok.

'I'm sorry, what was that?' I say carefully, quite sure this peculiar-looking, if seemingly well-intentioned fae must be misinformed. I cut my gaze to Law, but he just looks back at me and shrugs.

'You are fae, dear,' Sydok repeats, calmly overlooking my entirely disbelieving expression.

'But how?' I ask. 'My father is human, so is my mother. Two humans don't just go around making fae babies.'

Before the words are even out of my mouth, my tangled thoughts twist abruptly toward changelings. I know the stories, of course. Where human parents raise a fae child, unknowingly having had their own baby stolen, sometimes as an act of cruelty or revenge, sometimes so the baby can be raised in Faerie and kept as a servant. Or worse.

My attention snaps to Sydok, who is watching me with interest. 'Am I a changeling?' My words escape me in a strangled whisper, remaining strangely hushed, as if wary of the answer they might bring forth.

'No, no, nothing like that, dear,' Sydok says, shaking her head. 'Yes, your father is human, but your mother is fae.'

'But... how?' I ask, my mind too overwhelmed to fully form the questions careening around within it. Does my father know? Does Agnes?

'Your mother wanted to discover the world beyond Faerie, to explore the human realm. So, she glamoured herself to look human,' she pauses to tap her pointed fae ear, 'then journeyed to your world. When she got there, she met your father and fell in love. Out of that love, came you.'

Scanning the cat-faced faerie's features, I take a long moment to let this settle. Then, with suspicion creeping around my words, I ask, 'How do you know all this?'

Sydok blinks, whiskers twitching. 'Because I was the one who brought your mother back to Faerie.'

With that, I feel the truth click into place. I recall my father's words as he had lain frail and only halfway towards lucid, telling me of the strange-looking fae that had appeared at their door after receiving a plea for help from Agnes.

'You took my mother?' I ask, unable to hold onto the shake in my voice.

'Yes,' Sydok replies gently. 'I did as I was bid by my Queen.'

'The *Queen of Elphame* ordered you to bring my mother to Faerie?' Distantly, I am aware I'm repeating everything being said to me, just as I had when Agnes revealed she was a witch. But it's just too much. These immense, crushing revelations are too much.

Sydok takes a small sip of tea and nods. 'The Queen had not permitted your mother to travel to the human realm, much less stay there. She had searched for her but had been unable to locate her. Until your friend Agnes reached out for help. Unable to go herself, the Queen charged me with providing that assistance, to then return your mother to Faerie.'

'To return her to Faerie, even though she didn't want to go.' The injustice of this nettles me, slipping shards of something sharp into my words. 'What about us? What about my father? Me? We needed her.'

'I was not bid to bring you and your father to Faerie, dear. Only your mother.'

Sydok's expression is kind, her words filled with sympathy, but neither soothe the sting as the truths continue to unspool inside me. It doesn't lessen my fury over what the Queen did. It doesn't make my heart hurt any less thinking of all I have lost by having my mother taken from me.

Pushing through the anger, those hurts, I hurtle toward another. 'My father told me you saved my mother, that she was dying, and you brought her back.' I breathe in an infuriated sob rather than letting it go. 'He said you could have saved my brother too, but you didn't.'

Patiently accepting my ire, Sydok's purred words soften further. 'I was not bid to bring your brother back to Faerie. Only your mother.'

'But you could have saved him!' My voice cracks and I fail to stop the sob from breaking loose this time. I want to hit something, possibly the Queen. I want to make her hurt. I want her to feel this loss, this powerlessness, this fury over what has been done to me, to my family.

Sydok gives me a moment, before continuing. 'I am so very sorry, dear,' she purrs, genuine apology as evident within her words as the sorrow in her expression. 'But I had to do as I was bid.'

'What kind of creature is this Queen?' I spit, refusing to be placated. 'That she would care nothing of a baby's life? Nothing of my life, my father's life? We *needed* my mother, and the Queen took her from us. Why? Why would she do that?'

'Hester and Beatrix were close,' Sydok explains, as if that could possibly validate what the Queen had done. 'She wanted your mother returned to her so she could once again be part of her court.'

'But that's not fair,' I say, hating how childish I sound. Then, wondering what Law is making of all this, I glance at him. His inscrutable expression gives nothing away, but there is a certain tightness in the set of his jaw.

'When it comes to the Queen's court, what the Queen says goes,' Sydok replies, drawing my attention back to her. The regret in her words mixes with something that sounds oddly like my own frustration. 'Fair doesn't come into it.'

I force myself to take a breath, then another, and compel my thoughts to slow, to quiet. I am still livid with the Queen, I am still outraged over what she did, but I cannot do anything about that. For now.

What I can do is find out more about my own truth. To arm myself with it.

'So then, I am fae. I have magic.' My words sound abnormally flat to my ears. 'How could I not have known this until now?'

Sydok places her empty cup on the table, taking this shift in questioning in stride. 'Because I bound your magic, dear. I bound you and removed your Second Sight.' She pauses, her gaze assessing my undoubtedly obstinate expression. 'I knew it would not have been safe for you in the human realm, living with magic and the ability to see beyond to our world. Not without someone there to guide you. If your mother had remained there, she would have been able to teach you, to guide you in the ways of the fae.'

She pauses again, that unexpected flicker of frustration now flashing behind her eyes. 'As it was, you needed to be protected from your magic. Otherwise, you might have caused harm to yourself, or to others.'

'That's what you did to me while my father held me, while I was asleep,' I confirm, moving past incredulity and creeping towards acceptance. Towards curiosity. Over the fact that I am fae, the fact that I have magic. After a beat, I add, 'Why is my magic returning now?'

I think of the tiny flash that exploded behind my eyes following my fury at Donald. Of the spark when I grasped Law's hand. Of the light that exploded out of me when the kelpie attacked.

'The binding would only ever last so long,' Sydok explains. 'I'm just glad it lasted as long as it did. If your magic had returned before you were an adult, when your hormones were fully in charge, things could have gotten very messy indeed.' A wry smile reveals sharp canines, before she continues, purred voice contemplative. 'It's loosening now, but it *is* possible your magic escaped around the binding before. Did you ever notice anything unusual happening around you? Anything you couldn't explain? Like the glimmers you have seen recently, it would have likely occurred at a time of emotional upheaval. When you were angry or upset, perhaps.'

Casting my mind back, I search my past for anything inexplicable or mysterious, but there is absolutely nothing I can think of prior to that flickering spark that found me as I faced down Donald's maddening fucking smirk.

I shake my head. 'No.'

'Just a thought.' Sydok's shrug is easy, but her sharp smile tells a different story. Before I get the opportunity to question the meaning behind that smile, she pushes on. 'Unfortunately, there is no way for me to remove the binding fully without harming you in the process, but it should continue to loosen over time. And as it does, you will notice your magic more and more.'

I nod as another thought distracts me. 'What about when I met Law? There was a spark between us when we shook hands. I wasn't angry or upset then.'

Slightly aroused, perhaps.

'That was likely your magic recognising its opposite,' Sydok explains, crossing her legs neatly in front of her and acting as if that had been an entirely ordinary thing to say.

While I try very hard to process this, Law leans forward in his chair and speaks for the first time since entering Sydok's home. 'What do you mean?'

'The magic you and Elspeth hold are in opposition, dear. Elspeth's magic allows her to manipulate Aether. Or it will, once she can connect with it. Your magic, Law, as you know, is accessed through Nether, which is Aether's opposing force.'

Law considers this, looking as grim as I have ever seen him.

'What is Aether?' I say, unsure of whether I am asking Sydok or Law.

It's Sydok who answers.

'Aether is the unique essence that flows through, well everything, really. Some say it is the essence the gods breathed into the world as they created it, as they created everything we see around us. The seas, the earth, the trees. From the shortest blade of grass to the tallest mountain, it all contains Aether. As such, it is considered a powerful celestial element, a fifth element, as it were. But a much more powerful element, as it can bind the other four.'

'What do you mean it can *bind* those elements?' I ask, feeling no more enlightened than I had been prior to her explanation.

'It provides control over them,' Sydok replies patiently. 'By manipulating Aether, you will have control over earth, air, fire and water. In theory anyway. Those who access magic by way of Aether are not exactly common.' Her shrugged smile conveys her acceptance of the fact that the extent of even *her* wisdom has its limits. 'I am unsure of how powerful your magic will be, of how strong your connection with Aether will be. It was hard to judge your access to it as a child, and now your magic remains bound, even if the binding is loosening.'

'All I've seen of my magic so far is light,' I say. 'Is that... normal?'

Really, what the hell is normal about any of this? I sigh inwardly.

'It is as I was explaining earlier. That is your magic – or Aether, really – escaping around the binding,' Sydok says. 'Once the binding has loosened fully, you will be able to work on your connection with Aether, and from there, use it to manipulate the elements, though to what extent, I am uncertain.'

'And what of Nether? It's an opposing force, you said.' I look to Law, trying to gauge his reaction. His expression tells me little, but the shadows on his skin spiral in agitation.

'Nether is another celestial element, like Aether,' Sydok says. 'But where Aether flows through everything that makes up our world, the world of the living, Nether flows through the realms of the dead. If you think of it in the same way as Aether – that the gods used it to create all you see here – it is said that Death used Nether to create the Underworld.'

'The Underworld?' I ask.

'The world of the dead,' Law replies, voice void of emotion.

'A subterranean dimension where all souls go when they pass on,' Sydok says gently. 'As it is also a celestial element, Nether is not one that can be perceived in any physical sense within this realm.' Sydok looks to me. 'This light you described, that is your magic creating a visual representation of Aether. Otherwise, we would not be able to see it.' Lifting a hand to indicate Law, she continues. 'Law manipulates Nether when he accesses his magic. We cannot see Nether, just as we cannot see Aether. As I understand it, Law's magic allows him to draw from Nether and mix it with an element of our physical realm that we *can* see, which in his case is shadow.'

I nod dumbly, thoughts scattered and mind racing. Having taken in so much, it now staggers between vastly overwhelmed and wanting to find out even more.

Seeming to sense this, Sydok leans over to pat my knee. 'You take some time to think on it, dear.' She stands to clear away the cups. 'Perhaps I can get you two something to eat?'

I manage a weak smile in her direction, before my gaze travels to Law.

Lounging back in his chair, he appears to have entirely regained his usual composure. But while that placid, carefully neutral expression tells one story, the turbulent twists of shadow that roil over his skin articulate another.

Chapter 13

Whether Law senses my desire for solitude in my thoughts, or he simply prefers to remain in his own head as we continue on our journey, we walk through the rest of the afternoon in relative silence.

Surrounded by extravagantly luxuriant foliage and dazzling flora, I am far too consumed by my churning thoughts to pay attention to any of it. Instead, I place one boot in front of the other, turning over everything I'd not had the opportunity to fully process as Sydok pitched truth after truth at me, trying to make it fit with what I thought I'd known about myself, about my life.

I think of my mother, this woman whom I'd thought dead up until a few days ago, who is actually a faerie belonging to the Queen of Elphame's court. I think of the Queen, who I've travelled all this way to find, but who may in fact be the source of my troubles rather than a solution. I think of my father and the loss we've both suffered as a result of the Queen's demands, and of how Agnes, my best friend, kept the truth from me not just of her being a witch, but of my mother being fae. Of me being fae. Of me having bloody goddamn magic, for fuck's sake.

Betrayal. Loss. Fury. Confusion. Disbelief. Wonder. I spiral through all of it, trying to make sense of everything, while at the same time, trying not to sink into it, trying not to let it overwhelm me.

At times like these, it would always be Agnes I would go to. To talk it over and sort through what was useful and what to cast aside. To help me work out how to get my head straight so that I could move forward, move past whatever my problems were, so I could focus on the practical, on getting things done.

But Agnes is not here. I am stuck in my own head and must work through all of this on my own.

Or you could just push it aside and deal with it later.

Tried and tested, this has often been a method I've fallen back on. One that doesn't require quite as much soul searching, as much pain, as much effort as processing and moving past those difficult emotions. Pushing it all to one side, I can shove it away where I don't have to think about it, so I can still move forward, so I can still get things done.

Not something Agnes would approve of, but it will have to do for now. I have things to do. I can deal with the rest of it later. Maybe.

With that neatly tidied away and definitely never coming back to bite me, I turn my mind to Law, considering whether his own silence is one of churning thoughts or simply respect for my own. From the look of him, he is as relaxed now as he had been at the cottage, even as each of those revelations had rolled out of Sydok's mouth and flattened me with their enormity.

Well, up until the point when talk had turned to his magic. At that, barely concealed tension had edged the effortless lines of him, causing my overwhelmed mind to take note, but even now, I'm not sure what it means.

I'm certain there is something there. I just can't put my finger on what it might be.

I continue to mull it over, dusk drawing ever closer, until we finally reach the bothy that will serve as shelter for the night.

Set some way back from the path, it is a simple stone building tucked away within the surrounding trees, featuring a high-set roof and plain wooden door. Inside, it holds just one large room, but unlike Sydok's cottage, its interior dimensions thankfully match those of its exterior. Exposed timber beams brace the vaulted ceiling above bare stone walls, which are empty of adornment apart from simple metal sconces filled with floating balls of faelight that chase away the dusk. Along the far wall, several pallets provide a neat, if somewhat basic place to sleep, while at the centre of the room, a hearth creates a focus, around which a circle of mismatched wooden chairs gather.

'Will we have this all to ourselves tonight?' I ask, taking off my pack and hanging it over the back of a chair. A distinct chill emanates from the stone around me, and I opt to keep my cloak on, eyeing the unlit hearth.

'Perhaps,' Law replies. 'Bothies can be used by anyone in need of shelter. It might be just the two of us, or we might be joined by other travellers.' His words are not exactly tight, but they hold less of their usual ease.

Noting it, but unable to discern the cause of it, I choose instead to turn my attention to the hearth. Knowing it will only get colder as night sets in, I take out my flint stone and kneel to light the thoughtfully set kindling. As it catches, I take some of the smaller logs stacked next to the hearth and add them carefully to build up the fire.

Observing my efforts, Law says, 'You may not need that stone for much longer.'

Unsure of what he means, I tilt my head in question.

'Power over the elements,' he explains. 'Gaining control over your magic should mean you have fire at your fingertips.'

Despite being one of those far too overwhelming thoughts I'd decided to push to the side earlier, the notion that I might be able to conjure fire whenever it suits me is undeniably intriguing. I consider it, what it might be like to simply snap my fingers and for fire to appear. But then, what if I snap my fingers and set myself on fire? Or set someone else on fire?

It is intriguing but it is also intimidating and more than a little terrifying.

'What's so wrong with that?' Law asks, reading either my silence or more likely, the picture of daunted horror on my face.

I consider lying, shoving it down again, but after taking a moment to measure the concern in Law's own expression, I opt to let him in.

'It's absolutely fucking petrifying, that's what's wrong with it,' I say, my voice sounding somewhat strangled. I hadn't meant for quite that much truth to spill out of me, but now I've started, I find I can't stop. 'It's huge. It's crazy. It's intimidating. It is magic. Magic! I have fucking magic in me, and I have absolutely no clue what to do about it.'

In no way overwhelmed by my outburst, Law calmly assesses me. 'I could teach you.' Then, in a very un-Law manner, he hesitates, appearing unsure of himself. Like I might scoff at the very idea of such an offer. With some of that earlier tension returned to his words, he continues. 'If you like.'

I frown, running my eyes over him, wanting to understand this unexpected shift. But there's nothing. Despite his tight tone, he appears as easy as ever as he stands in front of me, one hand resting on the back of a chair, the other in his pocket. Features relaxed, his unflinching grey stare measures me right back, while shadowy whorls shift lazily below his rolled sleeves and at his open collar.

Tug.

The wrench toward him is almost brutal. It's physical, yes, but there's more there, I can feel it. With my gaze fixed on his and nothing but a sparking hearth between us, I can't deny how much I have come to appreciate him, to enjoy him, his company, his way. While I'm clearly hopeless at reading him when he is determined to give nothing away, I want that not to be the case. I want to see him better so I can know him better. And I want for him to know me in return.

The depth of that want should scare me. But somehow, it doesn't.

I blow out a breath. Articulating my emotions has never come easy, but I'm resolved to make the effort. 'I would like that, Law,' I offer, allowing the affection I feel for him to paint my words. 'I'm glad I have you here with me for this. I don't think I could do it alone.' Conceding this is especially difficult. For me, admitting I need help is even harder than expressing my emotions.

Shadows coiling faster now, Law regards me, something flitting across his features that is too fast for me to grasp its meaning. 'I'll do what I can to help,' he says, his words now an unreadable monotone.

I wait for him to continue, to perhaps voice his own feelings on the situation in which we find ourselves. Failing that, for him to hitch a brow and fend me off with some flyaway comment meant as a distraction.

Instead, he nods once and starts towards the door. 'There will be washing facilities outside,' he says over his shoulder. 'I'll go and get cleaned up. You can go after, if you like.'

What the fuck?

I gape at his retreating back, my traitorous eyes burning. Then, urging my attention to the hearth in front of me, I force a deep, shaky breath as I try and fail to tamp down the rather substantial bubble of hurt rising in my chest.

***

Enveloped in velvety darkness, the bothy feels warm and surprisingly comfortable, lit by golden faelight and the now heartily roaring fire. Having eaten dinner – me from my pack, and Law from provisions Sydok had provided – we are settled on opposite sides of the hearth, watching the flames pop and crackle between us.

'What are you thinking about, Red?' Law asks, breaking the not quite comfortable silence.

We've spoken little since earlier, both choosing to wrap ourselves in the mundane tasks of eating and washing instead of conversation. I had used the little bar of soap and bucket to wash my hair and body as best I could, but I'd been unable to do anything with my dress without spending another night in my underclothes. Law is now wearing a different shirt, one made of pale grey cotton, though where it came from, I have no idea.

With his earlier reaction – or lack thereof – being another thing I had flung to the side so I wouldn't have to think about it, I answer honestly when I say, 'My mother.' Feeling very much like a wobbly tooth I can't stop worrying, I can't seem to stop my mind from probing and prodding thoughts of her. No matter how far I push them away, they just keep on bloody coming back.

'Understandable,' Law replies. 'Anything in particular bothering you? Perhaps there are answers I could provide.'

I lean back in my chair and stretch my feet toward the fire, trying to decide where I might start. I sigh. 'Mostly, I want to know why she didn't come back for us.' My eyes flick from my boots to Law's face. 'She travelled to the human realm once, why couldn't she do it again?'

Sydok's explanation had made it obvious my mother had little say in her return to Faerie, but the notion that she'd never thought to come back to us is one I cannot wrap my head around. If the hurt that followed Law's odd reaction earlier was a bubble, this hurt is a boulder.

'Like Sydok said, what the Queen says goes,' Law says, a slight frown creasing his brow. 'Your mother defied her by travelling to the human realm. The fact that she did that – and then had to be sought out and returned to Faerie – would not have made Beatrix receptive to further requests your mother may have made to go back to you.'

'If she loved us, she could have disobeyed the Queen,' I protest, that same impotent anger I'd experienced earlier rushing back. 'She could have come back to us without her permission.'

'No one in the Queen's court would – or could – defy her like that,' Law says evenly. 'She's simply too powerful. If she wanted your mother to stay within her court, to remain in Faerie, her power as Queen would have made it so. Even if your mother had wanted nothing more than to return to you, if Beatrix had not also wanted that, it simply would not have happened.'

The conviction in his words washes away my anger – towards my mother, at least – but I still can't stop probing that wobbly tooth. 'If only Mama could have stayed with us. How different our lives would have been.' Thoughts of growing up with a mother, a brother, a fully present and happy father, blaze through me. 'She could have taught me how to use my magic.' I pause, considering. 'It could have changed things. I could have used it... to protect myself.'

'Against the kelpie, you mean?' Law asks.

While being able to protect myself against that murderous fucking horse certainly would have been preferable to relying on Law to rescue me, my thoughts had instead skipped back further, to my time with Malcom.

I wrestle with whether or not to tell him, with whether I want to open up to him after I'd made the effort earlier and got nothing from him in return. It's one thing for him to keep his past from me, it's another for him to bury his emotions and not let me in.

'Yes, there is that...' I start, then waver.

Cautiously, I consider this thing between us, of what it might be. Of what it could be, if I only give it a chance. Turning it over in my mind, I realise I still very much want to give it a chance. To give Law a chance.

Fighting past that instinctive desire to keep everything locked down tight, I step off the ledge. 'But mostly, I was thinking about Malcom.'

'Malcom?' Law says sharply. 'Your husband?'

'Yes,' I say, unsure how to go on from there.

'Why would you need to protect yourself from your husband?' Law asks, jaw clenched in a way that suggests he already knows the answer.

I eye him, weighing my words. 'Malcom could be violent. Not at first. But later, after we had been married a while. Little things would annoy him, and he would blame me. He was a quiet man, he kept a lot to himself. But I could always tell when that switch in him flipped, when his quiet manner would flip to silent anger. From there, I knew it wouldn't be long before his anger would spill out onto me.'

With the dancing flames having drawn my gaze, I force myself to look up at Law, who now sits in unnatural stillness, expression drawn taut with anger of his own.

Observing my attention, he asks, 'Why didn't you leave?'

I let out a low laugh, although there is little humour in it. 'Wives don't leave their husbands,' I say wearily. 'Or they don't where I'm from.'

'Was there no one who could help?'

'I never told my father, although I'm sure he suspected. It's not so uncommon for men to beat their wives, after all. I told Agnes and she did what she could to help. Gave me balms and powders to help me heal. A tonic to make sure I never fell pregnant.'

Law's lips thin. 'Did he force you to...?' He leaves the rest of the question hanging, but I know well enough what he is asking.

'No, he didn't,' I say truthfully. 'It wasn't so bad all the time. We could have weeks, sometimes, when life was almost normal. It was like living on a knife's edge, though. I just never knew...' I stop, mouth dry.

A heavy moment passes.

Law is the one to finally break the silence. 'What happened to him?'

'It was his heart,' I say. 'That's what the doctor concluded, anyway.' I pause for another long moment, gathering myself. 'We were both at home. I was clearing up after dinner. I was being too loud, I imagine. Malcom often complained that I was too loud. He'd come home from work cloaked in one of those quiet furies of his. I suppose I knew it was coming. Even with my back to him, washing the dishes, I felt that switch in him flipping, pushing him over the edge from a kind of unfocused fury to... to intent.'

I am surprised by the clarity of my recollection. I have worked hard over the years to push down any thoughts of Malcom, mentally locking it all away in a box deep within me.

Now, the memories return with a vividness that scorns the years that have passed between that night and this.

'I heard him stand, the chair scraping on the floor behind him. I tensed, knowing what was coming.' Even now, I feel that cold sense of frustration that would surge over me in those moments. The exasperated rage that would come from knowing I could do nothing to stop what was about to happen. The first few times, I'd tried to fight back, but it had been pointless. Spending his days at the forge, Malcom had been a wall of muscle.

'But it never came,' I continue, feeling oddly numb now, detached. 'It was as it always was. My entire focus was on locking down, tensing in anticipation, unsure of where the blow might land. When it didn't, I turned, saw him crashing to the floor. He was clutching his chest, but it didn't look like it was his heart that was paining him.' Pausing, I lick dry lips. 'He looked like he couldn't breathe. Like he was... a fish on land, gasping but not actually getting any air.'

Twisting my hands in my lap, I exhale the peculiar truth of it. The truth I had not dared to mention to the doctor or the bailiff, too afraid they might call it witchcraft or worse, something they could blame on me. While I hadn't rushed to his side, hadn't tried to help him, I had not been the cause of his death.

With the same numb detachment, I continue. 'After that, it was all legal paperwork and doctor's reports and dealing with the minutiae that comes with packing up one life and moving to another. I did all I could to stamp it down – the memories, the emotions... his death. I packed it all away in the same way I packed up my trunk. There was no real grief. Only relief. I had to work so bloody hard to keep the smile from my face when I finally left that hateful fucking house.'

I blink, looking up from the flames to find Law, several emotions racing one another across his face. I give him a wan smile. 'So, you see, it would have been nice to have a little magic back then.'

Seeming to hesitate, he then moves in one fluid motion, so that within the space between heartbeats, he is out of his chair and crouching in front of me. He places one hand on his knee and the other on my armrest. He doesn't touch me, but his intense expression reaches out instead.

'Perhaps you did,' he suggests, one coiling shadow creeping along his forearm onto the hand that rests next to me. As if it wants to reach out to me, like it feels the same pull towards me that I feel drawing me towards Law.

'What do you mean?' I ask, searching the intensity within his slate gaze.

'Sydok said your magic may have escaped around the binding. Maybe you used it to protect yourself without realising.'

'I could have done that to him?' I ask tentatively, unsure whether I am horrified by the prospect or electrified by it.

'Stolen his breath? Without a doubt. Fae with a powerful enough connection to air magic can do such a thing, so I don't see why you couldn't. Or your emotional connection to Aether could, at least.' Law ponders this, seeming in no way dismayed by the notion that I may have in fact, murdered my husband. 'But it might mean we'll have to start working on your control over Aether sooner rather than later. We can't have you wandering around, unintendingly dispatching folk to the Underworld.'

I choke out a startled laugh. If I had been thinking sensibly, there would be nothing funny to be found in a conversation such as this. But, feeling curiously empty after pouring out my past, I find I cannot push down my amusement as I take in the ever so slightly wicked look on Law's face.

Without thinking, I angle in to kiss him.

The kiss is brief, but I gather in the feel of his soft lips, his warm exhale of breath as I surprise him. Then I pull back, looking him in the eye, gauging his reaction. I want more, but only if he does too.

Answering my unspoken question, Law chases my lips with a kiss of his own. Leaning into it, his mouth gently brushes mine, then slowly, as if giving me the opportunity to pull back, he deepens the kiss, one hand lifting to cup my cheek. Cradled against his touch, the rightness of it surges over me and I part my lips on a fluttering sigh, his tongue running along their seam to seek out my own.

I reach out, bunching my hands in his shirt, realising I want more, so much more, and tugging him closer to get it. Taking the hint, he shifts to kneel before me, and I part my legs to allow his body to fit between them. The heat of where we touch is heady, and I breathe in the even headier scent of him, unable to deny the inexorable rush that comes from having this feared fae kneeling before me, centring all of his attentions on me.

I lean back in my chair, dragging Law with me, wanting to taste more, feel more, know more. Breath ragged now, my hands seem to move unbidden to find the hem of his shirt, pulling it up to explore the muscled planes of his torso. Relishing his low groan, I smooth my hands over his skin, unsure whether I imagine the small sparks that seem to fizz under my fingertips.

As the heat of his kisses tracks down the column of my throat, to my neck, my earlobe, I am almost overwhelmed by how much I want him. His name flies from my mouth, an answer to which I do not know the question. Another raw grown escapes him and he cups my hips, hauling me toward him to bring the centre of me flush with his torso. Through the folds of my skirt, I feel the hard length of him there, making me ache as I wish there was much less fabric between us.

Again, his mouth finds mine. His touch is heat, it is hunger, it is everything.

My arms wrap around him and I tangle my hands into his hair, using my nails to caress the velvet stubble at the nape of his neck that I have longed to touch for days.

'Elspeth,' Law breathes against my lips, the smoky sound of his voice sending another shiver of desire straight to my core.

I tug him closer, his solid chest pressing against my breasts, causing my taught nipples to graze the fabric of my camisole and a jagged moan to escape me. Somewhere in the back of my mind, I dazedly wonder how far this might go. With every sensation heightened, everything in me is calling out for Law, yearning to be closer to him, yearning for more.

Without warning, he pulls back, his jaw compressed so tight it looks like it hurts.

'What is it?' I ask, flushed and breathing hard.

'We shouldn't,' he starts, 'I shouldn't have done that.'

'But I thought...' Mind and body reeling from the sudden loss of him, I can't wrap my head around his sudden change of heart. Hurt and need and confusion punch at me from all angles. I'd felt him. I'm quite sure he'd been enjoying himself just as much as I was.

He stands swiftly, cocking his head as if listening out for something.

'Red, I'm sorry,' he says, running his hands through his hair. I can still feel the softness of those strands as they'd twisted through my fingers. I ball my hands into fists to push away the sensation. 'We can talk about it later. Right now, we have company.'

I scoot back in my chair and look at him askance. I can't hear anything. 'What are you talking about?' I bite out.

In answer, Law nods to the door, just before it bursts open and three fae males step in, cold swirling around them to sweep through the bothy.

Chapter 14

In a flurry of movement, the three fae step quickly inside and close the door behind them, nodding their greetings as they set their bows and quivers neatly beside the door, then remove heavy woollen cloaks.

Well aware I am gawking but quite unable to stop, I take the opportunity to study them while their focus is elsewhere. Looking mostly human, each one has certain characteristics I'm far more familiar with seeing on animals. One has the floppy ears of a hound and a long shaggy tail that extends through a hole in the back of his trousers, while another has the ears and snout of a pig, though if he has a curly tail, he's keeping it hidden. Feline in appearance, the third male reminds me of Sydok, but without her asymmetry he has two cat's eyes, two cat's ears, and a sinuous cat's tail that curls out behind him.

'Evening,' the male with the pig snout says, settling himself into a chair by the hearth.

'Nice night for it,' Law says, lifting his chin in reply. Leaning back in his own chair and crossing his long legs in front of him, he looks nowhere near as ruffled as I feel. Trying for subtlety, I attempt to smooth my hair and rearrange my skirts.

'Certainly is.' The male with hound ears smiles a dopey grin, as he too makes himself comfortable in front of the hearth.

'How's the hunting?' Law asks.

'Can't complain,' replies the porcine fae. 'Mordant over there got himself a doe this afternoon.' He gestures to the male with the features of a cat.

'Left her outside,' Mordant says, shuffling his chair closer to the fire in an attempt to warm himself. 'I dressed her, but the cold should keep her well enough until tomorrow.'

'Set a few traps around this way as well,' the pig-faced fae says. 'We'll check them in the morning to see if anything interesting happens into them overnight.' Then, seeming to remember he is talking to strangers, he continues, 'The name's Samient, by the by. Over there, as I mentioned is Mordant, and this fellow here is Timias.'

With his hound ears pricked, Timias raises a hand in greeting, comfortable in a way that makes me think he and his companions are not familiar with Law and his daunting reputation.

'Law,' Law says, then gestures in my direction, 'And this is Elspeth.'

More than a little distracted by how convincingly Law has smoothed over his demeanour, I flick my irritated gaze from him to smile quickly at each of the fae. Feeling all kinds of knotty and jagged myself, I'm also still somewhat embarrassed by my dishevelled appearance. I am quite sure these males know exactly what activities we'd been engaged in before their arrival.

Samient confirms this by saying, 'Sorry to interrupt your, um, evening.'

'Nothing to apologise for,' Law replies amiably. 'You are as much entitled to use this bothy as we are.' He turns to face me while continuing to talk to the other fae. 'Your timing could have been better, though.' He focuses his grey regard on me, trying to communicate something I am unable to interpret.

In an attempt to distract myself from the chaos of emotion swimming within me, I drag my attention from Law and aim a question at the three males. 'Are you hunters?'

'Yes, mistress,' Samient replies, seeming to be the voice of the group. His glistening snout twitches as he talks, causing the thick hairs surrounding it to bristle unpleasantly. I try hard not to stare. 'We move around a lot. We go where the hunting is good.'

I consider this, wondering what etiquette might apply to the hunting of animals, when you appear to be at least part animal yourself. Weighing up whether this would be an appropriate question to ask, I choose to err on the side of caution and keep my curiosity to myself.

'It must be hard being away from home so much?' I feel this is safer ground to tread.

'It can get lonely indeed, mistress,' Timias chips in, puppy-dog eyes accentuating his already forlorn expression. Reaching into a pocket of his tunic, he slips out a flask, opens it and takes a long pull. He passes it to Mordant, who does the same.

'Do you have sweethearts at home?' I ask. To my eyes, they appear not far into adulthood, so I have no idea if the question is appropriate or not. Given Law's age and the way he looks, they could easily be pushing two hundred and have a dozen grandchildren between them.

'Not me, mistress, nor Samient,' Timias replies, not giving any indication that my question had been an odd one. 'Mordant does, though he doesn't get to see her much.'

'Causes me no end of grief,' Mordant sighs, passing the flask to Samient. I hope it doesn't come to me next. I'm getting tired of declining offers of food and drink here in Faerie.

'Can't decide which is worse,' Samient puts in. 'Having someone and not seeing her, or simply having no one at all.'

'What I wouldn't give to have someone to curl up with on a night like this,' Timias says. His ears droop so dramatically, I have to work hard not to reach out and scratch between them in an attempt to cheer him up.

Law stiffens and sits forward in his chair. He appears to be listening out for something. Something I obviously cannot hear with my disappointingly average human ears. Scrubbing a hand over his face, he mutters something that sounds like, 'You really shouldn't have said that.'

I open my mouth to ask him what he means, just as he stands and sweeps his eyes over the three males. 'Please don't think us rude, but it's time for us to retire.'

'Not at all,' Samient replies, one of his little piggy eyes winking in a disturbing manner. 'Don't mind us.'

I eye Law. I don't feel tired, and I'm not sure I want to go anywhere with him, never mind bed.

'Trust me,' he murmurs, something urgent cast against his features. It's an expression I've not seen on him before. 'Please,' he offers.

Hurt and confusion still cling to me, but I realise I do trust him, or at least, I trust his instincts. And given what happened at the lake, I owe it to him to listen to those instincts now. From the look on his face, this request is not an idle one. It has purpose.

'Fine,' I say tightly, waiting as he gathers our cloaks and my pack, before following him to the sleeping pallet at the far corner of the room. I settle next to him with my back against the wall, ready to ask what the hell is going on, when he clasps my hand in his and silently hushes me. He gives me another of those looks and I hush.

Indignant, but curious all the same, I turn my attention to the three males, watching a moment as they resume a quiet conversation, passing the flask around as they talk. Thus distracted, it's some time before I notice the corner in which we sit seems much darker than it had been before.

I look around sharply, wondering if my eyes are playing tricks on me. A glance above tells me the sconce on the wall is no longer lit, but it's more than that. Cloaked in a much heavier darkness, it's as if we are somehow wrapped in shadow, concealed within this corner of the already dark and ill-lit bothy.

Peering through the dark, I search Law's face, seeking an explanation. Seeming to sense I'm about to question him again, he squeezes my hand. Hard.

The door bursts open, wrenching my attention from Law, my jaw dropping at the sight of three of the most breathtaking females I have ever seen. Apparently unbothered by the cold, each one steps out of the curling haar wearing nothing but a green silk evening gown that leaves very little to the imagination. Pale-skinned and delicate in their features, all three are utterly exquisite. So much so, I feel almost hypnotised by their beauty, like I might struggle to look away if I happen to try. But, as captivated as I am, as entrancing as they are, I can tell there is something not quite right about them.

Apparently, Timias does not feel the same. Standing so fast he almost knocks over his chair in his haste, he bounds over to the females, acting in much the same way as I would expect of an over-enthusiastic puppy.

'Ladies,' he says, bowing low before the newly arrived fae. I'm glad to see he is still thinking clearly enough to skirt around them and close the door, cutting off the chill night air creeping across the stone floor to where we sit.

'Welcome, welcome,' Samient says as he joins the party by the door, also bowing extravagantly. Mordant stands but remains by his chair.

Do none of these males think this strange? I would pass it off as a fae thing if it were not for Law's unusual behaviour. He remains quiet beside me, holding my hand, his grip still ominously tight.

'Won't you join us in a drink?' Samient says, sweeping one hand gallantly to the circle of chairs around the hearth, as if welcoming the females into a grand sitting room.

'What an enticing offer,' one of the females replies, voice so rich I feel like I should be able to taste it. Red lips curving into a smile, her face reveals an expression so gloriously radiant, it almost hurts to look at it.

'My name is Rivena,' she continues, artfully swishing luscious locks of the deepest black, allowing them to tumble alluringly down one side of her face. Working in harmony with her hair, her inky eyes play perfectly against pale, almost translucent skin. Gesturing to the two females beside her, she says, 'These are my sisters, Edane and Aemylia.'

I narrow my eyes, assessing each of them in turn. While there is some similarity in their refined beauty and pallor, I wouldn't mark these three as sisters. Still, it's nowhere near the strangest thing about them, so I let it go.

Having apparently turned into awkward adolescents, Samient and Timias almost trip over themselves to guide the females to a seat, then, once settled, Samient shyly passes Rivena the flask.

Quiet up to now, Mordant asks, 'If you don't mind me asking, how do you ladies find yourselves out on the road this late at night?'

Good question, Mordant. At least he still seems to have some sense about him.

'We travel here and there,' Edane replies, her voice a softly bubbling stream. With hair of gilded honey, pale blue eyes and fragile features, she appears the most delicate of the three. Although there is absolutely nothing delicate about the amount of cleavage she is revealing.

'Much like you.' Rivena showcases another of her devastating smiles and passes the flask to Aemylia.

'Oh yes, yes we do,' Timias pipes up. If his tail weren't tucked under him, I'm quite sure it would be swishing eagerly right now.

'So, are you boys interested in having some fun?' Rivena asks, standing from her chair to find another in Samient's lap.

If I hadn't witnessed such wanton acts at the wedding, I would have wondered if this kind of forward behaviour was normal among the fae. Mentally shrugging my shoulders, I suppose it must be.

Samient stammers something unintelligible while Aemylia sashays over to Timias. She flicks a curtain of poker straight brown hair over her shoulder and drapes herself over him, leaning in as she caresses the wiry fur of his ear.

I wonder what Mordant's take on this will be, and whether he will stay true to his sweetheart. Curiously I watch as Edane saunters over to him, bending to whisper something in his perked feline ear and giving him an obvious eyeful of her magnificent cleavage. Evidently persuaded, Mordant tugs her onto his lap, grabbing her perfectly rounded arse with palpable appreciation. Straddling him to reveal what appear to be cloven hooves instead of feet, Edane lets out a high, tinkling laugh that raises the hair on the back of my neck.

Whether this is normal fae behaviour or not, I can't shake the sense that something here feels... off. Law's own behaviour doesn't help. I cut my gaze to him. He is held taut by that strange fae stillness, barely breathing and as silent as graves. If this situation were in any way normal, why draw me into this shadowy darkness? Why hide unless there is something to hide from?

Unsure what else I can do, I turn my attention back to the fae situated around the hearth, unsurprised to find things becoming all the more intimate.

Having unbuttoned Samient's shirt, Rivena uses her tongue to pay special attention to what lies beneath, her deft hand working his cock through the fabric of his trousers. Still straddling Mordant, Edane slips her dress over her shoulders, and with his slitted cat's eyes blown wide, he gives her breasts his full and enthusiastic attention. Not wasting any time, Aemylia releases Timias's straining erection and lowers herself onto it, causing an excited yip to escape him as he clamps both hands over her ample hips.

Sounds of pleasure cloud the bothy, the scent of lust as potent as the breathy gasps and animalistic grunts that fill the air, and I can't help but feel my own arousal stir, despite the peculiar threat I sense.

It is around the same time I smell the coppery scent of blood that I also notice the red rivulet dribbling down Samient's chest. With his head tipped back and back arched in pleasure, he has exposed himself fully to Rivena, lost to the fact that she is now licking blood from various bite wounds across his torso.

Stunned, I dart a look at Law. Through the thick, shifting shadows, he shakes his head in warning. I whip my gaze back to the scene at the hearth to see Edane with her hand in Mordant's hair, twisting his head back, lapping blood from a messy wound on his neck. While I can't see much of Timias with Aemylia surging up and down on his lap, the brunette's mouth is planted firmly on his throat.

This time, it's my turn to clutch Law's hand in a death grip. Communal sex, fine, I can pass that off as a fae thing. Drinking blood, not so much. This feels wrong with a capital W. They may be near immortal, but even fae are sure to perish if they lose enough blood. How much more can these males lose before things turn perilous?

Beside me, Law lets out a near silent sigh. He removes my hand from his and places it on my chest, seeming to signal that I should stay where I am. Then he stands and steps into the light, leaving me alone and enveloped in darkness.

'Rivena, I think you've had enough.' Law's voice rolls over the room, sounding almost as seductive as Rivena's. Facing away from me, his stance is relaxed, but he is keeping his shadows coiled tight to his body, as if readying for attack.

Lingering a moment longer, Rivena flicks her tongue to trace a crimson stream trickling down Samient's chest, before raising her head to take in Law.

'Law, darling, I thought I could smell you,' she says, jet eyes heated with desire. 'I couldn't nail it down though, not with the animal scent and lust pouring off these three.' She looks disdainfully at Samient, whose head now lolls at an awkward angle. Seeing his piggie ears twitching and chest rising and falling, I am somewhat comforted by the fact that he seems to be unconscious rather than dead.

With that thought taken care of, my mind hurtles towards another. Rivena knows Law.

What is it with this male and outrageously attractive women?

Forcing that thought aside for later, I turn my attention to Mordant and Timias, who have both collapsed into in a similar state of oblivion as Samient. Ceasing their activities, Edane and Aemylia also shift to gaze at Law.

'Just leave them be,' Law says. 'They're harmless.'

'They are hunters, my darling,' Rivena purrs, her sneer revealing a row of needle-sharp teeth. 'They are far from harmless.'

I do not much enjoy hearing Rivena call Law her darling. It forces something cold and oily to twist in my gut.

'Unless they are inept,' Aemylia says, voice husky. Edane releases another tinkling laugh, making me shiver.

'You know what I mean, Rivena,' Law says, tone even. 'Let them go and be on your way.'

'You've changed,' Rivena pouts. 'Not so long ago you would have happily joined in. Admittedly not in the bloodlust, but there would most definitely have been lust involved.'

I grit my teeth and force a few deep breaths, working hard to keep each one even.

Abruptly, Rivena snaps her head in my direction, nostrils flaring. Uncurling from Samient's lap, she stands. 'Law, dearest, why are you hiding a human over there?'

Chapter 15

Dread cloaks me like a shroud. Having apparently kept her power tightly reined up to now, Rivena lets it roll off her, wild and entirely unrestrained. I feel it lave me, and I can't help but tremble in its wake.

I am unsure of how Law had known of Rivena's impending arrival, but I think I understand now why his first thought had been of concealment. Her beauty may be devastating, but her magic is something else entirely. It makes me want to bow down to her, to worship her, to throw myself at her feet and do whatever it takes to please her.

Law still stands sentinel in front of me, surely feeling that vast, terrible magic wash over him, just as it washes over me. My eyes flick to him and I am unnerved by the depth of my concern for him. Can he possibly be a match for such a thing?

I am frozen in place, barely daring to breathe as Edane and Aemylia stand, scenting the air and looking curiously towards the shadows in which I hide.

'She is none of your concern, Rivena,' Law says, tone hard.

'Ah, so the human is a she?' Rivena drawls. 'Is she your little pet, perhaps? Come on Law, let us all play with her.'

'I can't wait to taste her.' Edane drifts closer, eyes widening as she peers into the darkness. 'I do so adore the taste of human.'

'No one will be tasting her.' There is danger in Law's words now, his rigid frame matching their severity.

I swallow, its click audible in the shifting darkness. I have to think, to force my mind past Rivena's seductive wash of magic. I consider the fact that these fae seem to think me human. Which is not the whole truth, as I know now. Perhaps I can use that to my advantage.

Gathering my focus, I reach inside to feel out my magic.

Disappointingly, but perhaps not unexpectedly, it takes me no time to realise what I'm doing is pointless. I have never felt even an inkling of power inside myself. I have no idea how to feel it out, never mind access it and bend it to my will. When the kelpie attacked, the burst of magic that escaped me did so entirely of its own accord. While I'm experiencing quite a bit of the same terror I'd felt then, I also feel just as removed from my so-called magic as I had prior to knowing it existed.

Fuck it. If I can't use magic to defend myself, I can use iron. Quietly, I reach into my pack, draw out my dagger and unsheathe it. Digging down deep to scrape together some courage, I stand, then step out of the shadows with the dagger concealed behind my back.

'Oh, she is a pretty little thing, Law,' Rivena says. 'Feisty too, from her expression. I can see why you'd want to keep her to yourself.'

Law lets out another sigh, louder this time. Determinedly facing the three females, he doesn't glance around at me, wisely choosing to keep his focus on Rivena as all three drift subtly closer, a yearning hunger edging the very lines of them.

'She is not yours, Rivena,' Law intones.

'Does that mean she is yours, my darling?' Rivena replies, voice remaining playful even as her eyes narrow.

The hurt from earlier still clings to me, but I find myself unwilling to dismiss this thing between us. It is new, confusing even, but not something so fragile I can so easily throw it away. Which may explain why, at Rivena's question, my heart stutters at the thought Law might consider me *his*. While I am certainly not a possession to be owned, I know that, given enough time, one can own the heart of another. He had pushed me away, but he hadn't explained why. I *want* to know why.

'She is mine to protect,' Law replies.

I'm not sure how I feel about that answer. Although I suppose this is not the time to unpack his choice of words. Especially not with the way Rivena is looking at me. While her posture is relaxed, she seems coiled, ready. She has a hungry look on her lovely face that is twisted by something ugly. Jealousy, perhaps?

Aemylia tilts her head to one side, making a show of looking me up and down, appraising me. 'She would make a passable sister, I suppose.'

'If she survives,' Edane chips in, sounding almost cheerful.

'She will be no sister of yours, because I will not let you touch her, let alone bite her.' I wonder if Law's expression matches his grim tone.

Beyond that I must let my confusion show, as Rivena takes the opportunity to enlighten me on the meaning behind their conversation. 'If we bite you, you will become one of us, pretty one,' she says, as if talking to a child. 'Would you like that?' She smiles, putting those alarmingly sharp teeth on full display.

I feel the threads of her magic winding their way over me, endeavouring to steal my will, and I push against them, battling to keep my mind my own. Shoving the magic back, I grip onto my intense distaste for this faerie who keeps calling Law her darling. Onto how I like the condescension in her tone just as much as I like the idea of becoming one of these horrifying creatures.

'And what are you exactly?' I grit out, frustrated that I am once again having to ask a murderous fae to explain its nature to me.

'We are baobhan-sìth,' Rivena says, her silken drawl drawing out the pronunciation so that it undulates over her tongue... *baa'van shee*.

Teeth clenched in concentration, I continue to drive back her magic. I feel it creeping and crawling, seeking to seduce me, and know I need to create some sort of distraction, if only to slow the surge of magic just a little. With Rivena too far away for me to do any damage with my blade, I fall back on a tactic that's always worked so well for me in the past.

Giving lip.

'Right, so. How will this work?' I ask. 'You bite me, and I join the sisterhood. I get a green dress just like yours – they do look magnificent, by the by – then follow you ladies around, seducing unsuspecting males so I can fuck them senseless and drink their blood.' With my hands still clasped behind my back, I shrug. 'Thank you, but I think I'll pass.'

Law coughs out a laugh.

'Yes, I definitely see the attraction now, my darling,' Rivena purrs at him. 'She will make a wonderful addition to our trio. And then perhaps you will return to us too.' Her tone still sounds playful, like she is toying with Law, but there is a touch of pleading fraying its edges. There is definitely history there, and I'm becoming all the more certain Rivena had not been the one to end it.

'Neither Elspeth nor I will be joining you, Rivena,' Law says, his tone revealing no trace of his earlier amusement. 'This is the last time I will say it. Leave. Or I will make you leave.'

Rivena's expression remains carefully neutral, but there's an air of exhilaration illuminating Edane and Aemylia's dazzling features, causing me to wonder whether the threat of violence excites them. My breath hitches at the stark need I see there, and I grip the handle of my dagger tighter, desperately wishing I could wipe my sweating palms on something.

But there is no time for that, there is no time for anything, before the three baobhan-sìth descend on Law in a chaotic flurry of green silk and razor-lined snarls.

Law, who is there... and then abruptly, not.

While the movement is fast, almost too fast for me to catch, I'm sure I see him *step* into his own shadow, to then reappear within Edane's.

I seriously need to talk with Law about this magic of his.

Materialising behind Edane, he draws a shadow dagger made of the same inky substance as his broadsword and drives it into her back, skewering her through the heart. Before her slumped body falls to the ground, Law steps back through her shadow, emerging this time behind Aemylia.

Taking only a second to stare in horrified disbelief at her fallen sister, Aemylia whips around and ducks back swiftly from Law's blade. She has no weapon of her own to counter his attack, but she has undiluted fury – and those sharp fucking teeth. Her expression seething with wrath, she growls low in her throat and leaps at Law, hitting the ground and stumbling awkwardly, as he steps back into shadows to appear within mine.

Wholly distracted, I had watched this play out in the space between a handful of heartbeats, mouth agape, attention fixed firmly on Law. And foolishly, not on Rivena. Having sidled embarrassingly close without my notice, she launches herself at me just as Law grabs my shoulder and the world goes black.

One sickening heartbeat later, I am somehow looking back on the room from just beside the door. Before the enormity of this has the opportunity to settle fully in my mind, I'm hit by a sudden rush of vertigo and only just manage to turn my head to the side before I vomit violently.

By the time I straighten to wipe my mouth on my sleeve, Law has once again disappeared from my side. Dazedly, I watch as he appears in front of Aemylia, where he bends low to sweep her legs from under her, and as she tumbles backward, his dagger arcs.

Aemylia is dead before she hits the floor.

Not even waiting for her sister to fall, Rivena charges at me, letting out a feral snarl as she hurdles furniture like she is in no way constrained by the evening gown she wears.

I breathe down my lingering nausea while steadying my stance, gauging her approach and forcing myself to wait until the last possible second to draw my dagger. I brace for impact and feel the soft slide of flesh as it parts against the sharpened iron tip, gripping tight as Rivena's momentum drives it in all the way to the hilt. Vaguely aware of a scent of burning, I twist the dagger in a vicious upward motion, ensuring it causes maximum damage before I rip it back out.

Taking three quick steps back to assess the situation, I eye Rivena as she looks down in disbelief at the gaping, blistering wound in her gut. She sets trembling hands over the brutal, jagged slash, making a futile attempt to quell the black blood that gushes from it.

'Iron,' she spits, looking up, her face twisted in a mix of rage and agony. 'You bitch.' Her mouth sprays black blood in accompaniment to the insult, but I don't feel even a thread of her magic press against me now.

Law materialises beside me, choosing not to step into my shadow this time, but the shadow of a nearby chair. He glances at my dagger, then regards Rivena coolly.

'How could you do this?' She staggers towards him, gazing at him beseechingly as her tone turns pleading. 'You loved me.' Black tears mix with the inky blood that now flows freely from her mouth. 'How could you?'

Expression cold, Law stares her down, coils of shadow snaking furiously over his skin. 'You brought this on yourself, Rivena.' I shiver slightly at his icy tone. 'I gave you fair warning.'

Rivena's pale skin is ashen now, her lithe form shrunken. She pulls back her lips in a sneer and turns to me, revealing sharpened teeth that are now as black as her blood-stained dress. 'I will not let you have him,' she snarls.

Moving faster than I would have thought possible from someone apparently so close to death, she lunges at me. Barely thinking, I spring back to give myself more room and brace for her attack, then with a swift, sweeping movement upward, I plunge my blade up through her chin and into her brain. Before her dead weight can pull me down, I yank the dagger free and skip neatly to one side, letting her corpse collapse on the ground beside me.

Into the sudden silence, my breaths come hard and ragged, skin prickling, adrenaline surging through me in waves. Keeping my dagger loosely in hand, my attention drifts from Rivena to Law. I eye him cautiously. I'd sworn to him I brought no iron into Faerie, and I am altogether uncertain how he will react to that lie.

Cool remoteness fading from his features, he allows his own shadow dagger to dissipate and his lips to curve in the barest hint of a smile. 'Very impressive, Red,' he says, eyes sparkling. 'You barely needed me to save you at all this time.'

Chapter 16

My body begins to shake as adrenaline abandons me. In a breath, Law is there, wrapping me in his arms and steadying me. Circling my own arms around his waist, I lean heavily against him, inhaling deeply as I attempt to slow my harsh attempts at breathing.

His head bent over mine, he says softly into my hair, 'Are you well, Red?'

I suck in a slow, trembling breath. 'No. I don't know. My mind feels numb. Or maybe empty, but also too full. And I might vomit again.' I hesitate, desperately trying to marshal my thoughts. 'I've never... killed anyone before.' *Oh really?* my mind prompts. I shove that thought aside and pull back to look up at him. 'I just killed her, Law. I can't... I don't know what to think.'

'I know,' he replies, soothing gentle circles on my back. 'She didn't give you much choice in the matter, though.'

Missing the warmth of him, I let my head fall back to his chest and calm myself listening to the steady beat of his heart.

'If I could make a request?' he says after a long moment, his voice a deep rumble against my ear.

I nod, knowing he will feel the gesture.

'Could you perhaps move the blade elsewhere?'

I realise I still have the bloody dagger gripped in my hand and release it immediately so that it clatters to the ground.

'Thank you,' he says, barely suppressing a shudder. 'It's far from comfortable having that much iron so close to my person.'

While my mind still lingers on Rivena and the sickening feel of her flesh sliding along my blade, I absently consider this new piece of information. I had no idea iron affected fae to such an extent that it could cause pain on contact, never mind scorch faerie skin and burn away what lies beneath.

From there, my scattered mind flutters to another thought. Why am I able to hold the dagger without feeling so much as a twinge? I am half fae. Shouldn't that mean iron would affect me too?

Another flutter. Even though I held iron in my hand, Law hadn't hesitated to embrace me, all the while knowing such proximity to my dagger would be at worst fatal, at best, extremely uncomfortable.

The last flutter carries my mind back to Rivena. To Law's relationship with her.

'Hey Law,' I say.

'Hey Red,' he replies, a smile warming his voice.

'I think we need to have a serious discussion about your choice in females.'

I feel him stiffen. His words come out stilted. 'My time with Rivena was a lifetime ago. I was... different then.'

Waiting in the silence that follows, I finally pull back to look up at him again. 'Is there any further explanation forthcoming?'

Law looks as uncomfortable as I have seen him.

'I'll take that silence as a no.' My words come out sharper than I had intended, my patience for his reticence worn thin. Irritation filters through my shock, urged on by the unexpressed emotion following our broken kiss. I start to pull away, just as he leans down and brushes his lips against my forehead.

Leaving a whisper of warmth there, he straightens and says, voice low, 'It scared me'.

Startled by this change of direction, I ask, 'What did? When?'

'When I knew they were coming. Red, I know what Rivena is capable of.' His eyes flit to her body and he revises his choice of tense. 'Was capable of. It scared me to think of what she might do to you. That's why I wanted to conceal you from them. I knew if Rivena saw us together...' He pauses, gathering his words. 'I knew it wouldn't end well. Especially if she suspected how I feel about you.'

Questions of how he had known of the baobhan-sìth's impending arrival scatter in the wake of my more pressing enquiry. 'How do you feel about me?'

Grey gaze intense, Law's eyes search my face, and I wonder whether he can hear the wild pounding in my chest. 'I like you, Red. More with every passing minute, it seems.' He breaks away from me, turns, and drags a hand through his hair. Abruptly, he swings back, and words spill out of him in a cascade of anguished sincerity. 'You draw me to you, you pull me in. I can't explain it. I've never felt anything like it. It's like there's a tether, somehow, a connection. Like there's something inside me that pulls me to you...'

His words falter and he studies me, searching for my reaction while at the same time, looking like he wants nothing more than to stuff all that spilled vulnerability back where it came from.

I let out a long, shaky breath, hunting for the right words to reassure him, to tell him I feel the same way. That I am as baffled by it as he seems to be. That, somehow, through all of this awful shit I am wading through, it is the one thing that feels right.

But, as I try to find those right words, to form them, my eyes fall to the floor, where I see Rivena. Nothing more now than an ashen, lifeless husk, black blood pools around her, spreading, reaching for me, for Law, even after death. The sight of it turns my stomach, reminding me I had been the one to spill that blood, to take that life. The life of another being, who had lived and breathed and yearned and loved, and perhaps even died because of that love. For Law.

'Perhaps we should have this conversation a little further from the corpse of your former paramour?' I suggest, swallowing down my nausea alongside a reluctant dose of regret.

A careful mask of nothingness chases the fleeting surge of disappointment from Law's features, before he nods tightly and gestures towards the chairs circling the hearth.

Settling there, my attention falls on Samient, Timias and Mordant, who remain slumped where the baobhan-sìth abandoned them, each in varying stages of undress, but all thankfully still breathing.

Law drops into a chair beside me.

'Are they going to be alright?' I ask.

'Well enough,' he replies. 'They'll have lost some blood, but not enough to do any real damage. Fae heal fast. They will likely sleep off the worst of it.'

'But they won't become baobhan-sìth, will they?' I eye the bite marks peppering their bodies, my gaze lingering worriedly on the tattered wound at Mordant's neck.

'No. Only females who are bitten become baobhan-sìth.'

'Could they have died, though?' My chest constricts as I am hit by the sudden realisation that perhaps we could have left the baobhan-sìth to feed. That maybe they would have drunk their fill and gone on their way, leaving Samient, Timias and Mordant to sleep off the effects, much as they seem to be doing now.

While I consider seducing males to drink their blood to be morally grey at best, if the baobhan-sìth had been planning to leave the three males breathing at the end of it, had we been right to intervene? To kill them for it?

'Yes,' Law says, chasing away that thought. 'While Rivena didn't always drain them dry, Edane and Aemylia usually did.' He pauses, clearing his throat. 'Rivena liked to play with her food.'

He doesn't elaborate, and I am glad of it. I also feel far less remorse over the fact that the baobhan-sìth are now dead.

'So, you saved them,' I say, tilting my head toward the three slumbering fae.

'I suppose I did,' he sighs. 'But it doesn't make up for those I didn't.'

I hear the gravity within his words but don't know quite what to do with it, so I circle back to one of the questions I had pushed aside earlier. 'What I can't understand is where the hell they came from. How did you know they'd turn up like that?'

'It was part of their magic,' Law explains, leaning forward to rest his elbows on his knees. 'There was seduction – I'm sure you felt enough of that rolling off Rivena – but their magic also allowed them to listen out for lonely males craving female company. They would prey on anyone, but they were drawn to hunters most of all. It was the scent of blood that attracted them.'

'When Timias said he wanted a female to curl up with, that's what brought them here?' I ask, tamping down the fear that needles me. If a throwaway comment like that could invite such terror to our door, what else might Faerie have to throw at us?

Compelling myself to think past that, past just how out of my depth I feel, I look to Law as he nods. I assess the heaviness that lines his still carefully neutral mask and add quietly, 'You knew the baobhan-sìth would likely kill them?'

Law nods again.

This time, I stay silent, waiting for more.

His dark eyes seek mine. His mask wavers as his throat bobs.

'I do not seek out trouble, Red,' he says after a long moment, jagged emotion escaping his words now. 'As much as everyone thinks of me as this dangerous, despicable creature, I try to avoid causing trouble, causing suffering, whenever I can.' Seeming to echo my earlier thought, he continues, 'There was a chance Rivena would feed and leave them alive. My main priority was keeping her from you, so I opted to give her that chance instead of simply raining down death without seeing how it might play out first.'

His gaze slips to the three males on the opposite side of the hearth. 'I know it's not right. Not fair to Samient, or Timias, or Mordant. But I chose the path I hoped would end in less pain. Less death.'

He pauses, scrubs his face, then looks back at me, mask discarded, eyes brimming with bleak torment. 'I was not always this way. I was not... good. I caused others pain. I had no issue with killing. It was why Rivena and I were once such a good fit. It's why I have this reputation now.'

He spits the word, and the pain in his face, the desolation in his voice, causes something sharp to twist deep inside my chest.

'What changed?' I ask.

'Eachlair Ürlar,' Law replies. 'The witch we met at the tavern the first night?'

I nod, indicating I remember.

'We... crossed paths many years ago. You could say she used her magic to allow me to see the error of my ways.' A bitter smile twists his expression, failing to conceal the shame behind it.

I see it, just as I hear the sorrow tucked away within his words. I know he has not given me the whole truth. But I also know how hard truth telling can be. I'll take this for now, hoping the rest will come later when he is ready to tell it.

'And you changed because of that?'

A humourless laugh escapes him. 'She turned my entire existence upside down. There was no way for me to be the same male I was before I met her.'

I take my time weighing my next words, watching the inky swirl that wraps around Law's neck then dips below his collar. 'But if this happened so long ago, why is everyone still so afraid of you? You said you don't want to cause any more pain or suffering. Surely, they would have caught up to that by now. No matter how bad the reputation, it always fades with time. People, fae, they forget.'

'I said I don't want to cause pain or suffering, not that I do not.' His jaw clenches as he grinds out his next words. 'It is a large part of what I do for Nicnevin.'

Fucking Nicnevin.

I shove down my swelling hatred of the hoary old crone, take a breath, then say, 'You said at the wedding that you have no choice in what you do for her. So, you have to do as she asks, even if it means hurting others?'

My loathing is echoed within Law's reply. 'That's about the sum of it.'

'But how? How does she make you?' I don't doubt what he is saying, I just cannot wrap my head around how Nicnevin could make him do something that seems to conflict so grievously with his morals.

'Nicnevin and I, we have... an agreement. It binds me to her service.' While there is still that same loathing in Law's words, the smile that stains his face is not one I have seen before. It makes him look infinitely sad.

He doesn't give me time to respond, eyes flicking back to the hearth as he continues, 'I'll understand if you don't want anything more to do with me. I wouldn't want to have anything more to do with me. Not knowing who I once was. Who I still am.'

I can't stand to see him look so wretched. All his sorrow, his guilt, how heavy it must be to carry, to never be able to set it down. I can't imagine what it would feel like to want to do better, be better, but to be forced along the same path, to remain that same person everyone fears. To be hated for something you have no choice in doing.

'I'll still make sure you get there safe,' he says, breaking into my thoughts. 'That you get to the Queen.' He sets his jaw, his brows drawing together to focus more determinedly on the fire. In his features, I see his ready acceptance of my rejection. In his words, I hear his belief that I will no longer care for him because he deems himself to be less than.

Heart aching, I stand. Dragging his eyes from the hearth, he looks up at me, his defeated expression making way for one of confusion as I move towards him and cup his face. Curled tendrils twist up his throat to meet my hands.

'I see you, Law,' I say softly. 'Who Nicnevin forces you to be is not who you are. While I can't comment on who you were prior to your… exchange with Eachlair Ürlar, you say you've changed, and I believe it.'

I smooth my thumbs along his cheekbones as he stares up at me, grey gaze hesitant. 'While we haven't known each other long, the way I have seen you act does not suggest to me that you are bad. The way you have treated me, the way you have treated others, it has always been with kindness and respect, despite your reputation, despite the fear. God knows, with that magic of yours, you could make anyone bow down to you, you could easily make them feel small. But you've not done that. You've not sought out ways to cause others harm. You've not revelled in causing pain.'

I blow out a breath, my mind pushing forth an image of Calder, decapitated on the sand. Of Edane and Aemylia, impaled and bleeding, lying only a few yards from where I stand now. 'The only time you hurt anyone was because you had to,' I press. 'To protect me.'

His lips thin, like he wants to protest this, unreadable emotion warring behind his eyes, before gradually clearing, leaving his expression softer. He swallows, appearing to come to some sort of decision as his arms circle my hips, pulling me close. Resting his head against my stomach, he exhales, slow and heavy. 'You deserve better,' he says, weary resignation weighing down his words. 'Malcom, he was not a good man. Now, me.'

I run my hands through his hair, dragging my fingers across the velvet at the back of his neck. 'Nothing is so black and white as all that. No one is all good or all bad. I judged Malcom for the bad things he did. For the fact that he chose not to stop doing those bad things. You may have done bad things–'

'Horrific things,' Law interrupts.

'Horrific things,' I amend. 'But you do not choose to do them now.'

A grim sense of stubbornness outlines his reply. 'But I do still do them.'

I feel the warmth of his breath against my belly. 'And that is something we will have to remedy.'

Law pulls back to look up at me, and again, something flits across his expression that I can't quite read. 'We?' he asks, and I'm happy to see some of that anguish fade as one brow quirks.

'You told me before that you like me,' I begin, before hauling in a deep breath, trying to dredge up confidence I don't feel. 'I like you too Law. I feel that same... connection.' I kick myself for not being able to express my emotional self better. *Ugh, words.* Defiantly, I push more of them out of my mouth, hoping they don't sound as awkward to Law's ears as they do to my own. 'I don't know what it means, whether it's some kind of fae thing, but I do know I like who you are. I like the way you are with me.'

Recalling the misery that soaked his words earlier, I continue, hoping my expression conveys just how much conviction I have in my own. 'What you've shown me is that you are good. If there's something that's preventing you from being so, something that is causing you pain by forcing you to be something you are not, then we will work out how to fix it.'

Law's charcoal gaze locks on mine as he pauses to consider this, something he is trying very hard to conceal snaking beneath his features.

‘Fine. But first we get you to the Queen,’ he says finally. ‘You have to save your friend before you start thinking about how to save me.’

Chapter 17

As we set off from the bothy a few hours past dawn, my gaze twitches unwillingly to the spot where Law had dragged Rivena, Edane and Aemylia, the burden of having taken a life still twisting uncomfortably under my skin. Seeing nothing there now but three indents in the grass, I shudder, imagining the three of them winding away in coils of ash as the sun rose over the bothy. I am not sad to have missed it.

We make our way back onto the main path and I eye Law curiously, wondering where his head may have taken him after all that had happened. Having once again smoothed over his emotions, he has been his usual composed self since waking this morning, and now as we walk, he appears just as relaxed, hands in his pockets, dark shadows shifting lazily across his throat and down the back of his neck.

Could he really have collected himself as thoroughly as that? I know I certainly haven't.

'You're staring, Red,' he says, a hint of a smile curving his mouth.

I startle. 'I was just wondering how you were,' I reply quickly. 'Last night, it was... a lot. For both of us. Your former lover tried to murder me, then you watched me kill her. We also shared a few heavy truths. That kind of thing can take its toll.'

'Has it taken its toll on you?' he asks.

'I asked first. Don't start avoiding my questions again.'

'You didn't actually ask a question.' Law looks back at me, eyes sparkling.

'You are so infuriating.'

'You love it.'

I'm surprised to realise, in a way, I do.

While he may occasionally exasperate me, while he may still hold back, he is someone I very much enjoy being around. Putting aside how easy he is on the eye, he is also funny, thoughtful, and smart. More than that though, with him, I feel comfortable enough to show him my true self, without holding anything back. I can be entirely Elspeth; the Elspeth I have allowed to bloom in the years since Malcom's death.

To me, that means something.

I lived five years with Malcom, second-guessing myself, my actions, even the manner in which I spoke. With Law, I feel no need to censor myself, to worry about how he might react to something I say or do. Through it all, he has taken everything I have thrown at him in stride. Despite the insane amount of power he has, his sheer ability to cause harm, he holds none of that over me.

I let out a small grin and enjoy the one I get in return.

'Maybe I do,' I admit. 'A little. But I wanted to know how you are. Do I actually need to say the words? How are you feeling, Law?'

Law blows out a breath and turns his attention back to the path. 'I think you know by now how much I enjoy talking about myself, Red. I'm not... this is not something that comes easily to me.' He rubs the back of his neck, losing some of his earlier composure to awkward discomfort.

'No,' I say dryly, 'I had never noticed you try to distract me from subjects you don't want to talk about, or that you reroute conversations you don't want to have. Or that sometimes you just stop speaking when the topic turns to something you don't want to discuss.'

Law's smile is wry. 'Looks like you pay attention too.'

'Yes, I do,' I reply. 'Answer the bloody question.'

He puts up his hands in a gesture of surrender. 'Alright, fine. I'll talk. Or I'll try to. Will that do?'

I roll my eyes and motion for him to get on with it.

He sighs, looking put-upon. 'Fine. How do I feel about Rivena and her harpies being dead? I'm not feeling all that conflicted about that one. While I'll admit I wasn't in favour of seeking out their demise, I'm not sorry they're gone. They preyed on the innocent for decades. Now they can no longer do that.'

He shrugs, looking to me for approval.

'And?' I prompt.

'Those heavy truths?' Another shrug, although the gesture is not quite as easy as he had perhaps meant it to be. 'How do I feel about pouring out my soul to you?' His gaze flicks to mine, then falls back to the path. 'Not all that comfortable. Although that has everything to do with me, and nothing to do with you.'

I offer him what I hope is an encouraging smile, waiting to see if there is more.

There is.

'How do I feel about you pouring out your soul to me?' At this, he surprises me by catching my hand and raising it to his lips. 'Privileged.' My heart flutters at the sincerity in his expression, enjoying the warmth of his hand in mine as he lets them fall, but keeps them clasped together. 'I don't have words to express how I feel about everything Malcom made you live through. But if he were still breathing now, he wouldn't be for much longer. I'd put aside my moratorium on causing pain and suffering, just for him.'

'Um, thank you?' I say, not altogether sure of the etiquette surrounding new lovers offering to kill former husbands.

'You're welcome.' He winks, squeezing my hand. 'So, has this similarly uncomfortable outpouring of emotion answered your question to your satisfaction?'

I snort my amusement. 'Yes, and I appreciate it.'

'Outstanding. Well then, I will go one step further and let you know the emotion I am *currently* feeling on this bright and beautiful day is, overwhelmingly, lust.' He pauses, cutting a knowing smirk toward me. 'Towards you, just to be clear.'

Spluttering a laugh, I use my shoulder to shove him in protest.

'What?' he says innocently. 'Things were getting rather heated last night.'

'Before you pulled away,' I remind him. The memory of that hurt still nettles me, despite the fact that I am reasonably sure I understand his motive for doing so. That he feels he is somehow unworthy of me. Of us.

'Yes,' he admits, something dark dancing just behind his eyes.

'*And* your former flame turned up,' I say teasingly, wanting to lighten that look by adding a little levity back into the conversation. 'That would have likely killed the moment regardless.'

Law accepts my offering. With a small curve of a smile, he says, 'Yes, I imagine it would have.' Making a show of looking around us, he continues, 'Still, there are plenty of hidden spots around here if you want to continue where we left it last night?'

A laugh escapes me as he sends me one of his most wicked grins. Quite without my permission, my mind wheels over the heady sensations of last night. Liquid warmth pools at my core as I remember his lips exploring my mouth, my neck, my earlobes. The feel of his hard length pressed against me.

I clear my throat. 'While I am also in favour of continuing things–'

'Yes, I know that,' Law interrupts.

'Excuse me?'

'I can tell that you are in favour of continuing things,' he replies, a roguish glint in his eye.

'How?' I ask, suspicion tightening around the word.

'Fae have an extremely sensitive sense of smell.'

Realisation dawns on me. Scandalised doesn't even cover it. 'You mean, you can smell when I'm...?' I can't even finish the question.

'Yes,' he replies, that knowing smirk firmly back in place. 'You were getting nicely warmed up a moment ago.'

My mind flits over the many, many instances I have let my imagination run wild in Law's presence. He had known what I was feeling all of those times? Heat surges to my cheeks.

'But that's... that's mortifying.'

'It's damn intoxicating, actually,' he says, dipping his shoulder to give me a little nudge in return.

My ears burn with embarrassment. 'Well, either way, we're not stopping in the middle of these woods to attend to your... lust.'

'We'd be attending to your lust too,' he teases, drawing me to a stop. He releases my hand to brush my hair back from my neck, then bends down, grazing his teeth over my earlobe. Surrounded by the hypnotic scent of him, my body arches towards his and I relish the warmth of his breath against my neck, a flash of heat igniting where his teeth touch skin.

Law curses, jerking back. 'Did you feel that?'

'Was it another spark?' I ask.

'Yes. But bigger this time. Did it hurt?'

'No,' I say, considering. 'It felt incredible. Why? Did it hurt you?'

'No,' he admits. 'It was just, unexpected.'

With his lips so close, his expression so thoughtful, I have to work hard not to reach up and kiss him. But I know we have to keep moving.

Kissing him would lead to touching him and touching him would lead to... all sorts of other things that would certainly be enjoyable, but would also delay our journey. I want him. I want him so much. But I also need to get to the Queen. I need answers for Agnes. For myself.

I compromise by dragging a finger over his bottom lip. He bites it, tongue flicking over my fingertip.

'Later,' I promise. 'We need to keep moving.' I turn and start walking, then, as he falls into step beside me, I continue. 'That spark has given me an idea, though. It might just help to keep your mind off other matters.'

'It would have to be a spectacularly distracting idea,' Law says.

I bite my lip in consideration. Ignoring the way his gaze catches on the movement, I press on. 'I was thinking about your offer – to help me to work on my magic.'

'Definitely not as distracting as other pursuits, but admittedly, it is important,' he says, interest piquing his expression. 'And it is something we can work on as we walk.'

I nod my agreement. 'Right, so last night, I tried to feel out my magic after Rivena discovered me. I thought I might be able to use it against her.' I huff a laugh, recalling the intense surge of Rivena's own magic. I could never have been a match for that. 'Stupid, really. But, anyway, I couldn't sense anything. Not even the tiniest of those little sparks.'

Law contemplates this. 'Your efforts were likely hindered by Sydok's lingering binding,' he says after a moment. 'There's only so much you'll be able to do with it still in place.' Hesitating again, he continues. 'You are also quite old to be first learning how to handle your magic. That will impede your efforts as well.'

'So, I'm old now, am I?' I laugh, unable to take offence at his careless wording. 'I thought I was too young to have experienced anything at all?'

Unphased, Law says, 'It's all relative. You are young in terms of a fae's lifespan, but still, most fae start learning how to control their magic around the time they learn to walk and talk. It would be dangerous to be around them otherwise.'

'Can you remember learning to control your magic?' I ask. I can't imagine how overwhelming it would be for a small child to have to learn to control the kind of power he has. Or perhaps the amount of power a fae has increases as they age? I have so much to learn.

'I don't remember much of that time,' Law replies, looking very much like he wants to shut down again.

'Did your mother teach you? Your father?' Not for the first time, I realise just how little I know of Law's past.

'I never knew my mother or my father,' he says evenly. I can't read much from his tone, but the agitated swirl of shadows at his neck suggests this is not a topic he likes to discuss. 'I assume they are dead.'

'I'm so sorry, Law,' I say, heart twisting at the pain he must feel not knowing. 'Who raised you?'

'A fae named Balgaire. Apparently, I turned up on his doorstep when I was around 10 years old. I have no memory of my life before that, but according to Balgaire, I had my magic. He taught me though, helped me shape it.'

He seems to have nothing more to say on the matter, and I decide not to push him. I appreciate how much he is trying, but I can also tell how hard he finds it talking about his past.

'So, you remember some of that?' I prompt. 'You can use it to help me shape *my* magic?'

Law casts a glance in my direction, angling a small smile my way. 'Of course, Red. We can't have you relying solely on that dagger you told me you did not have.'

I can feel the comforting weight of my blade, now clean, sheathed, and safely back in my pack. Law had not mentioned it last night as we cleaned up the mess left by the baobhan-sìth. He had simply left it on the ground where I dropped it, ensuring he gave it a wide berth as he dragged bodies around.

'Yes, well,' I start, 'I'd have had to be seven kinds of stupid to come to Faerie and not bring anything to protect myself with.'

'Valid point,' Law says. 'But you could have told me you had it.'

'I didn't know you then. I didn't know if I could trust you.'

I blink, considering him, the way he is considering me. My mind flashes back to that first night in the tavern, over everything we've been through since then. Aside from the many hours spent in each other's pockets, walking, talking, and attending to all the mundanities of life on the road, we've also had to deal with some fairly staggering – and in some cases, life-changing – encounters.

The wedding, the kelpie attack, meeting Sydok. Everything that happened in the bothy. Even though it had all occurred over an extremely short period of time, I can't help but feel like those experiences have amplified everything, moving our relationship far further along than it otherwise should be.

There's also that mysterious *pull* we both feel towards one another.

I still have no idea what to make of that.

'Do you trust me now?' Law asks. He assumes the same effortless manner I have come to know as typical of him, but there is a certain tautness in his posture. I wonder whether it has anything to do with his confession last night. About him believing himself bad, of me deserving better.

'Yes,' I say, knowing somehow, that it is the truth.

He nods once, breaking that tightly concealed tension within his frame with a crack of his knuckles. 'Alright then. Let's start with the basics. How to recognise your magic.'

Chapter 18

'So, I can't see it or feel it, but I'm somehow supposed to be able to use it to control the elements around me?' I ask, frustrated.

Under Law's instruction, I've spent the morning working on clearing and focusing my mind, which, according to him, should help me to visualise the Aether around us. But despite trying a multitude of breathing techniques and various exercises designed to centre myself, my mind has stubbornly refused to remain clear or focused, leaving the source of my magic maddeningly elusive.

'You can't see it or feel it *yet*,' Law explains patiently. 'As the binding loosens, you should be able to sense Aether around you more and more.' He hesitates. 'As I understand it anyway.'

'But you can't sense Aether?' I ask.

'No, I have no sense of Aether because I don't use it to access my magic,' he responds, a certain stiffness in his voice. 'I manipulate Nether to access my magic. But from what Sydok said, it sounds like the principle of it should be the same.'

Law's manner had been as smooth as ever through the morning's instruction, but I observe a sharpness behind his features now. I can't help but compare it to the tension I'd seen in him at Sydok's cottage.

A query for later, perhaps.

Instead, I ask, 'How does it feel when you access your magic?'

Law considers my question. 'How does it feel? You know, that's surprisingly hard to answer. It's not something I think about. When you do something every day for years, decades, you stop thinking about how it feels. You just do it.' He chews the inside of his lip. 'Let me think on it properly for a moment. I'll see if I can visualise it to better explain it.'

We stop walking and he closes his eyes. As he takes time to consider his magic, I take the opportunity to drink him in, delighting in watching his face at rest. The curved arch of his dark brows, the gentle swirl of shadows over his skin. His expressive mouth, showing neither smile nor frown. When he opens his eyes and rests his gaze on me, my breath hitches.

'Enjoying the show?' he asks, eyes dancing.

'Very much,' I admit. 'Feel free to think some more.'

'No need. It's your turn. Close your eyes.'

I cock one brow, but do as I'm bid. 'This had better not be some trick so you can have your wicked way with me.'

'No,' he replies easily. 'Your eyes will be open and on me when I have my wicked way with you.'

The promise in his words sends heat surging over my skin. I can't help but picture his body, the hard lines of him. My fingertips tingle at the thought of what it might feel like to run my hands over his taught muscle, to draw patterns in the shadows coiling over his skin. My core clenches as I wonder what he might feel like inside me.

He chuckles softly.

'Stop that,' I say.

'I couldn't, even if I wanted to,' he replies, voice several shades rougher than normal.

I force my eyes to remain closed and instead try to focus on what we were doing before my mind hopped into the gutter. 'What am I supposed to be doing?'

'Listening,' he says. 'When I first met Balgaire, I could already access my magic. I have no memory of how that happened, but I can remember how he taught me to manipulate Nether, to control it more fully.'

I nod my acknowledgment, supposing Law will see the gesture even if I can't see him. Then, realising I am standing here with my eyes closed, surrounded by all the dangers of Faerie, I wonder at the fact that I don't feel vulnerable in this moment.

Law continues, unaware of my thoughts. 'His lessons trained me to visualise Nether in a way that allowed me to perceive it, even though Nether – like Aether – isn't something we can actually see. Once my mind was able to create a visual representation of Nether, it became easier to control it, to allow it to flow through me and power my magic. From there, I was able to learn new ways to make the shadows work for me.'

He takes my hands in his and I nod again, allowing the velvet of his voice to wrap its way around me.

'Now, when I use magic, I just let Nether flow through me. I no longer think about visualising it to draw on it. But, if I close my eyes now, I can see it when I focus on it. To me, Nether looks like a network of dark veins hidden within the earth. While some are thin, almost threadlike, others are much thicker. But they all connect, creating a web that flows under my feet wherever I go.'

'What about when you're in water?' I ask, wondering what happens if he ever travels by boat. Or goes for a swim. 'Does Nether run through water as well?'

'No, only through the earth. But I can channel it from the earth through water. I've never been anywhere I haven't been able to access Nether.'

'But what–' I start.

'Don't get distracted, Red. This isn't about my magic; it's about yours. The point I was making is you must find a way for your mind to visualise Aether so you can more easily access it. Once you can do that, the next step will be to manipulate it and use it to control the elements.' Law squeezes my hands. 'Try to clear your mind and then shape your intentions. That will give your magic the direction it needs to do what you want it to do.'

I take a deep breath and try once more to clear my mind. I think about the little blue spark that danced between us when I first touched Law's hand, attempting to focus on finding that spark inside me. If I can find it, I can shape it. Or my intentions. Or something.

Nothing.

Sighing, I open my eyes, letting our hands drop to start walking again. 'It just feels so impossible. I can't feel or see anything magical at all. I've been trying all morning and I'm no further along than when I started.'

'It will take longer than a morning,' Law laughs. 'Especially still bound.'

He pauses, taking time to consider his next words. 'Alright. When we've seen your magic escape the binding, it's been visible as a silvery, blueish light. That could be how you will see Aether when your mind is able to perceive it fully.'

'How do I know where to look for it though? You see Nether as a network under the earth, but where is all this Aether I'm supposed to somehow sense?'

I can't help but feel discouraged. I'm in a magical realm, surrounded by magical beings. I'd really like to be able to access my own magic now I know I have some.

'Everything the gods created contains Aether, which means it is everywhere, in everything,' Law explains, patient despite my irritation. 'By my reckoning, once you can perceive Aether, those things should become visible to you in terms of the Aether each one contains. Once you can see that, you will be able to draw from it, using it to manipulate the elements, just as I draw on Nether to manipulate shadows.'

As Law talks, I'm reminded of our dinner at the tavern, of how much I'd enjoyed listening to him describe the Seelie and Unseelie courts, and how far I'd fallen into his explanation. I realise I have gotten similarly lost now when I glance over at him and see that he has stopped talking and is staring at me, expression curious.

Gathering myself, I manage, 'But you're not sure?'

Law shrugs his reply. 'No one is. Sydok wasn't exaggerating when she said those who access magic by way of Aether aren't common.'

'How does everyone else access their magic?' I ask. 'Do they manipulate Nether, like you?'

Law's smile is stiff. 'No. Accessing magic through Nether is... unusual,' he says. 'Most fae are elemental by nature, so those who have magic typically have an affinity with a certain element, they draw their power from that element. For some, that may allow them to manipulate the element itself, for others, the element provides them with a way to manipulate their own magic in other ways.

'Like the kelpie,' Law continues, inspiring a small shudder in me. 'Kelpies draw their power from water. They need it to shift between forms.'

'That's why Calder didn't shift until we were by the lake,' I say. Not sure I want to know the answer, I ask, 'And he really would have eaten me if you hadn't arrived when you did?'

'For kelpies, their true form is the horse. Most choose to live their lives underwater in that form, but may on occasion, shift to hunt on land. That's what he was doing at the wedding, most likely. Hunting. Or perhaps, finding you there was just a happy accident.'

'He said he could smell me.' I wrinkle my nose at the memory. 'He said humans were a delicacy.'

'I've heard that, yes,' Law says. 'They tend to eat mostly fish, seals, crabs, that kind of thing. When they hunt on land though, they typically entice their prey back to the water where they have more control over their magic. If I hadn't found you, he would have likely drowned you, then dragged you into the lake and hidden you somewhere. Lodged you under a rock to let the water soften you up a bit.'

'And then he would have eaten me,' I finish, stomach turning.

Despite this rather nauseating thought, I realise my stomach is making itself known for other reasons aside from revulsion. I am hungry.

I catch the sound of running water in the distance and tilt my head towards it. 'Is there a river near here?'

'Yes, not far,' Law replies. 'We'll come out beside it in a moment. There's a bridge further down, but I thought we could stop to catch something for lunch before we cross.'

'We're going to catch our lunch?' I ask, not sure I'd have picked Law for a fisherman.

'I'll catch, you cook. I thought you'd be keen to eat something fresher than whatever still lingers in the depths of your pack.' Law glances down at my bag. 'As much as I would like to smell that haggis again.'

I consider my rations. While I have enough food to last the rest of our journey, I would very much like to eat something that's not bannock, haggis, or dried fruit.

'Yes, that does sound appealing,' I admit. Eyeing him carefully, I ask, 'Are you carrying a fishing net somewhere on your person? Or do you plan on luring the fish out of the water with your effortless charm?'

'Oh, the latter, most assuredly,' he replies, giving me a mischievous half grin.

It's not long before we step out past the edge of the forest and into the sunshine. With woodland at our back, a narrow valley dips before us, through which, a deep, slow-moving river winds its lazy way between lush banks of emerald greenery. I follow Law down toward the river's edge, spying a stone bridge in the distance.

Cerulean in colour, the river bubbles softly as it tumbles over boulders on the riverbed, sweeping past sparkling swathes of white sand where it meets the land on each side. Walking a little further upstream, Law stops where a bend in the river has created a natural pool, which, protected by a bank of large rocks, is filled with gently eddying water unaffected by the river's current. Surrounding the pool is a small beach so blindingly pristine, I have to shade my eyes to look at it.

With the canopy no longer providing cover, the sun beats down, feeling more like an unusually hot summer's day than the frigid autumn I'd left behind at home. Uncomfortable in my cloak, I remove it and place it next to my pack, then hitch up my skirt to position my dagger in the side of my boot. It's not exactly comfortable carrying it this way, but it will allow me easy access if I need it. Even if I'm only leaving to collect firewood, I refuse to take any chances. I call over my shoulder to Law, then head back up the valley and into the woods.

Nothing tries to murder me, so it doesn't take long to collect a good haul. With my attention on the grassy knots under my feet, I navigate my way slowly down the slope to the river. About halfway, I glance up to check on Law and almost drop the stack of firewood.

Stripped to the waist, he stands in the river, crystalline water sweeping past his thighs as he tosses out a net made of shadows. Dark trousers slung low on his hips, the muscles in his back reveal the effort he puts into every throw as he casts the net wide, then drags it back and repeats the process. Inky spirals shift with each movement, sinuous and graceful as they dance over his skin. Those coiling shadows, the sharply defined lines of him. It is undeniably hypnotic.

Stop staring, you pervert. I give myself a mental kick, snapping my mouth shut and telling my feet to start moving.

Arriving back at the beach, I drop the firewood on the sand and turn my attention to my next task. In this heat, the last thing I want is to be near a smouldering fire. Still, I ignore the trickles of sweat tickling my back, building up a base of kindling, while sneaking glances at Law. The view is even more delightful now I can see it in greater detail. Distractedly, I strike the flint stone and blow gently on the sparks to encourage the kindling to catch, which it does, just as Law lets out a whoop of satisfaction. I quickly stack on some smaller sticks, looking up to see him scooping up a fish caught in his shadow net. Tightly muscled arms working to keep the large fish under control, he wades to the shore, where he unceremoniously bashes its head against a rock and lets the shadow net dissipate.

'Nice catch,' I say, smiling as I look up at him.

Glistening with river water and radiant with triumph, he is even more breathtaking than usual. Holding the fish cradled in one arm, he uses his free hand to push wet hair out of his face, grinning back at me with barely concealed delight. Closer now, I can see an array of white scars mars his otherwise perfect skin, disappearing from sight as shadowy whorls move and twist over his torso.

Interrupting my ogling, he steps toward me and hands me the fish. 'You can do the honours. Seeing as you're so handy with a blade.'

'Don't pretend you couldn't whip out some shadow dagger to clean and gut this thing just as easily as I could,' I reply, taking it from him. Preparing fish is far from my favourite thing to do, but I've had plenty of practise, living in a coastal village with the sea at my back door.

'You're right, I could,' he admits.

I expect him to say more, but he just curves his mouth into a teasing smile, then bends to feed the fire some larger sticks. Putting some distance between him and the fire's crackling heat, he takes a seat on the sand on the other side of me.

'Clever trick with the net,' I say, removing the dagger from my boot. 'Are you going to tell me any more about what you can do with your magic, or do I need to wait for events to unfold, and you unveil a different trick for each one?' I move to the river's edge and hold the fish firmly by the tail, cut its throat and let it bleed out into the water.

Law watches me as I use the dagger to remove the fish's gills. 'I don't know. Isn't it more intriguing not knowing what will come next?'

I wash off the blade in the water, make a clean slice along the belly of the fish, then scoop out its entrails. No matter how many times I do this, the feel of those slimy guts always makes me gag. I throw them out into the middle of the river, so they won't spoil the sand.

'Wouldn't it be useful for me to know more about such magic, oh wise teacher?' I ask, tone playful. 'You know, show me a trick or two so I know what I could aspire to?'

I give my hands a quick wash as I clean my dagger, then remove my boots and stockings. Picking up the fish, I step into the water, the current tugging at my skirts as I wade in past my knees. The water is not as cold as I'd expected, and I enjoy the feel of it against my heated skin as I submerge the fish to clean it. As I walk back onto the beach, I eye Law. He looks pensive, but he still hasn't responded.

'Well?' I prod.

Suddenly, my feet won't move. I am mid-stride, stuck in place. I peer over the top of the fish to see if I have stepped in something. But no, there are my feet, held in place atop perfectly normal, perfectly pristine sand. I try to move them again, but they won't budge. I can't even wiggle my toes.

'What the hell?' My gaze races up to find Law. His expression is utterly serious. No mischievous smile, no glint in his eye.

'I pinned your shadow in place,' he says, tone even. 'You won't be able to move unless I release it.'

'Well, do you feel like doing that? This fish is heavy.'

In an instant, my feet are free. I wriggle my toes, then step towards him, passing him the fish. 'Here, hold this, I need to look for some leaves to wrap it with.'

'Are you angry?' he asks.

Frowning, I look him over, legs bent in front of him as he sits on the sand. Muscled torso gleaming in the sun, shadows pass over his skin, seemingly agitated in their motion. His face now unreadable, something vulnerable lingers at the edges.

'No, I'm not angry, you eejit,' I say, answering honestly. 'I was startled. You could have given me some warning.'

'Sorry,' he says.

I turn away and make my way back up the hill, my eyes on the shrubbery. 'It's fine, Law,' I throw over my shoulder. 'I asked you to show me more of your magic and you did. Next time, just tell me what you're going to do before you do it.'

More and more, I can't help but notice the strange relationship Law has with his magic. I think back on the unease in his expression when he explained his magic to me. The tone in his voice as he talked about Nether. The way he reacted to Sydok's account of it all. Aside from him using his shadow net to catch the fish, there's never been anything casual about the way he's used his magic. It almost feels like he is ashamed of it, or uncomfortable with it, at least.

It is something I will have to deal with, but I choose to put it off for now. I have other plans in mind.

Spying the perfect specimens, I reach down and tug them off their stalk. I walk back to Law and take the fish from him, giving him a quick grin to put his mind at ease. Wrapping the fish with the leaves, I place it on the sand and rinse my hands in the river. Then I use a stick to separate the fire so that it will die down faster. Carefully, I place the wrapped fish among the glowing embers.

With nothing else to do for now, I pull my dress over my head and arrange it on the sand next to the fire to dry. I turn back to Law and see that he is watching me. Tugging in a deep breath to steady myself, I take the few steps over to where he sits and hold out my hand. 'Feel like a dip?' Butterflies catapult around my belly and I am more than a little surprised to find there is no shake in my voice.

I want this.

I'm quite sure Law wants this.

But that doesn't make propositioning the most beautiful male I have ever met any less intimidating.

Several excruciating heartbeats pass, before a smile spreads slow and steady across Law's face. Warmth curls through me as he reaches up to take my hand. Then he is in my space and all I can see is him. Heat radiates from his body, the scent of him surrounds me, and I wonder if I might simply wilt and die right here from desire. My other hand finds its way to the tightly defined muscles of his stomach. I watch, breath held, as the shadowy coils on his torso gather around my hand in greeting.

Momentarily side-tracked, I look up and ask, 'Is that normal? Reacting like that to touch?' Rivena's face flashes in my mind, and I push away the extremely disagreeable thought of anyone else touching him like this.

'No. Only to you.'

I consider this, knowing he cannot lie. If my magic is reaching out for him, perhaps it makes sense that his is reaching out for me. It's something worth thinking about.

But not right now.

With a confidence I do not feel, I shift past him and move towards the pool, putting a little sway in my hips as I walk. I climb carefully over the rocks and step into the water, finding it surprisingly warm. I bend my knees to dip below the surface, emerging to look back at Law and pushing my hair from my face as I turn.

My breath falters at the sight of his raw, naked desire.

'Well?' I say, as close to sultry as I can manage. 'Are you coming in?'

Darkened gaze fixed on me, Law follows me over the rocks, stepping with the easy grace that never seems to leave him. My eyes skip down his torso, following the line of hair that leads from his navel to his low-slung waistband. His trousers are still wet from the river and they cling to every inch of him.

I can't help the small smile that creeps over me at the sight.

Chapter 19

I let myself float back to the rocks that frame the far end of the pool. Law steps into the water, dips down and stands. Water cascades from him, streams of droplets catching the light as they trickle down his flawless form. Slowly, he makes his way toward me, the water in the pool eddying around his torso, seeming to want to caress him just as much as I do.

I drift, waiting, heart refusing to beat in any way that could be described as normal. Anticipation in me twines with apprehension over what is about to happen. It is new, yet it's not. I have been intimate many, many times. But not like this. Not with Law. Who has seen decades come and go. Who seems so at ease with his sexuality.

What if after all the leadup, after all the attraction that has sparked between us, it doesn't live up to what he had expected?

What if it is a disappointment?

What if *I* am a disappointment?

My mind skims over the many moments between us that have led to this. To me brazenly inviting this outrageously attractive male to join me in such deeply intimate activities. Where I will be vulnerable, lay myself bare.

Flashes of Law skip through my mind; of the way he has looked at me, of the way he has talked to me, of the way he has made me feel. He has been forward about his attraction, but he has never taken advantage of my vulnerability. He has opened up about how he feels about me, but he has never made me feel scared or exposed. At all times, he has treated me as an equal, as someone of value. In all he's done, he has shown affection, tenderness, care.

I have to trust that. To trust him. To trust myself.

Glancing down, I see the white cotton of my camisole and knickers is all but translucent in the water. As I look back up at Law, I notice this has caught his attention too.

'You really want this?' he asks, voice rough, gaze steady.

Knowing it to be truth, yet not sure I trust my own voice to work, I nod.

Then, he is everywhere.

He scoops me up, his arms surrounding me, protecting my back as he pushes me hard against the rocks, kissing my mouth, my jawline, my neck, my shoulder. My legs fold around his waist and I knot my feet behind his back, gasping as I feel the solid length of him press against me. I let my hands roam, relishing the feel of taught muscle working in his back, the gorgeous definition of his chest, the soft skin at the back of his neck.

Savouring the intensity in his movement as he joins me in a deep, lingering kiss, I feel him slip the strap of my camisole off my shoulder, pulling it down at one side. He circles his thumb around my nipple and a deep, pulsing ache rushes to my core, my head tipping back as an involuntary moan escapes me. He draws his tongue down the column of my throat, another smooth movement exposing my other breast, and he dips his head, kissing his way down to it. Lighting up at the heat of his attentions, my breath hitches as his tongue rolls lazily around my nipple, before he takes it in his mouth and nips it between his teeth. Letting out a much louder gasp at that, I dig my nails into his shoulders, swirling my hips to gain some friction against him.

Suddenly, I am weightless, as Law grips my hips and lifts me up onto the rock behind me. I spill back onto it, catching my weight on my elbows as he follows, caging me with his arms and driving his hips into me. The pressure of it is exquisite, but I want more, need more.

'Elspeth, you are beautiful.'

My eyes fly to his, finding his sharp, charcoal gaze as dark as I have seen it. Crowding my body in the best possible way, he stands above me, muscles tensing through those broad shoulders as he leans down to draw me into another blistering kiss.

Almost overcome by my need for him, my attention is swept to the sensation of his fingertips curving over my waist, tracing down over my hip to find the sensitive skin at the back of my thigh. I shudder as he draws languid circles there, his tongue continuing to explore and leaving sparks in his wake. I arch my back in demand, the ache between my legs almost painful now.

'Law, I need...' I hitch out, unable to articulate what exactly it is I need through this haze of aching, all-consuming hunger.

'You need?' he prompts, his tone a murmured, silken promise. He skims his hand across the soft skin of my inner thigh, promising so much more as he drags his thumb down my centre.

Without me telling them to do so, my hips buck against his hand, my desire to be touched there leaving me gasping. I try to marshal my thoughts. 'I need...' *Fuck.* I can't think straight when he is touching me like that.

'Use your words, beautiful. Tell me what you need.' He pushes aside the fabric of my knickers and massages a leisurely figure-of-eight, applying just enough pressure to make me see stars.

Deep, intense arousal crashes over me and I find I am no longer able to hold myself up. I drop back on the rock, utterly exposed as I reach above my head, hands twisting in my hair. I look up at Law looking down at me, naked desire barely held in check, inky coils shifting swiftly over his skin.

Momentarily, my thoughts flash to Malcom, to his heaving, short-lived exploits in the bedroom. With him, there had been no build up, no attentiveness. After a few rough caresses he had expected me to be ready. Then it had been several short thrusts, and blessedly, it was over.

'Hmm?' Law brings my focus back to the present, hooking his thumbs through the sides of my knickers, tugging them down and tossing them on the sand. He takes a long moment to let his gaze roam over me, skimming over every dip and curve. 'I want to hear you.'

'I need...' *Oh my god, oh my god.* My mind stumbles as his fingers find a new tempo. *Oh. My. God.* I have absolutely no idea what I need. My brain has been replaced by senseless slush. I force it to push out some words. 'More of you.'

Brow raised, Law gazes down at me, his smirk telling me he knows exactly what he is doing to me and how it has stolen my every coherent thought.

'Your wish,' he says, dipping his head, languishing attention on each nipple in turn, before dragging his tongue lazily downwards, 'my command.' Then those smirking lips are on my core, and I very nearly pass out from the sudden, dizzying pleasure that focuses all of my awareness, all of my everything, right where his mouth meets me.

This, this is something I have never experienced before. I'm not even sure Malcom had been aware this is something people do.

Another moan escapes me. It is ragged and wild and sounds nothing at all like me.

While Law had certainly been deft with his fingers, he is even more adept with his tongue. Back bowing with my need to feel more of this, more of him, I feel the pressure in me swelling with every sweep of his tongue. Panting now, I can't help but cry out as he slips one finger inside me. Dazedly, my gaze finds his and I am unable to look away. I drink in the lines of his shoulders, the desire written all over that painfully beautiful face, all the while losing myself to the burning need inside me as he adds another finger, and thrusts them expertly to complement what he is doing with his mouth.

Absolutely lost to desire, to sensation, my head falls back, and my eyes flutter shut, feeling nothing but the heat of Law's skilful attention between my legs as, deep within me, that coiled pressure continues to surge. Just when I think I can't take any more, that I might just *break* from the exquisite pleasure of it all, I sense it, the approaching plateau. With every muscle in me tensed and my breath held tight, I pause on that plateau for the most delicious of moments, before I crash over the edge and feel it shatter over me in waves.

My breath returns to me, harsh and wild.

Even under my own attentions, I had never felt anything like *that*.

Utterly boneless, I sense long moments pass, until finally I regain some of my composure, and crack open my eyes. I tilt my head up to find Law. He is still between my legs, skimming kisses along my inner thigh. Not entirely sure of my ability to hold myself up, I manage to prop my weight on one elbow and reach out to stroke his hair back from his face, dragging a fingertip along the top of one pointed ear. Leaning into the caress, he looks up at me, his expression edging towards smug.

'That was…' I start, voice still husky with desire.

'Was?' he prompts, eyes sparkling as his mouth, that exceptionally skilled mouth, curves up playfully at one side.

'Fucking spectacular,' I finish.

Law laughs softly, his lips spreading into a full smile. 'Happy to be of service, mistress,' he says, standing, water streaming off him as he leans down to kiss me.

His touch is gentle, a soft caress of greeting rather than an expectation of more. I taste myself on him and realise I *do* want more. I want more of Law, want him to experience some of that same bliss he'd just gifted me. While I may not be in any way as experienced in providing pleasure, my every sense is heightened with arousal, and I am eager to try.

Circling my arms around him, I deepen the kiss, relishing the warmth of his mouth as my tongue explores, caresses, tastes. 'And what about you?' I breathe into him. I glide one hand over the taught muscle of his torso, coming to a rest over the extensive bulge in the front of his trousers. 'Are you not in need of some… servicing?'

Law smiles as I continue to kiss him. 'Perhaps.'

Not in *any* way confident of my skills in this department, I push him back as I sit up, reaching forward to unbutton his trousers. Somewhat shakily, I manage to work the buttons loose, before drawing his trousers down over his narrow hips. Soaked through, his trousers descend into the water carried by their own weight, revealing his cock, hard and ready.

What made me smile earlier, now makes me wonder if I could even fit something of that size inside me. Is this another fae thing? Are all fae males hung like horses?

My ever-expressive face must display some of my trepidation, because Law breathes a laugh, catching me up in a kiss that soon makes me forget about anything other than his tongue and his now roaming hands.

My hands find themselves exploring him in return, curving over his torso to his back, where they seem to want to slip down to study the arse I've been admiring for days. Perfectly formed under my touch, it absolutely does not disappoint. I tug him to me and find the very centre of me becoming much better acquainted with his cock. Scooting my hips closer, I circle them as I press against him, relishing the sensation as much as the growl of pleasure it elicits.

Emboldened as much by that vocalisation as by the stark look of yearning laid plain against his face, I keep his gaze as I push him firmly away and hop into the water. Noticing my camisole still snagged around my waist, I lift it over my head and let it drift away in the pool. With nothing between us now, Law stands as naked as I am, shifting vines of shadow dancing over every perfect plane of muscle and sweep of his skin. Urged on by the heat behind his eyes, I suck in a deep breath to steel myself and point to the rock behind him.

'Sit,' I order.

His brow quirks but he does as he's told. In one graceful movement, he is out of the water and sitting on the rock, leaning back smoothly on his arms and giving me the perfect view of his sharply defined chest and shoulders. With only his knees remaining in the water, I part them and step in close. Tearing my gaze from his face, I glance down at his cock. It stands to bold attention between us. I let out another shaky breath and reach for it.

This kind of thing had never been part of what I'd done with Malcom. He really hadn't needed help to climax any sooner. So, instead of calling on experience, I move partly on instinct, and partly using what I have gleaned from ribald stories divulged by punters after imbibing a touch too much ale.

Marvelling at the hard feel of him under such a velvety soft touch, I glide my hand up and down, wondering just how much pressure I should be applying. As if in answer, Law's hand closes around mine, encouraging a little more weight from my grip. Seemingly satisfied, he removes his hand, and I glance up to check his reaction. I don't think I could take it if he were laughing at my efforts, or worse, pitying me for them. Instead, his gaze is steady, darkened now to near black and heavy with desire.

Reassured by this, I allow my other hand to join in, moving both together as I slide them up and down his cock, savouring the flutter of his long, serrated exhale against my overheated skin. His breathing becomes more ragged as I continue, the muscles of his torso contracting in pleasure while shadows shift and stutter over him. My eyes trail up his body to find his face. No teasing smirk curves his lips now, only dark, cavernous desire.

Deciding I want to drive that desire further, I bend down to swirl my tongue over the tip of his cock. Licking the bead of liquid that rests there, I taste salt and something darker, something smooth and deep and silky.

He expels a weighty, jagged moan. 'Fuck, Elspeth, that mouth.' Wrapping his hand in my hair, he cradles the back of my head.

I swirl my tongue again, and at another of Law's low muttered curses, I am encouraged to continue my explorations. Gradually hastening the glide of my hand and adding some weight to my grip, I use my mouth to suck and my tongue to explore. I revel in the feel of him, the taste of him, the way short, sharp breaths escape him, the way his hips flick to meet me. My own arousal stirs, and I clamp my legs together to gain some friction there, relishing his reaction as I hollow out my cheeks and take more of him into me.

'Elspeth,' he says unevenly some moments later, untangling his hand from my hair. 'I'm going to come.'

Knowing what is coming but not quite what to expect, I continue, increasing the speed of my hand, flicking the tip of his cock with my tongue. Suddenly, his every muscle under me tenses, and my mouth is filled with warm, salty liquid, which, I have to admit as I stand and swallow, isn't entirely unpleasant.

His head tipped back, Law's chest expands and contracts rapidly, breath escaping him in a harsh, shuddering rush. A mad beat pulses at his throat and the muscles in his legs tremble slightly under my hands. I allow myself a curve of a smile, enjoying a small measure of accomplishment.

Opening his eyes, Law sees that smile and responds with a lazy grin of his own. Reaching forward to brush his lips against mine, he says, 'Well that was fucking spec–'

I give him a gentle push and cut him off with a kiss.

'You don't need to say that,' I say. 'I've never done... and I'm sure you've done... had it done plenty. I'm just saying... Shit, what am I saying? This is new to me. I've never had, never done anything like this before.'

Law lifts my chin so that I meet his grey gaze, which, while no longer as dark, looks far smokier than usual. 'I'm not asking you to be anything you're not, Red,' he says, voice rough. 'I'm willing to take whatever you're willing to give. And, if it's anything like what you just gave, believe me, I'm more than happy to accept.' His eyes twinkle as he moves his hand up to my cheek, where he brushes my cheekbone with his thumb, before pushing a tangle of my wet hair back from my face.

Wondering just how wild my hair must look, I lean into his touch, echoing his earlier movement while enjoying the warmth of his hand. A soft breeze sweeps over my wet skin and I shiver, goosebumps springing up over my body.

'Time to get out,' Law says, running his hands over my arms.

Nodding, I reach down and pass him his trousers, before moving to the other side of the pool to retrieve my camisole. I spot my knickers on the beach and climb out of the pool to collect them too. Seeing that they are covered in sand, I wash them in the river, before hanging them over some greenery to dry, as close to the fire as I can get them without setting them alight.

Using my cloak to dry myself, I wring out my hair and step into my spare underclothes, leaving my damp dress out to dry a while longer. My eyes find Law, sneaking another look before he dresses. Having dried himself with his own cloak, he twists the water out of his trousers, then casually opens some kind of shadowy hole in the air and throws his trousers into it.

I gape at him.

'What was that?' I squeak, incredulous, although I know I really shouldn't be. What I've seen of his magic has already proved to be extensive.

'A portal.'

I check his face for any of the tightness that typically follows questions about his magic, but I see none. Maybe the sex made him more amenable? It had often worked that way with Malcom.

'Um, alright,' I laugh. Encouraged by his open expression, I continue, 'Do I get any more of an explanation than that?'

'My magic allows me to create pockets of shadow to hold things in. I open portals to access them.' As if in demonstration, he opens another, removes a dry pair of trousers and slips them on.

I can't help but be impressed. 'Are those the same trousers?'

'No,' Law laughs. 'It's not that kind of magic. The pockets just hold things I place inside them. I put that wet pair in to deal with later. This pair, I suppose you could say I packed them before we left.'

'So that's where you got the clean shirt from at the bothy,' I say, remembering my wonder over where it could have come from, given the fact that he'd travelled with nothing but the cloak on his back.

Curious now, I wonder how far I can push this new sense of openness. 'What else have you got in there?' I ask. 'Do you have any cake? Ale? A pillow?' Oh, what I would have given for a feather pillow the past two nights.

Law laughs again. My heart swells with happiness at the sound. I want this from him, to be open with me, for him not to feel like he has to close himself off.

'Unfortunately not,' he says, not sounding in any way remorseful. 'I only packed the essentials.'

'You don't consider those essential?' I snort. 'I think I should help you pack next time.'

Kneeling down in front of the fire to check the fish, I glance up at Law, just catching what looks like sadness flit across his face. Then it is gone, replaced by one of his playful smiles.

'Next time, Red?' he asks, tone teasing. 'Where are we going on our next adventure?'

I had only been joking, throwing out words without really thinking. But the thought of what will happen after we see the Queen suddenly weighs on me. My time with Law has been short, yes, but also, meaningful. Substantial. Important. To me, at least. I want to know him better, to know if there is anything more to this thing. Can I call it a relationship? Am I even allowed to ask for more?

I'm still set on finding the Queen, asking for her help with Agnes and hopefully getting some answers regarding my mother, but I know there is more beyond all of that. Will Law be a part of it? Does he want to be a part of it? How would that even work, with his life in Faerie and my life in the human realm?

Overwhelmed by uncertainty, I force a weak smile. 'Surely the next one is yours to pick.'

Law studies me. Whatever he reads from my expression leads him to change the subject rather than push. Nodding to the fish, he asks, 'Is that ready yet? I could eat a horse.'

Happier to go with it than face down those unknowns, I use a stick to poke the fish out of the fire and onto the sand, the leaves surrounding it now charred and black. Carefully, I remove the wrapper, breaking the skin on the fish to pull apart the flesh beneath. Flaking perfectly, steam rises from within, signalling it's cooked through.

'Ready,' I say. 'Got any plates in those pockets of yours?'

'Sadly, no,' Law responds.

'Essentials, my arse,' I mutter, reaching out into the nearby greenery to find leaves we can use instead. 'Head or tail?' I ask as I cut the fish in half.

'You choose.'

Passing him the head so I don't have to look at its bulging eyeballs while I eat, I decide to see how much more I can find out about his magic. I don't know when his sex brain will wear off, and I want to make the most of it.

Using my dagger to pull flesh from bone, I scoop some fish into my mouth, breathing rapidly to cool it enough to swallow. Perfectly tender, it tastes delicious. Perhaps one of the most delicious things I've ever tasted. Although that could have more to do with my limited diet over the past few days than my skills as a cook.

'Can you make anything out of shadows?' I ask lightly.

Law arches a brow, taking his time as he chews. He swallows slowly. 'There are limits,' he says finally, 'but mostly, yes. Anything I can imagine, I can create. Although larger things require more magic, so it drains me more. The same applies to shadows I hold onto for a long time.'

'But if you channel Nether, how does it drain you?' I ask. 'I imagine it as there being a never-ending supply of Nether. Like air or water.'

'It's not about how much Nether is available, it's about how much of my own magic I drain as I channel it. Big magic means more of a drain.'

'Have you ever run out of magic? Drained yourself?'

All of this is so foreign to me. It feels like I'll never get a handle on it. And it doesn't help that I can't get even the slightest grip on my own magic to start to feel it out.

Law smiles in between mouthfuls. It's an easy smile, and one I appreciate even more given what we are discussing. 'Yes, plenty of times. It's important to push yourself, to know your limits when you practise using magic. Otherwise, you could easily get caught out when the outcome matters a lot more.'

'What about what you did at the bothy, stepping into one shadow and stepping out of another?' I ask, scooping up another large chunk of fish and popping it into my mouth.

'It's just as you describe it,' he says. 'I use shadows to step between two spots. I don't really know *how* it works. Magic is like that sometimes.'

'And you took me with you,' I prompt, remembering how dreadful I felt afterwards.

'Not something I'd usually do, but the situation called for it.'

'Could we not have just hopped from Nicnevin's estate right to the Queen's palace like that? Stepping from shadow to shadow?'

I don't particularly like the thought of doing such a thing, but if it could have cut our journey down to moments instead of days, I would have happily considered it as an option. I still haven't gotten over the fact that we have to walk the entire way instead of travelling by horse. Iron horseshoes and fae don't mix, apparently.

'It doesn't work like that,' Law explains. 'I have to be able to see the shadow I'm stepping out of. Also, doing it drains my magic. I couldn't step from one shadow to the next to the next, indefinitely.' After a brief hesitation, he continues. 'There would also be the Queen's wards to contend with. Her palace borders are shielded against any kind of magical invasion.'

I chew thoughtfully. 'So, no stepping through shadows to get into the palace,' I muse. 'What exactly is the plan, then? Is one allowed to simply walk into the palace and ask to see the Queen?' I consider how that situation would play out in the human realm. There, if a commoner walked into Edinburgh Castle and demanded audience with King James, it would be far likelier he'd be escorted to the king's dungeons than to the king's court.

'Don't worry, I have something in mind,' Law replies, scooping up the last of his fish and tossing the carcass into the shrubbery. 'Alright, we should leave soon if we want to arrive at the tavern we're aiming for before nightfall.'

He stands, pulling on his boots and shirt. I am more than a little sad to see all that beautiful muscle hidden away. Again, this must show clearly on my face, because Law lets out a soft chuckle.

'Later, Red. There's always later. Don't think I'm done with you yet.'

Chapter 20

Set over three squat arches through which the tumbling river flows, the bridge I spotted earlier appears much larger now than I'd anticipated from afar. As I weigh up whether the incongruence had been caused by some skewed sense of perspective, or perhaps as a result of odd faerie magic, my mind is somewhere else entirely when I step onto said bridge and a thunderous roar surrounds me.

Admittedly somewhat startled, I halt mid-stride, darting a look at Law in an attempt to gauge this new threat.

Law sighs, looking entirely unmoved. 'Don't worry. It's just the bridge troll. Grumpy bastards, the lot of them.'

I have no time to question him about what a bridge troll might be, or why it might tend towards cantankerousness, as I am suddenly face-to-face – or rather, face-to-crotch – with one of the most disturbingly ugly creatures I have ever seen. Having vaulted over the wall of the bridge, it now towers over us in the middle of the walkway, clearly intent on blocking our path across. I can only assume it had been hiding under one of the bridge's arches, as the monstrous creature is soaked to the skin.

I falter back a step, my eyes wide as I take in its massive, sloped shoulders and vast, quivering belly, which flops over squat legs and huge knobbly feet. Up top is a disproportionately large head, mostly bald apart from a few thin patches of course grey hair. With one of its eyes bulging out alarmingly, its face is not made any easier to look at by a painfully bulbous nose covered in festering sores, and a gaping hole of a mouth, in which I count a total of three rotten brown teeth.

'To cross the bridge, you must pay the toll,' it rumbles.

Sending a wary eye over the creature's long brawny arms, I note the spade-like hand clutching a cudgel that is almost as broad as I am. I'm not keen to speculate on what that cudgel might accomplish if we do not have the required toll.

'And what might that be?' Law asks.

'One silver coin,' it replies.

'Seems a bit steep,' Law drawls, seemingly quite bored.

'That is the toll,' it says. 'You must pay it, or you cannot cross.'

'Perhaps we can go about this another way?' Law tries.

'What way?' the troll demands, eyes narrowing.

'I give you a riddle. If you answer correctly, you can bash me around the head with that admirably sized cudgel. If you cannot answer, we cross without paying the toll, with my head still intact.'

The troll ponders this, breathing heavily through its mouth as it deliberates. 'I accept,' it says eventually. 'I would like to see the inside of your skull.'

'Alright,' Law starts, pushing his hands into his pockets. 'What can run but never walks, has a mouth but never talks, has a head but never weeps, has a bed but never sleeps?'

Tapping the cudgel on the ground, the troll contemplates this, gears turning visibly. While it is thinking, I also consider what the answer might be, smiling when I figure it out.

We watch the troll think for a few painful moments, opting to look elsewhere as it idly picks something grotesque from its ear, before finally, Law prompts, 'We're somewhat pressed for time. Do you happen to have the answer?'

Bushy grey eyebrows close in over its eyes, almost concealing even the bulging eye from sight. 'Do not rush me, faerie. You provided no limit on the time allowed to answer.'

'I suppose I didn't,' Law admits. 'Still though, if you could be a bit swifter, it would be much appreciated.'

'Stop distracting me,' it says. 'I am trying to think.'

'Come on,' goads Law. 'I gave you an easy one.'

The troll releases a warning rumble, eyeing Law irritably.

'Tick tock goes the clock,' Law says, unbothered by the troll's furious scowl.

'I am still thinking, faerie,' the troll growls. 'Shut up, or I will shut you up myself.'

I stand back, watching the exchange quietly. I am quite sure the troll could do some serious damage with that cudgel. Even with the impressive range of Law's magic, I wonder if he should not provoke the creature quite so much.

'Law, perhaps we should just pay the toll and be on our way?' I ask, nervously scanning the troll's darkening demeanour.

'Do you have a silver coin in that pack of yours, Red?' Law responds.

'No,' I sigh. 'Silver coins are not something I generally carry on my person.'

'Then we will have to wait for our friend to come up with an answer.'

'But what if it answers correctly?' I say under my breath. I glance over at the troll. It appears to be deep in thought, mouth hanging open, breathing out a foul stench with each exhale. 'I quite like your head. It looks much better on you than it would smashed around that cudgel.'

'You say the sweetest things,' Law replies, giving me a quick wink. Not bothering to keep any kind of hush to his own voice, he continues, 'My head is in no such danger, though. Our repulsive friend does not have the grey matter required to provide the correct answer.' He turns away from the troll, sauntering back to the foot of the bridge, whistling as he goes.

Frowning, I wonder why he feels the need to aggravate the troll in such a manner. I cut my attention to the creature, just as its own unfocused gaze sharpens and narrows on Law. Back turned, whistling tunelessly, Law does not see the intent transforming the troll's expression. Nor does he see the creature surging forward, raising its admirably sized cudgel, mind seemingly set on dispensing with the silly riddle, along with the faerie that issued it.

But I do.

I watch the cudgel arc high into the air and time...

slows...

to...

a...

crawl.

Thinking of nothing but protecting Law, I throw up my hands and throw my will out into the world.

Beneath my feet, the stone shakes violently, causing me to stumble as I try to keep my balance. Working to right myself, I see the troll similarly wrongfooted, carried off-balance by the weight of the massive cudgel swung above its head. Drawn by its own momentum, the troll lurches backwards, losing its footing before landing heavily on its back. I feel rather than see its head cracking the stone.

Before the ground is settled beneath my feet, Law is on the troll, shadow sword drawn against the thick rolls of its neck. 'Yield,' he demands evenly.

'I yield,' the troll replies, slurring slightly. It drops the cudgel.

Law steps back, drawing his sword from the troll's neck but keeping it in hand. He watches carefully as the troll sits up, rubbing the back of its head with one huge hand. It looks thoroughly dazed as it gazes at me with a queer expression.

'You magicked my bridge,' it says, hurt in its voice as it eyes me suspiciously.

Heart still beating wildly, I look around to see the previously even stonework under my feet now cracked and dishevelled, mortar crumbling and shards of stone sticking up at odd angles. While the bridge still seems stable enough, it's definitely going to need repairs if it is to remain standing for much longer.

'Did I?' I murmur, quite sure I'd never be capable of such a thing. Perhaps Law had known what the troll was doing somehow, and he had *magicked* those ferocious tremors. His magic always seems to be manifesting itself in new and surprising ways, I really wouldn't be all that shocked if that had been another one of his tricks.

I look to him in query, finding him relaxed but on guard. 'Did I?' I repeat, aiming the question at him this time. 'Law?'

'Well, it wasn't me, Red,' he throws back over his shoulder, apparently unwilling to take his eyes from the troll again.

Stunned by the possibility that I could have made the world shake in quite such a violent manner, I open my mouth, then close it again. 'But, how?' I manage after a moment.

'Perhaps we should leave the questions for later?' Law suggests, stepping back again so that he stands beside me. Opening another of his shadowy portals, he reaches in and pulls out a pouch. From the sound it makes when he tosses it into the troll's lap, I guess it must be filled with coin. 'For the repair of your bridge. Are we free to pass, troll?'

The troll removes its hand from behind its head, using giant fingers to fumble with the pouch strings, before peering inside. A glint of silver shimmers within. Much more than one would need to repair a bridge, I suspect.

'You may pass,' it grumbles.

'Much obliged,' Law says.

Reaching out to take my hand, he steers me around the still seated troll. With its attention firmly on the silver in its hand, it doesn't even bother looking up as we pass. Law waits until we are safely on the other side, then squeezes my hand and lets his broadsword dissipate. 'Excellent work,' he says, grin splitting his face. 'I knew you had it in you.'

'Wait, what?' I splutter. Much slower than it should, realisation dawns on me. 'Did you do that on purpose?'

'If I say yes, will you promise not to drop a bridge on me?' he replies, eyes dancing.

'That troll could have killed you,' I yelp, knowing that said troll can probably hear us.

'There was not even a remote possibility of that happening,' he says. 'I knew what it was doing. If you didn't stop it, I would have.'

'So, you purposefully provoked it? Hoping it would attack, and I would use my magic to save you?' I can't decide if I should be furious or appreciative.

'I did,' he admits, with no remorse whatsoever. 'You'd been struggling to access your magic using the techniques I taught you, so I thought I'd try another tack. Sydok said you could access your magic when your emotions were high, so I decided to raise the stakes. Trolls are famously quick to anger. I just gave it a push.'

'But the troll,' I say, 'will it be alright? Its head took quite a knock.'

'It will be just fine. Trolls are not only grumpy, they're also notoriously hard-headed.'

Mind racing, I stumble on something else as I run over it all again in my head. 'You had the silver to pay the troll all along?'

'Yes,' he acknowledges. 'But I still say one silver coin is too high a price to cross a bridge.'

'And a pouchful of silver isn't?'

'Ah, but I didn't pay a pouchful of silver to cross a bridge, I paid a pouchful of silver for you to get your first meaningful grip on your magic.'

'Law, I can't pay you that back,' I stammer. 'I don't have that kind of money.'

'I know that, Red. I wouldn't expect you to. I am, however, more than happy to raid Nicnevin's deep pockets for such a cause.'

His hand still warm in mine, I turn my attention more fully on him. I take my time studying his perfect profile, watching as inky shadows coil leisurely over his throat and along his jawline. I don't know what to make of this male. He just keeps surprising me.

'This won't cause problems between you and Nicnevin, will it?' I ask. Even after such a short acquaintance, I know without a shadow of a doubt that Nicnevin is not someone you'd want to cross.

Law chuckles. 'Don't worry about that. We can call it backpay.' Something hard races across his face, before clearing quickly. Dropping my hand to rub both of his own hands together, he turns a delighted expression in my direction. 'Right, let's see if that loosened anything up. Another magic lesson is called for, I think.'

Still too wary to be swept up in his excitement, I reply, 'Fine. But no more provoking large trolls with big bloody cudgels.'

'No more trolls,' he agrees. 'But we are on Unseelie lands now, so who knows what we will find for you to throw your magic at next.' He sounds almost gleeful at the prospect.

'Wait, what?' I say again. 'Bloody hell, Law, are we safe?'

'Of course we are,' Law replies, his most mischievous smile playing at his lips. 'We have you to protect us.'

Chapter 21

My anxiety turns out to be entirely unwarranted. The fae we pass on the path through the rest of the afternoon are certainly numerous, but not one seems in any way inclined to cause us trouble.

I identify a pack of pixies, small in stature and round of belly, looking much like the one who'd stolen my pack on my first day in Faerie. The pixies giggle as they pass but make no attempt to stop and talk.

I see a tiny, wizened fae walking beside a gigantic brown bear. While I have to look twice to make sure my eyes aren't wilfully deceiving me, the fae and bear appear to be carrying on a quite normal conversation as they pass, apparently discussing the rising cost of bread at market.

I spot tall, willowy fae who look like they'd blow away on a strong breeze, and small, sturdy characters who make walking on such short legs look like very hard work indeed. I see ancient fae wrapped in shawls and leaning on sticks, and boisterous young fae sporting vibrant hair and extravagant garments made from shimmering fabrics.

While I observe them all with barely concealed curiosity, most pass by without even glancing at me. I do, however, notice that they all try conspicuously hard not to look at Law. That reputation at work again.

As we walk, I also take note of the changing backdrop. Having left the lush woodland behind on the other side of the river, we wind our way over meadow and heath, climbing and descending hills that often leave me gasping for breath.

True to his word, Law continues to challenge me with my magic, although I find it hard to concentrate with so many remarkable sights passing us on the path. Having explained that I had used earth magic to unsettle the bridge, he goes on to test my abilities in small ways, trying to conjure more earth magic from me, while at the same time working on my ability to visualise Aether.

'I can see it!' I almost yell. 'Oh, it's gone again.'

'Keep your focus,' Law says smoothly. 'Try again.'

Having attempted – and failed – many other small tasks, my current challenge involves stacking the layer of soil in my hand into a pile. As instructed, I focus on it, letting my consciousness loosen, attempting to use my magic to assess the soil, rather than simply seeing it with my eyes. Taking in steady breaths, I imagine the soil piling up to create a small mound, sending my will towards it.

Focusing so intently on the soil, I am unsure whether the hazy blue shimmer that materialises within it is real, or simply a trick my eyes are playing on me because I want so much to see it there. Optimistically deciding on the former, I take a moment to breathe deep, halting my steps so I can focus further.

I place all my attention on the thin layer of soil, watching as the shimmering haze within it becomes less translucent, pulsing softly to reveal a silvery shade of blue. Observing each pulse, I can't help but think of it as a heartbeat and respond by slowing my breathing to encourage my own heartbeat to match it. As the rest of the world falls away, my focus narrows to the pulse of my heartbeat in my ears and the pulse of blue within the soil, waiting patiently for them to beat as one.

When it finally happens, I feel it rather than see it. The sensation is small, soft, but I feel the shift deep inside me. Before, all of my *self*, everything I considered Elspeth, had been contained within me. Now, it feels like there is something, something *vital* connecting my inner self to the outer world. Specifically, to the blue haze pulsing in my hand.

All at once, I am attuned to it, connected with it. I feel it. Know its power.

All I need to do now is channel that power.

Knowing I must shape my intentions, I tug gently on the power held within the blue haze, visualising the layer of soil as a small mound, willing it to be so.

Heart still beating in time with each blue pulse, I watch as slowly, oh so slowly, the soil starts to move. Gathering together, it piles up to create the small mound I had visualised.

Elated, I let out a whoop of joy, looking up to find Law grinning at me wildly.

'Did you see that?' I say grinning back at him, delight pitching my voice much higher than usual.

'I did indeed,' he replies. 'How did it feel?'

'Incredible,' I admit, although the word doesn't even begin to encompass everything I'd felt in the moment. Momentous, perhaps. Life-altering. 'I felt this connection, with the Aether. It wasn't just seeing, it was feeling. I could feel its power.'

I glance down at the pile of soil in my hand. Something that feels very close to devastation bottoms out in my gut. The pulsing blue haze is gone.

'What? Where did it go? I can't see it anymore!' I am unsure why I am quite so frantic, but the idea of losing that connection is suddenly unbearable.

Law places his hands on my shoulders, steadying me. 'It's there. It will always be there. You just lost your focus on it. Take a breath and look again.'

I take one shaky breath, then another. Focusing my attention on the pile of soil, I let my consciousness relax and allow my mind to open, reaching out to feel for that connection. Faster this time, the blue haze materialises within the soil. It pulses once, twice, and by the third pulse, my heart is beating in time with it. Joy fills me as the connection snaps into place. While I would struggle to fully explain the sensation, I can't deny the rightness that settles inside me once that link is made.

I decide to try something, sending my will towards the soil, gently pulling on the power held within the Aether it contains. Slightly surprised to see it actually work, I watch as the soil gathers itself into a tight ball. Delighted with what I've created and revelling in the delicious sense of connection, I will the ball to roll around my palm.

At the edge of my focus, Law lets out an amused chuckle.

'Catch,' I say, willing the ball out of my palm and flicking it at him. But, while my intention had been to throw the small ball to him so he could catch it, somewhere between me throwing it and him catching it, I lose focus and the ball crumbles.

'Hey!' he exclaims, soil spraying his shirt.

'Bloody hell, sorry,' I say quickly. 'That wasn't what I meant to do at all.' I reach out to brush the soil from his shirt, looking up to give him an apologetic grin. His eyes sparkle with amusement and warmth fills me at the sight. I rise on tiptoe to brush a kiss against his lips.

'What was that for?' He leans into it, chasing mine with his own much fuller kiss. 'Not that I'm complaining.'

Smiling as we separate, I say, 'It was a thank you. For helping me with this, for helping me find my magic. Finding that connection...' I sigh, satiated at the thought of it, 'it made me feel like I discovered something I didn't know I was missing.'

While this is certainly true, I refrain from telling him that I also couldn't *stop* myself from kissing him. That doing so, touching him, being closer to him simply feels right to me. So much so, I'm not sure if this is something I should be wary of, should be guarding myself against. Do I really want to be at the mercy of such a strong pull towards someone I've only just met, and know so little of?

'You're a good teacher, you know,' I continue, trying to distract myself from spiralling into those thoughts. Determining what Law and I have together will have to wait until after I get answers from the Queen. Until after I save Agnes. That's what's most pressing right now.

Urged on by that thought, I straighten my pack and start walking, brushing the last of the soil from my hands onto my skirts. Having stopped on a craggy hill, we are not far from its peak, but I can't make out what's beyond it.

Law falls into step beside me. 'And you are a passable student.'

I move to give him a playful shove and suddenly he is no longer there. I whip my head around, searching for him, only to see him reappear in the shadow of a large boulder at the side of the path up ahead.

Smiling that mischievous smile, he calls out, 'But you still have a lot to learn.' Waiting for me to catch up, he continues, 'Soon you'll see Aether in everything, all the time, not just when you focus on it. You'll feel the connection constantly. Before long, it will become part of you, allowing you to call on it without even thinking.'

I consider how wondrous it had felt finding that connection. I can't imagine what it might feel like to have that link, to feel tied to all that power, all the time. Will it overwhelm me? Will I ever take it for granted?

We reach the peak of the hill, and I finally see what lies beyond it. From where we stand, a narrow path twists its way down the steep, rocky descent, leading to an expansive crescent-shaped bay. Unlike the pristine sand lining the river, this beach is stony and black, the water edging it the darkest indigo. While the skies remain clear and the weather warm, there is something about those seas that fills me with unease. I know I would never willingly wade into that water, no matter how hot the weather.

'That's where we're heading?' I nod my head in the direction of the bay.

'Certainly is,' Law replies. 'We need to make another short stop once we're down there.'

I sigh inwardly. I really don't want to slow our journey with any unnecessary detours.

As if sensing this, Law continues, 'It shouldn't take long, but it is important. Remember the plan I mentioned? This should help us get into the palace.'

'Are you going to enlighten me on what this plan of yours entails?' I ask, shifting my gaze up to his. A soft breeze rises up from the bay, sweeping his hair back from his face and drawing attention to the sharp angle of his cheekbones. I restrain my desire to reach out and touch them, to tangle my hands through his hair and pull him into another of those long lingering kisses that make me forget where I am.

Instead, I curl my fingers into fists and press my lips into a firm, distinctly unkissable line. Damnit, it really shouldn't take this much effort to keep my hands to myself.

Law cuts his attention to me, his lips quirking like he knows what I'm thinking. 'It starts with some light shopping and ends with us hopefully gaining access to the palace. Are you in need of any more detail?'

'Some light shopping?' Dubious, I look from the barren landscape that surrounds us down to the rocky shore below. I have no idea where Law imagines he will carry out this shopping trip, never mind what he might be looking to buy.

'Yes, we should be able to find everything we need in the market down there.' He tilts his chin toward the bay.

'Have you started seeing things in your old age?' I ask, amused. 'There is no market.'

'Are you quite sure about that, Red? Perhaps you should look a little harder.'

I squint down at the bay, seeing nothing but black rock and water of the darkest, deepest blue. Wondering if this might be like my ability to perceive Aether, I slow my breathing and relax my consciousness, letting my mind open to what I imagine must be some kind of magic.

I am rewarded by the unveiling of not just a market, but an entire island swarming with a warren of market stalls. From this distance it's difficult to make out the details, but it certainly looks... lively.

'We're still on Unseelie lands, aren't we?' I ask, unable to keep the nervous edge from my voice.

'What gave it away? The grizzly collection of rotten heads mounted on the gates, perhaps?'

'Perhaps,' I reply. 'Are you sure this is a good idea?'

'Not at all.' Law angles one of his smiles my way. 'But I'm sure you'll keep us safe.' He extends a hand, and I reach for it without thinking. Shadows snake along his forearm to the tips of his fingers, greeting my touch. 'Come on. We can make back some of the time lost to this market with a shortcut.'

'What kind of shortcut?' I ask warily.

'Probably best if you don't get too much time to think about it.'

Before I have the opportunity to mull over this cryptic response, he wraps me in his arms, and the world goes dark.

Chapter 22

I open my eyes, then squeeze them shut as a wave of nausea washes over me. Bile rises in my throat, and I work hard to swallow it back down. I absolutely do not want to vomit again.

Tucked against Law's chest, I steady myself with the hard feel of him, his warmth, the scent of him surrounding me. Taking a few deep breaths to centre myself, I crack open one eye to see where we are.

Shoving past the stubborn sense of vertigo still threatening the contents of my stomach, I force my attention toward the slick, dark walls of what I assume is a cave. Sharp, rocky ground lies uneven beneath my feet, and I breathe in salty air, noticing for the first time the splash of gently lapping waves. Soothed by the familiar sound, I take a long moment to appreciate the cool darkness enveloping us, before finally feeling steady enough to open my other eye. When I am sure I'm not going to vomit, I step back from Law and his obvious concern.

'Let's not do that again.' I wince, my head continuing to spin. 'I don't know how you make that look so easy. My insides want to be on the outside right now.'

'Decades of practice.' He rests a comforting hand on my shoulder, dragging his thumb along my collarbone. 'I can go to the market if you'd prefer to stay here?' He looks around uncertainly, as if assessing the cave's suitability to hide a fragile half-human.

'No, I'll go with you.' I square my shoulders and will my stomach to settle. I appreciate his concern, but I have two feet, and I need to stand on them. Checking my pack is still in place, I blow out a much sturdier breath. 'Time to adventure into my first Unseelie market.' I give him my most determined grin. 'Lead the way.'

Law eyes me, then nods once, and turns to exit the cave. I trail close behind, making my way out onto the beach, where I have to lift a hand to shade my eyes, squinting against the glare. As my vision adjusts, I realise it's not the sun that is dazzling me, but the beach beneath my feet. From above, it had appeared rocky and black. Now it's in front of me, all around me, I see it's actually made up of a faceted multitude of gleaming jet. It's absolutely breathtaking.

My gaze skims to the indigo water washing softly against the shore. Almost luxuriant in its colouring, it is also eerie enough that there would need to be a very compelling reason for me to ever venture into its depths. And thankfully, I won't need to. Before us extends a walkway set flush with the water, leading out to the small island sitting squat within the bay. On the breeze, the sounds of market day drift toward us. It is familiar, yet not, and I nervously untuck my hair from behind my ears, before stepping out onto the walkway. It feels solid underfoot, despite being slick with water, small waves lapping against it and occasionally overtaking it.

'Security against thieves,' Law says, answering the question tipped on my tongue. 'The walkway sinks when the alarm is raised, leaving thieves either stuck on the island or at the mercy of the sealife that prowl these waters.' He nods to a dark shape gliding silently by, cutting its way close to the walkway before heading further out into the depths.

'So, they either get eaten by whatever the hell that was or they end up with their head on a spike,' I conclude. 'A worthy deterrent, I'd imagine. I'll be sure to keep my hands off the merchandise to avoid any misunderstandings.'

Not wanting to end up in the drink, I raise my eyes briefly from my feet to glance at Law. He strides confidently beside me, shirt sleeves rolled up and collar unbuttoned to expose inky spirals twining at his throat. Unlike me, he wears no cloak. Thinking of how he had concealed his appearance from the crowds at the wedding, I ask, 'Do you not need to cover up here?'

'No, not here,' he replies evenly. 'Considering who we might be rubbing shoulders with, I'd prefer for them to know exactly who I am, lest any of them contemplate an interest in you.'

I am still pondering the threat within his words when we reach the end of the walkway. Stepping out onto more of that same sparkling jet, I can't help but notice the island exudes a certain sinister air. It's an impression that is only intensified by the gruesome collection of decapitated heads decorating its gates, assorted in their states of decay. Swallowing thickly, I urge my attention beyond the gates and the sizeable guards that lurk beside them, to find endless rows of market stalls displaying their wares to passing fae, some of whom hurry stall to stall, as others leisurely peruse what's on offer.

We walk out into the first row of stalls, Law's cool composure an obvious contrast to my sweaty uncertainty. Feeling the many sets of eyes that conspicuously track our progress, I try – and likely fail – to mask my unease under their gaze. Of the fae that turn our way, one has the skin of a lizard, whom as we pass, bares dagger-sharp teeth, scenting the air with his tongue. Another with armour made of shells clicks his crab's pincers ferociously, his bulging fish eyes following Law with interest.

But while each and every gaze is most certainly unsettling, I am disconcerted most of all by the attention of what appears to be half-fae half-spider. This living nightmare tracks me with a dozen inky black eyes, a gruesome set of fangs glistening with venom below. I shudder. As if spiders aren't appalling enough in their small, furry form. This one has to be life-sized and staring straight at me.

Seriously contemplating retreating into the depths of my own cloak for concealment, I compel my attention toward each stall's wares rather than meeting the eyes of those we pass. In an attempt to distract myself, I step in closer to Law and ask, 'What are we here to buy?'

'We need to find you a dress,' he replies, stopping at a stall to examine the fabrics on display there. From his demeanour, I have no doubt he has already catalogued each threat in this market, and he is entirely unconcerned by every single one.

'What's wrong with this dress?' I ask, offended by the implication that Law has something against my choice in clothing, as much as by the fact that he might think buying a dress, of all things, could warrant such a delay in our journey.

I look down at the item in question, dirt soiling the hem, its worn fabric rough to the touch. Buying nice dresses had never been a priority for me. I'd never felt the need to impress anyone by dressing in a certain way, but more than that, I simply don't like wasting money on such frivolities. Back at home, pretty dresses would only have ended up ruined as I foraged in the woods, or sweated through and stained during the brewing process.

'Nothing at all,' Law replies, picking up a ream of creamy velvet in a sensuous shade of blush pink. 'But it may stand out somewhat at the Queen's Winter Welcome Ball.' He places the fabric back and eyes another gauzy ream.

'The Queen's Winter Welcome Ball,' I repeat, tone questioning. 'I didn't realise we held an invitation to the Queen's Winter Welcome Ball.'

'We don't,' he states simply. 'But that doesn't mean we won't be attending.'

'And that's your plan for getting us into the palace?' I ask, pushing aside the thought that one would *definitely* need a formal invite to gain entrance to such an event.

Law holds the fabric against me. Studying its pale purple colouring, he responds, 'Yes, it is. And yes, this is the one.' He turns to the fae standing patiently behind the stall piled high with ream upon ream of lavish, colourful fabrics.

This fae appears more human than most I'd seen on the sprawling market island, but there is definitely something about him that would set him apart at home. Murine, I think, as I watch his nose twitch. There's something about his nervous, scurrying movements that bring to mind the mice Cheetie keeps from my grain stores.

'Admirable choice,' the fae squeaks, cutting nervous glances up at Law. 'And what are we creating today?'

'A dress,' Law says simply.

'For this lovely lady, I assume?' the fae quivers, gesturing shyly at me.

I'm not sure how I feel about being dressed by Law, much less the idea of attending a royal ball. Moving closer to him, I keep my voice low as I say, 'Is this really necessary?'

'It is if you want any chance of gaining an audience with the Queen,' he replies. 'Appearance is everything in the royal court.'

Catching something tight flit across his expression, I say carefully, 'Making a dress takes days, Law. We don't have that kind of time.'

'Not here, it doesn't,' he says, hitching his mouth up at one side. Turning to the fae, he continues, 'How long will it take?'

'A gown for the royal ball,' the fae considers, nose twitching furiously. 'I can have that finished up for you in around an hour.'

'And who is paying?' I ask, knowing I certainly don't have the coin for such an extravagance.

'Nicnevin, of course,' Law replies, tone sharp despite his languid smile.

'Of course,' I sigh, resigning myself to my fate of being dressed like a doll. At home, I'd paid so little attention to what I wore, it would have been laughable to even think of having a gown made in this manner. Here in Faerie, that leaves me with the problem of not knowing what to ask for during such a process, while also being absolutely clueless as to what passes for fashion. I'll just have to hope Law knows more about Faerie fashion than I do.

I sweep my gaze over him. I have to admit he does look well put-together. But that likely has more to do with Law and less to do with his choice of clothing.

Sighing inwardly, I watch uncertainly as the mousy fae steps out from behind his wall of fabric and stops neatly in front of me.

'This will only take a moment,' he squeaks. Displaying the first hint of confidence I've seen in him, he twists a measuring tape out of nowhere and with practised movements, proceeds to take my measurements.

***

To pass the time while we wait for my dress, we stroll through the market, now with my hood carefully raised. While I have no doubt Law could keep me safe here, I don't enjoy the attention we're receiving. Watchful eyes follow us as we wander the rows of stalls, and I am cautious to keep my gaze lowered and – remembering what happens to thieves – my hands neatly tucked away.

Despite my unease, I can't help but be mesmerised by the weird and wonderful merchandise on display. I'm moving in closer to inspect what appears to be a mechanical insect with a glistening human eyeball rolling around on its back, when I hear someone call out to Law. I turn sharply towards the voice, finding a male stalking up to us, his expression illuminated by a broad white smile. Nervous about what kind of characters might frequent an Unseelie market, I shoot a glance at Law, a sense of relief washing over me as I take in his easy stance and wide flash of a grin.

'Struan,' Law says. 'It's been a while. It's good to see you.'

'And you!' the fae, Struan, replies enthusiastically, clasping Law's shoulder in greeting.

I can't imagine Law enduring the touch of someone he does not trust, so I relax further, taking time to assess the newcomer as the two exchange pleasantries.

Taller than Law, Struan is also much bulkier. Everywhere. And it's a feature he certainly makes the most of with his chosen ensemble. Worn open at the front, his sleeveless tunic perfectly showcases thick, powerful arms and a sharply defined wall of muscle across his chest and stomach. Despite his size, he moves with that flowing fae grace that seems to be innate among their kind, but there is none of their ethereal beauty in his features. His face is harder somehow, its edges starker. Conspicuously contrasting that severity, his sparkling amber eyes light up his expression, where an easy smile seems a permanent fixture.

But while his eyes and his smile and his muscled form are indeed diverting, my gaze snaps again and again to the velvety wings that rise majestically behind him.

Observing my attention, Struan raises his brows, wings flaring wide behind him. 'Struan, mistress,' he rumbles, amber eyes glinting as he holds out his hand in greeting. 'As Law has so rudely refused to introduce me, I must do so myself.'

'Elspeth,' I respond, my hand meeting his massive one. Instead of shaking it, as I had expected, he raises it to his lips and kisses it. I cut a quick, questioning look toward Law. He shakes his head, amused.

'So nice to meet you, Elspeth,' Struan says, gently releasing my hand. 'Now, what would a lovely creature like you be doing with a scoundrel such as this?'

I pause, wondering how much I should tell this unknown, if admittedly very charming fae.

Sensing the reason behind my hesitation, Law cuts in, 'Elspeth has business at the palace. I am her escort.'

Glancing between us, Struan nods, apparently unbothered by the lack of detail provided. 'Not a destination you will make before nightfall. I insist you stay with me tonight and carry on your journey tomorrow.'

'We wouldn't want to impose,' Law replies, some of the ease in his voice replaced by what sounds like apprehension. 'There's a tavern I was planning on stopping at just over the border.'

I assume he means the border between Unseelie and Seelie. I wonder if that means Struan lives here, on Unseelie lands.

'Do not worry for her safety, brother,' Struan says, his voice softer now. 'I know she is human,' he continues, nostrils flaring to scent the air, 'or partly human, at least. No one would be bold enough to harm her within the bounds of my lands.'

I scowl. All these fae *scenting* me is really getting a bit much.

Warily, I watch Law as he appraises the male who had called him brother. Considering Struan's open, earnest expression, he appears to come to a decision. Although his features are still somewhat guarded, he replies, 'In that case, we'd be glad to accept your kind offer of hospitality.'

Struan beams. 'Excellent, excellent,' he says, clapping a hand on Law's back.

'We just need to pick up a package, and we can be on our way,' Law says. 'Do you have everything you came for?'

'I do now,' Struan responds heartily. Tucking in his wings, he steps back, gesturing to us. 'Lead the way.'

Chapter 23

In Struan's amiable company, the walk to his estate passes quickly. His manor – I am unable to come up with any other word for it, as *house* certainly wouldn't do it justice – is a thing of immense dark beauty. Where Nicnevin's mansion had most definitely seen better days, what stands before us is as imposing as it is magnificent. A masterpiece of glittering black stone and gleaming grey glass, it erupts out of the earth, jutting out at sharp angles as it reaches high into the sky.

Admiring the myriad blood red roses that line the manicured gardens, I breathe in their irresistible scent as we reach the towering front door. At a quick flick of Struan's hand, the door swings open, but I have no time to marvel at this before he ushers us inside and we are swallowed by opulence.

Walking into the warmly lit foyer, my steps falter and I gape. I can't help it. Everything is just so... luxurious. The front door closes silently behind us, and Struan guides us through the foyer to the sumptuous sitting room beyond, where sinuous silk curtains line smoky grey windows and sinfully soft carpet welcomes our footsteps. Expansive and elegant, it is a space that still manages to feel inviting, filtered as it is into cosy, comfortable nooks. In one nook, there are golden day beds heaped with velvet cushions, set around matching tables piled high with plated delicacies. Over by the fire, overstuffed lounging chairs conspire together, calling out to me and making me wish I could sink into one and not emerge until morning.

When I finally drag my gaze away, I find Law and Struan propping up a bar made of sleek mahogany, each with a glass in hand. Heads together, they talk quietly, their conversation swallowed by the clink of ice against glass, large shards of it swirling around rich amber liquid.

Law notices my attention and offers me a small, private smile, eyes twinkling as they crinkle at the corners. At the sight of it, a leisurely heat unwinds low in my belly. It is desire, certainly, but there is comfort in it, too. I still have reservations about staying overnight on Unseelie lands, but I trust that Law knows what he is doing. Struan's charm has gone a long way towards settling my nerves, but without Law's confidence in him, my guard would remain much higher.

'Drink?' he asks, raising his own glass in question.

Remembering what he said at the wedding about not suggesting I imbibe if the occasion were Unseelie, I wonder whether that same warning applies when sojourning in Unseelie manors. I suppose not if he is the one offering.

'Why not?' I reply, making my way over to the bar.

Law considers the options, before reaching for a glittering crystal decanter filled with clear liquid. As he pours, it fizzes and sparkles like no drink I have ever seen. I accept the glass, and sniff it warily.

'What is it?' I ask, my eyes narrowing as I recall the terrible turn of events following my run-in with faerie wine.

'Fleurdelis,' Law responds with an encouraging smile. 'Try it. I think you'll like it.'

My attention shifts to Struan. Open and affable as ever, he nods. 'It came from a marvellous batch.'

I sniff it again and take a small sip, a slight moan escaping me as the liquid slips over my tongue. Delightfully effervescent, it hints at the sharpness of bramble, before rolling through with the sweetness of strawberry, ending with a delicious pop of something decadent I can't quite name.

'Wow,' I say, taking another, much larger swallow. 'I need to learn how to make this.'

'Glad you like it,' Struan says easily. 'Now, I'm afraid you'll have to excuse me. I have arrangements for our gathering to oversee.'

'Gathering?' I ask, distracted by the touch of bubbles bursting over my tongue.

'A small one, yes,' Struan replies. 'Happening upon you and Law at the market was most fortuitous. Now you can both attend the soiree I had planned for this evening. It's been an age since I've seen Law attend any event. It will be good to finally see him enjoy himself a little.'

Law's carefully guarded expression tells me he had known about this gathering and is not particularly enthused by it, but will go along with it for Struan's sake. 'You heard what I said,' he says, his voice a low warning that has no effect whatsoever on Struan.

'Yes, yes, brother, I heard you.' Struan tosses back the rest of his drink. 'I'll have Darach show you to your room. Let him know if there's anything you need while you're here.' At Law's nod, he shifts that glinting amber gaze to me. 'It's been lovely meeting you, Elspeth. I very much look forward to getting to know you better.' The innuendo in his words is unmistakable and I force down a blush. Throwing me a quick wink, he places his empty glass on the bar, and strides out of the room.

'So that's Struan,' Law says, swallowing what remains in his own glass and raising his brows.

'How do you know each other?' I ask, knowing there is a fairly good chance I will not receive an answer.

'We've been friends since we were boys,' Law says, trying for a smile but not quite getting there. 'He was once madly in love with my sister.'

'Sister?' I cough, bubbles shooting up my nose. 'I didn't know you had a sister.'

'I didn't tell you.' Sadness paints his words the deepest blue. 'I wasn't alone when Balgaire found me on his doorstep. Florie was there too. She was nothing more than a baby, still wrapped in swaddling. But she grew up quickly enough, kept Balgaire on his toes with her antics.' He smiles more fully at this, though I can see sorrow behind it.

'Where is she now?' I ask delicately, hoping that sorrow doesn't mean what I think it does.

'She's with Nicnevin,' Law replies, voice sharpening on her name.

Slightly startled by this, I wonder both at Law's tone and the fact that Florie may have been at Nicnevin's mansion during my own time there.

In the face of Law's now shuttered expression, I tuck away my questions and turn my attention to the elderly fae shuffling through the door dressed in a butler's uniform.

'Darach,' Law greets him, some of the warmth returning to his eyes.

'Master Law,' the butler replies with equal affection, bowing first at Law, then at me. 'Master Struan asked me to direct you to your room. If you would care to follow me?'

***

I am decidedly uncomfortable as we enter the crowded ballroom later that evening. Struan had clearly downplayed the size of his *small* gathering. If this is his idea of small, I wouldn't like to guess at what he'd consider large.

Just as sumptuously decorated as the sitting room we had been in earlier, the ballroom radiates a dreamy sense of opulence within its much larger dimensions. With a plush velvet canopy draped languidly across its soaring ceiling and plenty of shadowy corners to get lost in, the grand room still somehow manages to feel intimate. High tables edge the dancefloor, where small groups gather, many chatting animatedly as they drink from crystal glasses. On stage at the far end of the dancefloor, a band plays lilting music while a male singer with an indulgently rich voice serenades the room.

Heels clicking on the polished timber floors, I'm all too aware of eyes cutting in our direction as Law and I make our way to an unoccupied table. In black trousers, black shirt and a tailored grey doublet that brings out the charcoal in his eyes, Law is devastating, although he seems not to notice the many admiring glances the crowds turn to offer.

Darach had delivered both the doublet and my dress to our room shortly after guiding us there, dutifully averting his eyes from the sight of me sunk deep into the ridiculously large and exquisitely comfortable bed.

As much as I would have preferred to stay sunk and skip Struan's *small* gathering in favour of much-needed sleep, I had forced myself to get up and play the role of appreciative guest. After a long soak in the lavish clawfoot bathtub, I'd slathered myself in an array of gorgeous smelling lotions, then applied some rouge to my cheeks and stain to my lips. Pinning up my hair to hide the tips of my ears and adding cascading emerald earrings to bring out the green in my eyes, all that had been left to do after that was grit my teeth and brave the dress.

Made from lustrous ivory silk, the gown is unlike anything I've ever seen before, never mind worn. Sumptuously cut and sleeveless, it drapes softly through a high neckline, sweeping down into a deep twist at the base of my back. Tracing each curve like a caress, it trails my body to sashay to the floor, where intricate beading shimmers like sunlight on water. It is breathtakingly fae and utterly beyond the likes of me. But still, I feel like I might be warming to it under Law's shamelessly appreciative gaze.

He stands close beside me now as a server delivers our drinks, skimming a hand over my exposed back and making me shiver despite the warmth of the room.

'I knew that dress would look sensational on you.' Struan's voice drags my attention from Law, and I hide behind the rim of my glass, trying to conceal my blush. With Law's hand gliding ever lower, I had been busy pondering our chances of escaping to one of the ballroom's shadowy corners, where he could remove the damn dress and replay some of his moves from earlier. I don't need Struan knowing that, though. Obviously.

Struan raises a brow, mouth spreading into a wicked grin that tells me he knows exactly to what depths my thoughts had just plunged.

'Fuck,' I mutter angrily.

Law coughs out a laugh and says, 'Nice gathering, Struan. Just a few of your closest friends?'

'You know how it is, brother,' Struan smiles. 'One whiff of a party and every Unseelie within a hundred miles comes running.' Golden eyes mischievous, he slides his gaze to me. 'No one can resist the opportunity to attend one of my little soirees.'

Casting my eyes over our charming host, I wonder whether his guests come for his parties or for him. He is no longer exposing quite as much carved muscle, but the outfit he wears does little to conceal it. Reminding me of the rippling seas surrounding the Unseelie market, his silk jacket and trousers cut close to his body, revealing a deep indigo that shifts to black as he moves. With a crisp white shirt complementing his broad white smile, his entirely enchanting ensemble is only enhanced by those glorious wings that rise magnificently behind him.

But, while I can certainly appreciate Struan's powerful good looks, my appreciation doesn't tip over into desire. His form is far too close to that of Malcom's for it to truly appeal to me. I grimace, recalling the many times my husband's thick, corded arms had caged me in bed, where I'd suffered his clumsy thrusts and damp grunts against my neck.

Pushing aside the past, I drag myself back to the present, catching more of the easy conversation between Law and Struan. I like seeing Law like this. His customary stance is unaffected and effortless, but he seems genuinely happy to be in the company of his old friend. Continuing to sip my drink, I let them catch up, scanning my surroundings and ogling our fellow partygoers.

Standing in groups around each of the high tables that line the dancefloor, fae talk and drink, an excited sense of anticipation crackling among them. While I still feel very much exposed in what I consider a brazenly revealing gown, many of the fae around us reveal far more skin than would ever be deemed decent back in the human realm. Though, with the arrival of what I assume to be the evening's entertainment, I suppose any sense of decency at this gathering may soon be cast aside.

Winding their way through the crowds, a group of sinuous fae draped only in the most delicate wisps of fabric leave lingering touches and sensuous kisses on those they pass. A mix of male and female, the dancers – I will think of them as such until they prove otherwise – are as eerily graceful as their looks are ethereal. With lithe movements, a pair slink over to Struan. Up close, their skin shimmers a pale silver hue, and I can't help but admire their willowy forms as the male leans in close to graze Struan's earlobe with his teeth. Meanwhile, the female opts for a more direct route, skimming her hands up his bulky thighs to rest on what lies at their apex. Entirely unabashed, Struan turns to give the male a long, lingering kiss, before shooing the pair away to attend to the rest of his guests.

'They seem... friendly,' I offer, as Struan shifts his attention back to us.

At home, one simply wouldn't see such a show of affection. Unless you were in a bawdy house, perhaps. Even there, it would be highly unusual to find members of the same sex enjoying one another openly. But, while it may remain one of society's biggest taboos, I have never been able to drum up any indignation over the idea that some men love men, and some women love women. To me, love is love. It doesn't matter where you find it.

'They're paid to be friendly,' Struan says with a shrug, dragging a thumb over his lower lip. 'I've been told this is your first Unseelie party, Elspeth.' He grabs a drink from a passing tray, then tilts his glass to me in toast. 'Law suggested I amend my original lineup, so the evening's entertainment will be far more sedate than most of my guests are accustomed to. Still, I'm sure it will be an entirely pleasurable experience for all.' Amber eyes glint over amber liquid as he tosses back his drink.

'Thank you?' I say, unsure of how to respond.

'Probably for the best,' he replies. 'I wouldn't want to scare you away by revealing any of my... darker passions.' He gives me a broad grin that edges towards savage, and I wonder whether I imagine that glimpse of sharpened canines. 'Not yet anyway.'

'Very considerate of you,' I manage, shooting a look at Law. Again, he simply appears amused by Struan, rolling the ice around his glass and not showing even the slightest hint of concern. Whatever dark passions Struan holds, Law obviously trusts him to keep them in check while I am in residence.

Carefully scrutinising the crowds, Struan then centres his attention back on me. 'Now, everything seems to be moving along smoothly enough. I wonder if I could ask a favour of you, Elspeth?'

Uncertain what he could possibly want from me, I nod in response.

'I need to borrow Law for a short time. It won't take long. There's just something I need his assistance with.'

I skim my gaze from Struan to Law, wondering what might call a consummate host such as him away from a party such as this. As for Law, apart from the stuttering, staccato movements of the inky whorls at his throat, he looks as calm and collected as ever.

My regard returns to Struan. 'As long as Law is happy to provide that assistance, I am also quite happy to remain here.' I gesture to the dancers – I'd been right in my assumption; they do seem to be dancing – now performing some kind of sensuous routine on the dancefloor. 'I have plenty to keep me entertained while you're away.'

'You are most generous, mistress. Please save me a dance.' Struan sweeps up my hand to gift it another kiss, bowing over it deeply. 'It would be an absolute travesty if that sensational dress – and the mesmerising female wearing it – did not make it onto the dancefloor this evening.' He aims a playful smile at Law. 'When it comes to dancing, Law doesn't have anything on me.' His smile widens, becoming almost feral when his eyes find mine. 'I'll show you how to move.'

I swallow, unable to push out a response before Struan winks at me and strides away. Raising my brows, I turn to Law, wholly unsure of what to make of his enormous winged friend.

Law shrugs, unaffected. 'He's...' he hums, considering his words, 'Struan.'

'Right,' I reply, drawing out the word.

'Will you be alright here on your own?' Tone serious now, concern traces his brow, and his hand moves from my lower back to tighten on my hip.

'Yes.' I narrow my eyes. 'Will you be alright *assisting* Struan?'

His jaw tightens. 'I won't be gone long,' he says, noticeably not answering my question. 'Struan has assured your safety, and I trust him.' Expression clearing, his eyes darken. He leans in, his murmured words tickling my ear. 'And when I return, I'll be the one to take that sensational dress – and the mesmerising female wearing it – out on the dancefloor. After that, I want to see much less dress, much more you, and much less of this fucking party.' Gripping my hip, he tugs me closer, pressing his lips to just the right spot below my ear.

Eyes fluttering, I nod, unable to talk past the rush of heat surging over me.

Straightening, he slips his hand around to the curve of my arse. The touch is possessive, knowing. 'Try to have fun while I'm gone.'

I nod again dumbly, wondering where the hell my voice has disappeared to as I watch the cut of his sharply tailored form make its way through the crowds. Shoving down my nerves, I glance around, trying to take comfort in his assurance that I am perfectly safe under Struan's protection.

Since Malcom's death, I have worked hard to assure my own safety, taking it upon myself to learn how to defend myself, to learn how to use a dagger effectively. Feeling the weight of said dagger tucked against my leg helps to shake loose some of that lingering unease, but I'm under no illusions here. If events were to turn against me now, I would be seriously out of my depth. Even with my newly found magic.

Through the rest of the day, I had taken small, quiet moments to work on my connection with Aether, thrilling at the sense of rightness that washed over me each time my heart had fallen into rhythm with its pulse. But the magic I managed had been minor, insignificant, entirely unequal to the task of protecting me should I need it to. Although, thinking back on the damage I'd inflicted on the troll's bridge, I suppose what my magic is capable of may depend on how dire my situation.

My gaze focused on the dancers and my attention slipping away elsewhere, I jump when a cool voice beside me drawls, 'What do you think of the show?'

What I want to say involves a suggestion that fae should be forced to wear bells to prevent them from sneaking up on me, but what leaves my mouth as I shift toward the source of my irritation is, 'It's absolutely charming.'

The source of my irritation turns out to be an exceptionally attractive male with pale blonde hair tied in a tight braid that extends down his back. But while I am completely unsurprised by his staggering good looks, I am somewhat taken aback by the horns that grace the top of his unfairly beautiful face. Sweeping up dramatically from his forehead and making him seem even taller, those curved horns frame sharply defined features and even sharper blue eyes.

I search his expression for any indication of intent behind his attentions, but his appraising regard gives nothing away. 'And you are?' My tone skirts rudeness, but I am in no mood to welcome more fae with murderous intentions into my life.

'Broden,' he offers, along with a smile. It is not as broad as Struan's or as eloquent as Law's, but it softens the sharp lines of his face into something that feels a lot like warmth.

'Elspeth,' I offer back, willing to give him that, if not much else.

'Pleased to make your acquaintance, Elspeth,' Broden continues, his voice still cool, smooth as undisturbed water on a lake. 'May I ask how you know our host?'

'He's a friend of a friend.'

'Struan is a friend to many.' Broden gestures to the now packed ballroom. More guests have filtered into the luxurious space, many of whom seem to be enjoying the intimate attentions of Struan's *dancers*. 'Is your friend anyone I would know?'

I know I must remain on guard, must keep this unfamiliar fae at a distance until I understand exactly what he wants from me, but as he looks me over with those piercing blue eyes, I feel my suspicion soften.

Odd. I work to bolster my guard once more.

'Perhaps,' I say, trying to retain some mystery.

Another piercing look pins me in place. Another flutter encourages me to lower my defences. I have the unmistakable urge to open my mouth and convey to Broden anything he might want to know. 'Law,' my mouth spits out, quite without my meaning it to. *Bloody hell, Elspeth, shut up.* 'I'm here with my friend, Law. Do you know him?' Again, I don't mean to say it, but something at the back of my mind soothes me, letting me know it's absolutely fine to talk to Broden about this.

'Indeed, I do,' Broden replies evenly. 'Law and I have a long and storied history.'

Noting what he didn't say, I push against the sense that I should let Broden know anything Broden wants to know. 'Are you and Law friends?'

'You could call our relationship many things, but a friendship is not one of them,' Broden admits with a wry smile. 'No matter, though,' he breezes on. 'What brings you to these parts? I can't imagine an exquisite thing such as you would ordinarily attend an event such as this.'

With effort, I manage to tear my eyes from Broden to scan the crowds around us. That light, crackling feeling of anticipation I'd noticed earlier has rolled over into something heavier, something almost hedonistic. Lust, abandon, wildness, greed. It's only now I see the air is thick with it. Everywhere, all around, fae gyrate, grind, heads thrown back, completely uninhibited. Absently, I wonder what they might have been drinking to lose themselves so thoroughly.

Broden takes my hand, snapping my attention back to him. His touch is cool against my now fevered one. Somewhere inside me, I know this is wrong, that I don't want this fae touching any part of me. But again, those thoughts are soothed by a sense that all is well, that I have nothing to fear from Broden. That I should open myself up to him.

'I asked you a question, Elspeth. Please see to it that you answer.' Despite his sharp tone, the sharpness of his gaze, I feel nothing but kindness, a warmth washing over me. I am clay, ready to be shaped in Broden's hands.

This time I answer immediately, wanting to please him. 'We're on our way to meet with the Queen of Elphame. Law is my escort. I don't know the way.' Broden's eyes narrow, and I continue, needing to tell him more. I want to please him with my willing acquiescence. 'I need to ask the Queen's help, you see. My friend Agnes, she's a witch, she's in the most terrible trouble. The Queen knows her, so I'm hoping she can help.' I know I am rambling but still feel the need to push more words out of my mouth. 'I also want to find my mother. She's in the Queen's court. Or, at least, she was. Her name is Hester.'

Broden's eyes flare. He is silent a moment, appearing to take time to process my rush of words. Vaguely, I notice my desire to talk slowly dissipate.

'And what business is it of Law's that you meet with the Queen?'

With his question, that desire reforms, insistent and impatient in my mind. 'Nicnevin asked him to,' I say quickly. 'Well, I don't think she *asked*, as such. I don't think Law has much say in what he does or doesn't do where Nicnevin is involved.'

'Why then, is Nicnevin involved?' In much the same way as Nicnevin had dripped disgust onto her words when mentioning the Queen, Broden's tone sounds unnervingly similar as he sneers Nicnevin's name. Not a fan, then.

'She said she couldn't let me get eaten by angry pixies. She was the one who brought me into Faerie, and she said she felt responsible for me. Or words to that effect, anyway.' I am rambling again but I'm unable to stop the words from escaping me. Although it's not quite that. I need the words to escape me. I want to offer them to Broden as a gift.

'Prince Broden.' Law's words are a low growl. He steps in close, his reassuring touch meeting the small of my back. 'If you would kindly remove your hand – and your allure – from Elspeth.'

I breathe in the warmth and comforting scent of him, then exhale slowly as light fingers retreat from my mind. Missing the pressure, I feel suddenly, inexplicably empty. Broden drops my hand and steps back. Gradually, my body adjusts to the space, and my mind becomes my own again. I am free to consider what I actually think of him. What I shared with him.

'What did you do to me?' I spit, disgusted with myself for letting go of so much precious information. None of what I said was anyone's business but my own.

'A truth is always better shared,' Broden replies, infuriatingly unapologetic.

'Answer my question,' I demand, specks of blue sparking at the edge of my vision.

'Prince Broden is a master of mind magic,' Law cuts in. He moves to my side, directing his words towards me, but keeping his gaze locked on the horned fae in front of us. 'He specialises in using what we call allure. It allows him to alter someone's feelings, adjust their emotions, and modify their responses to give him what he wants.'

I feel dirty, violated. Rivena's incursion into my mind had been a slow, sinuous seduction I had been able to push back. Broden's had been a full-frontal assault.

'My guess is what he wanted from you was information.' Law's tone is as abrupt as I have ever heard it. The line of his jaw is rigid, coiled tension clear in the shadows snaking at his neck. I know he is powerful, I've seen what that power looks like. Right now, he looks to be working damned hard to pin that power down. To not let it slip and shred the fae prince standing before us, whose sneer is fixed in place, sharpening his features further.

Wait a minute. Fae prince? My muddied mind only now catching up, I realise Law had addressed him as Prince Broden. Twice.

'You're a prince?' I ask, shock replacing disgust, at least temporarily. 'As in, son of a Queen?'

'Yes, Elspeth. The Queen you seek is my mother.' Broden sounds bored now, although I can't quite tell if it's an act. He slides his gaze to Law. 'I understand you are to be her escort. How, pray tell, were you hoping to gain an audience with the vaunted Queen Beatrix?' His tone shifts to smear an ugly sneer over the word *you*.

'That is none of your business,' I snarl, delighted I am no longer under his influence and can answer as I please.

'Let me guess, then,' Broden says, looking exaggeratedly thoughtful. 'Given tomorrow evening will see heavy crowds attending the palace to celebrate my mother's appallingly tedious and abysmally named Winter Welcome Ball, you hope to slip in among them.'

Am I that transparent? Even when I'm not spilling my guts, I still can't keep a bloody secret.

'I see from your expression that I am correct, Elspeth,' Broden drawls. 'I am sorry to dispel your hopes, but that will not work. Not only will there be heavy crowds, those crowds will be heavily guarded. My mother has increased her security. She told me she senses an incoming threat.' His gaze moves coolly over Law then returns to me. 'So, my question to you is, do you want to meet with the Queen or not?'

'You know I do,' I snap. 'What are you really asking?'

A smile twitches at his lips. 'Whether you want my help.'

Chapter 24

Judging by the look on Law's face, Broden's response is as much of a surprise to him as it is to me. 'Why would you help us?' he asks guardedly.

Broden tsks. 'I would not be helping you, Law. I would be helping Elspeth. Think of it as my way of apologising for my behaviour.'

I can't bring myself to believe his motives are in any way noble. There is no way this imperious prince would ever lower himself to help me.

'Seriously, what would you gain from doing such a thing?' Law delivers the question I had been poised to ask.

'Let's just say it would be a mutually beneficial arrangement,' Broden offers, an entirely untrustworthy smirk dancing under his calculating gaze.

'In what way?' Law snaps back.

'In that you both will be allowed to enter the palace unmolested and I will attend my mother's ball on the arm of a fascinating, intelligent, and not to mention, dazzling young woman. Is that not enough?'

I snort as Law replies, 'Not for you.'

'Sadly, that is all I can give you,' Broden sighs. 'Perhaps I hope to use the opportunity to win her affections. Maybe that is what I hope to *gain*.'

I snort louder this time. Yes, I know how to dazzle males, right enough.

'Before we agree to anything, I want your word on a few things,' Law replies, startling me with his unexpected acquiescence.

'I'm listening,' Broden says, boredom oozing from every pore.

'I need your word that you will ensure entry for both of us into the palace during the Winter Welcome Ball tomorrow, and that you will introduce Elspeth to your mother. You will also give your word that you will not use allure on Elspeth, you will not hinder her efforts to speak with the Queen, and you will not have us removed once we have gained entry.'

'You have my word,' Broden replies.

'Say it,' Law prompts, irritation escaping around his words.

Broden rolls his eyes, but dutifully repeats in monotone, 'I will ensure entry for each of you into the palace during the Winter Welcome Ball tomorrow, and I will introduce Elspeth to my mother. I will not use allure on Elspeth, I will not hinder her efforts to speak with the Queen, and I will not have you removed once you have gained entry.' He brushes an invisible speck of dirt from his shirt, muttering, 'It's as if you have some reason not to trust me, Law.'

Law's expression is as taught as his tone. 'I can't imagine what that might be.'

Neither male elaborates as I glance at each of them in turn. Wanting this awkward encounter to be over, I prompt, 'The plan for tomorrow, then?'

'Meet me at the main palace gates tomorrow at eight. I will escort you inside, where you will gain an audience with my mother.'

'Fine,' I say. With a mockery of a smile, I add, 'I look forward to it.' Once again, I celebrate the fact that while fae are bound to the truth, I can tell as many bald-faced lies as I like. Broden's sour expression suggests he knows exactly how sincere my comment had been. *Fuck you*, my face says, while my lips offer up, 'Goodbye Broden, it's been an absolute pleasure.'

Broden turns on his heel, throwing over his shoulder, 'Tomorrow, eight o'clock. Don't be late.'

I wait until he is out of earshot, then round on Law. 'Why is he helping us? I don't understand.'

Law rubs his jaw, an inky swirl curving thoughtfully over the back of his hand. 'I'm not entirely sure. Did you tell him Hester is your mother?'

Sheepishly, I nod. While I know I had no control over the matter, I still feel weak for letting Broden manipulate me.

'It could be that.' Law's tone is questioning, uncertain. 'As Sydok said, your mother and the Queen are close. Maybe Broden thinks that bringing you and your mother together will frustrate the Queen.'

'Why would our meeting frustrate the Queen? And why on earth would he want to *frustrate* her anyway?'

'Beatrix is known to be... possessive,' Law says, before moving on quickly. 'And Broden and the Queen are always at odds. The animosity between them is something of a poorly kept secret at court. It's widely known their relationship is far from loving. I'm quite sure he longs for the day when she will hang up her crown.'

'You mean abdicate?' I ask, wondering whether royal succession works the same way here as it does at home.

'Yes, one day, the Queen will abdicate,' Law says, gesturing to a passing server to bring us two more drinks. 'We fae are not immortal, but we are extremely long-lived. Royals in power may choose to abdicate when they have achieved all they hope to achieve, when they feel their successor is ready, or simply when they have had enough of ruling. When Beatrix chooses to abdicate, assuming she doesn't die first, the crown will pass to Broden.'

I don't like to think what might happen to Faerie with Broden at the helm. I say as much to Law, but he only laughs wearily.

'Broden is no worse and no better than Beatrix,' he says, before thanking the server and handing me my drink.

I am unsure what to make of this, but understanding his exasperation at decisions made by the crown, I decide to set it aside. We have a plan in place for tomorrow, and there is no point worrying over what may or may not happen before then.

Sipping my drink, I savour the tart sweetness and tickle of bubbles, my gaze drifting to the dancefloor. Brows zipping together, I consider just how deeply Broden must have absorbed my attention. Somehow, the scene before me is even more debauched than it had been earlier. I'd been thinking of Law's promise of a dance, but I see now there is not much *dancing* going on.

Plenty of writhing, though.

Plenty of body parts being thrust into an assortment of orifices.

There are blindfolds and ropes being used to distract and withhold, whips and chains being used to punish and titillate.

But no dancing. Definitely no dancing.

I think of the intimacies I'd witnessed as we left the wedding. 'Do all fae gatherings end in a mass release of bodily fluids?'

'One way or another,' Law muses. 'We won't see anything like this at tomorrow's ball, though. The Queen wouldn't want to dirty her floors.'

Chuckling, I say, 'Do you mind if we get out of here?'

'More than happy to.' He throws back his drink and offers me his arm.

I look around, trying to find Struan so we can let him know we're leaving. I cannot see him, and my attention snags on Law's face instead. He looks tired. Edgy. Putting it down to our messy interaction with Broden, I link my arm in his and let him guide me out of the ballroom, that ridiculously large and exquisitely comfortable bed calling to me.

Chapter 25

Heart punching in my chest, I wake abruptly, gaze sweeping the unfamiliar room for any sign of danger. It takes a long moment for me to remember where I am, and to realise that whatever peril had crept through my dreams and woken me, had not followed me into wakefulness.

After our swift exit from the party, Law and I had retreated to our room and fallen into bed, too exhausted to even bother closing the curtains. Now, moonlight spills through expansive panes of smoky grey glass, washing the room in pale silver.

Tucked against Law's chest, I relish the solid warmth of him at my back. Surrounded by the lingering panic left by my unremembered dream, I try to focus on his arm wrapped over me, on each steady inhale and exhale, his breathing relaxed and smooth in sleep.

Gradually my heartbeat slows, that surge of adrenaline leaching out of me, until all that's left is a determined restlessness that lets me know sleep will not be returning any time soon. Of course, it takes no time at all for my mind to decide these quiet moments are ideally suited to replaying over and over the events of the past few days in Faerie.

During the bright hours of daylight, I have always found optimism, hope, confidence much easier to come by. While life seems to have taken pains to throw challenges my way, I still push to see the brighter side of things, to not let those challenges break me. To come out on the other side and look back on how it has made me stronger. I pride myself on my pragmatism, on my ability to put things behind me and keep moving forward. You can't face new challenges when you're looking back over your shoulder at the last one, after all.

So, I keep busy, I keep moving forward.

But when those daylight hours fade and the quiet, dark hours of night slide in, there is nothing to keep me busy, nothing to keep my mind occupied. I can't move forward when I am lying alone in the dark. That's when my doubts creep in, when negative thoughts find a way to make me doubt myself, doubt my choices.

As I replay my conversation with Broden, silently wincing at all those details I so happily provided, I wonder what I could have done differently. Whether there might have been a way I could have stopped him from so effortlessly invading my mind. If I'd had more control over my magic, would I have been able to block him out? Law had seemed not at all worried Broden would use his powers on him, so perhaps there is a way to shield oneself from that kind of magic. If there is, I will have to learn it. I never want to feel that vulnerable again.

Thinking over everything I revealed to Broden, I keep coming back to one thing. Nicnevin. Broden had asked why she would help me. In my desire to divulge every single detail, I had regurgitated what I remembered of Nicnevin's own response to that question.

While at the time, my mind had still been somewhat foggy, I recall something about her feeling responsible for me. Is that right? Is that how she had worded it?

While I'd been suspicious at the time, I had fallen back on my pragmatism. I had regretfully concluded I would likely struggle to make it to the Queen's palace on my own, and Nicnevin provided a solution: Law. Not ideal, but I had tried to protect myself as best I could, by obtaining his word that he would not harm me on our journey. Both he and Nicnevin had seemed happy enough with this, so we made our deal, and Law and I had set off on this grand adventure.

While my suspicion over Nicnevin's motives had ticked through my mind from time to time since then, there had been far more pressing concerns to occupy my attention. My worry over Agnes and my desire to get the answers I need from the Queen to help her. My deepening attraction to Law and that strangely magnetic pull I feel growing stronger with each passing hour. My shock at finding out my mother is fae, that I am half-fae, and that not only do I have magic, but I will need to learn to use it if I want to keep myself safe in Faerie. Where so many things seem to want to eat me or murder me or use me.

Had Nicnevin's motivation been to use me? What could she want from me? What could she hope to gain from helping me? Wracking my brain, I can't come up with anything solid, anything with enough weight to make it worth her while. There is absolutely no way she would have helped me out of the goodness of her heart. I doubt Nicnevin even has a heart, and if she does, that ancient, shrivelled thing would certainly not be pumped full of goodness.

I go over it again and again, my thoughts spiralling, making the rest of me feel as restless as my mind.

Roused perhaps by the furious turmoil of my thoughts – or more likely, by the agitated twitching of my limbs – Law stirs behind me. His sleepy sigh tickles the back of my neck, and his arm tugs my body closer to his.

I am abruptly much more aware of where his skin touches mine, of the hard panels of his chest pressing against my back, of his lean, powerful thighs tucked up against my own.

I want to get out of my own head, but much more than that, I want to indulge that pull towards him. To feel him, to know him. I want to let go, to let everything go so I can keep moving forward. With Law.

This may be a job for him, but while I cannot comprehend Nicnevin's motivation for sending him, I am certain that for Law, this is more than just a job. I can't help but believe he feels something for me in return.

If the presence of his hard length pressed against my back tells me anything, I know he certainly feels that for me. I let out a soft sigh as he kisses the back of my neck. Then, just as it had when we'd woken tucked together in the woods, his hand brushes my stomach, seeking its way lower.

This time I do nothing to interrupt its progress.

Savouring the sensuous sensation that comes from feeling skin against skin, I drag in a sharp breath as his hand sweeps lazy strokes beneath the band of my silk knickers, drawing my muscles taut with each pass that caresses lower, ever lower. Parting my thighs to allow him access, a heady wave of arousal careens over me as those lazy strokes drift to the very centre of me.

Feeling my wetness, my desire for him, Law exhales a low groan.

'You're so wet for me, Elspeth,' he murmurs, his words brushing dark velvet yearning over my skin. 'I love the way you feel.' His tongue trails the shell of my ear. 'I love the way you taste.' A whimpered moan flies from my lips as those deft fingers of his move to touch, to tease, to caress. 'I love the way you sound.'

Mesmerised by his soft words, by the hunger in them, in his touch, the pressure inside me builds rapidly. My need for him nearly overwhelming me, that tightness coils inside me, all too eager to find its release. Almost embarrassingly quickly, I am at that exquisite precipice of pleasure, breath held, every muscle tensed. Silken words of desire at my ear and skilful strokes at my core balance me there, before tipping me over the edge.

Mind scattered, I am left panting, but in no way sated. My desire is too great for that. I want more. I want Law. I want to feel him inside me.

Turning to face him, I reach out my hand to cup his jaw and move in to touch my lips against his. It is a gentle touch at first, a warm brush of skin against skin. But feeling his body so close to mine, knowing its potential, I can't hold back for long. I deepen the kiss, drawing my body closer to his, sweeping my leg over his hip. Law lets out another rough groan and wraps his arm around my back, closing the remaining distance between our bodies so that the only thing between us is a thin layer of silk. With the hard press of him now impossible to ignore, that urgent need for him becomes even more demanding.

I push him onto his back and straddle him, relishing the way his hard cock now presses perfectly against my centre. Rolling my hips to heighten my pleasure, I look down at him lying beneath me, a snap of desire hitting me low in the belly. Black hair ruffled from sleep, he stares back at me with a shameless gaze glittering with an urgency that matches my own.

'Beautiful,' I breathe, running my hands over the carved muscle of his stomach up to his chest. I luxuriate in the feel of him, savouring the way those shadows follow my touch, how they reach out only to me.

One side of his mouth kicks up in a smile, making my heart stutter. 'That's supposed to be my line.'

I pull the silk camisole over my head, discarding it carelessly while Law's gaze trails over my body. I shiver as his touch follows in its wake. Rocking my hips, my arousal notches upward as his hands skim the curve of my breasts, lingering on the peaked bud of my nipples, before sweeping down over the sensitive skin at my waist and settling on my hips. His firm grip there tells me of his impatience, of his need to feel more of me, in the same way I need to feel more of him. Right now, though, he seems willing to let me take the lead, perhaps making sure this is really what I want.

This is really what I want.

Reaching between us to slip the fabric of my knickers to one side, I lift my hips and guide him to my entrance. I take him in slowly, adjusting to accommodate the impressive length of him. While I had been hesitant upon seeing that length uncovered at the river, now, all I feel is the rightness of it as I sink down onto it.

Once I am fully seated, I stop for a moment, loving how complete I feel, how full. Realising I've kept my eyes closed to focus solely on sensation, I open them now, finding Law's eyes searching my face. I let my mouth curl into a satisfied smile.

'You're magnificent,' he responds, giving me a sensuous grin of his own. 'You feel–'

Tightening the muscles within me, I steal his words, taking no small amount of pleasure in seeing that grin transform into an expression of lust, of need, of want.

'I feel?' I prompt teasingly, playing his game from the river against him.

'So...' he hums, an uneven sigh escaping him as I swirl my hips, 'fucking...' I lift them and sink back down, somehow deeper than before, 'good.'

I can't help but agree as I begin to rock my hips.

'Just good?' I mock.

'More than good,' he says sombrely, his tone at odds with the taunting flicker in his eyes. His hips thrust upwards, appropriating both my breath and my intended reply. 'Perfect.'

I sigh, letting his words trail over me, savouring that delicious feeling of fullness. My hips rock, heightening my pleasure. Law's hands grasp them, urging my movements on, while still letting me take the lead.

But that's not what I want.

Leaning down, I graze my teeth against his ear and whisper a challenge, 'Alright then, let's see what you've got.'

In the space between heartbeats, I am on my back, my knickers gone. Pinned beneath him, I look up at Law and absorb the intensity of his gaze. Playfulness banished, all it contains is the barely restrained need he seems to have kept on a tight leash up to now. At my challenge, he finally seems willing to let that leash loose.

Good. That is what I want.

Drawing himself out until only the tip of him remains inside me, he locks his charcoal eyes on mine and drives into me. Losing him, then feeling his return pushed all the way to the hilt, I can't help but gasp at the intense rush of pleasure, lined as it is with the most exquisite edge of pain.

He pauses there, waiting, gauging my reaction.

'More,' I breathe.

He draws out just as fully, then drives into me.

Pausing there again, he drags his gaze down my body to where we are joined. 'I love the way you take me.' His cock twitches inside me. 'You feel perfect. You are perfect.'

My mindless response is lost to the darkness surrounding us as he plunges into me again. And again. And again. I writhe against the sensation of it, of having him, then not having him, of feeling him fill me up completely and then withdraw. I smother a scream as that coiling pressure swells inside me.

Seeming to sense this, Law slows his pace, bringing his body closer and murmuring against my ear, 'Not yet, beautiful. You will come for me again.' He bites my earlobe. 'But not yet.'

As my mind tumbles, he moves on to use his mouth to tease each of my most sensitive parts in turn. His touch lights up my ear, my neck, my wrist, my nipple. As he works his tongue, his hips keep a steady rhythm, no longer driving into me but keeping me on the edge. I grip his shoulders, curving my hands round to his back, marvelling at the way the hard muscle there moves under his skin. At all that power within him that's entirely focused on me. On my pleasure.

I catch his chin and draw him in for a kiss, loving the way his tongue sweeps inside my mouth as his cock surges in and up to what feels like the very centre of my being. I am filled up with Law and it is as incredible as I had ever dared to imagine.

Pushing himself up, he draws back and cages me with his arms. Worlds away from the way Malcom made me feel when he'd done the same, I take the opportunity to admire his broad shoulders, his gorgeously defined chest, his abdominal muscles that carve down to a V, pointing to the part of him that is currently providing me so much pleasure. I allow my gaze to trail down that V, my arousal increasing at the sight of him sliding in and out of me, adding to that steady build of pressure gathering low in my belly.

My eyes flutter closed, savouring the sensation.

'Eyes on me,' Law says, hitching one of my legs up over his shoulder.

Remembering his promise that I would want my eyes open and on him when he had his wicked way with me, my gaze finds his, grey gleaming in the shadows, heady desire lining his features. I gasp as he drives harder, at the dizzying sensation delivered by the deeper angle of his thrusts. He moves one hand to stroke my centre, and that pressure inside me coils ever tighter.

Knowing Law has one hand propped beside my shoulder and the other working its own kind of magic at my core, I'm momentarily distracted from just how fucking good it feels when a soft caress brushes against my stomach. Startling slightly, I look down to see an inky shadow shifting over me, kissing my skin with the lightest of touches. I draw my eyes up to Law's, and see the question within them.

'Yes,' I answer. 'Fuck, yes.'

Law's response is immediate. More shadows curl in closer, skimming over every part of me, caressing my body like silk. Shadows curve against my neck, trail down my inner thigh and across my breasts, the sensation so utterly exquisite I wonder whether I might just pass out rather than climax.

My hands gripping the sheets, Law drives harder, faster, his hand moving to keep pace as shadows curl and twist against my skin. The coiled tension inside me keeps building, building, pushing me right to the edge, where I hold onto that decadent sense of anticipation.

'Come for me, beautiful.'

At his words, I let go, plunging over the edge and into the abyss.

Breathing hard, pleasure sparkling through me, I open my eyes and see Law is close now too. Focus draws his brows together in a tight frown as he pulls back into a kneeling position and throws my other leg over his shoulder, plunging into me faster, harder, deeper. Each time he drives in, a rough, breathy moan escapes me, which Law responds to with a hoarse moan of his own. Again and again, he thrusts into me, returning to me that same coiling pressure deep down in my belly.

Fucking hell. Surely not again?

But I have no more time to think, distracted as I am by Law's hips moving in jerky thrusts, somehow driving deeper, filling me up, driving, driving, driving, before his body tenses violently. Head thrown back, darkness explodes from him, forcing back the pale wash of moonlight and drenching the room in inky black. Throbbing, pulsing, his explosive release detonates inside me, sending me crashing over the edge for a third, mind-shattering time.

Heart hammering, sweat cooling on my skin, it is some moments before I eventually come back to myself. With the room still entirely black, I can't see Law, but I hear his breathing coming fast and hard above me.

'Law?'

I slide my legs off his shoulders to rest at his hips, and reach a hand to his chest, feeling his heart thundering just as hard as mine. Slowly the darkness creeps back, shadows receding so that I can see him again, soaked in moonlight and utterly breathtaking. I curve another smile at him, expecting him to offer one of his own in return.

Instead, he leans down, gifting me the most heartbreakingly tender kiss, it almost makes me want to cry.

'Hey Law,' I breathe against his lips.

'Hey Red,' he breathes back, then grants me another heartrending kiss.

Chapter 26

As the darkest hours edge towards dawn, I wrap myself closely around Law, drifting in and out of sleep. Feeling the rise and fall of his breath, his heartbeat against my ear, I know he is awake. Know that something is on his mind. Outwardly relaxed, it's the shadows shifting over his skin that give him away.

Turning my head to kiss his chest, I look up at him. Eyes open, he stares up at the canopy above our bed, seeing it but seeming a hundred miles away.

'Thinking about tonight?' I ask, voice soft, not wanting to disturb the darkness surrounding us. While sleep had touched me, it had been light, fleeting, leaving me plenty of time to consider what might await us when we finally reach the palace.

'Among other things,' Law replies in equally hushed tones.

'Anything you want to talk about?' I ask, not liking the lines of tension bracketing his mouth.

Law pauses, considering. Feeling the moment stretch, I'm unsure whether he will answer. Whether he will brush aside whatever he is thinking about and come out with something light, distracting, to sweep away my concern.

Instead, he takes a deep breath and begins to talk.

'At the bothy, after Rivena, I told you some of my past, a sketched outline of it, at least. You deserve more than that, though. This thing between us, I feel it, it's... powerful. But I don't want it clouding your judgment. It's not fair to you, allowing you to follow that pull, without knowing more of what you're being pulled towards.'

As much as I've been longing to hear Law talk about himself, his past, to understand what makes Law, Law, my heart clenches at the sadness in his soft words. Like he is getting ready to say goodbye.

'Law, I told you. I see you. What I see of you is good. Our past doesn't define us. We learn from it and keep on moving forward.'

'But I cannot move forward,' he sighs. 'Not when my past continues to wrap itself around me. It ties me up and keeps me living a life I yearn to leave behind.'

'You mean Nicnevin? This hold she has over you?' I still don't understand that hold, the scope of it, how it works. I need to know more if I'm to help Law escape it.

'Yes,' he says, before pausing again, considering his next words. Gently, he rolls out from under me, leaning his back against the headboard and setting his elbows over bent knees. I pull myself up too, tucking my legs under me as I sit close, curled towards him so I can study his face.

'My working for Nicnevin wasn't always coerced. I chose to work for her. I delighted in carrying out the tasks she set for me. I thrilled at their violence, the power it gave me. Growing up, I'd always felt a darkness inside me. I don't know if it was my connection with

Nether, but as I grew older, the need to release that darkness grew stronger. More intense.

'When Nicnevin and I crossed paths, I think she must have sensed that darkness, my need to use it, to wield it. She said she had a job... a contract for me, that she would make it worth my while. But from that very first one, it was never about the coin for me. I would have done it simply for the way it made me feel.'

Tension radiates through his body, his hands clenching into fists in front of him. 'Killing someone should be hard. You felt it, with Rivena, I know you did.' He glances at me, then his attention shifts away, focusing on the shadows instead. 'It was written all over you, despite the necessity behind her death. For me, killing wasn't hard. It wasn't anything. Using my power though, feeling the release of that darkness inside me, that was everything. That was a rush I couldn't stay away from. After every contract I carried out, I wanted more. It was... an addiction.'

Remaining silent beside him, I let Law talk. This is a truth he needs to tell, and he's right, it is a truth I need to hear.

'That is until I was tasked with ending Eachlair Ürlar. I don't know the reason behind Nicnevin's request. I didn't ask, I never did. The what and why of it didn't interest me. That was Nicnevin's business.'

He exhales heavily, his pulse beating visibly at his throat. 'The leadup was the same as any other contract. I scoped out my target, decided on the best way to access her. I knew she was powerful, so it would be best to catch her off-guard. As it turned out, she was far harder to catch off-guard than I had anticipated. She was waiting for me and knew exactly why I was there. She took me down hard. I'd never felt power like it. But even that did not take the thrill out of it for me. The challenge only made it more enticing. She took me down again and again, until eventually, I knew it was over. She had me. I assumed she would kill me. I would have done the same in her place, obviously.'

He unclenches his fists and runs a hand through his hair. 'Except she didn't. She told me she had something else in mind. Killing me would be too easy. She wanted to know that I would suffer. To endure that same pain I had caused so many others. She cursed me to feel the pain of those I hurt, to feel what they feel. Their terror, their helplessness, their agony.

'Afterwards, I wasn't even sure the curse had worked. I didn't feel any different. I still felt that darkness inside me, the desire to let it out. So, I took another contract from Nicnevin. I was cautious about it, but I supposed, maybe the curse wouldn't be that bad. I thought that maybe I could still glory in that release of darkness I craved so much, while putting up with whatever the curse gave in return.'

He breathes out the softest of laughs, a bleak smile brushing his face with shame. 'I was wrong. So very wrong. It was excruciating. I felt it all, everything Eachlair Ürlar said I would feel. The fae I was sent to kill, I felt his tortured vulnerability at seeing me, knowing he was powerless to stop me. I felt his mindless terror and his agony as I ended him. It surrounded me, enfolded me, took me over.

'I had never seen that when I killed before. I had never thought past the incredible rush I felt releasing that darkness. The way it made me feel.'

He turns to me, expression hard. 'You asked me once which court I belong to. It's true, I am now courtless. But once, I was Unseelie. I was one of those fae uninterested in restraining my wilder instincts. It's how I was raised, how all Unseelie are raised. We are taught to indulge those instincts, to follow our desires, no matter how debauched. I felt that darkness, that desire, so I let it roam free, I followed it where it took me. I grew up surrounded by those who did the same. We did what we wanted and cared little for whoever got hurt along the way. The strong survive. The same principle applies to Seelie, they just go about it in a different way.'

He turns to me again, his features grim now, imploring. 'I'm not telling you this to excuse my actions, nothing can do that. I'm only trying to explain to you the world in which they were nurtured. The party last night? That was nothing, just sex. All fae enjoy sex. Like Struan said, he altered what was on offer as a favour to me. You don't need to experience a true Unseelie party. With you being human – even part-human – it would not have been... safe.'

Taking another deep breath, he continues. 'So, there I was, feeling everything, experiencing everything, being on the receiving end of all that pain and suffering I had so long doled out. Needless to say, it changed my attitude somewhat.

'After that, I took some time away. I holed up and considered my life, such as it was. Whether it was worth continuing. My entire existence had been centred around finding new ways to release my darkness and heighten that rush. But the only way to do that was to hurt others. I didn't want to hurt anyone anymore. Feeling their terror, their torment, how could I possibly put anyone through that again? But if I wasn't me, who was I?'

Law closes his eyes, rolling his head side to side, seeming to want to release the tension I can see so clearly within him.

'It was Florie who pulled me back.' The smallest of smiles touches his lips as he says her name. 'Florie was never like me. She never had that darkness inside her. Yes, she knew how to raise hell, but she never revelled in the suffering of others. She found me and I explained everything that had happened, poured out everything I was feeling. She didn't try to sugarcoat it, didn't try to make me feel better. She basically said the same thing as you: learn from it, move on, do better. And with her help, I did.'

I break my silence, offering up a small smile of my own. 'She does sound very wise.'

Law's grey gaze shifts back to me, eyes warm. 'Indeed. I think you'd like her. I think she'd like you.'

Encouraging him to continue, I reach out to take his hand in mine. He allows it, staring down at our clasped hands as he goes on. 'It was hard. Extremely hard, I'm not going to lie. But I worked every day at pushing down that darkness, making it smaller so that it no longer had such a hold on me. Eventually, I felt strong enough to return to Nicnevin, to tell her I would no longer work for her. As you can imagine, she was not best pleased. I had carried out the dirtiest of her dirty work and now she would have to find someone else interested in the task.' He sighs deeply. 'Except that she didn't.'

'What? Why?' I ask.

'Florie,' he replies. I'm just about to ask what he means by that, when he sucks in another deep breath and continues. 'Not long after I told Nicnevin to find another lackey, Florie was attacked. Badly. Every healer I took her to told me there was nothing they could do, that she wouldn't survive. But she had to survive. She was my baby sister. I had to do whatever I could to save her. So, I took her to Nicnevin.'

At my questioning look, Law explains, 'Nicnevin is a necromancer. She deals in the dead. While her magic is... wide-ranging, one of the things she can do is converse with Death. Death's decision is absolute; once you're dead, you're dead. But, if you know the right way to talk to him, you may be able to persuade him to wait a little while before he takes a certain soul. Or take one earlier, should the occasion call for it.'

I startle at this. I know Law cannot lie, but I had still not entirely believed him at the wedding when he said he'd met the Grim Reaper.

'I asked Nicnevin to treat with Death on my behalf, to ask him to spare Florie. Which she did. But not without first demanding something in return.'

I think I know what that something might be. 'You,' I say.

'Me,' Law confirms. 'In return for her saving Florie from Death, I was to continue in her service. While she initially pushed for unending service, we negotiated. I would be bound to carry out a specified number of contracts before gaining my freedom. Knowing what those contracts would entail, I knew I could not survive if I were to be forced to carry them out indefinitely. I would have preferred Death to take Florie and me both. But with a limited number to deal with, I could endure that. For Florie.'

Law's hand slips from my grasp. He scrubs his face, his mouth a tight line. 'I'm aware it's not right. In carrying out these jobs for Nicnevin, I am essentially trading the lives of those I kill for the life of my sister. But it's the decision I made. She deserves to live.'

I choose not to say that many of those on Nicnevin's hit list probably deserve to live as well. By the tortured look on Law's face, he is well aware of that fact. Instead, I say, 'Where is Florie now? You said she was with Nicnevin.'

'That was another part of our deal. Nicnevin keeps Florie until I have completed the required number of contracts. She has put

Death on standby, as it were. Florie will remain in Nicnevin's care, held somewhere between life and death until my last contract is completed. She's in no pain, she's not aware.'

'Fuck,' I utter, unsure of what else to say. Then, taking some time to process what he has told me, a question comes to me. 'How many contracts do you have left on this agreement between you?'

'I cannot say.' Seeing my follow-up question before I ask it, he clarifies, 'It's not that I do not know, it's that I physically cannot tell you. Before sending me here with you, Nicnevin used a geas to prevent me from conveying certain details to you. She is wily, among other things. She's always thinking of every angle.'

'A gesh?' I ask, unsure of the word.

'It's a form of magical compulsion. If someone places a geas on you, you are compelled to follow whatever conditions are contained within that geas. If you fail to comply, you die.'

'Right, so. Dramatic then. What else did she forbid you from telling me?' I ask, mind spinning. Why on earth would Nicnevin not want me knowing that?

'I cannot say,' Law says, adding, 'Sorry.'

I nod. 'Can you tell me why she sent you with me?'

'No.'

'Can you tell me what she wants from me?'

'No.'

I curse again in frustration. 'Fucking magic,' I spit. 'Fucking Nicnevin.'

'I know,' he sighs. 'I've said the same thing more than a few times myself.'

A nauseating, mind-splintering thought crawls over me. 'What we have, though, that isn't part of it, is it? Did she ask you to seduce me?' I hold my breath, wanting to know the answer, but also not wanting to know the answer.

Law's features soften instantly. 'No, never. I could never fake this.' His expression turns regretful. 'I just couldn't say no to it. When I started to feel that pull, I pushed back. You don't deserve this; you deserve more than me. Much more than me. But as much as I tried to fight it, I couldn't. You kept surprising me, kept drawing me in. Part of it was that pull, but the rest was all you. You're incredible. You keep taking everything Faerie throws at you and you keep on going. You're smart, you're brave, you're good.'

I have never been good at taking compliments, though. I suddenly don't know what to do with my hands, where to look. Instead of looking at Law, I stare out the wall of windows. See that dawn is breaking.

Law gently draws my chin so that I have no other option but to look at him, to take in his earnest expression. 'You are too good for me, Elspeth. But I am not good enough to give you up.'

I have no words. I need time to process everything he has told me, to go over it all in my own time and come up with my own questions. Hopefully ones he is able to answer. Beyond that, though, there is one thing I know without doubt.

I am not willing to give him up either.

Climbing into his lap, I rest my head on his chest, and as his arms circle me, everything else slips away, so that all I can feel is the way he pulls me close and holds on like he will never let go.

Chapter 27

Despite my spiralling thoughts, I manage a few more hours of sleep before I have to drag myself from bed. Making use of Struan's lavish bathroom facilities, I wash and make myself presentable. Pulling on my dress, I am almost sad to say goodbye to all the opulent silks Struan so kindly provided. I shake my head, chiding myself for such indulgence, before putting on my cloak and swinging my pack over my shoulder.

Making our way downstairs, Law and I see plenty of fae passed out in varying stages of undress, but no Struan. Law leaves me in the sitting room, stepping through shadows to search the rest of the house for him, returning a few moments later.

'I found him,' he says. 'But he wasn't what you'd call suitable company. Or in suitable company, either. He passes on his greetings, such as they were, and told me to tell you that he hopes to see you again soon.'

'His night must have been a success,' I suggest.

'Something like that,' Law returns, tone grim. He heads for the foyer and holds the door open for me to step through.

'What was it that he needed your help with? I forgot to ask you last night.'

'It's probably best you don't know the details,' he says, tone not any lighter.

'Ah,' I reply, getting a strong sense that it would be best to talk of something else. As we start down the path that will lead us out of Struan's estate, I consider another question about last night my mind had tripped over.

'Broden,' I start, not entirely sure talking about the prince will improve Law's mood, but needing to know, nonetheless. 'What was he doing there last night? He is a Seelie prince. Why would a Seelie prince attend an Unseelie party?'

'For the same reason anyone attends an Unseelie party,' Law says. 'For the entertainment.'

'But I thought Unseelie parties were all about debauchery. And the Seelie are all about... *not* debauchery.' I stumble over my wording, unable to come up with an appropriate converse to debauchery. Can one be undebauched? That doesn't sound right.

Law arches a brow at me, smiling. 'Like I said, not all Seelie are as restrained as the Queen would like to think. Her son, especially.'

I mull that over. I'm not particularly surprised. 'One more question about Broden, then I'm done.'

Law nods at me to continue.

'How does he have mind magic? I thought you said fae magic is usually elemental.' I simply cannot work out how manipulation over the mind could tie back to any of the four elements.

'Typically, yes. But there are exceptions. Us, for example. We are anomalies, just as the royals are. Each member of the royal line is gifted with some degree of mind magic. Broden, as you experienced, specialises in allure, altering emotions. Beatrix specialises in telekinesis, although as Queen, her magic is more multi-faceted. Having the crown gives her access to more power, meaning she can do a lot more than simply move things with her mind.'

'That's mildly terrifying,' I say.

'So is she,' Law replies. Reaching into a pocket of shadow at his side, he pulls out two large packages and hands one to me. It's warm and it smells heavenly. 'I scrounged these from the kitchens,' he says, unwrapping his package to reveal two thick slices of freshly baked bread, in between which are layers of crispy bacon and fried egg.

My mouth instantly fills with saliva. Realising I am absolutely done with stale bannock, chewy haggis, and tough pieces of dried fruit, I follow Law's lead, unwrapping my own package and taking an enormous bite. I almost moan with pleasure.

'What happened to your vow to not eat Faerie's food?' Even though he says it around a mouthful of bacon, I hear his teasing tone plain enough.

'Fuck it,' I say, delighting in the smoky, greasy taste as I take another huge bite.

Law lets out a loud laugh, then takes another bite of his own.

'After all we've been through, I think I trust you enough to know you're not going to enchant me with food.'

'True,' he says lightly. 'I've found other ways to enchant you.' His grin is as sinful as the glint in his eye.

My mind races back to earlier this morning, to what he had done to me with his hands, his tongue... his shadows. I shiver. He's not wrong. Still, I don't need to stroke his ego by confirming it. I have a feeling he knows exactly how skilled he is.

Finishing my sandwich, I fold up the wrapper and tuck it in my pocket, where I discover the rowan ward I'd hidden there before leaving home. Amazingly it is still there, after all we've been through. I pull it out, inspecting it.

'How do you feel about rowan?' I ask, wondering if Law will have the same reaction to it as iron.

'Mostly indifferent, why?' He takes the ward from me to examine it more closely.

'It's supposed to offer protection against magic cast by faeries,' I muse.

'I hope no one's staked their life on that,' he says, twisting a spiral of shadow around it before handing it back to me.

'What about oatmeal?' I ask.

'What about oatmeal?' he replies.

'Some people put oatmeal in their pockets to protect themselves from fae.'

'That's ridiculous,' he scoffs.

'Why is it any more ridiculous than iron?'

'I suppose,' he concedes. 'But you would have to impale me with iron to put me down. Coming into contact with it is admittedly very uncomfortable, but I can't imagine a pocket full of oatmeal would make me feel uncomfortable. I like oatmeal.'

Keeping a leisurely pace, the rest of the day passes by easily enough, as I pepper Law with questions and marvel as he answers every single one. While my feet hurt, while I am utterly and absolutely sick of walking, I soak in this easy time with him, letting it fill up some of those empty spaces inside me.

Late in the afternoon, the countryside recedes, making way for Paridell, the city in which the Queen's palace resides. Having visited Edinburgh on numerous occasions, I see some similarities between the two cities, but it's mostly just the bustle and noise. Paridell is remarkably cleaner for one thing. And it doesn't smell anywhere near as bad as Edinburgh, where residents cheerfully throw shit and piss out of their window to land on the street – and anyone who happens to be walking along it.

Even putting aside the dirt, the stink, the overcrowding, I have never felt comfortable being hurried along within the hustle of city life. It's too busy, too rushed for me. In that, Paridell feels the same as Edinburgh. As we are jostled along Paridell's streets, I become intimately acquainted with all manner of fae, who seem to come in all shapes, sizes and colours. Law remains unphased, but keeps a firm grip on my hand, guiding me towards the tavern where we will dress for the ball.

Making our way up the rickety tavern stairs, we arrive at our room. Sparse yet comfortable, it gives us everything we need. A washing bowl, some towels, a bed. This, I walk over to, swinging off my cloak and pack, before sitting down heavily to unlace my boots. Kicking them off, I lie back and let out a groan. I am exhausted. My feet feel like I have been walking for weeks rather than days. And it's not like I got much sleep last night.

I shimmy further up the bed so that I can lie on it fully, patting the space beside me as I look up at Law. 'Come and keep me company.'

Both dark brows rise in question.

'Not like that,' I sigh, wondering where on earth he could find the energy.

Shrugging off his own boots, he joins me on the bed, curling in behind me in what I now consider my favourite way to sleep. Breathing in the scent that now feels like home, it is only moments before I'm asleep.

It is dark when I wake, Law still tucked behind me. I startle, worried that we have missed our meeting with Broden, that I have lost my chance to speak to the Queen.

Law brushes the back of my neck with a kiss, murmuring, 'It's fine, we're not late. We still have plenty of time before we need to leave.'

I take a deep breath and allow that sudden rush of anxiety to fade. Everything is fine. We have a plan. The plan will work. I will help Agnes. And then we will work out how to help Law.

'Can we not just kill Nicnevin?' I ask.

'Hells below, Red, you woke up in a violent mood. I think I like it.' He draws my body closer to his, biting my earlobe.

'Seriously. Won't that solve your problem?'

Sighing, he says, 'I admire your reasoning, but given my propensity towards killing, do you not think I would have considered that?'

'Yes,' I huff, annoyed the answer can't just be simple for once.

'It was part of our deal. If I kill Nicnevin – or arrange her death – Florie will die as well.'

'Damnit. I'll keep thinking.'

'You do that,' he says. 'Let me know what you come up with.' Moving down from my ear, his mouth finds its way to my neck, along my shoulder, his mind obviously occupied elsewhere.

Suddenly, so is mine. Abruptly, all I can think of is the fact that not only do I *not* know what will happen at the ball, but I have no idea what will happen after. I need to return home to help Agnes.

Will Law come with me? Or will his agreement with Nicnevin make that impossible? She could easily send him away to carry out another contract and he will have no say in the matter. I might never see him again.

My heart hammers in my chest, panic washing over me as tears sting my eyes.

In a movement so fast, I have no time to track it, Law rolls me onto my back, pinning my body under his. Kissing away my tears, he doesn't ask me what's wrong, he just holds me, making me feel safe, anchoring me as my panic recedes.

'I don't want to lose you,' I whisper into his neck. Knowing there is more to this than the pull we both feel, but in no way ready to put a name to it, I say instead, 'I cannot lose you.'

Law draws back, the quiet anguish in his face telling me he feels the same. A sad smile touches his lips, and he lowers himself to brush them over my own.

'Make me forget I might lose you,' I breathe against him.

Given the way he just kissed me, I think the sex might be the same. Sad, tender, slow. But that's not what Law gives me. Knowing that's not what I need to drag my mind away from what might happen between us, he sweeps me away with the hardness of his passion. Rough, fast, and utterly mind-shattering, it makes me climax once, twice, leaving me gasping for breath.

Coming back to myself some moments later, I reach out to kiss him. 'Thank you,' I say, not for the sex, but more for knowing me well enough to give me what I'd needed.

'Any time, my love.' He is lying on his back, eyes closed, breath still coming hard.

I startle at the endearment, wondering if it had been a slip of the tongue. It's easy enough to get swept away in the wake of sex like that. Deciding to tuck it to one side, I gift him another kiss, before rising from the bed and throwing over my shoulder, 'I will hold you to that, you know.'

'I'm counting on it.'

I turn to look at him lying stretched out on the bed, and take a moment to drink in the sight of his naked body. Coiling shadows twisting over hard muscle. A face that is heart-wrenching in its beauty. Effortlessly contained power, effortlessly powerful grace. All within one male that just called me his love.

'You're staring,' he says, eyes still closed.

'I'm moving,' I reply, hurrying to the wash basin to clean myself up.

I have not yet looked in the package that holds my dress. All I know is it is purple, the colour of heather. I've not tried it on, have no idea if it fits. I just hope that mousy wee fae who made it knows his business.

Chapter 28

'That little guy really knows his business,' Law says, stepping back to admire my dress.

Using the darkened windowpane to assess the gown myself, I am apt to agree.

Exposing a lot less skin than the one I'd worn last night, it is still just as flattering. Scooped low through the neckline, it curves close within a structured bodice, cinching in my waist, while still allowing me to move without feeling restricted. From the hip, diaphanous layers float to the floor, creating a sense of movement, even as I stand still. Loose auburn waves cascade over one shoulder, complementing the colour of the dress, while exaggerating my pale skin and the green in my eyes. With no makeup or jewellery conveniently arranged on the vanity, the only other item I added to the ensemble is the dagger concealed at my thigh.

I glance at Law's reflection, and can't help but appreciate his own sleek look. Dressed in the same inky black as the coils that shift over his skin, he wears a tight-fitting black leather doublet retrieved from one of his shadowy pockets, paired with black leather trousers and a black shirt.

'Presentable enough for a royal ball?' I ask nervously, directing the question toward the mirrored windowpane. I remember how he told me appearances were everything in the Queen's court, and I am gripped by a sudden dread that I will not be allowed in. That I will be picked out as different, as something that does not belong among those polished fae with their refined grace and devastating beauty. With Law beside me, I see the disparity between us well enough.

Law turns me towards him, cupping my face in his hands. 'More than presentable.' He leans down and distracts me with another of those kisses that leaves me reeling. 'Perfect.'

As we walk Paridell's still crowded streets, I take strength from the warmth of Law's hand in mine, my mind skimming over everything I hope to achieve over the course of the evening. I push aside the factors I have no control over. What Nicnevin's motives might be, what Broden hopes to get out of this, whether I will see Law again after tonight. My mind stutters over that last one, before I firmly move that thought to the side as well. Instead, I focus my will on positive thoughts. The Queen *will* offer to help Agnes. I *will* find my mother. It *will* all go to plan.

Realising my jaw is clenched so tight my teeth hurt, I work to loosen it.

It's not long before we reach the palace gates. A crowd of elegantly dressed fae assemble in front of them, waiting patiently as guards check their invitations, before moving on beyond, into the palace grounds.

We stop at the edge of the crowd, and I look around for Broden, then up at the large clock that illuminates the town square. Eight o'clock. We are on time, so where is he?

Law squeezes my hand to alleviate my worry, and I shift my searching gaze up to meet his. His features are arranged in their usual relaxed manner, but still, I wonder whether there is a tightness behind his eyes. Is he as anxious about tonight as I am?

I get no more time to ponder this, as Broden is abruptly beside us. *Bells*, I think irritably, *they all need to wear fucking bells.*

'Elspeth,' Broden drawls, bowing as he sweeps up my free hand and brushes his cool lips against it. I force myself not to snap my hand back. Or slap him with it. Straightening, he releases my hand, tilting his chin in Law's direction. 'Law,' he says, his voice as cool as his lips had felt against my skin.

'Prince Broden,' Law replies tonelessly.

I glance between the two males. I can almost taste the animosity rolling off them.

One dark, one light, the difference between them is especially severe tonight. Cutting a stark silhouette against the night, Broden is dressed in a smartly tailored ivory doublet paired with a white shirt, pale blond hair flowing loose down his back. Cobalt eyes feature within his chiselled face, crowned with graceful horns that arch high above his head.

'Pleasantries accomplished,' I sigh. 'Can we go?' Not only am I keen to break the tension between Broden and Law, I also want to get on with this. To move forward.

'As you wish,' Broden says, holding out his arm.

Reluctantly, I drop Law's hand and link my other arm through Broden's. Touching him feels *wrong*.

My mind flashes to the way I'd felt as he used his magic to bend my will to suit his own. To how out of control it had made me feel. I flash back further, remembering the way Malcom had made me feel the same. While my husband had preferred to use physical over mental force to gain control over me, it had levelled me just the same, making me feel small and useless. Leaving me with that same frustrated feeling of powerlessness, of having no control over... well, anything.

Still, I have Broden's word that he will not use allure on me tonight. I have to trust that in order to get what I want.

With Law walking a few steps behind, Broden guides us toward the gates, the crowd parting before us as if compelled by some magical force. Knowing the fae prince's power, I suppose compulsion may indeed be involved. As we reach the heavily armed guards, Broden nods imperiously, and the guards let all three of us through.

I release a small sigh of relief, mentally ticking that first feat from my list. We are on palace grounds and one step closer to the Queen.

Unlike Edinburgh Castle, whose grimy stone walls sit high above the city atop the dramatic volcanic mass of Castle Hill, the Queen of Elphame's palace looks out over sprawling gardens, lush with night-flowering blooms and manicured lawns. Its vast turreted façade is made from sharply cut white stone that's almost blinding in its brightness, looking much like something out of a faerie tale, which I have to admit is apt.

Making our way along a gravel path that cuts through the grounds, we proceed in silence towards the palace's imposing doorway. With no desire to make small talk with Broden, I listen instead to passing snippets of conversation, allowing my focus to rest on the beauty of the gardens, and drinking in their delicious scent.

Upon reaching the doorway, Broden stops and turns to Law. 'This is where you leave us,' he says, derision dripping from both his regard and his words.

Law nods, as if he had expected this.

Surprise washes over me and I immediately drop Broden's arm.

Having grown so accustomed to Law's steady presence these past days, it had never been a consideration whether he would remain at my side for this. While I know Nicnevin had tasked him with escorting me to the Queen, it staggers me to think he's simply walking away now his task is accomplished.

A swirl of panic and sadness and lack of control courses through me, and instantly Law is there, taking my hands and gifting me one of his most luminous smiles.

Coiling shadows curve around my waist. 'I'll still be there, Red,' he says, glittering grey gaze focused entirely on me. 'But I can't be seen to be there with you. The Queen and I are not on the best of terms.' The tension bracketing his mouth suggests this might be something of an understatement. 'If you are to gain her assistance, I cannot be at your side when you request it.' He aims a look of barely concealed loathing towards Broden. 'Which is why I agreed to Prince Broden's offer. While his reasons remain suspect, he has promised to introduce you to the Queen, which is beyond the scope of my ability.' A certain sorrow edges his expression, before sharpening and shifting once more to Broden. 'Just know that I will be there, watching over you. Watching over *everything*.'

'What are you, some dark guardian angel, now?' Broden's air of detached boredom cracks, if only for a moment. 'Give me strength.'

Law ignores him, bending down to cup my face in his hands. He bestows upon me yet another of his mesmerising kisses, leaving the world to fall away, unheeded and unneeded. With my eyes closed, I sense rather than see the tiny blue sparks that flicker toward his touch, relishing the sharp way they spark and how it contrasts with the soft warmth of his lips.

Broden coughs pointedly and we pull apart. Instantly, I feel the loss of Law, and as he melts into shadows, I can't help but think of how the brief smile he gives me looks very much like one of goodbye.

With his hand gripping my unwilling elbow, Broden jerks my attention back to him, steering me through the doorway to the ballroom beyond. My feet hurry to keep up, and I force my focus onto where I am, toward what I am here to do.

Grand both in proportions and design, the ballroom is a space that was clearly built to impress. I crane my neck to get a better view of the soaring domed ceiling above, where sweeping panes of stained glass splash the room with colour, despite night having fallen dark and heavy outside. Framing the already crowded dancefloor, white stone walls shimmer with winter-themed decorations, below which are arranged a multitude of highly polished wooden tables laden with food. While there is no band in sight, music lilts through the air, playing a jaunty tune I can't quite place, but know I have heard before.

Continuing to take it all in, my gaze comes to rest on a raised dais at the far end of the room, where an impressively ornate throne is placed beside a smaller, but no less elaborately embellished chair. I wonder whether that's where Broden usually sits, positioned lower than his mother and scheming over new ways to *frustrate* her.

Laughing softly to myself, I search the shadows for Law. Disappointed as I am not to find him, I'm not all that surprised by my inability to spot an almost three-hundred-year-old fae who specialises in cloaking himself in darkness.

I shift my attention to Broden, and see that he, in turn, is scrutinising me. 'So, what does one usually do as one waits for the Queen's arrival?' I ask, clipping my accent so that it sounds more like his.

'One might get a drink,' he proposes, his cool expression warmed slightly by the curve of a smile.

I raise my brows, lacing my words with barely concealed contempt. 'And if one chooses not to drink in the company of those she does not trust?'

'Well, aren't you charming this evening,' he drawls back, that trace of warmth gone as quickly as it had come.

'I'm not here to charm you,' I snap. 'I'm here to speak with the Queen.'

Broden's mouth tightens to a thin line, but he doesn't respond. Instead, he signals a server to pass him two of the drinks on her tray. Pressing one of the glasses into my hands, he slides me a razorblade smile and murmurs, 'Trust me, you'll need it.'

Proud of how I manage to keep the violence I feel for this pretentious prince from spilling out into action, I turn my attention back to the room, where a flurry of activity disturbs the space around the doorway. It takes no time at all for silence to fall, weighty and reverential, the crowds drifting apart and bowing low as they make way for their Queen.

While I have grown accustomed to the beauty of the fae, nothing could have prepared me for just how lovely Beatrix is. No, lovely isn't the right word. Enchanting. Spectacular, perhaps. My mind can't seem to conjure up one word that encompasses just how startlingly beautiful she is.

Everything about her is golden, from the honeyed gold of her wavy, waist-length hair to the shimmering tones of her pale golden skin. Even the gauzy fabric skimming over her lithe body shifts through burnished shades of gold. At her wrists and throat, delicate gold chains hold tiny gems that glitter sunshine as she walks, playing the perfect complement to the intricately embellished gold crown sitting atop her head. This nestles gracefully between arched horns, which are remarkably similar to Broden's.

As captivated as I am, it takes some time for my eyes to glide from the Queen's shining beauty to her glittering entourage, which fans out behind her and holds a face that haunts my most sacred of memories.

It is my mother. She is here.

My heart beats wildly, stunned by the sight of her, and I seriously consider whether it might just burst out of my chest. Hers is a face I haven't seen in more than two decades, but I would know it anywhere. Especially since it has not changed at all in that time. I blink, concerned my eyes are playing tricks on me, then I remember. She is fae. She looks not that much older than I am now, but she has likely seen centuries come and go.

Despite that huge and terrifying strangeness, despite being faced with the undeniable truth that she is fae – a creature I thought belonged solely to myth and legend only weeks ago – all I see is my mother.

She is the one who sung me sweet lullabies as she rocked me to sleep, who wrapped me in her arms and chased away fears of monsters under the bed. She is the one who told me stories and held my hand and kissed my forehead and made me feel loved.

Seeing her now, right *there*, all the emotions I have pushed down, ignored and swept to the side return in a rush.

All the hurt, the pain, the loss of all we could have had, it very nearly overwhelms me.

I suddenly want nothing more than to run to her and feel those warm arms wrapped around me once more. I stumble forward, only to be wrenched back in place by Broden's steely grip.

'Let me go,' I snarl, trying to tear free of him.

'Not yet,' he snarls back, his grip painfully tight. Through gritted teeth, he continues, 'My mother does not like to be approached until she is seated on her throne. You will do yourself no favours by angering her with your ill manners.'

Breathing hard, I absorb his words, understanding the importance of them, but remaining infinitely furious at him. Mostly, I recognise, because he is Broden.

'Fine,' I say finally. I pull my arm away and this time he loosens his grip and lets me go.

Silently, we watch the Queen make her way to the dais, graceful steps carrying her up to stand in front of her throne. Serene in her expression, she gazes over her audience, before opening her mouth to address the hushed room.

'Thank you all for coming tonight,' she begins, her tone a bright and sunny summer's day. 'Our Winter Welcome Ball is one of my favourite events of the year. It marks the end of autumn and the gathering of our bounteous harvest, giving us the opportunity to celebrate in style as we welcome in winter.' She pauses for applause, beaming her appreciation. 'But this is not a time for speeches. It is a time for merriment! I invite you all to fill your plates high and your glasses even higher, as you welcome in another winter and celebrate with me.'

A glass appears in the Queen's hand as if from nowhere. She raises it to the crowds, who raise their own glasses in return. 'Cheers,' she offers, her golden tones rolling around the toast.

'Cheers,' the crowd replies dutifully.

Tilting my untouched drink in salute, I murmur *slàinte mhath*, hoping the words will bring me the luck I need. At my side, Broden does not return his mother's toast, but does take the opportunity to drain his drink. It's the second he's tossed back, having grabbed another during Beatrix's big entrance.

I watch as she makes herself comfortable on the throne. 'How long do we have to wait?' As desperate as I am for the Queen's help, I'm impatient now to put this meeting behind me so I can talk with my mother.

'Not long now,' Broden replies absently, swiping another drink from a passing server's tray.

'Should you be drinking so fast?'

'Who are you? My mother?' he retorts. Gaze sharp on mine, he slings back another pointedly large mouthful. 'It's a party, isn't it?'

'Whatever makes you happy, Broden,' I sigh.

'*Prince* Broden,' he prompts. 'I would appreciate it if you made even the slightest attempt to respect my station.'

'You're not *my* prince,' I say, returning my caustic focus to him. 'And after the way you acted last night, you proved you are in no way deserving of my *respect*.'

His cobalt gaze sharpens further. 'You are treading on thin ice, Elspeth Reade,' he says softly, shocking me with his knowledge of my surname. 'You are lucky I am bound by my word this evening.

I would watch the way in which you speak to me if we happen to meet again.'

A biting chill rolls off him, but sensing no tendrils of allure snaking their way through my mind, I force down my unease with a shaky breath. Hesitantly, I tear my eyes from him and shift my gaze back to the dais. Where my mother now sits on the ornately decorated smaller chair beside the Queen's throne. *What the hell?* My eyes flick to Broden, finding a satisfied smile trailing his lips. It makes me think Law may have been right about his motivations somehow involving my mother. I just can't figure out his angle.

Before I have any more time to ruminate on the matter, Broden swaps his now empty glass for another full one, then holds out his arm. 'Shall we?' he says, his tone infinitely colder now.

I cannot think of anything I would like to touch less than this appalling fae's arm, but I take it anyway, knowing the importance of propriety in situations such as this. Placing my own glass on a nearby table, I allow myself to be led forward, the crowds parting for us once again. Time stretches dizzyingly as surge after terrifying surge of emotion crashes over me, each one threatening to knock me down while I try desperately to get a handle on what I am about to do.

There is so much riding on this. I cannot fuck it up.

All too soon and not soon enough, I find myself standing in front of the Queen, and belatedly, I remember to bow, seeing Broden going through the motions of obeisance at my side. Straightening, my attention snags on my mother, whose expression remains smooth, betraying no emotion whatsoever.

I haul my gaze away, and force myself to focus on the golden royal before me. Propriety, once again, demands I act a certain way. I can't imagine the Queen would appreciate my approaching the throne, only to ignore her completely and strike up a conversation with my mother. I need to do this properly if I am to get what I want.

'Mother, may I present Elspeth Reade,' Broden's lazy drawl intones beside me.

I chance a quick glance at my mother to check for any sign of recognition.

Nothing.

I lower my gaze in what I hope is a sign of respect, managing a tight *your majesty*, before following it up with a small bob of a curtsy.

'Elspeth,' the Queen says warmly, offering another of those serene smiles when I raise my gaze to meet her cobalt one. Another feature she has passed to her son. 'May I say how lovely it is to meet you.'

'And you, your majesty,' I reply, with a touch more confidence now.

'What brings you to our little gathering?' the Queen asks, suggesting she might have the same issues with proportions as Struan. 'Could it perhaps be the charms of our compelling prince?'

I note a little less warmth in the Queen's tone when she mentions Broden. I also wonder at her use of the word *compelling*.

'As charming as Prince Broden is,' I begin, ignoring the scoff from him as he tips back his drink, 'I came to you for another reason. I came to beg a favour.'

'Oh yes, and what would that be?' Beatrix asks, shining a beatific smile my way, like she cannot imagine anything she'd like to do more than grant me a favour.

As hesitant as I am to acknowledge it, I can't help but feel there is something not quite right about all this golden serenity. It all seems a bit too... staged.

Unbidden, the memory of everything I'd pushed aside after meeting with Sydok comes rushing back. My anger at the Queen, my fury over her actions. Knowing she was central to everything I'd come to Faerie for, I'd shoved down all of those painful, negative emotions, understanding that if I didn't have her, I essentially had nothing. No one to answer my questions, no one to turn to for help.

Now, as my gaze rests dubiously on this all too bright and sunny monarch, I wonder if I had perhaps been wrong. If I should have listened to my gut instead of pushing my emotions aside. If I should have looked elsewhere for answers, found someone else who could help.

Still, I am here now. I have to ask.

'I travelled from the human realm, your majesty,' I say, rolling as much respect into my words as I can. 'My good friend, Agnes Sampson is in dire need of your aid.' Again, I glance at my mother, wanting to see if she will react to the name of the woman she'd once considered her best friend. But there is nothing. Almost vacant, her features are as smooth as glass. I frown, but quickly shift my attention back to the Queen.

'I remember Agnes,' Beatrix says. 'Part of my North Berwick coven. Dedicated witches, all.' She says this with pride, as if she is responsible for such success. Which, in a way, I suppose she is. 'What kind of trouble does she find herself in?'

I describe the situation in Scotland as best I can. How a craze for hunting witches has swept the country, leading to the deaths of so many innocent men and women. How under the allegation of witchcraft, they have been hunted, tortured, burned at the stake.

'Agnes herself was taken up,' I finish, 'Following the arrest of another in her coven, Geillis Duncan. Both of them have been imprisoned in Edinburgh. It is imperative I find some way to help them.' I honestly don't feel one way or another about Geillis Duncan, but I don't want to see her burn. If I can, I will help Geillis and Agnes both.

'I understand, child,' the Queen says thoughtfully. 'As much as I would like to help those of a coven into which I passed power, however, I'm not sure I would be quite so apt to help you.' Her warm tones cool significantly over the word *you*.

Breath hitching, my armpits prickle as a wave of shock, and what I'm certain is the Queen's power wash over me.

Calmly observing my astonishment, Beatrix continues, 'Yes, I know who you are, Elspeth Amoretta Reade. And you are *supposed* to be quite dead.'

Chapter 29

My stomach hollows out as my eyes flick from the Queen to my mother and back again. My mother remains impassive, her blank expression void of emotion. Beatrix's far too perfect features are marred by an ugly smirk.

Should I run? It certainly feels like I'm in danger.

Subtly, I touch the dagger at my thigh and make the decision to stay. While it's yet to be seen if this is, in fact, the stupidest decision I will ever make, I really do want to know what Beatrix will say next. I may be a woman grown, but as hard as my father tried, he never did manage to kill the curiosity in me.

And then there is Law. I know he is watching all of this. So, whatever *this* turns out to be, I won't be alone in dealing with the fallout. If staying here does turn out to be monumentally idiotic, I don't *want* him to charge in and rescue me. I'd like to be able to rescue myself. But, just say I can't... It's nice to know there is something dark lingering in the shadows to counter whatever this far too golden creature chooses to throw at me.

Beatrix sighs, then kindly indulges my curiosity. 'I will certainly have words with Sydok about that *oversight.*' She tsks, sounding eerily like Broden. 'It would appear she failed me when I sent her to collect your mother. I don't suppose she killed your father either, as I requested. I am quite certain she disposed of your brother. Your mother was rather distraught about that upon her return.' Both her expression and her tone suggest she thinks there is something weak, revolting even, in grieving the death of one's own child.

Beside her, my mother sits glassy and vacant, appearing entirely unmoved by Beatrix's words. I want to shake her for it. I want to shake the emotion – any emotion – out of her, for her to give any indication that the mother I knew and loved is still in there. But then, if she is still in there, how could she possibly remain at this monster's side, letting her talk about our family this way?

Does she simply not care?

Shoving aside that agony, I hiss at Broden, 'Did you know about this?'

'Actually no,' he replies airily. 'Not the finer details, anyway.' He looks around for another drink, sighing when he cannot find a server. The crowds that had parted to allow us access to the dais have long since reformed, carrying on with their celebrations, cheerfully unaware. With a martyred expression, Broden sighs again. 'But I did know who you were. And I was quite sure bringing you here would result in something... dramatic. These parties get so tedious after the first two hundred years or so.'

I have never felt like I want to stab anyone more than I want to stab Broden right now.

Instead, I grit my teeth and try a new tack. 'Mama?' I say, trying to catch her eye.

No response, not even a flicker.

This can't be normal. What the fuck is wrong with her?

'What did you do to my mother?' I ask the Queen, keeping my tone even, knowing anger has got the better of me in the past, and it likely won't get me anywhere good right now.

'She is no longer your mother,' Beatrix replies, voice as cool as Broden's now. 'She is *my* consort.'

I work very hard not to let my disgust translate to my expression. While I have no problem with my mother finding love with another woman, I have a very big problem with her loving this abhorrent individual.

'Why can't she be both?' I ask aloud, trying for diplomacy.

'Because *your mother* proved that she cannot be both,' the Queen spits. She takes a moment to visibly gather herself, then continues in a much smoother tone. 'Do you know how many times I had to have her dragged back from our borders? She did not know I had tasked Sydok with the disposal of you and your father, and she kept trying to return to you, again and again.'

While her tone makes it clear she finds this behaviour utterly repellent, something inside me cracks at her words. My mother tried to come back to me. She didn't abandon me. But what is wrong with her now?

Beatrix peers down at me with the same revulsion she had dripped over her words. With a delighted sneer, she clips out, 'So I fixed her.'

'What do you mean *fixed*?' I breathe, skin crawling.

'She was broken, so I fixed her,' she replies, her tone sing-song. 'I had all those irksome feelings she had for you, for your brother, for your father, removed.' The way she says this makes it sound like removing complicated emotions would be as easy as removing an ingrown toenail. Deliberately, her gaze shifts to my mother. 'Admittedly, she is a lot less lively these days, but the upside is, she is *mine*.' Pausing a moment, she adds, 'And she still has her uses.'

In no way ready to give up on my mother, but at a loss as to what I can possibly do to help her here – standing at the Queen's feet with only a few sparks of magic and one iron dagger at my disposal – I decide instead to uncover her plans for me.

'So, you have your consort, and I no longer have a mother. What happens now?' I'm honestly quite surprised by how confident this comes out.

Beatrix taps the arm of her throne with one long, elegant finger, taking her time to consider this. 'I am in two minds about that,' she says at last. 'To kill you or let you live…' Her glower is anything but golden. 'I've decided that despite that glimmer of power I sense in you, I do not consider you a threat. Hester is mine, there is no way for you to change that. And as much as my son might desire drama, there shall be none. Partly because you are nothing but a weak child barely worth my attention, and partly because I do not wish to give my son what he wants.' Cutting her gaze to Broden, she snaps, 'He's had far too much of that already.'

Ouch. Law had undersold it when he said Beatrix and Broden's relationship wasn't exactly loving.

I remain quiet as she goes on. 'So, Elspeth Reade, I will let you live. Consider it my gift to you at this most wonderful of celebrations. You may stay, you may drink, you may dance. And at the end of the evening, you will leave my palace and return to the human realm.' She leans forward, narrowing her eyes to continue in a low hiss. 'If you do not, if I see you again after tonight, even once, your life will be forfeit.'

Immense power pours off her and I almost stagger under the weight of it, leaving me in no doubt as to the sincerity behind her words.

I don't know what to say. Thank you doesn't seem appropriate. She quite obviously just threatened my life. And she admitted to *fixing* my mother. She also refused me the one thing I came to Faerie to find: a way to help Agnes.

Fuck. Fuck. Fuck.

Drawing on all of my reserves, I steel myself. This old bitch does not get to see me fall apart. Instead of falling apart, I bow stiffly and say, 'Understood, your majesty'.

Not waiting for Broden, I turn on my heel and push my way through the crowd, snatching a drink from a server's tray as I stalk towards one of the ballroom's many doorways.

In the shadowy hallway beyond is where Law finds me.

With my glass now as empty as I feel inside, I set it down and haul in a deep shivery breath. I know I will get through this, that I will find another way to help Agnes. That I will find a way to help my mother. I just need to keep it together for now.

I search Law's face, knowing without asking that he heard every word of my conversation with the Queen. I see my own desolation mirrored in his features, and I am reminded that I am also supposed to be helping *him*.

I need to keep it together. But I am so ready to fall apart.

Breathing deeply, I try to swallow down the tightness in my throat, the burning tears threatening to fall. One escapes regardless, rolling silently down my cheek. My eyes find Law's, and seeing his expression so filled with sadness, a sob escapes me next. Its wretchedness wrenches at the cracks tearing me so violently from within.

And I crumble.

Law catches me as I fall, gathering me up as I fall apart, wrapping me in his arms and enveloping me in a tender swathe of shadow.

I will put myself back together.

Soon.

After that, I will move forward.

Chapter 30

Gathered in Law's arms, I breathe him in and allow my mind to wander to Agnes, to all the ways she was always there for me.

When I was wee, Agnes was the one to make me laugh when the world got me down, her skilled hands ready to tend to scrapes and bruises and other childhood hurts. As I grew, she remained there, at my side, with a cup of ale and a willing ear when I needed to put the world to rights, and her healing ointments when my battered body required them.

Agnes had been there for me, a balm to my spirit and body, my only true friend. I don't know how I will help her now, but I'm sure as hell I will find a way to do so. I may not have the Queen's magic to help me, but I do have some of my own. That will have to do.

As for my mother. My mind hitches on that. Is she still in there? Had she even recognised me? I'm unsure how I can help her when I don't know how badly she is broken.

Thoughts of my mother twining through my mind, I'm certain I must be imagining her voice as it reaches out to me, little more than a whisper.

'Elspeth?' There it is again.

I pull back from Law's embrace, and turn towards the sound.

Standing some way down the hallway, my mother waits, looking uncertain, and oh so very breakable. She is dressed in a gown of the palest blue, her hair arranged in a crown around her head, its deep brown making her skin appear even fairer. Earlier, I had marvelled at how she seemed not to have aged. Now I can see that's not quite true. Faint lines mark her features, adding to her fragility, making it seem like she might crack, fracture into pieces and float away. My chest tightens painfully to see the mother I had known, who had been so strong, so steady in memory, now look so broken.

'Mama?' I whisper, keeping my voice soft, not wanting her to break apart at my words.

'My darling, beautiful girl.' Her tone is equally soft, the smile on her face agonisingly tender. 'How you've grown.'

'You remember me?' I breathe, stepping away from Law to move closer to her, keeping my movements light, terrified if I move too suddenly, I might scare this delicate creature away.

'I could never forget you. You are part of me, just as Wylyam was.' Wylyam is the name my parents had given my brother, the name that graces the small headstone I still visit so often.

'But the Queen said that... that she had removed us somehow.'

I'm still unsure how one would remove feelings, emotions. My mind snags on Broden. Before I met him, I wouldn't have believed my own emotions could have been manipulated in such a way. Had he been involved in this? Was he capable of removing emotions, in the same way as he had altered mine? But that alteration had only been temporary. At Law's demand, Broden's hold over my mind had vanished. Could he have left that compulsion there if he wanted to? My skin crawls at the thought.

'Beatrix certainly tried,' my mother sighs. Outwardly, she appears tranquil, if terribly sad. If she was once as strong and steady as I remember, the fight in her is long gone now. 'It left me... changed, empty in many ways. But you cannot remove love like that, the love you have for a life created inside you. Of course I remember you, Elspeth, my brave, curious little girl.' Her eyes brighten, the same green as my own. 'You were the light of my life. My love for you, for Wylyam, for your father, I held that in my heart, through all of Beatrix's attempts to cut it all away.'

'Then why do you stay here? With her?' I blurt, venom for the Queen staining my words.

'He knows,' she replies, glancing at Law, a soft smile touching her lips.

My gaze whips Law's way. 'What?'

Before Law has the chance to respond, my mother continues, 'He knows how magic can bind. How, even when love moves you, magic has the power to make you do things you would rather not do.'

My reeling mind careens over the fact that my mother seems to know Law, or at least, she knows of his agreement with Nicnevin, of how he kills to keep his sister from dying.

She drifts, her attention shifting from Law to me. 'Beatrix placed a geas on me that bound me to her. She tried to cut away my love for you so I could love her more. I did love her once, before I travelled to the human realm and found your father, before I created you. She wanted my love back, tried so hard to make that happen. But you cannot force love. Beatrix knows that, deep down. Which is why she compelled me to stay. I cannot leave. I am hers, until she decides I am not.'

'If she knows you do not love her, why does she keep you so close?' I can't imagine how awful life would be spending it with someone you had to compel to make them stay.

'Ego is a powerful thing, my sweet.' She hovers uncertainly, looking like she wants to reach out, to touch me, but something stays her hand. 'Beatrix is powerful too. What would it mean if she did not have the power to hold onto my love? She has made herself believe she has that love, that she gained it back when she removed all traces of others from my heart.' She pauses, hands fluttering at her sides. 'And, as she said, I have my uses. She keeps me close to make use of those.'

The Queen's words return to me. She'd said the same thing, but my mind had been in turmoil, and had skipped over the odd phrase to focus on whatever it could grasp.

'What uses?' I ask warily.

My mother's gaze finds Law's once more, then slips back to me. 'I am the Queen's shield.'

Confused, I prompt, 'What do you mean?'

'When I am with her, my power acts as a shield so no magic can touch her.'

A shield? How would that even work? Law had said some fae magic was an anomaly. Is my mother's magic an anomaly too? Is that why I am different, why I access magic through Aether?

'You were born with shield magic?' I ask.

'No,' she sighs. 'That magic was a gift. When Beatrix and I first fell in love, I felt so protective of her. I wanted to shield her from all the dangers she faced as a young queen. But what could I do with a little air magic? I wasn't particularly powerful, and I disliked feeling powerless to protect the one I loved so very, very much. So, I asked Beatrix to gift me the power to help her, to protect her. She was wary at first, she didn't want me to get hurt either. Over time, though, I wore her down, and eventually she made me her shield.'

Law's shadows curl tenderly at my back, reminding me that he is there for me, while giving me the space I need to take this in. Absently, my mind flits over all of the other times he has done this, when he has stood solidly by my side, giving me strength with his presence, but not intruding. Letting me take the lead, rather than taking over.

Warmed by those thoughts, I gently push them aside to focus on my mother, whose gaze is drifting again, seemingly lost in the past.

'Over the years, I continued to protect her, our love for one another as strong as it ever was. There was something in me, though, something that over time, grew more insistent. I wanted to know more of other worlds. Beatrix and I travelled every inch of Faerie, but she never allowed me to travel to the human realm. I don't know why. Perhaps she thought the human realm too dangerous for me. Perhaps she knew how much I would love it, and how much I would want to stay.'

Her gaze remains unfocused. It reminds me unnervingly of my father's.

'In the end, the promise of what the human realm held grew stronger than my desire to remain at Beatrix's side. So, I sneaked away, hiding any trace of where I might have gone. I left her a note begging her not to follow me. She didn't listen.'

Her eyes find mine, a keen sharpness in them now. 'When Sydok returned me, Beatrix was beyond furious. She knew my heart was no longer wholly hers. And, as she tried harder and harder to make it so, what love I had for her, waned away. Now, I mostly feel empty, trapped. I remain at her side because I am compelled to do so. I present Beatrix a shell, while I live with you, Wylyam, your father, in my heart.'

I realise tears have escaped me once more. They spill down my cheeks, hot and heavy, my heart wrenching with anguish at seeing my mother so obviously in pain.

She steps closer, seeming to float towards me on a breeze, and as she lifts one pale hand to brush away my tears, I lean into the touch and my tears fall harder. 'I'm so sorry I couldn't come back to you.' Those faint lines on her face appear to deepen, crack further. 'I tried, you have to know I tried.'

All of her pain, all of my own, is suddenly too much to bear. A wretched sound, somewhere between a sob and a scream crawls its way out of me, and then, my mother is there, wrapped around me, surrounding me with everything I remember from my childhood. Warmth, safety, love.

Long moments pass, and still I cling to her. Breathing her in, trying desperately to hold onto the shape of her in my mind, I wonder whether I imagine some of the strength I remember in her making a break for the surface.

Eventually, it is my mother who pulls back first, with me still wholly unwilling to let go. As her warmth leaves me, what remains is an even stronger determination to find a way to save her, to wrench her away from the Queen's clutches.

She takes a small step towards Law. Her breathy tone filled with warmth, she says, 'Your love for her is strong, true. I know it is hard, but take that strength and hold it close. It will make it easier for you to do what you have to do.' She reaches up to touch Law's cheek, in the same way she had touched mine, full of love, compassion. Law surprises me by closing his eyes and leaning into the touch ever so slightly.

She lowers her hand, drifting back so she can look at both of us. 'Do not be afraid of that pull you feel towards one another.' My mind stumbles, hitching over her leap from Law's love for his sister to this strange, new thing that extends between the two of us. A small smile dances on her lips. 'Trust that your magic knew what it was doing when it brought you two together.'

Utterly confused now, I stutter, 'What do you mean?'

'Magic craves balance, my sweet girl,' she replies. 'I know this is new to you, and that is my fault. I should have been there to teach you, to guide you in our ways. I should have been there to help you shape your magic, to help you understand it better. That is something you will have to figure out on your own now.' Glancing at Law, she goes on, 'Hopefully with some help along the way.'

'But what do you mean by magic craves balance?' I push.

'That pull you feel toward one another, that is your magic seeking out its opposite.' My harried mind races back to something Sydok said, about my magic recognising its opposite in Law's. That's why my magic sparks when I touch him, and presumably why the shadows on his skin reach out for me. 'Aether is drawn to Nether as its opposing force. They balance one another out.'

A rush of unease washes over me. Has everything I have felt for Law been some kind of trick? Have I somehow been brought along for the ride as my magic sought out his? Is any of it actually real? I chance a look at Law. His expression is hard, unreadable, much as it had been at Sydok's.

'Hush those panicked thoughts, Elspeth,' my mother chides, apparently having no problem reading my rattled expression. 'Magic may have brought you two together, but it cannot alter the way you feel. Whatever you feel, in your heart, that is real. Trust in it.'

Law opens his mouth, then shuts it again. Emotion wars behind his features, shadowy and uncertain. When he eventually speaks, there is a finality in his tone. 'Nether is not to be trusted. I know it to be the source of my darkness. I cannot allow it to pull Elspeth towards me.'

A much sadder smile touches my mother's lips now. 'Nether is neither good nor bad, it simply is. Just as Aether was used to create life above, Nether was used to create the worlds below. One is not better than the other. I know you struggle with holding onto that darkness of yours, but understand that its source is not Nether. I'm not sure where it came from, but I do know that.' She reaches out to place her hand on Law's chest, over his heart. 'Stop feeling so ashamed of your magic. It is not evil, nor dark, and neither are you. You allowed the darkness inside you to overcome you once, but you pushed it back. I know you will continue to do so – and that you will do what you must to gain control over your life. So you can cast aside the last of that darkness and live in the light.' She cuts her gaze to me, as if I might be that light.

'How can you be so sure?' Law pushes, echoing my thoughts. How can my mother possibly know all this?

'I have lived a long time,' she replies, something ancient flashing behind her eyes that somehow conveys the many centuries they have seen. 'You don't live as long as I have without learning a thing or two.' Her brows lift. 'Or picking up a few tricks along the way.'

Before I can truly appreciate the flicker of humour in her expression – the one I remember illuminating my childhood – it is gone, replaced by one of grim resignation.

'I must get back to the Queen,' she says. Her green gaze searches mine. 'Do as Beatrix says. Leave tonight and find a way to help Agnes. I do so wish I could help you, but I know you are capable of great things, Elspeth. You will save her.'

Eyes shining, she gives me a tight smile, then looks to Law, nods once, and turns to walk away with more purpose than I had thought her frail form capable of.

Standing there, swaying slightly, I try desperately to draw strength from her words, to force myself not to run after her and cling to her to make her stay. I take a few deep breaths to steady myself, hastily papering over the cracks inside me that seem so eager to pull me apart. Determinedly, I push down my anger for the Queen, my irritation for Broden, my anguish for my mother, and turn to find Law, once more solid and sure at my side. 'What do we do now?'

Which is when all hell breaks loose in the ballroom.

Chapter 31

'Do you trust me?' Law says.

Torn between my desire to run after my mother and the strange sharpness in Law's tone, I twist my attention away from the sounds of chaos to study his face. It is smooth, inscrutable.

'What?' I snap. 'What does that have to do with anything right now?' I am impatient. I need to know my mother is alright.

'Everything,' he says, tone far too even.

I glare at him. That smooth mask stares straight back, but there is something flickering at the edges. It is a plea, I think. To listen.

Knowing he would do the same for me, I take a breath and search my heart for the answer. Thankfully, my heart is easier to interpret than Law in this moment.

'Yes, I trust you,' I say.

Regret chases relief from those flickering edges, before that too is smoothed away. 'Remember that. Trust that I would not hurt you, or anyone else you love.'

'What the fuck, Law?' Confusion churns through my impatience now, making my words snap harder.

'I don't have time to explain,' he says, tone grim. 'It would be best for you to stay here, out of harm's way, but I know you will not, even if I ask you to. Instead, I'm going to ask that if you must follow me into the ballroom, to stick to the shadows as you did in the bothy. I can better protect you from there.'

I open my mouth to say that I don't need to be protected, just as Law leans down and brushes his lips over my forehead. He carries on quickly, his words urgent. 'Yes, I know you do not want to be protected or saved or rescued, but this is Faerie. And there is much you do not know.' Straightening, he looks me over, concern pulling his brows together. 'Do you have your dagger? Are you ready?'

I tap my thigh. 'Yes, and yes.' *I think.*

'That will have to do.'

His mouth a tight line, he grabs my hand, and I have no time to prepare before the world disappears from under me and I am wrenched into darkness. Two violent lurches carry us to a shadowed nook at the far side of the ballroom, where Law drops my hand and steps again into the midst of the crowds.

Willing myself not to vomit, I haul in deep breaths to steady my mutinous stomach, my gaze hunting the vast space around me, trying to locate the source of the uproar. Out in the hallway, the clamour of the crowds had been panicked, wild almost. I'd been expecting to find fae rioting or fleeing for the exits. Instead, they are all ominously still, inexplicably silent. I cast my eyes over those closest to me, seeing only glazed looks, vacant expressions. It's like they are mesmerised. No, that's not quite right. Enthralled. They look to be enthralled by something. Or someone.

I search beyond the crowds, and it doesn't take long to find who that someone is.

Nicnevin.

As ancient and unnerving as I remember her, Nicnevin stands alone, a broad, empty circle between her and the enthralled fae packed around her. Her attention directed towards the dais, she is muttering to herself, her gnarled fingers tapping out a rhythm at her side.

'What exactly is it that you want, Nicnevin?' The Queen's tone is bored, haughty, with no trace of that golden sunshine her words had resonated with when she earlier addressed the room. Up on the dais, she lounges on her throne, appearing entirely unphased both by Nicnevin's presence and the bizarre thrall her subjects are under.

I breathe a sigh of relief seeing my mother perched next to her, seemingly unharmed, and her blank, expressionless mask back in place. With only two guards flanking the dais, I can only assume Beatrix's calm comes from knowing she has her shield at her side.

'Your head, Beatrix,' Nicnevin rasps in reply, ceasing her muttering but continuing to tap out that same jagged rhythm. Her lips curve to reveal something that might resemble a sweet smile on any other face, but on hers, it could easily sour milk. 'Not only has it remained on that scrawny body of yours for far too long, it's also not worthy of wearing that crown.'

'*You* want to wear my crown?' The Queen touches the tangle of gold resting between her horns, a delicate sneer cast over her impeccable features. 'We've done this dance before, Nicnevin. It didn't end well for you. What has changed that makes you think you can get those twisted old hands on my crown now?'

'Well, now, that would be telling,' Nicnevin rasps back, violet eyes flashing. 'I wouldn't want to ruin the surprise.'

'Oblige me, then, with how you managed to get this far past my wards,' Beatrix says, much of the insouciant boredom within her tone falling away, replaced by an edge of annoyance.

Concealed within shadows, I observe the exchange, while continuing to scan the room for Law. Stepping in and out of darkness, he is hard to keep track of, but when I manage to catch a glimpse, his attention is focused wholly on Beatrix.

Now I know of Nicnevin's desire to remove the crown from the Queen's head – and her head from her shoulders – I have no doubt this is why she'd sent Law as my escort. She'd needed past Beatrix's wards to gain access to the palace, a feat she or Law presumably couldn't have managed alone. Somehow, she'd known I would make it past those wards just fine, bringing Law along with me.

'I had some assistance,' Nicnevin replies smugly, confirming my suspicions when her eyes flick to Law.

Beatrix follows Nicnevin's gaze to search the shadows in which Law no longer stands. She tsks her irritation and drawls, 'Marvellous effort, Nicnevin, dear. You are clearly getting better at this. You are here, and you apparently have my subjects enthralled. I fail to see what comes next, though. Even if you command every fae in here to attack me, it *will not work*. You know any kind of magical assault will be repelled by my shield.'

Well, that explains why everyone on the dais has retained control over their senses. Distracted for a moment, I wonder why *I* am not under Nicnevin's thrall. Perhaps my mother's shield extends to me somehow? Or maybe my humanity provides me immunity, in the same way iron levels full fae, but has no hold over me.

Unable to come up with an answer, I drag my focus back to Nicnevin. The Queen has her shield, as well as her own considerable magical defences. So, what is her angle? And why is she drawing this out? If this were *my* grand coup to overthrow a fae as powerful as the Queen, I'd want to get it done. I wouldn't stand there chatting about it.

I study the conniving old battleaxe, holding court within a sea of enthralled fae, and I think I have my answer.

She is enjoying this.

Seeing the wicked delight dancing behind her eyes, my stomach turns as I truly appreciate the sick, naked desire searing her expression. I don't know how she plans to take down the Queen, but judging by that gloating, exultant look on her face, she believes this battle already won. She's simply taking her time to enjoy it.

'Isn't it a pity, then, *dear*,' Nicnevin responds, rasping voice almost gleeful now, 'that you will no longer have that shield.'

Given how fast everything plays out next, I have no time to consider that, yes, Nicnevin was perhaps right to draw out her moment, as there is absolutely no opportunity for posturing in the tumult that follows.

As Nicnevin's exhilarated rasp slithers over the word *shield*, my gaze instinctively cuts to my mother. Sitting smooth and upright in her beautifully embellished chair, the nod she gives is almost imperceptible. If I had not been watching her so closely, I would most certainly have missed it. By the speed at which Law arrives at her side, it's apparent he had been watching closely as well.

My mind stutters. Law should not have been able to step into my mother's shadow with her shield in place. She must have lowered it. But why?

Before I get any more time to vacillate over this, my mother and Law vanish.

They are there one breath and gone the next, and I know without doubt that Law has stepped her somewhere. Still unsettled from my own journey through shadows, my stomach hollows out now. Law had asked if I trusted him. I said yes. Had I been too hasty? Perhaps he stepped my mother to safety, or maybe he took her somewhere to kill her. Where I wouldn't see it happen.

Only a few short hours ago, he'd admitted to a propensity towards killing.

Law is a killer.

He has killed for Nicnevin.

With Nicnevin's geas in place, he'd been unable to divulge his role in all this. What if his role involves killing my mother? Taking her out so the Queen no longer has her shield.

I shake myself. *No.*

What about that nod? My mother had nodded, presumably after she lowered her shield. It looked to be a signal.

And, in the hallway, she'd known a remarkable amount about Law. What had she said? That he knew how magic could bind. That, he understood how even when love moved you, magic had the power to make you do things you would rather not do. Had my mother known of Nicnevin's plans? That she would use her control over Law to force him to do this?

Despite knowing this, she had shown nothing but warmth for Law.

Law, the killer.

Something else she said to Law spins through my mind. She'd told him she saw the strength in his love, that he should hold onto that, as it would make it easier for him to do what he had to do.

'Any time, my love.' Law had said that. He had called me his love. Even now, I warm at the memory.

At my mother's words, I thought she'd been referring to Law's love for his sister, but could she have possibly meant his love for me?

My mind races back and forth over our exchange in the hallway, and a wave of sick, all-consuming frustration washes over me.

Fucking magic. Fucking bindings. Fucking secrets.

All I want is the truth.

Furious, I reach inside myself, searching for that truth, pressing my mind over all that's happened since I woke in Faerie. A few short days and a lifetime ago.

Every memory, every recollection; everything comes back to Law.

How he cut down Calder, Edane, Aemylia, soaking up their agony, all to keep me safe. How he guided me to Sydok, then pushed the bridge troll to anger, just so I might get a better grip on my magic. How he guided me toward that magic, calm and patient, and was so utterly delighted when I was finally able to shape it. How he bared his soul to me as he told me of his struggle with the darkness inside him. How he gifted me those heartbreakingly tender kisses and called me his love.

I recall more of my mother's words.

'Whatever you feel, in your heart, that is real. Trust in it.'

It had not been what Law told me, but what he had shown me. How he had acted. It is those actions that tell me everything I need to know. Law may be a killer, but it is not by choice. Whatever is happening now is not under his control. But he had known what was coming and had asked me to trust that he would not hurt me, or anyone else I loved.

It seems my mother had trusted Law, and I *know* now that I do too. I am certain he stepped her to safety, that she must have – somehow – known he would do so.

I wrench my attention back to the present to see Beatrix sweep her gaze over the empty chair beside her. She lets out a snarl, rounding back on Nicnevin, her perfect features distorted with fury. In one sharp, graceful movement, she rises to her feet, tearing her gaze from Nicnevin to take in the more immediate threat.

Chapter 32

Clearly still under Nicnevin's thrall, the crowds of fae surrounding the dais no longer stand in vacant, motionless silence.

Now, they attack.

Fast and brutal, they launch at the Queen.

First to reach her are her own guards, who, having been previously sheltered from Nicnevin's control by my mother's shield, are closest to Beatrix when that shield vanishes.

Despite the odds being very much stacked against her, Beatrix moves with graceful composure, sending each guard flying with a quick flick of her wrist, their bodies crumpling like paper, their armour crushed.

Knowing the Queen holds the power of telekinesis, I understand she is using that power to fend off her attackers. But seeing it in action, seeing her move objects with only her mind, my own mind struggles to keep up.

Fae after fae after fae surges at her, swinging a sword or simply swinging fists, only to be ripped apart or crushed or effortlessly flicked away like they are nothing more than dolls. Even fae who attack with magic find themselves similarly repelled, as Beatrix smoothly dispatches assaults involving air, water, earth and fire.

She is one against many, but she looks unstoppable.

I'm not sure if this is how Nicnevin imagined things going, but if this were *my* coup, I'd be leaning towards concern right now.

My eyes flick from the chaos on the dais to Nicnevin. Still muttering and tapping away, her own gaze remains fixed on Beatrix, presumably orchestrating the attack with... With what exactly? Law said she was a necromancer, but these fae aren't dead. How is she controlling them?

Well, clearly some of them *are* dead, but that had been the Queen's doing. I just hope Nicnevin doesn't reanimate them somehow to continue their attack.

For my own part in things, I choose to hang back for now, remaining concealed within shadows, as Law had requested. With him and my mother now hopefully somewhere safe, my pragmatic side assures me that remaining clear of the melee is the wisest course of action. While I feel for the fae Nicnevin is puppeteering, I know the help I could offer them is limited. As for that bitch of a Queen? I feel absolutely no desire to wade in and help *her*.

Tugging my attention back to the dais, Law steps out of the darkness, my mother no longer at his side. Shadows coiling around him, he takes a long moment to assess the Queen, appearing to weigh up her defences and the fight she has left.

Moving impossibly fast, Beatrix continues to fend off every assault, but her motions no longer hold the same fluid ease, that effortless lethality. Broken bodies piled up on all sides, she snarls frustrated rage, her movements becoming ever so slightly sluggish. She is tiring.

I can see it. Law can see it.

Those inky vines churning around him, he steps toward Beatrix in a blur, giving her no time to defend herself as his dagger arcs. But somehow, she does. With a howl of fury, she shoves one of her attackers at him, leaving him no choice but to step away. Moving at a blistering speed, he dances around her, stepping in and out of shadows, his form blurring as he tries to get close enough to attack. Every time, though, she knows just where he will step, slipping away fast enough to defend each assault. Instead of flicking Nicnevin's thralls away, she starts repurposing their bodies, using them to absorb blows meant for her, then pitching them at Law. Or where he had been only an instant before.

Nicnevin pulls back her own attack, apparently smart enough to see what she's doing is hindering Law rather than helping him. Enthralled fae retreat from the dais, leaving Law and the Queen alone, whirling around one another, attacking and parrying at a speed that is almost too fast to follow.

Using that vast, roiling power of his, Law had dispatched the baobhan-sìth and kelpie with ease, but Beatrix is proving to be a far more formidable opponent, matching both his skills and his speed, despite her growing fatigue. My mother's words return to me as I try to keep up with their movements, and I wonder how many *tricks* the Queen has picked up over the centuries. Whether Law is a match for them.

My mind focused on their fight, I almost miss the prickle at the back of my neck, the stinging sense fostered during my marriage to

Malcom that tells me someone is lingering behind me, waiting to cause me harm.

I know he is there, that someone, but I have no time to spin around before a heavy arm hooks my throat, tightening with such force, I stagger back into him. He is big; stronger and taller than I am. My mind races, telling me I won't be able to use my bodyweight to drive him into the wall behind us. So instead, I slam one boot into his instep, then throw my elbow into his torso. As his body reacts to this, I reach up and find his ear, using all my strength to tug it in a savage downward motion. The arm around my neck loosens slightly, and I make the most of the extra space between us to pitch my head back into his face, bending my knees and jerking them straight to add momentum to my movement.

With a satisfying crunch, the arm around my neck drops and I duck quickly out of range. Whirling around, I rush a few steps back, needing to put some space between us before I decide whether to run or continue to fight.

Fury slashed across his features – along with a pleasing amount of blood – Broden stands before me, weighing me up in turn.

Taller than me, heavier than me, the fae prince also has fae strength and speed on his side. But it would seem he overestimated those advantages, while underestimating me in his attack. He'd clearly not expected me to fight back, and so, had not been prepared for me to launch any kind of defence.

From the look he is giving me, I don't suppose he will make the same mistake again.

His body coils, and I anticipate his lunge, spinning to the side so he crashes past me rather than through me. He changes direction with unnerving ease, launching himself at me again, barely giving me time to weave away. Moving swiftly, he steps in closer, using his powerful upper body to send a vicious swing at my head. Just in time, I duck and spin away, landing a punch in his side as I rotate. Knowing I cannot allow him to get much closer, I'm hindered in my ability to do any real damage. I may be fast, but I am not fae fast. If I move in closer to attack, he will use his superior speed to catch my movement and do much worse to me than I could ever do to him.

Still, I am not willing to give up.

I know I got lucky with Rivena. Just as Broden had initially, Rivena underestimated me, and I'd been able to use that to catch her off-guard. She had also not been expecting to slide onto an iron dagger.

I don't know what Broden wants, whether he wants me incapacitated or dead.

Right now, I don't particularly care.

I draw my dagger from its sheath, silently thanking Law's foresight to request a slit to the thigh in the skirts of my dress. Seeing the dagger, Broden's face arches into a sneer, but he takes no time to pause before he hurls himself at me again. Spinning and weaving, I continue to remain just out of his reach, while taking every opportunity to swipe at him with my blade.

Somewhere at the back of my head, my thoughts wander to whether I could add my magic to my defence. But caught by the speed of Broden's attack, I cannot calm my mind adequately to focus on my connection. I've not had enough practise. It simply won't come fast enough.

I'm just glad Broden can't use his own magic on me. If that had been an option, this would have been over before it even began. As it is, he is bound by his word to not use allure on me. And while I am enormously grateful Law got that much out of him, right now, as my body tires, I wish his promise had encompassed all kinds of attack, physical as well as mental.

Broden comes at me, again and again. Breathing ragged, my movements slow. I don't know how much longer I can keep evading him. I spin past him, thrusting my blade at his ribs, but I am too slow. He grabs my wrist and twists it viciously, the dagger clattering to the ground out of my reach. I wrench out of his grip, but don't move fast enough to dodge his brutal uppercut. It catches me on the jaw and sends me flying.

Landing hard, I shake my head, jaw on fire, silver edging my vision. Broden launches toward me, and I scramble back, but careen into a table before I can find my feet. He snatches my arms and hauls me upward, spinning me away from him before I have the chance to strike out. Locking one arm around my neck, he wraps his other around my body to trap my arms at my sides, pinning me tightly against him and lifting me off the ground. I struggle in vain, my kicks landing without force. Then, with barely a grunt of discomfort, he starts walking us toward the dais, compelling the crowds to make way.

No doubt sensing the pull on her own compulsion, Nicnevin swings around, her searching gaze quickly finding Broden. Her eyes narrow, assessing this new wrinkle in her plan. Muttering and tap-tap-tapping, she aims her thralls at us, and I watch in horror as the fae closest to us coil in attack.

I feel rather than hear Broden's heavy sigh, and I am momentarily side-tracked by just how much boredom he manages to imbue into the gesture.

Then, I tense, unable to do anything else to defend myself against the incoming assault.

I am more than a little surprised when it does not come.

Surging towards us, the fae fall to the ground, limp and unmoving. I sweep my gaze to Nicnevin, and find she is just as shocked by this turn of events as I am. Still, she does not let that shock hold back her next assault. With more muttering and tapping, she swiftly compels more fae to turn and pitch themselves at us.

Again, they fall, limp bodies tumbling bonelessly to the floor.

Broden doesn't wait for Nicnevin's next attempt. One moment we are surrounded by enthralled fae, the next, they hit the ground. All but four of them. Those four fae swarm Nicnevin. One lands a particularly vicious blow to her head, and she slumps to the ground, as boneless as her thralls.

Quite predictably, this gets the attention of both Law and the Queen, who stumble away from one another up on the dais. Neither looks to be in great shape. They eye each other warily, taking a moment to evaluate the scene before them.

A slow smile twists Beatrix's lips, Law's eyes darkening as he takes in Broden's hold on me. I wince, realising I am in need of rescue yet again.

Fuck.

Chapter 33

'Make one more move towards me or my mother and I will snap her neck,' Broden commands into the silence. 'Disappear into those shadows, Law, and Elspeth will be dead before you reappear.'

Breathing in the alcohol lacing Broden's words, I realise this is the first I've heard him speak since my disastrous audience with the Queen. Now I find myself back at her feet, and just as powerless as I was then.

Well, perhaps more so now.

Gritting my teeth, I arch and wriggle and struggle against Broden's grip. It is steel. I try to kick my legs, but with my hips pinned, I can't put any real weight behind it. Disliking my efforts, Broden locks his arm tighter around my throat, compressing my airway.

A nervous, fluttering panic edges towards me and I stop fighting. For now.

'What do you want, Broden?' Law replies. Dual midnight daggers in hand, his stance remains guarded, opaque expression giving nothing away. With his attention on Broden, he remains wary of Beatrix's movements at the far end of the dais, who, seemingly persuaded her role in this little debacle is done, strolls casually to her throne and pours herself into it. Straightening her crown, she dabs a smear of blood from her lip, that unpleasant twist of a smile fixed firmly in place.

Law's regard flicks over Beatrix, then falls on me.

I'm sorry, I mouth, unable to push the words past the crush on my throat.

His charcoal gaze darkens to black, before sliding up to meet Broden's reply.

'I want you to drop your weapons and step back,' Broden says, tone glacial.

'I won't do that,' Law returns.

'You will.' Broden wrenches my neck to an agonising angle. 'If you want Elspeth returned to you with her head still attached to her body.'

Law stares back, impassive. 'I have a job to do. If you really think she means so much to me, you don't know me at all.'

My heart misses a beat, then punches out violently in my chest. Frantic, I search his face, but it is as blank and expressionless as my mother's had been. I can't tell if he is playing Broden to make him think I mean nothing to him. Or I actually mean nothing to him.

'Any time, my love.' His words echo through me, and I clutch onto them as Broden's grip stiffens at my throat.

'Surely, you don't expect me to believe that,' Broden drones, words dripping with contempt. 'If you didn't care, you would have made your move by now.'

He starts walking us forward, picking his way through the fae heaped in limp piles on the floor. Unable to strain even slightly against his resolute, restrictive grip, I am forced into taking short, shallow breaths. I am now worryingly lightheaded, silver sparks dancing at the edge of my vision.

A thought flits across my faint, flyaway mind. *My sparks. My magic.*

Dragging focus toward me, I search for my calm centre, that gorgeous connection.

But there is nothing.

No calm centre, no connection.

Sydok said my magic would be more responsive during times of emotional disturbance.

I am feeling very fucking emotional and very fucking disturbed right now.

So where is my magic?

Law stands his ground as Broden steps closer to the dais, while on her throne, the Queen lets out a delighted laugh, like this is the best entertainment she has had in years.

Perhaps it is. Broden did say these parties were tedious.

My vision darkens and tears sting my eyes. I curse, furious at myself for getting caught in this position. For putting Law in a position where he has to choose between me and his sister. I'm not entirely sure I would blame him if he let me die.

Well, I might be somewhat upset.

Broden steps us up onto the dais, and I know I don't have long before I inevitably pass out. With only the smallest trickle of air making its way past his grip, my vision swims, the world going in and out of focus as I cling to consciousness. I black out for a moment, and see in the next that we are suddenly standing beside the throne.

'Broden, you have outdone yourself,' Beatrix says, gazing up at him, her golden countenance battered and bruised but no less beautiful. 'I really am quite impressed.' She couldn't sound more condescending if she tried.

'That's nothing, Mother. Wait until you see what I have for you next.'

Abruptly, Broden's arms are no longer around me. With no air in my lungs and nothing to hold me up, I crash to the ground, heaving in deep breaths, blinking furiously to clear my vision. Then, I am not on the ground, but in Law's arms and I am watching in utter confusion as the Queen screams and screams, clawing at the dagger protruding from her rapidly blackening chest.

That's my dagger, my trembling, tangled mind tells me.

Vomit surges up my throat, and I swallow it down. Hauling in ragged breaths, I lean heavily against Law, who stands solid and unmoving beside me in the middle of the ballroom. I twist to look up at him. 'Was that you?'

A desolate shake of his head. 'No. It was Broden.'

I fight to clear the fog from my mind. Had Broden picked up my dagger? How? It is iron. It would burn him, weaken him.

My eyes fly over him, searching for an answer.

Triumph lines the very essence of him. He looks exultant, victorious.

Perhaps when you're filled with as much hatred as it would take to kill your own mother, handling the pain that comes with carrying her murder weapon might not be too much of a problem.

Beside Broden, Beatrix paws helplessly at the dagger. Her body stutters jerkily, appearing one instant young, the next ancient. Glowing, *stutter*, ashen. Dazzling, *stutter*, shrivelled. Gradually her strangled screams die away, golden light ebbing from her body until she is nothing but a shrunken, desiccated husk.

Pale hair flowing around him, Broden towers over her crumpled form, his features betraying no emotion as he bends down and plucks the crown from her head. Setting it atop his own head, his austere mask cracks only to reveal a triumphant curve of a smile. A final drift of golden embers float up and away from the Queen, seeming to follow the crown, where they settle... and transform. Once a web of delicate gold and glittering gems, the crown reforms to create a broad golden circlet encrusted with gleaming sapphires. Broden closes his eyes and tilts his head to the heavens, breathing deep as he appears to accept the crown's magic, winding its way over him, turning his skin that same golden hue his mother's had once been.

'Elphame has a new King.'

I startle at my mother's voice, soft as it is. While I hadn't noticed her arrival, she stands beside us now, looking to be whole and well. I step away from Law's embrace and give her a fierce hug, drawing in the familiar, comforting scent I remember from childhood.

'Are you alright?' I ask, scanning her face.

She reaches out to skim her hand over my throbbing jaw. 'I should be asking you that.'

I carefully conceal my grimace. 'I've had worse. I'll be fine.'

Her expression tightens. 'I should have been there for you.'

'I'm glad you weren't.' Under my touch, her willowy form feels far too fragile.

Unwillingly, my gaze shifts back to the dais. Imbued with a gilded, golden light, Broden looks to be fixed in place as power flows around him, through him, into him.

'Shouldn't we leave?' I ask warily. Broden was powerful before. I don't like to think of the power he might hold now he is King.

My eyes find Law, searching for an answer. He gives me none. As motionless as Broden, he is somewhere far beyond my words, unmoving except for the tide of emotion crashing behind his dark, empty eyes.

'It will take a while,' my mother says into the strained silence. 'Usually, the passing of power occurs during the coronation ceremony. It takes some time for the magic to fully settle in its new host.'

'Broden seems distracted by it. Couldn't someone... I don't know, take him down?' By someone, I obviously mean Law.

'The crown will shield him during the transferral process,' my mother replies with a small sigh.

At her mention of the word shield, I start. 'The Queen. She's dead. That doesn't mean you are now bound to Broden, does it? To be his shield?'

'Fortunately not. Beatrix gifted me my shield magic, but her binding was personal. That came later.' Sorrow touches her words, and it makes me wonder if it derives from Beatrix's binding of her, or the fact that her former lover is now dead. I know love can be a tricky thing. It doesn't always let you feel the things you think you should feel. My mother spent centuries at the Queen's side, and now the Queen is dead.

'Did you know this was coming?' I ask.

'As her shield, I could often sense the outline of threats. I didn't know exactly what would happen, but I knew she faced great danger.'

My brows furrow. 'And you chose not to protect her from that danger?'

'Beatrix had more than enough opportunities to change. She chose her path and then chose to drag me along beside her. There comes a point when you realise change will not come to you, and you must do something to create change of your own.' Some of the strength I had sensed within her earlier seems to make its way into the light. 'Tonight, when I saw you, I saw all those years I had missed, all at Beatrix's hand. I knew the time had come for me to have a hand in my own destiny, to choose my own path.'

She drifts toward Law. 'For what it's worth, I am deeply sorry for how this turned out for you.' Reaching out a hand, she brushes his arm.

At the touch, he tears his gaze from the dais, focusing first on my mother, then on me. Waking from the reverie that had held him so motionless, his features fill with so much despair, it hurts me to look at him.

'I am too,' Law replies, a worrying hollowness to his tone. Whatever this was, I am certain it meant more to him than simply completing another contract for Nicnevin. Taking a deep breath, he gathers himself. 'We should go. I am in no shape to take on the freshly appointed powers of a new royal.'

I follow his gaze. Broden remains transfixed, expression teeming with something that looks a lot like ecstasy. Draped over the throne next to him, Beatrix sprawls, skin ashen, open eyes vacant and lifeless. Broken fae bodies litter the dais around them, extending far onto the ballroom floor, where they meet those of the fae once compelled by Nicnevin, then felled by Broden.

I have no desire to remain here, surrounded by such carnage, but responsibility tugs at me. 'Shouldn't we help them? The ones that still live, I mean?' The fae circling us look to be asleep, but in that sleep, they seem all too vulnerable.

'They are Broden's subjects now, the nobles that once served his mother,' Law says, tone still achingly hollow. 'He knows he will need their support as he transitions into his role as King. I have no doubt he will strip a few of their rank if they show too much sorrow over Beatrix's passing, but he will let them awaken so he can first determine who is smart enough to follow him.'

Torn between retrieving my dagger and never wanting to see the bloody thing again, I opt for prudence and turn to leave. Not only does the thought of physically removing the dagger from Beatrix's scorched, disintegrating chest make my stomach heave, I simply do not want to step that close to Broden – no matter how far from himself he seems right now.

Carefully picking my way past fallen fae, I follow Law and my mother as they step towards the main doorway. My mind slipping and sliding over what comes next, I almost miss the scratchy voice that beckons from the darkened doorway in front of us.

'Where do you think you are going, Lawrens?'

Somehow, Nicnevin is in front of us. The last I had seen of her, she'd been slumped on the ground, knocked clean out and dead to the world. Violet eyes trained on Law, she appears sharp, composed, revealing no sense either that she was comatose for some time, or more surprisingly, that she is disappointed by the outcome of the evening's events.

'We are leaving,' Law says, voice flat.

'And should I have need of you?'

'You know where I will be,' Law grinds out, moving to step around her. Nicnevin flashes out a gnarled hand to clasp his arm. He allows it. I know he could just as easily slip away. Or separate Nicnevin's hand from her body.

'You know you cannot leave this realm, Lawrens.' Her eyes narrow, her tone turning sly. 'Not while I *own* you.'

Law stills. I have witnessed that fae stillness cast over him before, but this is the first time I've seen the shadows on his skin halt, ceasing their endless shifting so they are as motionless as he is.

'I am aware, Nicnevin.' Betraying no emotion in his tone, in his expression, he is as dangerous in this moment as I have ever seen him. After a long, perilous pause, he forces himself to take a breath, and the coils at his neck begin to wind and twist once more.

Her cunning smile lined with triumph, Nicnevin turns her attention to me. 'Ah sprig, what a disappointment you turned out to be. It was all going so well until you inconveniently let yourself fall captive. If it hadn't been for you, I'm quite sure Lawrens would have put an end to Beatrix. I would have my crown, and Lawrens would have his sister back.'

My eyes fly to find Law, the truth of her words lying stark against his features. Stomach lurching, I hastily swallow down more bile, struggling to get enough breath into my body. He closes his eyes as if he can't bear to look at me, and I feel my mother's small hand make its way into mine.

'No,' I breathe. 'This was your final job. This would have brought Florie back.'

Law opens his eyes, the desolation within them telling me all I need to know.

'Not quite, sprig,' Nicnevin says. 'Lawrens still had a number of *jobs*, as you so sweetly call them, still to do. But, seeing as this one was so significant, I generously agreed to clear away those that remained to replace them with this one final task. I believe in providing my workers with proper incentive, after all.' She spreads her hands in a gesture meant to mimic benevolence. 'I amended our original agreement so that should he succeed, Lawrens would no longer be bound to me, and he would have his dear sister returned to him.' She pauses to smile that alarming smile, wide with malevolent promise. 'Should he fail, however, the number of contracts he would have to complete would double.'

'How many remain now?' I ask cautiously.

'None of your concern, little sprig,' Nicnevin replies brightly. 'All you need to know is he's unlikely to complete them within your lifetime.'

Icy horror washes over me. This is my fault. If I had evaded Broden… hell, if I had allowed Law to take me somewhere safe, instead of into the ballroom, as he had wanted, none of this would have happened. He would have killed Beatrix, and now he would be free. His sister would be free.

'Enough, Nicnevin,' Law snaps. While his tone is blisteringly cold, his gaze is warm as it finds mine. Some of that excruciating torment still lingers there, but he has reigned in much of it. 'I don't blame you for anything, Red,' he says, confirming once again, that my face is all too easy to read. Eyes blazing, his shadows reach out in a gentle caress. 'It was my choice to amend the agreement. If I had not, I would still be bound to Nicnevin, regardless of the outcome tonight.'

I open my mouth to argue, but he doesn't give me the chance. 'Nicnevin, we will take our leave now.' He glances back at Broden. 'I fear matters here will wind up soon enough, and as such, I have no desire to linger.'

Nicnevin shifts her unsettling gaze to the dais, nods in agreement, then turns back to me. 'I would say it has been a pleasure, sprig, but as you know, I cannot lie.' She cackles at her own wit, then spins on her heel and disappears into the darkness, leaving the three of us to make our own way out of the palace grounds and as far from the newly coronated King as possible.

Chapter 34

Startling awake, I open my eyes, remember where I am, then shut them again tightly. If I keep them closed, I won't have to face the day. Won't have to face what today will bring.

I pull Law's arm more closely around me, shuffling my body back so it fits more completely against his. He feels warm, solid, there. He shifts against me, and I breathe him in, my throat tightening as my mind wanders to when we will next wake up like this. If we will ever wake up like this again.

After making our hasty exit from the palace last night, we'd hurried back to the tavern, collected my belongings, then made our escape from Paridell. While Paridell is a large enough city and easy to get lost in, we hadn't wanted to take the chance Broden would take it upon himself to seek us out. Unsure of how high on the new King's list of priorities we might be, Law had pointed out that it was probably best we didn't linger long enough to find out.

And there had been Agnes to think of, as well.

Besides Law, I have no real reason to stay in Faerie. I need to get home to my friend. The clock is ticking, and I'm desperate not to let time run out for her. She has been in prison for more than a week now, and while I try not to think of everything that could have happened to her in that time, the bleak horror of it rolls over me whenever my mind strays to thoughts of her. Of how I have failed her.

Stop. It.

I force myself to think positively, to consider what I do have. I have my magic. Small as it is, it is more than any human at the courthouse will have. I also have my mother, her magic, and whatever *tricks* she has picked up over the centuries.

She had been positively giddy when I hesitantly suggested she might return with me to the human realm. Essentially homeless, she really didn't have anywhere else to go. But, as she eagerly accepted the invitation, she'd lit up with that same warmth I remember illuminating my childhood. Still fragile, she had seemed a little less empty, a little less like she might drift away on a strong breeze.

Knowing I can't hide from the day forever, I reluctantly open my eyes, taking in the lightly smoking fire and my mother lying asleep beyond it.

I still can't quite believe I will be returning with her to North Berwick. Worriedly, I wonder what she will make of our little home, what she will think of my father now he has grown old. I know she lived there long before I came along, but I also know she spent the years that followed in a royal palace, surrounded by unimaginable luxury. Will our little cottage be a terrible disappointment? Will seeing my father – old and grey and in his sick bed – make her too sad to stay?

Soft kisses on the back of my neck interrupt my mind's idle wandering.

Law. Out of all the unknowns today will bring, those surrounding Law are the ones I find most painful to consider. My mind has already spiralled over them dozens of times, unable to settle without knowing for certain what will happen between us. It is a new thing, but it is powerful. I simply can no longer comprehend my world without him in it. But that is what I am heading towards. That is what today will bring.

I must go where he cannot follow.

Squeezing my eyes shut, I push back tears. Seriously, I have cried more in the past week than I have in the past year, probably even longer. I need to get a grip on myself.

'Good morning, Red.' I hear his smile as he whispers in my ear.

No, I absolutely will not cry.

In the quiet hours that passed since the truth revealed itself, my mind swept back and forth over our time together, using my new perspective to press various details into place.

While I don't know the specifics, I can deduce the bones of it.

Before we even met, Law had known of my fae heritage, of my mother, and of her position at the Queen's side. I can only assume Nicnevin recognised my mother when she tore away my memory of her, then tasked Law with escorting me to the palace, where he could use my reunion with her to get close enough to kill Beatrix. I don't know if Nicnevin meant for Law to take down my mother alongside the Queen, but I'm willing to bet she didn't expect her to willingly lower her shield to aid Law in his endeavours.

I am not so wrapped up in Law that I don't recognise the hurt that comes from him deceiving me, but I am also not naive enough to think he should have placed some half-human he'd never met above his goal to free his sister. He had been given a contract – a contract that would have seen him and Florie freed from Nicnevin's clutches – and he had carried it out, while keeping collateral damage to a minimum. He had kept my mother safe, and he had worked to keep me safe, even as danger tried its damnedest to dance with me.

As for our relationship, he hadn't sought that out, hadn't used my attraction to him to his advantage. He had even admitted to pushing aside his own attraction to me, trying to keep me safe from that too. Keep me safe from him.

Having worked it over and over in my mind, I understand holding to the deception required of him had not been easy, but for the most part, he'd really had no choice. Firstly, it had been a job, *I* had been a job. Secondly, there had been a geas that physically prevented him from telling me truths Nicnevin had not wanted me to know.

But even though he had not been able to tell me everything, he'd done what he could to arm me, to inform me. He had insisted on our visit to Sydok, where I found out more of my own truth, about my mother and my magic. He had then helped me with my magic, going to extreme lengths to encourage me to gain control over it. Then, after Struan's party, he had laid himself bare, giving me every excuse I might need to push him away.

He had not *needed* to do any of that.

As far as I'm concerned, Law's task had been to get me to the Queen in one piece. Nothing more had been required. He could have just as easily escorted me to the palace, used me to get to my mother, and from there, to the Queen. Then, contract completed, he and Florie would have lived happily ever after, just like the faerie tales.

But this is no faerie tale, and as far as I can see, there's no happy ending in sight. Not for Law, not for Florie.

As for Law and I, what we have together? I know he is not to blame for any of this, just as, deep down, I know I am not to blame for anything I may have done to hinder his attempts to end the Queen. But I so desperately want to help him. *Just* as much as I want a future with him. I just don't know how to make it happen.

One step at a time, Elspeth. Agnes first, then Law. And Florie, too, I suppose.

Luxuriating in Law's closeness, I attempt to pull him even closer, but find his body is just about as close to mine as it will get. With our clothes on, at least. And they are most definitely not coming off with my mother lying a few yards away.

Seeing her shift and stretch, I know I can't put it off any longer. I need to get up. I need to face down the day and move toward my next challenge.

Twisting around, I brush a kiss over Law's lips, then sit up before that kissable mouth makes me tarry longer. My body feels old, more tired than I can ever remember it being. While I had hoped that we were finished with walking, our trek out of Paridell into the surrounding woodlands had not done my aching muscles any favours. Sleeping on the forest floor also hadn't helped.

As I work out the crick in my neck, I raid my pack to find what food remains. Laughing at Law's not-so-polite reply to my suggestion that he consume the remaining haggis, I share the rest of the bannock and dried fruit among the three of us.

All too soon, we are back on our feet and heading for the border.

Having been mercifully mostly unconscious during my flight within the *Sluagh*, I have no memory of passing through the veil when I crossed the border from the human realm into Faerie. But now as I trudge ever nearer to the boundary it creates, I feel the magic of it shimmer over me, there yet not.

During my time here, I have learned that Faerie essentially sits within the borders of the human realm, layered over the top of it, but inaccessible to those who do not hold magic. A human may travel over where certain borders of Faerie lie – creases where the veil is thinnest – but unless they carry magic, they will remain in the human realm rather than ambling into Faerie.

Following the contours of the human realm that lies beneath it, Faerie's lands often mimic those over which it is layered. Where large cities feature in the human realm, Faerie will also typically hold a large city. Where there is woodland below, there is often woodland above, where there is water below, there is often water above. But Faerie does not always hold to those rules. Which is one reason why I have found it so difficult to get my bearings here. That, and I am appallingly bad at geography.

With my mother's assurances that the border we are about to cross will lead to the human lands flanking Edinburgh, I can't help but assume Paridell is in fact, layered over Scotland's capital. Tallying the many hours Law and I spent on the road, I try and fail to guess where we may have started. Nicnevin's estate could lie near the outskirts of where Dundee sits in the human realm, just as easily as it could lie over Gretna.

Giving up on my incredibly imprecise speculating, I drag my attention back to what lies before us. Faerie's border. What I need to do before I cross it.

'Are you sure you can't come with us?' I plead. Turning to look up at Law, I arrange my features into what I hope is such a piteous expression, it might somehow change the answer I know he must give.

Law laughs. 'You know if there was any way for me to come with you, I would.' He glances at the veil's crease, glittering a pale shimmering purple in the watery morning light. 'Nicnevin's binding won't allow it. I can feel the veil repelling me from here.'

I know this. Know that if Law were to try to pass through the veil, he wouldn't make it to the other side. Not alive, anyway.

'Fucking magic,' I say, although I am too emotionally exhausted to put any real venom behind it.

'Language, Elspeth,' my mother scolds, eyes crinkling. 'I'll give you both a moment,' she continues gently, before turning and walking a little way off.

Watching her sit delicately on a rock, I turn my attention back to Law.

It's almost painful to look at him, not knowing when I will see him again. Not knowing when I will next see those eyes sparkle mischievously at me. When he will stagger me with a smile. When he will gather me up and make the world disappear with one of his kisses.

How can this be happening? How am I supposed to say goodbye to this?

A sad smile tugging at his lips, he looks down at me. 'Don't cry, Red.' He uses his thumbs to brush away tears I hadn't realised were falling.

'I'm not,' I lie, throat tight, voice cracking.

Laughing softly, he cups both hands to my face, bending to kiss my tear-stained cheeks, my closed eyelids, my lips.

I grab the front of his cloak to tug him closer, joining the kiss, deepening it, suddenly desperate to be surrounded by him. Enveloping me in silky shadow, he wraps his arms around me, and I revel in the way he feels. Hard muscle, warm skin. I soak it all in, how he feels, how he tastes, how he smells. I want to carry it all with me.

Gently, he pulls back, his gaze locked on mine like he wants to do the same.

I curve my arms around the back of his neck, stroking that velvety stubble I love so much. 'I'll miss you,' I say, only just managing to get the words past the tightness of my throat. If I say much more, I know the real tears will follow, and I will ugly cry all over this ludicrously beautiful male.

'I'll miss you too,' he replies, his quiet smile implying he knows just what I'm thinking.

'Tell me this isn't the last time we'll see each other,' I push, desperation sidling closer again.

His charcoal eyes glint softly. 'I sincerely hope this is not the last time we see each other.'

Just as Law cannot lie, he cannot speak a truth without being bound to it. In the same way as Broden had been bound by his word, Law cannot say we will see each other again without being bound by that truth. If he says it and it doesn't happen, the magic that binds him to his word will, quite literally, tear him apart.

'If you can't say it, you'll have to find some other way to make me believe it.'

Chasing my exaggerated pout with a kiss, Law takes up my challenge. Quite enthusiastically. My breathing is ragged when he eventually pulls back, gifting me one of his trademark roguish smiles.

'How did I do?'

'Very convincing,' I offer. 'Any more convincing and I might have to ask my mother to walk away a little further.' Smiling, I consider how he always manages to stop my mind from straying to places where hurt lies. He had almost made me forget why I wanted him to kiss me, why we are here. But I can't put it off any longer.

'I should go,' I say, regret a cold knife twisting in my heart.

Law nods. 'You should. You have a witch to save.'

'And then, a faerie.' I reach up to smooth my hand along his jaw, watching the shadows coil to my touch.

He turns his face to kiss my palm. 'I will hold you to that.'

'I'm counting on it,' I return.

Chest tight, despair hollowing out my insides, I lean around him and call out to my mother. I need to go now, or I will collapse into a puddle of misery and never get up.

As my mother approaches, I rise onto my toes and brush Law's lips with my own.

'Bye, Law,' I say, breathing him in one last time.

'Bye, Red.' His grey gaze is steady, his curve of a smile sad.

Compelling my feet to move, I turn away from him, throat aching, eyes on fire. As I force myself forward, I feel my mother's hand steal into mine, offering both her warmth and her magic as we slip through the veil.

Chapter 35

I don't look back.

I can't look back.

If I look back, I will do something stupid, like sprint back through the veil and melt into Law's arms. Melting is not moving forward. And I'm not entirely sure I could make myself say goodbye to him again.

Instead, I grip my mother's hand tighter, shove down the desolation, and try to get my bearings.

Swallowing past the thickness in my throat, the first thing I notice is how damned cold it is on this side of the veil. Far, far colder than when I left a week ago. This kind of cold feels closer to the depths of winter than early November.

Shrugging my hood over my head, I bite back a curse and squint into the distance, finding Edinburgh rising up against the bleak grey sky. Resigning myself to more bloody walking, I wrap my cloak closer around me as my mother does the same, and we both set off towards the capital.

Just as it always is, it's the smell of the city that hits me first. Long before we reach the hovels that line the outskirts of Edinburgh, before the busy sounds of so many thousands of people packed into such close quarters finds its way to my ears, the city's smell stretches out to greet me. It is foul, it is filth, it is potent.

Wondering why Paridell hadn't smelled anywhere near as bad, I glance at my mother, gauging her reaction to this reeking, filthy city. While her nose wrinkles ever so slightly, she seems enamoured by it all. As we make our way past the hovels and into the city proper, she cranes her neck to take it all in. The grimy buildings, the shit-covered streets, the very ordinary looking citizens that trudge through their day, looking nothing like the lithe, lovely fae Paridell had been filled with.

On our trek out of Paridell and on to the border, she had remained mostly quiet, keeping a gentle smile on her face and her thoughts to herself. I couldn't help but wonder if her seemingly contented silence was perhaps a result of shock. Within the space of a few short hours, she had rediscovered her daughter, then suddenly – and very violently – found herself no longer bound to Beatrix, and free to do as she pleased.

I consider it now, casting back my thoughts to how I'd felt when Malcom died. Dazed, unbelieving. Not quite willing to trust that it really might be over.

After crossing the border into the human realm, she'd kept her hand firmly in mine, seeming to gain as much strength from the contact as me. As we had drawn closer to Edinburgh, she started to ask a few questions here and there. Where did I live? What did I do with my time? Did Duncan still teach at the school? Had he found someone new to love? That last question had been timid, nervous.

In response, I had told her of my life, skirting around the worst of my marriage to Malcom to focus on my love of brewing, on my friendship with Agnes. As I spoke of my father, of his growing ill health, her expression had tightened, so I'd forged on, telling her of little things instead. Life in North Berwick, foraging in the woods, experimenting with new ales, expanding my business.

Now, as we draw closer to the courthouse, next to which I know the jail is situated, I fall silent. I take in the gathering crowds and wonder what they are gathering to see.

Edinburgh's citizens are just like those of any other city. Some are hardworking, some are lazy. Some are rich, some are poor. Individually, they can be smart, contained, thoughtful. As a group, as a mob, those smarts, that control, that consideration quite often abandons them.

I take a moment to evaluate the crowd surrounding the courthouse, trying to get a sense of the mood here, to measure the atmosphere. What I sense is a mob. Individuality abandoned, the mob exhales its sense of anticipation, its desire for entertainment.

Something is happening today. I just don't know what.

Checking my mother's glamour over her appearance remains in place, I steer our path toward an old woman standing on the crowd's milling fringes. Bundled up against the cold, she carries a grousing bairn on her hip, swaying back and forth to calm it as she keeps a close eye on the courthouse doors.

'What's happening?' I ask.

She cuts her attention sharply to me. 'Witch trial. A big one.'

Heart leaping, I push down the panic that surges over me. Just because this is a witch trial, doesn't mean it is Agnes's.

'Who's on trial?' I ask, voice stiff.

'Not sure,' the woman sniffs. 'All I ken is that it's certain to be more interestin' than that pile a laundry waitin' for me at home.'

Getting the strong sense I am being dismissed, I move away to find a space in which we can watch without being pulled into the mob. I know how quickly things turn ugly when the mob feels it's not receiving the entertainment it is owed.

I stamp down my dread, and force all my thoughts towards positivity.

This will have nothing to do with Agnes. This trial will be for some other unfortunate soul caught up in this ludicrous craze for hunting witches. Afterwards, the crowds will disperse, and we will make our way into the jail. We will find some way to get Agnes out of there, and then we will leave this stinking city and never come back.

If I think it hard enough, it will become truth.

Cloak drawn tight around me, I shuffle my feet to drive out the biting cold, waiting long, interminable minutes before the doors of the courthouse finally swing open, and Francis Drummond, High Court Judge of the Court of Justiciary, steps out to meet the waiting crowds.

'Citizens of Edinburgh. Today we bring to trial six women charged with the most heinous of crimes – that of plotting to murder our king, His Majesty, King James VI and his fair queen, Anne of Denmark.' Drummond's voice rings out icy and clear as it passes over the square, greeted by the mob's expectant silence. 'On this day, the 28th of January, in the year of our lord, 1591, these women will be tried for the crime of witchcraft, and for using that craft to raise the horrifying storms that plagued the king and queen's journey from Denmark early last year.' He pauses to clasp his hands over the rotund belly his ceremonial robes fail to conceal. 'Should they be found guilty, they will be sentenced and brought to swift justice.'

My lips thin. It sounds a lot like these poor women have already been found guilty, and this bit of theatre is all for the crowds.

Wait, what? January? That can't be right. It's only November. Samhain is only a week past.

As confused as I am, I don't get any time to consider this, before my attention is wrenched toward the jail's entrance, where six huddled figures are hauled roughly out onto the steps of the courthouse. Desperately scanning the wretched parade, it takes me no time at all to identify Agnes. Her shaved head bowed, she stands defeated, broken, weighed down by the jagged iron collar at her neck and the soiled, ragged dress that is no match for the bitter wind whipping across the square.

The panic that coursed through me moments ago returns, pressing down hard, made all the more substantial by such a profound sense of dread I find it hard to catch my breath.

No, no, no. I'm supposed to have more time.

What can I possibly do for Agnes as she stands up there, contained by masked, thickly muscled guards and in front of all these people?

'We have received testimony from many of Edinburgh's most honourable and respected citizens,' Drummond continues, before adding smugly, 'as well as testimony from His Majesty, King James, himself.' He pauses to sneer at the dishevelled group huddled in rags beside him. 'Using evidence gained from those astute and most dependable of witnesses, we have extracted confessions from each of the six women you see before you.'

The crowd lets out exultant whoops as my brain stutters. Finding out Agnes was a witch had admittedly been a shock, but I know without doubt that my oldest friend would never do such a thing. So why would she confess to it?

My mind skips back to Drummond's use of the word extracted.

I've heard whispers of the brutal ways in which confessions are extracted from witches. Pricking of the skin to search for the Devil's mark is common enough that most folks know of it. As is waking. Under this method, accused witches are deprived of sleep, until, not knowing where or even who they are, they confess to witchcraft, often admitting to bizarre and outlandish uses of their magic as a result of sleep deprived hallucinations.

The whispers, however, alluded to even more ruthless methods. Where the accused are put on the rack and stretched. Where their shins are broken and re-cast incorrectly. Where red-hot pincers are used to dig out their nails. Where their breasts are crushed to see if black poison drips from their nipples. Under the attention of such methods, whether the accused are witches or not, many confess to it simply to put an end to the torture. Even death can seem a kindness when the alternative is day after day of torment.

I can't tear my gaze from Agnes, whose own glassy stare remains cast down. Even from such a distance, I can see the sharp teeth set around the iron collar she wears – and the damage those teeth have done to her neck and throat. Blood and dirt streak every inch of her exposed skin. She looks gaunt, hollow. Utterly defeated.

Inspecting the five women who hunch next to her, I find further signs of the abuse they have endured. Ellen and Jonet's ears are missing, having undoubtedly been sliced off so they no longer hear the Devil's false promises. Deep scores mark Margret and Jeane's foreheads, where those testing them must have cut the skin, then waited to see if their familiars would come along and lick up the blood.

Drummond jerks my attention back to him, casting a hand toward the shambling figure closest to him and continuing his oration. 'As leader of this coven, Geillis Duncan has confessed to meeting with the Devil and entering into a pact with him to thwart the king's ships.'

Jeers and cries swarm over the crowd as the mob smells blood.

Drummond takes it all in, adjusting his robes before gesturing to Agnes. 'Her second in command, Agnes Sampson, attested to this in her own confession, in which she confirmed that on All Hallows' Eve in the year 1589, the Devil preached to her and her fellow witches in the old, ruined kirk on North Berwick's harbour.

'Travelling there on foot, by broomstick and some, sailing in sieves up the Forth, more than two hundred witches from across the country gathered in that kirk, where, illuminated by guttering black candles, they welcomed the Devil himself. Clad entirely in black, horned and fork-tailed, the Devil took to the pulpit and commanded his subjects disembowel seven cats, then bind their entrails to body parts they were to disinter from the kirk's graveyard.

'Mistress Sampson confirmed that these were tossed into the harbour and used in a spell of the Devil's to summon the storms that would later rein havoc upon the king and queen's crossing.'

Tears prick my eyes as Drummond's words are met by gasps and murmurs within the unruly crowds that surround us.

'Have no fear,' Drummond commands, voice rising to carry over the commotion. 'While this might be a terrifying truth to hear, no harm will come to you as long as you hold God in your hearts. These witches may have made a pact with the Devil, but the Church of Scotland has a covenant with God Himself. As long as you remain honourable, virtuous and decent, God will protect you from such horrors.'

He nods solemnly, letting his words sink in before continuing. 'As High Court Judge, I am God's servant in earthly matters. I remain in His service to carry out His will. As such, it is up to me to punish the wicked so they may not lead more astray. With God's hand at my back, I will ensure Geillis Duncan and her despicable coven no longer steer the unwitting toward the Devil's embrace.'

His voice having steadily increased in volume, Drummond's words now boom across the square, working to whip up the mob to such a degree that its desire for retribution, for blood, is almost palpable.

'Taking into account each testimony and confession, the Court of Judiciary concludes that these women are indeed witches. The Court also concludes that – with the Devil in their pocket – these witches are those responsible for raising the storms that near decimated the king's fleet.'

Boos wash over the crowd as some of the better provisioned members pelt rotten food at the women hunched on the steps. Half a rotten cabbage catches Agnes on the shoulder, and I flinch, my heart breaking at the way she makes no effort to shield herself, or even brush the wilted leaves from her dress.

Agnes is robust. She is bold. She doesn't take shit from anyone.

How bad must these past months have been to turn her into this... ghost?

Drummond makes no attempt to calm the mob as he continues, 'In conjuring those storms, these cruel and accursed women endeavoured to slay our most noble king and his new wife, in what the Court has established was an attempt to take down the royal line and sew chaos across these lands.'

I try to focus, heartbeat thundering in my ears. I throw a wild look at my mother and find that she is gone. Staring up at the courthouse steps with unseeing eyes, she has retreated once more behind that smooth, expressionless mask she'd worn at Beatrix's side. 'Mama?' I grasp her hand, squeezing hard. 'We need to help Agnes. What do we do?' My plea is choked, desperate, but doesn't penetrate her distant façade.

Revelling in the mob's attention, Drummond arches a grim smile of satisfaction, then roars, 'Under the Witchcraft Act of 1563, witchcraft in Scotland is deemed a capital crime. Under God, the Court finds these six women guilty of both witchcraft and treason. Their punishment is death.'

The mob goes wild.

I pull my mother closer, the crowds jostling around us, letting out thunderous bellows as more rotten food cascades towards the steps of the courthouse. There, the six piles of rags that had once been women cower in silence, not one of them looking out into the crowds baying for their blood.

Knowing I cannot fight the mob or the might of the Court, I cast around frantically for any other way I might help Agnes.

Magic. It has to be magic.

Another glance at my mother confirms both she and her magic are of no help to me now. As for Agnes's magic, Geillis's magic, the witches in front of us either cannot access their magic or are too broken to make use of it. In my racing mind, the Queen's death flashes before me. Agnes and her coven had been gifted their magic by Beatrix. Had her death resulted in the death of the coven's magic as well?

With no way to know for sure, I realise I have only my own magic to rely on. Still clutching my mother's limp hand, I squeeze my eyes shut, trying to focus on finding that beautiful connection to Aether.

Nothing.

Where is it? Where is it?

Frantic, my mind swerves towards Law. Just the thought of him makes my heart twist. *Not helping.* What would Law say? Feverishly, I try to think back on everything he taught me as he attempted to cajole my magic to the surface.

His velvet tones wind through me, making me think of those sinuous swirls that coil over his skin. *'Calm yourself, Red. Clear your thoughts.'*

I think back on the way in which I had connected with Aether on the road to Paridell, and attempt to slow my breathing, to calm my racing heart. But I have nothing to focus on. No pile of soil, no little sprout of a plant. I know Aether is in everything, but that is too big. I need some kind of focus in order to seek out a connection.

Trying to ground myself on the cobblestones beneath my feet, I think of the troll's bridge. Believing Law was in danger, I turned much of that bridge to rubble, with very little effort on my part. Now Agnes is in danger – very real danger – and I feel as connected to my magic as I did before I knew I had any. That is to say, not at all.

My eyes flash open, a shriek of frustration tearing from me. Wholly focused on the unfolding entertainment, the howling crowds around us pay me no heed. Another frenzied glance at my mother tells me she is somewhere else entirely. An exhausted hopelessness creeps over me, and I suddenly wish I could escape there too.

Wretched in my desperation, I watch as Agnes, Geillis and the four other women are rounded up and steered down the steps of the courthouse, toward the far end of the square. Dragging my mother along behind me, I follow the mob, rising up on my toes to see where they are being taken.

Then I see it.

The pyre.

They are going to burn Agnes at the stake.

Chapter 36

At one side of the gallows, an enormous unlit pyre looms. Drummond takes his place beside it, using the raised dais the gallows stand on as a stage to address the mob. I hover on tiptoe towards the back of the throng, unable to see much beyond the heads that crowd in front of me. I only catch glimpses of Agnes, who is glazed and vacant, perhaps having retreated to that same faraway place as my mother.

Knowing the best entertainment is yet to come, the crowds hush, anticipating the High Court Judge's next words.

'For their crimes, these witches will pay with their lives,' Drummond begins, rousing cheers from the mob. Following his gesture, one guard remains with Agnes and Geillis beside the pyre, while the rest drive the four other women up onto the dais. 'While no less wicked, the role of these four witches has been deemed by the Court to be lesser than that of the leaders of their coven. For that, their punishment is death by strangulation, after which, they will be set to the pyre.'

Shit, shit, shit. What can I do? What can I possibly do?

Addressing the four pitiful figures beside him, Drummond continues, 'Margret Doig, Jonet Fordyce, Ellen Hastie, Jeane Moncrief. Your confessions have been taken and punishment set. I will allow you no opportunity to sway these good and moral citizens that stand before you. Any evil that lingers on those wicked lips shall remain there until you reach the fiery pits of hell, where the Devil will surely be waiting to receive you. May these last moments provide you opportunity to reflect on whether making a pact with such a creature is worth losing your soul to endless and everlasting torment spent writhing in hellfire.'

Heads bent, the four broken women stare at the dais beneath their feet. A bleak sob escapes me as I again consider how persuasive Drummond's methods must have been to destroy these women so completely that they do not react to their own impending execution.

Guts twisting, shame floods me. Agnes, Geillis, these women, they were suffering for *months* while I was galivanting around Faerie. All for what? I returned with no cavalry, no magical solution. Agnes was alone, abandoned, tortured. And now she is going to die, as innocent as each of the five other women this smug bastard Drummond has decided to put to death.

Rage fills me, washing past the guilt, but I can do absolutely nothing as the masked ghouls on the dais take their places behind the women and await the High Court Judge's signal. Sweeping his gaze over the baying mob, Drummond slants a small smile and gestures with an imperious flick of his hand. In response, four garrottes snake around four grimy necks, and as the ghouls pull tight, the crowds go wild.

I force myself to watch, fury at my powerlessness lurching under my skin. Fists clenched as tight as my teeth, I watch Margret let out a silent scream, her skirts darkening as she loses control of her bladder. I see Jonet's hands fly instinctively to her neck, her fingers frantic but gaining no purchase on the taught rope at her throat. I watch helpless tears course down Jeane's face, leaving tracks in the filth as they stream over the tightening garrotte. I see but can do nothing as Ellen struggles weakly against the giant behind her, bare feet dancing in the air.

Lead in my stomach, I watch it all, until the last dregs of life leave those four shattered women in the most painful, horrific, and undignified way.

One by one, four bodies slump to the dais. Margret, Jeane, Jonet and Ellen no longer; they are corpses rather than people now. That unique essence that made each of them who they were, gone. While I had not known any of them more than to nod a head to, I feel sorrow for them all the same. Sorrow for all they had been, for who they had left behind, for who they were yet to become. Tears sting my eyes and anger tears through my gut, as their lifeless forms are dragged off the dais and slung unceremoniously onto the pyre.

Drummond folds his hands in front of him and waits for the crowds to hush. It doesn't take long. There is more killing to come, and the mob is eager to taste it.

'As leaders of their coven, Geillis Duncan and Agnes Sampson will now face a starker brand of justice,' Drummond pronounces. 'Just as their actions would have seen our glorious monarchs suffer, so now shall *they* suffer. In their wickedness, these witches schemed to use the seas to bring about the murder of our king and queen. Now we shall use fire to cleanse them of that wickedness.'

Stirred by the promise of such a gruesome spectacle, the mob roars its bloodlust. Howls slash the air as Agnes and Geillis are hauled to the top of the pyre, where they are secured back-to-back on the awaiting stake.

Terror gripping me, I turn to my mother. Grasping her shoulders, I shake her, the violence surrounding us leaching into the movement. 'Mama! We need to help Agnes. She is going to *die*.' I try desperately to make her focus on me. Another shake. 'Please, Mama. This is Agnes. Your best friend. My best friend. She needs us. Don't abandon us again.' I almost feel bad for aiming a blow quite so low. I know it was Beatrix's fault she hadn't returned from Faerie, that she had tried so hard to return. But I need to do *something*.

I search her eyes.

Not even a flicker.

Wanting to scream in frustration, I twist away from her and wrench my attention back to the pyre. It is aflame. Already, flames curl around the bodies of the four strangled women piled at the base. How long before those flames reach Agnes?

My attention flicks to Drummond. Seemingly satisfied with his role in the proceedings, he stands tall on the dais, a sick sense of delight cast at the edge of his features. He is enjoying this, the bastard.

I jerk back to my mother and grab her hand, dragging her forward, fighting through the mob to get closer to Agnes. I am sharp elbows and snarled words, brutal kicks and vicious glares. Panting, blood pounding in my ears, I finally stop five yards from the pyre, where the cloying scent of scorched hair and charred meat wraps sinuously around me. My stomach heaves and I force its burning contents back down, staring in utter panic at the flames licking Agnes's feet.

Focus. I must focus. Fire is an element. I have power over fire. I can stop the fire from reaching her if I can just concentrate hard enough.

I close my eyes and breathe deep, in through my mouth, out through my nose. With Law's words rippling velvet in my ear, I blot out the jeers of the jostling crowd, urging my focus to the crackle of the flames, the heat on my face. Trying not to think of how searing that heat must be for Agnes, I open my eyes and rest them on the flaming pyre, finding trails of pulsing blue coiling within the flames.

Aether.

I listen for my heartbeat, urging it to slow and find that rhythm.

One beat, three beats, five beats–

It's there. I feel it. That exquisite sense of connection.

I am Aether and Aether is me.

Thinking of nothing else, I use that connection to send my will towards the flames. I visualise them dying back, suffocating, snuffing out. And slowly, languidly, the flames follow my command. Instead of curling up, they die down, pulling back from Agnes's feet to hide in the scorched sticks of the pyre. I keep my focus solely on each blue pulse, refusing to let my joy overwhelm my concentration. Agnes's life depends on this. I will absolutely not fuck it up.

Infuriated shouts swarm around me as I push harder, and the fire dies back further. Drummond's men race around the pyre, throwing on more wood in an attempt to stoke the flames back to life. I grit my teeth, sending everything I have at the dwindling fire, and with one final surge, the pyre collapses, smothering the flames.

Exhaustion sweeps over me. I sway, clutching my mother's arm to remain upright. Dazedly, I stamp down any thoughts of triumph, my gaze flicking up to where Agnes and Geillis are bound. Skirts singed and smoke coiling around their feet, they are not safe yet.

'Witchcraft!' Drummond bellows.

Trembling, I turn toward the dais to find the High Court Judge, jowls quivering, eyes narrowed to furious slits. His wrath is a living, breathing thing.

Unnerved, the mob shifts, mostly silent but for a few unsettled jeers.

'Under God's gaze, these despicable creatures dare to defy His justice,' Drummond seethes, his words drenched in self-righteous fury. 'It will not stand. As God's hand upon this earth, I will not *let* it stand. If it be not fire, let them dance!' Motioning to the hulking brutes still skulking around the pyre, he shouts, 'Cut them down.'

The men hesitate, glancing nervously at the smoking ruins, where embers twist and dance over scorched wood and charred bodies. Another feverish yell from Drummond has them moving, climbing cautiously over the pyre, obviously wary of the possibility it might surge to life beneath them. Hurriedly, they cut the bonds that secure Agnes and Geillis to the stake, then drag them up onto the dais to stand under the waiting gallows.

Abruptly noticing the noose swinging above her head, the tremulous heap of rags that was once Geillis Duncan collapses on the rough timber boards beneath her. She is hauled to her feet while Agnes wavers on unsteady legs, unable to hold back the dry, smoky coughs that rack her.

Drummond speaks quietly to one of his men as the mob watches on, expectant.

The mob knows what comes next.

I know what comes next.

My best friend will *hang*.

A crushing, aching hollow unfolds inside me. It twists and roils and expands through my belly, reaching out cold fingers to fill my chest, my arms, my legs. It leaves me vacant, void, utterly spent.

It is more than the grief I feel, the desolate terror that now owns me.

I have reached the limits of my magic. It has deserted me.

With dread spiralling that icy, aching hollow, I watch Agnes. She wipes her streaming eyes, her glazed stare roaming the crowds before her. Our eyes lock. Recognition sharpens her expression, and a soundless moan escapes her. Her lips part around my name and she staggers forward, only to be shoved back into place by one of Drummond's brutes. Bracing herself against another racking cough, her attention flicks to my side. To my mother. Her eyes widen in wonder, but she has no time to react further before she's dragged up onto a waiting stool. Rough hands remove her iron collar and push the noose over her head, as a yard or so along the gallows, the same is done to Geillis.

Terror screams through me. I glance to my mother, only to find that same maddeningly vacant stare. I close my eyes, reaching desperately for any sense of my connection with Aether. But there is only that damned aching void. It is hollow, yet it fills me up, blocking me from that connection with its endless emptiness.

I want to fight them, those monsters up on the dais. But I don't even have a blade. The last time I saw my dagger, it was lodged in the Queen of Elphame's chest. And while I may be better at defending myself than I once was, I am under no illusion that I could take down five large, well-trained men.

No magic, no weapon. No hope.

Agnes is going to die. The woman who raised me, who seamlessly took on so many roles in my life – mother, confidante, friend, ally – is going to *die* right in front of me.

Paralysed by dread, I send out a silent plea to anyone who might help. *Help Agnes. Save Agnes. Please.*

Agnes reads all of this on my face, of course. Gaze locked on mine, she mouths the words, *'It's alright.'* Despite where she stands, despite the noose around her neck, her expression remains clear, her eyes filled with love. *'Be strong, Elspeth,'* she mouths, touching her heart. *'I love you.'*

Chest aching, my throat squeezes tight. 'I love you, too,' I whisper, a silent sob wrenching its way out of me.

Straining to think clearly, to consider my next move, my attention is dragged from Agnes to Drummond, whose words ring out over the mob once more. 'No man or woman stands above God's justice. While these depraved creatures may have evaded the pyre, they will not evade the justice of our Lord God. Whatever nefarious means saved them from fire will not save them from the noose.' Having smoothed over his fury, he stands proud and authoritative, an arrogant sneer curling against his lips. 'Now we shall see them perform the Devil's dance as God's hand tightens His grip at their throats.'

My stomach lurches, and I struggle to catch my breath as my eyes track back to Agnes. She stands high on a stool, noose at her neck, its rough fibres rending the abraded skin there. Tears burn my eyes as I take in the tenderness in her expression, one that is so at odds with her situation, I want to shriek at the unfairness of it all.

Agnes doesn't deserve this. Geillis, Margret, Jonet, Ellen, Jeane; none of these women deserve this. They stand here and die at the whim of misguided men, men with an agenda who can tell whatever story they want because they are the ones in power.

Fury at that all too familiar feeling of powerlessness thunders through me. My attention flicks to Geillis, head bent low, tears slipping silently onto the boards beneath her. Back to Agnes, her expression composed, seemingly resigned to her fate.

But what can I do? My magic is spent. My mother is similarly beyond my reach. Around us, the mob is getting swept up once more, Drummond's words rousing in them that eager sense of anticipation to see justice done. Grimly, I wonder whether I should just hurl myself at the haughty High Court Judge. Try to take him down… and all five of his monstrously large guards. It might work?

My uncertain gaze finds Agnes. She shakes her head, her features arranged in a stern expression I remember clearly from childhood. One that tells me she knows exactly what kind of mischief I am contemplating, and that I should seriously reconsider or face severe consequences. Deep down in my boots, I know such an attack is futile, that it would not save Agnes or Geillis. It would only get me strung up alongside them. And where would that leave my mother? My father? Law?

I have nowhere to direct my futile fury.

I have no power, no magic, no weapon, no allies.

I am just a woman.

I am out of time.

'Evil be gone,' Drummond roars.

Chaos tears across the howling mob as two stools tumble, two ropes draw taught, and two necks stretch. Above the clamour whips the *crack* of a snapped neck, leaving Geillis's body swinging lifeless. Mercy has touched her in her final moments. She will not dance.

Agnes knows no such mercy.

Heart in a vice, guts slithering, I force myself to watch through stinging, hot tears as the woman who has been by my side my entire life drops from the gallows to swing wildly beneath them.

Fingers grasping the rope at her neck.

Dirty skin turning an ugly shade of purple.

Her body bucking uncontrollably.

Feet dancing the Devil's dance.

I think. I might. Be screaming.

I am. I am screaming.

Agony rips out of me in searing, anguished wails, swallowed by the cheering crowds that move like the seas around me.

And still, Agnes dances.

Stretched, tormented moments pass while the crowds howl, while my screams tear away fragments of my sorrow-filled soul until eventually, I go numb.

My throat raw and cheeks dry, that aching void inside me finally, mercifully envelops my mind.

And Agnes stops twitching.

Chapter 37

Satiated, content, the mob slowly breaks up around us, Edinburgh's fine citizens tucking away their bloodlust to go about their day.

I stand adrift, lost among the scattering crowds, with nothing to grab onto.

My mother. She is beside me. But she is no anchor.

She is as lost as I am.

Pushing through my emptiness, I wonder vaguely what I should do next. In the past weeks, I've been urged ever onwards by my need to help Agnes. But now, Agnes is gone.

Gone.

No more warm hugs, no more wise words. No comforting shoulder to cry on or wicked jokes to drown out dark days. The friend who was with me through everything, who I could count on for *anything*, has slipped from this world and left me here, unmoored.

A strangled sob creeps around that aching void and crawls up my throat.

I force it back down. We need to move, or we will draw attention to ourselves.

I take one last look at Drummond. Haughty features composed in an aspect of smug satisfaction, he addresses his men, instructing them in their duties before hurrying down from the dais to whatever awaits him in the courthouse. I know they will remove the four bodies from the pyre and toss them in an unmarked grave, just as I know Agnes and Geillis will swing on the gallows for three days and three nights, their rotting bodies serving as a reminder to remain vigilant against the depravity of witchcraft. Or as a reminder of the Court's might should it choose to take against you.

Clasping my mother's hand in my own, I turn to leave, unsure of where we should go, but certain we must not stay.

'Friends of yours?' a deep voice rumbles.

In my anguish, I had not been aware of anyone standing so close behind us, but as I turn, I almost stumble into the cloaked figure that now addresses me. Tricorn pulled low over his face and clad entirely in black, he is a brick wall of a man, menace rippling off him as he towers over me. Instantly understanding he is seven shades of trouble, I bow my head and murmur an excuse me, attempting to pull my mother along as I step around him.

He moves to block my path. 'I asked if they were friends of yours,' he prompts, voice resonating with dark warning.

I take a breath to steady myself, craning my neck to look up at him. 'No,' I lie, doing my best to keep my expression clear, innocent. 'We're here for the show, like everyone else.'

'We both ken that is untrue, Mistress Reade.' Surprise steals my next breath as dread slithers over me. 'But then, how could I expect anythin' but deceit from a witch such as yersel'?' One ham hock hand snakes out from beneath his cloak, pushing up the tricorn to reveal his face. Scarred and broad, it is a face that radiates danger. While his size may be intimidating, it's the intelligence behind his eyes that reveals him as lethal.

'I'm no witch,' I stammer, unable to force anything more sensible past my fear and onto my lips.

'Do you ken who I am, Mistress Reade?' He waits a beat to watch the small shake of my head, then carries on, his rough brogue gravel under cartwheels. 'I am John Kincaid. Do you recognise that name? Do you ken what I do?'

My gut turns cold and oily. Everyone knows the name John Kincaid. Everyone knows what John Kincaid does.

Witch hunter.

'Ah yes, I see that you do,' Kincaid says. 'Now, I dinnae ken who your friend here is,' he pauses, gesturing to my mother, 'but, seein' as you witches gather in covens, I'd be willin' to bet good coin she is a witch too.'

Alarm courses through me, panic flooding me, despite the exhaustion. John Kincaid is Scotland's most esteemed witch hunter. Tasked by the Court, he pursues, stalks, and captures those accused of witchcraft. Then, witch or not, innocent or not, he ensures they confess to their supposed crimes so they can be brought to a trial such as the one Agnes faced today. Feared for his tenacity and utter lack of mercy, he has personally brought hundreds of men and women to trial. To their deaths.

Steeling myself, I stare up at Kincaid, aiming for defiant and most definitely falling short. 'She is not a witch, and neither am I, Mr Kincaid.' Impressed by my ability to keep the tremor from my voice, I continue, 'Agnes Sampson was a friend. We came here to attend her *trial*.' Somehow I manage not to snort my derision over that mockery of a word. 'There is no crime in that. You cannot accuse us of witchcraft simply for coming here today.' In truth, I know he could easily do just that. Kincaid has never let a little thing like lack of evidence stand in the way of taking down innocents.

'No,' Kincaid agrees. 'There's no crime in that, as you say.' He leans down to bring his face closer to mine, continuing softly, 'But I have testimony to prove your crimes as a witch, nonetheless.'

My shock knocks any show of defiance right out of me. 'What testimony?'

Straightening to tower over me once more, Kincaid motions to the gallows, where Agnes and Geillis's lifeless bodies swing in the sharp winter breeze. 'I have written confession from members of your coven, confirming you, Elspeth Reade, are a witch.'

'From whom?' I breathe, stomach plummeting to somewhere around my boots.

'The who of it matters not.' Kincaid lets loose a chilly smile. 'What matters is that you have made my job all the easier by comin' here today. Weeks, I have hunted you, and weeks, you have eluded me. I know not how. I found no sign, no trace. It seemed as if you had vanished.' Eyes narrowing, he leans down again, the gentle in his voice a warning. 'Like you had used witchcraft, wouldn't you say?'

Thoughts of betrayal sidelined, I scramble for some way I can talk my way out of this. But before I can refute his claim, he reaches into his cloak and swift as spiders, brandishes iron manacles, primed to clamp over my wrists.

I move without thinking, stepping back and pulling my mother with me. Readying myself to run, I feel her hand drop from mine. With a curse, I turn to her, reaching out to grab her wrist so that we can get the hell out of here. It is then I see her face is no longer a mask. Instead, her features reveal cool fury, that otherworldliness she had concealed beneath her glamour now frightening in its ferocity.

Kincaid gasps, an edge of fear lying stark within it. 'I knew it,' he murmurs.

'You will not threaten my daughter, Mr Kincaid.' My mother's voice is smooth as silver, brimming with peril. 'If you think to take her from me, I will destroy you.'

Kincaid visibly gathers himself, spitting, 'Witch, you will burn alongside your daughter. Witchcraft is a si–'

A whoosh of air surges from my mother and Kincaid flies back, landing on the filthy cobblestones, a good ten yards from where he had once stood. Having whipped his head against the stones, he moves slowly as he attempts to stand, passers-by turning to stare first at him, then at us.

'We need to go,' I urge. 'Now.'

I am entirely unprepared for a showdown, especially with the Court's extensive forces within shouting distance. My mother and her impressive show of magic are here now, but who knows when they might retreat, leaving me stranded and surrounded by the law. All it would take would be one yell from Kincaid–

'Witches!' Kincaid's cry reverberates around the square. Despite his knock to the head, his lungs seem to be working well enough. 'Witches!' he roars again.

'Run,' I breathe.

I turn to bolt from the giant in black, heartened to see my mother needs no more encouragement to do the same.

***

Slipping through winding side streets and a warren of shadowy back alleys, I finally find my way out of the city, my mother following close behind. Only slowing once we reach the hovels skirting the city's boundaries, I still push on to keep up a decent pace, unable to stop glancing back over my shoulder after every few steps.

Breathing hard, I angle a look at my mother, subtly trying to gauge how present she is after our hurried escape. She'd returned from that faraway place when she faced down Kincaid, but I'm afraid she may have gone back into retreat now the immediate danger has passed.

'Mama?' I try.

I shoot another glance over my shoulder. Kincaid's yells had not roused the Court's forces fast enough to allow them to get a good look at us before we fled, but I don't want to drop my guard while they might still be giving chase. Kincaid himself had been unable to keep to his feet after his head's conference with the cobblestones, so at least *he* won't be on our tail. Yet.

'Yes?' my mother replies.

Talking. That's a good sign.

'Are you alright?' While my breathing is still ragged, my question is tentative.

Following our emotional encounter in the darkened hallway of the Queen's palace, I'd been left with the strong impression my mother might float away on a sturdy enough breeze. Now, after witnessing her most recent retreat, after seeing what that level of emotional fragility looks like when things turn to shit, my concern most definitely remains.

Safe to say, things have been turning to shit a lot lately. If that trend continues – and given our current status on Kincaid's wanted list, it is more of a certainty than a possibility – I don't know how well my mother will cope.

'I'm sorry,' she murmurs.

Ducking sideways to avoid the low roofline of a hovel, I glance at her, throat contracting at the raw pain I see written across her face. 'For what?'

'For leaving you again.' She holds her gaze on the muddy path in front of her. 'I keep abandoning you, leaving you to fend for yourself. I am the worst kind of mother.'

'You didn't abandon me, then or now,' I say. 'I don't blame you for any of it.'

As infuriating as it had been to see her withdraw, I understand why she had fled. I remember well enough how I had retreated inside myself to escape the horrors Malcom inflicted upon me. Beatrix had thrown emotional torment at my mother for years. Today, she'd found herself faced with the agony of losing her friend, and her mind had fallen into retreat to escape further damage.

Urging conviction into my words, I say, 'Beatrix is to blame. No one else.'

Her reply is little more than a breath. 'But... Agnes.'

I claw back the grief that one small word unleashes. This is not the time to break down. Kincaid will be on our trail just as soon as he is able. That's if his men don't find us first.

Once we are safe, I will attend to the pit of grief within me, frozen and fathomless.

But where is safe?

'We just need to keep moving,' I say, pushing away thoughts of Agnes, of my mother's tortured expression.

'Where will we go?'

Her question echoes my own thoughts. But I don't know. The obvious answer would be North Berwick, to my home. I have been gone for months. Furious at how Faerie cheated me out of time, I am terrified by the thought of what those lost months have done to my father. I yearn to see him, to know how he is.

The only trouble is, Kincaid surely knows I will want to go home. It will be the first place he looks.

Suddenly it hits me. He said he'd hunted me. He will have already paid my father a visit. The witch hunter is certainly not known for his gentle touch. What might he have tried to get my father to talk?

I *have* to find out. Regardless of what it might mean for me, I need to know my father is safe. Once I am certain of that, I can work on a plan to move forward. That's what I'm good at, after all.

'We're going home,' I say, picking up my pace and throwing one more glance over my shoulder.

Chapter 38

Under the cover of darkness, I scrutinise the small cottage, hoping I will see no signs of danger, but remaining wary, nonetheless.

Having hopped on the back of a wagon heading out of Edinburgh, we had bumped along rutted roads, making good time as we hugged the coast all the way to North Berwick. While the grizzled farmer driving the wagon hadn't been all that keen on letting us hitch a ride, his wife had taken pity on us, insisting we ride with them instead of trudging along in the rain.

Soaked through and shivering, I curse the misery that is January, Scotland's bleakest month. I long for the warmth of Faerie's sunshine, for the heat of Law's body curled against mine.

'It looks clear,' I whisper, forcing the painful ache of that thought aside.

My mother shrugs in reply, looking vulnerable, and just as miserable as I feel. Freezing temperatures, sodden clothes and grief-dampened spirits seem to weigh heavy on her fragile form.

Taking a deep breath to steady my nerves, I stand, helping my mother up and putting a gentle hand at her back. I'd considered leaving her here and checking out the cottage alone, but decided against it. I'm not entirely sure she wouldn't wander off. While I am well aware she is hundreds of years old, I'm not overly confident regarding how well she will deal with real life, especially now she is in the human realm. She has spent much more time in the dream world than the real world over the past two decades, and as such, I don't fancy trying to wrangle her out of whatever calamity she gets tangled up in if left to her own devices.

Sighing, I think of how we seem to have swapped roles; one where I play the parent, and my mother plays the feckless four-year-old.

Quietly, I steal across the road, creeping up the path to the cottage door, where I stop to listen for any sounds from inside. It feels like an age since I was here last, when I'd bid goodbye to my father and marched off to meet Nicnevin. In reality – for me, at least – it's only been a week.

Silence. All I can hear is my own heartbeat pulsing in my ears, and my mother's quiet breaths beside me. Fuck it. I have to know my father has not been harmed by Kincaid. Nodding to my mother, I twist the handle and push the door open.

It's the smell that hits me first. That lingering scent of fermenting ale, the lavender in my father's soap, the smokiness of the hearth. It smells like home.

With my father's bedroom door open wide, my eyes fall on him, tucked up in bed, just as I had left him. He looks smaller, somehow, but all in one piece. I watch as his chest rises and falls and his eyelids flutter in sleep, relief coursing through me. He is safe.

I step slowly around the compact space, letting my gaze roam over the cottage, taking it all in to make sure everything is as it should be. With the hearth burning low and only one lamp lit by my father's bedside, the inside of the cottage is dark and shadowy. Even so, I would know it blindfolded. The chair beside the hearth is empty, but Mrs Ogilvie won't have gone far. Her knitting lies on the floor beside the chair, and on the sturdy kitchen table sit the remains of the pottage she must have served up for dinner. Reminding me I have not eaten a proper meal in a very long time, my stomach rumbles at the sight of it.

Later. I'll eat later. When I am sure it is safe.

From my room, Cheetie purrs and I give my mother a quick grin. She stands beside the front door, looking like she doesn't know where to put herself. From her hunted expression, I can tell she longs to go to my father, but is unsure whether she should.

'Would you like to meet my cat?' I want her to feel at home, welcomed. For however long we happen to be here. It likely won't be long with Kincaid giving chase, but I'd like at least a few warm moments here before I have to start running again. I will need to find somewhere safe for my father to hide, perhaps with my mother, until I can work out what to do about the notorious witch hunter.

And Law. He needs me too. He can't keep shredding his soul at the whim of Nicnevin.

My heart aches at the thought of him, of what that old bitch might be forcing him to do. I miss his enigmatic smiles and smoky voice, the strength of his arms around me and the way he makes me feel. Cherished, seen, safe.

My mother nods, letting out a soft curve of a smile in reply.

'Cheetie, Cheetie, come here boy,' I say in that sing-song voice reserved for fluffy animals and cute bairns.

I can still hear him purring, but he doesn't come at my call. Thinking he is probably curled up on my bed and refusing to move after gorging himself on pottage, I head toward my room to find the lazy little besom.

With no lamp in my bedroom, it takes a moment for my eyes to adjust. As they do, it's not just my cat I find stretched out on my bed.

Violet eyes stare up at me from the gloom.

'Good evening, sprig,' Nicnevin rasps. 'Dear Lawrens is in need of some assistance. Would you perhaps be interested in making another deal?'

Acknowledgements

This book would still be languishing on my laptop if it weren't for the love and support of my husband, Adrian. For all the time he gave me to write and edit while he covered bathtimes and busy weekends with our daughter, for the sounding board he provided, and for the incredible cover he created, this book is here – out in the world – because of him. Thank you, handsome husband!

I also want to thank my daughter, Amaya, for her patience over the past two and a half years as I have written and edited, and edited some more. Just kidding, she's seven, she has no patience at all. But she has put up with me disappearing into my office and losing myself to my book, which I hope she sees in time was worth it. As an aspiring author herself (*Dead Wedding Killers* is her latest masterpiece), she might one day choose to take her dream further, and I will be right by her side to help.

Next, I'd like to thank my beta readers for all their feedback and support. A big shoutout goes to my mum and dad, who got the expurgated version, and to my sisters, Catriona and Lisa, who got the version with all the spice. Thank you for reading it twice: once when I thought it was finished, and once when it was actually finished.

Lastly, I want to thank Lisa Egan for encouraging me to celebrate my book with a proper launch party. Lisa is one of those people who gives her all to supporting others, encouraging them and celebrating their achievements. I would never have had the guts to organise a launch without her, and I'm pretty sure it would have been pretty anticlimactic otherwise. *Here world, this is my book. Hello?*

And of course, I need to thank you all for reading! Reading is one of my favourite things in the whole world, equal only perhaps to writing. I hope you have enjoyed this little escape into Faerie, and will join me for the second book in the series, *A Darkness Set Alight*, out soon.

Follow me on TikTok (**@julesdalla**) and Instagram (**@jules_dalla_libera_author**) to keep up-to-date with all my bookish news and release dates, or check out my website **jdlbooks.com.au** to sign up for my newsletter.

As an indie author, it would mean the world to me if you could please review this book. Goodreads, Storygraph, Amazon, all of the places! Every review, every mention on socials, every word-of-mouth recommendation helps get my book out there and into the hands of other beautiful readers like you.

Thank you! Jules x

About the Author

Based in Lake Macquarie, Australia, Jules is a copywriter by trade. Having trained as a journalist, she dipped a toe in public relations, then found her way into copywriting, where she wound her words online for more than a decade.

As an avid bookworm her entire life, it's perhaps no surprise she uncovered a passion for writing her own books, finding as much joy in creating stories as she does in reading them.

Carrying with her an intense love of fantasy and a desire to create captivating worlds worthy of getting lost in, she wrote her debut romantasy, That One Small Spark, around a busy life writing real estate copy and running around after her very spirited daughter and two very needy staffies.

When she is not writing or residing in mum life, you will likely find Jules walking the dogs by the lake, decompressing at the gym, or adventuring overseas, usually with an audiobook in her ear or a book in her hand.

Printed in Dunstable, United Kingdom

76086106R00231